A Prayer for the Fallen

The Kelk Conflict: Assassination

Book 3 of *The Blacksword Regiment*

by

J. L. Doty

TELEMACHUS PRESS

Published by Telemachus Press, LLC
http://www.telemachuspress.com

Visit the author's website:
http://www.jldoty.com

ISBN: 978–1–951744–15–1 (eBook)
ISBN: 978–1–951744–16–8 (paperback)
ISBN: 978–1–953757–21–0 (hardback)

Version 2022.12.04

KEpuz!po!KJNEFTLUPQ:
Formatted using eTools for Writers 3.8.8, Dec 4 2022, 09:55:21
Copyright © 2013-2016 by J. L. Doty

Printed in the United States of America

10 9 8 7 6 5 4 3 2 1

A Prayer for the Fallen

The Kelk Conflict: Assassination

Book 3 of *The Blacksword Regiment*

Many fall and weep for their loss.
Some fall and claw their way back up.

1

Allies or Enemies

AS NIKAELA FOLLOWED Kristdokar down the passageway in the heavy cruiser *Konigsborge*, she couldn't forget John's last words to her, spoken only a few seconds ago: "You said if we survived, you'd have to find out if anything on me is forked." He had leaned close to her, so close their lips almost touched, and with a smug look on his face he had added, "Just let me know when you're ready to start the discovery process."

Her heart had raced and her face had grown hot, which angered her, because she didn't blush. *I am not a blusher*, she thought. *Nikaela Vreekande does not blush like some schoolgirl.*

And yet, she had blushed. How had John Mathius done that to her? A common-face!

Her thoughts were in turmoil as she and Kristdokar approached the two armed guards standing outside her stateroom. One of the guards opened the door and held it for them. Kristdokar did not slow down as she walked through the door, and Nikaela followed her.

They had set up her makeshift private stateroom exactly like John's by emptying a storage compartment, then dragging a medical bed into it, along with a table and four chairs. The tray containing the remnants of her first meal since her rescue remained on the table, and standing next to the table she saw a familiar face: Oberseergent Geltkarl.

Senior NCOs like Geltkarl intimidated Nikaela no end, but when their eyes met the older woman's face softened and she smiled. "Mistress Vreekande, it's good to see you alive and well."

Nikaela hadn't seen Geltkarl since Reisenar, when the woman had kept a very junior command boss alive. "Oberseergent Geltkarl, I didn't know you were here."

The NCO shrugged. "I accompanied Command Superior Brynjar as part of his team on *Drakan Helgis*. When I heard Brigadier Kristdokar needed people who could be trusted to . . . see to your best interests, I volunteered to transfer to *Konigsborge*."

Kristdokar nodded her approval. "Welcome to the team, Oberseergent." To Nikaela she said, "I've put Oberseergent Geltkarl in charge of protecting both of you."

With Geltkarl in charge, Nikaela would sleep a little easier. At the thought of sleep a jaw-breaking yawn forced its way out of her. After their escape from *Sycorax* and rescue from the disabled assault boat, she had slept, but it hadn't been enough.

"I'm not surprised you're tired," Kristdokar said. "We'll leave you so you can get some rest."

Nikaela looked at Geltkarl. "I'll sleep better knowing the oberseergent is protecting me."

••••

The makeshift private stateroom on the Kelk warship *Konigsborge* had all the stark trappings of a jail cell, though Kristdokar had implied John was not officially confined. Furnished with nothing more than a table, four chairs, and a medical bed, all of which had been dragged into an empty compartment to isolate him from the ship's crew, he couldn't help but feel like an inmate in a prison cell. And knowing the two armed guards stationed outside the door were there to protect him, not confine him, did nothing to alleviate the sense of incarceration.

After Kristdokar and Nikaela left him alone in the small compartment, he paced back and forth considering his situation. He desperately wanted to consult Primatov, because an officer of her rank would know a lot more than him. But Kristdokar had told him the red-hot Blacksword redhead had returned to the hunter-killer *Lightspear* to file a report. He wondered if that was true, wondered how far he could trust Kristdokar. She had told him Primatov would return in a few hours and they would then depart for Viktorkinde. He wondered if any of what she told him was true.

John and Nikaela had established a bond, and he had no doubt she would risk her life for him just as he would for her, as they had both done repeatedly now. But he didn't think his breschkada's loyalty had rubbed off on any of her Kelk comrades, especially a brigadier skalde who probably needed to balance John's continued well-being with political expediency, and any number of other factors.

That thought surprised him, halted him in his tracks and he stopped pacing. Never before had he been that distrustful, though it occurred to him it might not be distrust as much as a lessening of his naiveté, which would not be a bad thing. Nash Wakeland had certainly fooled him, had suckered John into his circle of deception like a child seeking the approval of a revered parent. Could he trust any of them? There would always be the Cranochs, the Merciers, and the DeLeons. How would he spot them when they came along? How could he detect their deceit before they turned his trust against him?

He thought of May, his roommate at O-School, and her lover Karya, and knew he could trust those two. He would never have any misgivings about Carla, Roark, Leeze, and several of his friends from his training platoon. Colonel Brightlaw, and Major Teal, probably he could trust them as well. And Sergeant Omuglu, he had not the slightest bit of doubt about her.

John scanned the small compartment and took in the table, four chairs, and the medical bed. Regardless of Kristdokar's assurances, he decided to test the limits of his freedom. He crossed to the only door in the compartment, wondering if he would find it locked. But when he gripped the door latch and pulled, it opened easily.

The two guards standing in the passageway turned their heads and looked his way. One of them stood only chin-high to John, and was rather stocky with a square face and rectangular jaw. The insignia on his sleeve displayed three clawed talons and a lightning bolt, a grandeseergent. John needed to refresh his memory of Kelk rank, but he thought the man held the equivalent rank of a Commonwealth staff sergeant. The fellow turned to face John squarely and said, "Maestra Mathius."

The sergeant's companion stood about the same height as John, had a narrow face with high cheek bones, and sported a carefully trimmed beard. His sleeves bore two clawed talons; an unterseergent, basically a corporal. The fellow glanced briefly at John, nodded and looked away, returning his attention to the passageway as if reluctant to have his scrutiny diverted from a potential threat.

It bothered John that two NCOs had been assigned to guard his door. That kind of duty would normally be given to enlisted personnel like a krieger or oberkrieger, their equivalent of privates second or first class. Kristdokar had told him the guards were selected from among *Konigsborge*'s crew for their "... attitudes regarding Commonwealth soldiers." They must have searched far and wide to find two who weren't inclined to execute John on the spot.

John resorted to his rudimentary Kelk. "I need toilet, maestra." He did need to pee, but he could have waited. This was more of a test.

The short sergeant's eyebrows rose. "You speak Kelk!" He had spoken carefully, as if he understood a rapid-fire burst of the Kelk language would be difficult for John to follow.

John shrugged. "A little."

The stocky sergeant looked to his companion. "Common-face speaks Kelk."

The tall, bearded one didn't take his eyes off the passageway as he said, "Shitty accent." He too had spoken carefully, probably wanted to make sure John understood how his command of the Kelk language was pure shit-of-bull.

The corporal said something else to the sergeant, but spoke too rapidly for John to follow. The sergeant glanced up and down the passageway carefully, then said to John, "Come with us."

John stepped through the doorway. The stocky sergeant closed the door, then did something and a green telltale above the door flashed red. He led the way down the corridor, with John following and the taller corporal behind him. They encountered no one, which was perhaps by design, and after a short distance stopped at an open doorway.

The stocky sergeant turned to John. "You wait here with Bergen."

John thought he might have just learned the corporal's name, though whether it was the man's family or given name, he had no idea.

John saw through the doorway into the head, and it looked much like any head on any ship anywhere: lots of plast and steel. He watched the sergeant enter the room with his hand resting on the butt of the heavy grav pistol strapped to his side. The man looked into each of the privacy stalls, and into an adjoining compartment that appeared to be a large shower area. Then he called out, "It's clear, Bergen."

The corporal nodded at John and said, "Go ahead, Maestra Mathius."

John walked into the head, chose a urinal and relieved himself under the watchful eyes of the sergeant. He wondered if the Kelk shared the same casual indifference to nudity as his Commonwealth comrades, but saw nothing there to give him any clues regarding that.

When he finished, the two Kelk NCOs escorted him back to his private compartment. The sergeant unlocked the door, and as they had done at the head, the short fellow entered the compartment with his hand resting on the butt of his grav pistol, while John and the corporal waited outside in the passageway. Then the sergeant emerged, declaring, "It's clear." He stepped aside so John could walk through the open door.

John hesitated, taking a moment to carefully compose what he wanted to say in Kelk. "Grandeseergent, how should I address you?"

The man paused and eyed John carefully with a look of uncertainty. His eyes shifted to his comrade as he said, "He knows our rank insignia."

The tall corporal nodded slowly. "Of course he does. Gotta know who outranks who, so he knows who to kill first."

The sergeant nodded sadly as if resigned to the inevitable. "He is a Blacksword, after all."

John couldn't determine if they were threatening him, or teasing him. They had again spoken slowly so he could follow their words, and it certainly was the same kind of mocking banter he often heard from his old platoon mates.

The sergeant returned his attention to John, shrugged his indifference and said, "I am Grandeseergent Matsen. And my tall handsome friend here is Unterseergent Kolbeck."

Bergen Kolbeck and *something* Matsen. "Thank you," John said, then stepped through the door into his private compartment.

They closed the door behind him and he hesitated for a moment. He had learned the door was not kept locked. He could open it, didn't have to knock and wait for them to do so. He had learned they peed pretty much like any other human, or at least they had urinals not too different from those he was accustomed to, which he should have been able to surmise without going through that little exercise. And he had learned they were not at all confident they could keep him alive on that ship. If worse came to worse, he might have to keep himself alive, if he could.

The meal they had given him—the first he had eaten in a couple of days—weighed heavily on him. And while he had slept after they had brought him back from hypothermia, he realized now it hadn't been enough. At least Matsen and Kolbeck seemed willing to keep him alive, even if only reluctantly.

He lay down on the medical bed still wearing the coverall they had given him, and sleep found him quickly.

••••

"You sure you don't want us to come with you?" Edward Fleming asked.

Standing in the Null team's bunk room on board *Lightspear*, and facing the Null team leader with his people behind him, some seated, some standing, Katrine shook her head. "Certainly I'd like you to come with me. But it wouldn't do any good, and it might look bad."

Fleming made no attempt to hide his concern. "We won't wear our Blacksword patches."

Katrine grinned. "Do you have any Blacksword patches left to wear?" They had just spent twenty minutes carefully stripping the Null team's uniforms of Blacksword patches so she could cobble together uniforms for Ensign John Mathius.

One of Fleming's people looked up from the task of repacking her uniforms. "She has a point, Cap'm."

Fleming grimaced and returned Katrine's grin. "But still, how about just a couple of us?"

"Cap'm Fleming," Katrine said, "you and your people do have a formidable reputation. But if a hundred million Kelk decide they want to kill us, you're going to need more than a few nullheads to stop them."

Fleming pursed his lips. "I was thinking more along the lines of personal protection against a small group of rogues. They're going to have the same problems we'd have if we brought home some Kelk, aren't they?"

Katrine was sorely tempted to take him up on the offer. Since Nygaard had flatly informed her that rejecting her invitation was not an option, Katrine had repeatedly considered approaching the councilwoman and Kristdokar with such a request. But each time she had come to the same conclusion. In the end, the presence of a few loyal bodyguards wouldn't make any difference, and such a request might be construed as a lack of faith in her Kelk hosts. "I'm afraid that in this, I must trust my Kelk counterparts."

Fleming closed his eyes and nodded once. "Then I won't press you further."

Katrine hefted the duffle containing John's new uniforms and threw the strap over her shoulder.

One of Fleming's people stepped forward and addressed him. "Sir, that thing we discussed earlier about the kid."

"Don't worry," Fleming said, "I didn't forget."

He looked Katrine in the eyes. "The kid breaks out of a jail cell and destroys a Kelk destroyer from the inside. And we heard on Trafalgar he killed five heavily armed Special Forces with a small knife. If he ever wants to transfer to Zeta Company and be a nullhead, tell him I'd be happy to put in a good word for him."

Katrine hadn't considered that. "On Trafalgar he only killed three with a knife. He killed the other two with a sidearm."

Fleming shrugged. "I know, but he took the sidearm away from them, didn't he? Offer still stands."

"And on *Sycorax* he did have some help, you know?"

Fleming's brows furrowed. "Yah, that young Kelk woman you told me about."

One of his female nullheads looked up and said, "Hey Cap'm, make her a nullhead too. Only fair."

Fleming's eyes widened, probably reflecting Katrine's own reaction; offer the Blacksword to a Kelk, truly an amazing thought. "I'll have to think about that."

With the duffle containing John's new uniforms slung over her shoulder, Katrine contacted Commander Neilosse through her implants, and the CO of *Lightspear* agreed to meet her in his office. A few minutes later she handed him a comp chip. "That contains my report to Colonel Blacksword. It also contains a special encryption key, and the coordinates of a communications buoy near the edge of Commonwealth space, the terminus of a relay chain that stretches back to Trafalgar. The Kelk have set up a similar relay chain, and the coordinates of its terminus are included as well. As soon as I leave, proceed with all due haste toward that buoy, and when you're within transition com range of it, transmit my report on that encryption key. It will land on Fran Thealone's desk within a day. I know she'll be watching for it and she'll read it right away, so wait there for further orders from her."

At four thousand lights, *Lightspear* could be within range of that buoy in about two days, so Thealone should receive the report within three or four. Katrine suspected it would stir up a political hornet's nest the like of which Trafalgar had not seen in a century or two.

"Colonel," Neilosse said. "As I said before, it's been a most unusual pleasure working with you."

They shook hands, Katrine again hefted the duffle with John's pilfered uniforms, then stopped by the small stateroom she had shared with three other officers. Katrine had displaced an ensign through the privileges of rank, and she found the young woman moving back into the space rightly hers. They shared a few words, then Katrine threw her own duffle over her other shoulder, and made her way to the air lock to board *Lightspear*'s small skiff. It took only ten minutes to cross to the Kelk cruiser.

Kristdokar met her in *Konigsborge*'s hangar bay, where she directed two Kelk enlisted men to take the duffels off her hands. "We've prepared quarters for you, and they'll deliver them there." As the two men carried the duffels away, she leaned close to Katrine. "We've filtered through *Konigsborge*'s roster and have identified quite a number of personnel we think we can trust with the delicacy of our situation. Those two are among them. We also have Command Superior Brynjar and a few other former members of First Liaison Company whom we already know we can trust. And the entire crew of *Drakan Helgis* was vetted carefully before departing from Viktorkinde, so we're using a few of them as well."

As they walked out of the hangar bay the pitch of the background vibration in the ship's hull increased a notch. In preparation for up-transit back to Viktorkinde, *Konigsborge* had begun accelerating away from the Sarkovie system with its sublight grav drive. They had wasted no time once Katrine had boarded the vessel. It occurred to her that in a few tendays, she and John would stand on a planet that no Commonwealth citizen had ever before visited.

Kristdokar led her to her own stateroom. As a flag officer on a large cruiser, the Kelk woman's quarters were quite lavish compared to what Katrine had grown accustomed to on a hunter-killer.

Kristdokar pointed to a seat at a small table and Katrine sat down. Then the older woman served them both tea, following the Kelk custom Nygaard had related to Katrine earlier that day: *In the Supremacy, under formal circumstances, it is customary for the more senior person to serve tea to the more junior.*

A small package about the size of a shoe box lay on the table near Kristdokar's teacup, but the brigadier didn't mention it so Katrine ignored it as well. Kristdokar spoke as Katrine sipped at her tea. "I should warn you our screening has also identified quite a number of people in whose presence you should not turn your back. I'll provide you with a list of names and photos, and we'll update it as it grows."

Katrine carefully placed the small teacup on the table in front of her. "Again, I am reminded of how there are many similarities between our cultures."

Kristdokar shrugged. "At least we have some understanding of what we're dealing with."

She reached out and slid the package across the table toward Katrine. Katrine raised a questioning eyebrow, and Kristdokar responded with, "Something you may need, Colonel."

Katrine opened the package, and in it she found a small grav pistol with both a shoulder harness, and a simple belt holster. As she examined the firearm, Kristdokar said, "The weapon is small, but its effect is not, though you're limited to six rounds. Since grav fields control the projectile, its accuracy is not reduced by the short length of the barrel. If you can't conceal it, then don't carry it. But if you can, you're welcome to wear it at all times. We intend to keep you and our breschkada safe, but if we fail, that may be your last resort. If so, don't hesitate to use it."

Katrine didn't try to hide the surprise on her face when she took her eyes off the weapon and looked at Kristdokar. The skalde grimaced uncomfortably. "I can see by the look on your face that like us, you do not allow just anyone to go armed on one of your warships. Well you're not just anyone. You're a target, and so are both of our breschkada. Captain Holverzon, his XO, Vice Skalde Nygaard, and Mistress Vagle, a young woman I'm about to introduce you to, are aware that we're making an exception for you. They're the only ones who know, so please keep it that way."

"You surprise me," Katrine said, recalling that she had said the same thing to Tarsik Obradour, and the wealthy little man had responded with, *Of course I do.*

Kristdokar appeared ill at ease. "We live in surprising and unusual times, something I would not have said a little more than a year ago."

The skalde introduced Katrine to Command Superior Ingrid Vagle, a lithe, athletic young woman with whom Katrine would share a stateroom. The young woman wore a heavy grav pistol in a holster buckled to her side. Katrine learned that Vagle was an experienced Special Forces combatant, would be armed like Katrine at all times, and would accompany Katrine everywhere she went.

Vagle showed Katrine to her new quarters, a small stateroom the two of them would share. The two duffels had been dumped on the deck. Katrine didn't waste time unpacking, but hefted the one containing John's new uniforms. "Let's go see Ensign Mathius."

Vagle stood with her back to the stateroom door, almost as if blocking Katrine's access to it. "You need to carry the weapon Brigadier Kristdokar gave you."

Katrine looked down at the uniform she wore: service khakis with a tunic tucked into belted pants. She had tossed the package containing the pistol on her bunk, and she glanced at it now. Dressed as she was, there was no way to conceal the weapon.

Vagle must have recognized her dilemma. "Do you have a coat?"

"Yes, I do." Katrine dropped John's duffle and plunged into her own. She retrieved a light-weight, khaki deck jacket.

Vagle nodded. "That should do nicely."

After Katrine donned the shoulder harness, Vagle helped her adjust the straps for a snug but comfortable fit. Then Katrine pulled on the jacket, but left it open.

Vagle nodded again. "Yes, that works. Now let's go see Ensign Mathius."

2

Continued Deceit

A KNOCK ON the door to Anders's cell brought him out of a deep sleep. He thought it odd that he was a prisoner in a cell, and yet someone had the courtesy to knock first before entering. He stepped out of the field of his grav bunk just as the heavy door ratcheted open and Brynjar walked into the cell. His implants told him the fellow had come in the wee hours of the early morning shift. Only about ten hours had elapsed since Kristdokar and he had told Anders they would stuff him into a lifeboat, and he'd be on his own to make his way to Sarkovie.

Brynjar nodded over his shoulder toward the door. "It's time to go, maestra."

The fellow had come alone, and as they walked out of the brig Anders glanced into the other two cells and noted that they were empty. The security station at the entrance to the brig also remained empty. And they encountered no one as they traversed the passageways of the destroyer *Drakan Helgis*. As long as nothing special happened, even larger ships tended to be very quiet in the wee hours of the morning.

Brynjar led him down a short corridor and through the personnel hatch into an assault boat. They stepped into it just behind the cockpit, where an NCO in full combat armor sat in the pilot's seat, while the co-pilot's couch remained empty. The NCO did not turn around and look his way, but scanned the instruments in front of her and continued preparations for departure.

Brynjar nodded toward her, leaned close to Anders and lowered his voice. "Everyone on *Drakan Helgis* has been carefully vetted, and among them I trust her above all others. But even she does not know who you are, or what your mission is. And she knows better than to ask."

The command superior led him to the back of the boat, where an empty set of full combat armor appeared to be seated comfortably on a couch. On the couch next to it rested an empty, multi-purpose vac suit, and next to that a set of rumpled and soiled coveralls. A tool kit of some sort lay on the deck nearby.

Brynjar pointed to the vac suit and coveralls. "You were wearing those when we rescued you. Strip down and put them on. And be very careful to bring nothing with you from this ship."

As Anders pulled off the clean coverall they had given him, Brynjar went to work donning the armor. While they worked at that, the pilot sealed up the assault boat, detached it from the destroyer, and launched it out of the ship through the open hangar bay doors.

The coveralls smelled of Anders's own stale sweat, and the vac suit wasn't any better. They had recharged its reactor pack cells and the oxygen and water supplies. Once he had the vac suit sealed up, he ran it through a full systems check, then dilated the helmet visor and sat down to watch Brynjar finish struggling into his combat armor.

Anders glanced forward, and saw through the boat's windshield that they were approaching a large structure of some sort in the middle of empty space. It floated in front of them with a slow tumble to its motion. He could only see a portion of it, and at first he thought they were approaching another ship. But as it completed one tumble, then another, he caught sight of a boundary of jagged and twisted metal and plast, with a debris field floating about it. They were approaching one of the three derelict pieces of *Sycorax*.

Brynjar clipped the helmet of his armor in place, dilated his visor and said, "That's the piece of *Sycorax* you were in when we found you. If you ever run into anyone who's been on that ship and knows its layout well, you may need to describe with some accuracy how you made your way to the lifeboat. So you and I are going to retrace your alleged route."

He bent down, picked up the tool kit, slung its strap over his shoulder, and said, "Let's go."

The tumble in the derelict piece of warship was not fast or pronounced, so the boat's pilot had no trouble attaching grapples to it and anchoring the boat hard against its surface. She evacuated the boat's cabin, then opened the personnel hatch.

The pilot had anchored the boat next to a damaged cargo hatch in the side of the derelict piece of *Sycorax*. The hatch appeared to have been blown open by explosive charges, probably the work of one of the rescue teams. Brynjar led the way, pulling himself through the open hatch, and Anders followed, taking care to avoid sharp knife-points of torn metal that might puncture his suit. Encased in combat armor, Brynjar didn't have to worry about such things. Floating in the eerily silent piece of ship, Anders quickly became lost as he followed the command superior, and only got his bearings when they reached the compartment from which he had been rescued. Its hatch still hung open on its hinges.

Brynjar spoke over the com. "The rescue teams found most of the compartments in this piece under vacuum, and they didn't keep any records of those that weren't. So keep it simple. Your story is that your compartment was under vacuum, as were all those between you and the lifeboats."

"Let me lead," Anders said. "I think I actually remember the way to the boats. And doing so will give me a more realistic story if I have to tell it."

Brynjar extended a hand toward the hatch. "Lead on."

Anders stopped at each intersection, thought carefully, and frequently made a wrong turn, then had to backtrack. But that would instill in him a very real memory of what he probably would have gone through if it had been for real. He worked his way to the outer hull, and eventually found three large round hatches with emergency markings telling him he had found his destination.

"The one on the right," Brynjar said. "That's the one we checked out. It's in good shape, and we've topped off its power cells."

It took some effort for Anders to turn the wheel to manually open the hatch. Sensing no atmosphere on Anders's side, the lifeboat had evacuated its interior so he didn't have to fight against tons of pressure. Beyond the hatch in the hull of the ship, the hatch in the hull of the lifeboat operated under power from the boat and opened with just the touch of a switch.

He was about to climb into the boat, but Brynjar stopped him by putting a hand on his shoulder. "When *Sycorax* broke up she was running on a course toward Sarkovie, so you've already got plenty of vector in that general direction, maybe even a little too much. As soon as you're free of this derelict, you'll have to make a slight course correction, then immediately start decelerating. You're probably going to decelerate all the way to Sarkovie to kill that vector, and you may even overshoot. But the boat's got enough reserves to handle it."

He pulled the tool kit off his shoulder and extended it to Anders. "A couple of things you might need. With the exception of some Sarkovie script, there's nothing in there you couldn't have acquired from this derelict with a little bit of ingenuity. And you can claim you pilfered drugs from the lifeboat's medical supplies and sold then on the streets to get the script."

There wasn't really anything more to say after that. Anders climbed through the hatch into what would be his new prison cell for the next ten or more days, or if things didn't go well, it might just be his coffin. He turned around to dog both hatches, but Brynjar had floated half way through them into the boat.

"We owe you a debt, friend," he said. "When this is done, I don't know if we can repay you, but I acknowledge that debt freely and openly. And if we both survive, and those old women in the Larscom don't do right by you, find me and I'll do what I can."

He saluted Anders as one officer to another. Anders returned the salute, then Brynjar backed out through the two hatches and closed the outer one. Anders closed the inner hatch, then strapped into the cramped pilot's couch.

He glanced around, took note of the ten bunk compartments, five on each side of the boat's center aisle. They were quite a bit smaller than the bunk compartments on board ship, and each could be sealed against vacuum. Two of them also offered extensive, automated, emergency medical care. Filled to capacity with ten spacers, the boat would be incredibly cramped.

He opened the tool kit Brynjar had given him. It contained a grav pistol along with some extra loads and charged power cells, and a small wad of local Sarkovie currency. It wasn't much, but it would make the whole ordeal a little easier.

He ran the lifeboat through a full systems' check, and as promised it passed with flying colors. He initiated the launch sequence and it detached from the derelict.

He checked his present vector, and as Brynjar had said, he was coasting in the general direction of Sarkovie. Anders accelerated the boat away from the derelict to get some distance between him and it, then performed the small course correction to put him on a vector that would make it easy to enter a low orbit around Sarkovie. All he had to do now was endure ten days of absolute boredom, then survive reentry. He hoped he could also survive the distrust of some very unhappy and dangerous people.

••••

With just about everyone trying to kill him since he had been abducted from Trafalgar, John's body had spontaneously resurrected his old Novalis III reflexes, which seemed to give him a hyperawareness of his surroundings. It helped that he could set his implants to monitor nearby sounds while he slept, and wake him if anyone entered the room. Otherwise, he might not have slept at all.

When someone knocked softly on the door to his stateroom, he awoke immediately. Checking his implants, he learned he had slept for another five hours, but from the way he felt he suspected he could still sleep a few more.

He swung his legs off the medical bed and stood, still wearing the rumpled coverall they'd given him. He sniffed at his armpits and didn't detect any odor yet, but still, he'd have to ask for a spare.

The knock sounded again.

He crossed the short distance to the door and opened it. Colonel Primatov stood facing him, a large duffle slung over one shoulder. Behind her stood an athletic looking female Kelk officer wearing the uniform of a command superior. John still wasn't conversant enough in Kelk writing to decipher the stencil above her left breast pocket, so he couldn't read her name. The two armed guards standing to either side of them were not the fellows he had met earlier. Matsen and Kolbeck must be off duty.

"Colonel Primatov," he said, stepping aside. "Please come in."

Primatov smiled and said, "John," then marched past him with the Kelk officer in tow. The way the younger Kelk woman walked bothered him, and it took him a moment to realize something in her bearing made him think *predator*.

One of the guards in the passageway closed the door. The colonel tossed the duffle on the table, then turned to face John. "Get enough sleep?"

John shrugged. "Close enough."

Primatov nodded toward the young Kelk woman. "Meet Command Superior Ingrid Vagle. She's my bodyguard, for which she is apparently imminently qualified."

John acknowledged the young woman. "Mistress Vagle."

With no expression on her face, she nodded. "Maestra Mathius." She had large, almond-shaped eyes that gave her face an almost child-like appearance, which was completely at odds with the predatory way she moved.

Primatov opened the duffle and pulled out a roll of khaki cloth. She shook it out to reveal the tunic of a ComSecCorps naval ensign. "Your new uniforms, Ensign Mathius. I know you haven't made a choice yet on Naval or Infantry Ops, but I had to scrape this together from *Lightspear*'s crew, so I didn't have much choice."

John hesitated. "Are you sure I passed my exams? I never heard one way or another."

She gave him a sardonic grin and glanced momentarily upward, as if looking to the heavens for guidance. "You wouldn't have made it to final exams if you weren't going to pass them. But I did check, and you did. Scored somewhere in the top thirty percent of your class. Congratulations, Ensign Mathius. You graduated from O-School."

She handed him the tunic, then glanced into the open duffle. "I cobbled together uniforms, stole a piece here and there from almost every officer on *Lightspear*. Not sure how well they'll fit."

Vagle said, "We can have them altered properly."

Another knock on the door interrupted them. One of the guards in the passageway opened the door and admitted a young enlisted man carrying a tray of food. The fellow placed the tray on the table, then turned and left.

Primatov said, "Enjoy the food, John. I have to go. I have a meeting with Skaldes Kristdokar and Nygaard."

John had not heard of Nygaard before, and the mention of her name tweaked his curiosity. "Nygaard, who is that?"

Primatov grinned as if at some joke. "Vice Skalde Nygaard, the third most powerful member of the Larscom Executive Council. You and Mistress Vreekande have drawn the attention of some very powerful people in both the Commonwealth and the Supremacy."

John didn't like the sound of that.

3

The Kelk Thing

THINGS HAD FINALLY started to go Macus DeLeon's way. Seated in the reception area outside Senator Palmutter's office, he thought about the events of the past year, and his duties working as an aide on the senator's staff.

After that fool John Mathius had ruined Macus's chances for a good military career, he thought it might take years to engineer a recovery. Even finagling an appointment as an aide to Palmutter had merely been an act of desperation, an excuse to get out of his term of enlistment. At the time he had thought serving as a glorified gofer on the senator's staff would prove to be a dead-end waste of time. If he could have gotten away with it, he would have put in a month or two kissing the senator's ass, then resigned and found something with more of a future. But there were limitations on what he could get away with, and that might have gotten his ass bumped right back into ComSecCorps. Resigned to a dead-end year of tedious boredom, he came to Trafalgar, did his job as one of the senator's lackeys, and kept his eyes open for any opportunity that might come his way.

Even his sex life had suffered. The senator had two female aides on staff, one quite pretty, and the other not so. The pretty one had rebuffed all of Macus's advances, making it clear she wanted nothing to do with him. So he'd settled for fucking the not-so-pretty one, whom he nicknamed Dog-Face. She had a good body, but to maintain his reputation, when he went out he needed someone on his arm who could make him look good. So he never took her out in public, and went to some effort to ensure that word of their relationship did not get out. She satisfied his needs at a basic level, but nothing more.

Macus's first real opportunity to shine came when he learned the senator was most interested in the incident on Reisenar. He dropped a few hints that some of his former platoon mates had been present during the altercation there. And when the senator questioned him on the matter, he played up his considerable knowledge of, and intimate relationships with, several of the soldiers involved, especially his dearest friend

John Mathius. It had been Macus's idea that Palmutter should give a guest lecture to Major Boremeir's SysComGov class, pointing out that with Macus's help, the senator could corner young Cadet Mathius after the lecture. Mathius had proven to be ignorant of any real information, but in a paranoid sort of way, that had sparked Palmutter's interest even more, and Macus's standing with the senator had improved considerably.

Later that year, when his parents had come to Trafalgar, Macus had taken steps to ensure Palmutter met them in person. The meeting went well, and it reminded the senator that Macus's parents were both Blacksword officers. After that the senator demanded even more of Macus's time.

The crowning glory of the entire year had come just after O-School finals and before the graduation ceremonies. Someone had abducted, and quite possibly murdered, John Mathius. ComSecCorps tried to hush it up, of course, but the hit-job had apparently been an open gunfight right in the middle of the academy campus, with several fatalities. Macus had quietly approached a few of the young, cadet eye-witnesses. All had been sworn to secrecy, but when he told them he was one of Mathius's dearest friends from the Recruit Depot on Miriteen, he learned quite a bit. None of them had been close enough to the actual fire-fight to confirm the demise of the poor fool. Macus had even contacted Mathius's roommate, May Forester, to tell her he was worried for his dear friend, who seemed to have disappeared. She appeared suspicious of his concern, but he did confirm that no one had heard from John Mathius since that night.

Yes, the year had ended in a most magnificent fashion.

"The senator is ready for you."

Macus brought his thoughts back from the past and focused his attention on the senator's receptionist. She wasn't bad looking, and for a moment he considered the possibilities there. He gave her a smile and said, "Thank you."

He stood. On the other side of the room, Faith Carlton also stood. Blond, tall and lithesome, with a body every man in the building had taken note of; she was the prettier of Palmutter's two female aides. Macus politely indicated with a wave of his hand that she should precede him. She nodded, gave him a cold smile, and walked past him to the senator's office door. He followed her, caught up with her, opened the door, and held it for her. She gave him an even colder smile, as if to say, "It's going to take a lot more than a simple act of courtesy to get inside my pants, you limp dick."

At least she wasn't fucking Palmutter. Not that the old fart hadn't tried, but everyone in the office knew she had turned him down rather bluntly, then threatened to make a sexual harassment claim against him if it affected her standing within his organization. Macus admired the way she recognized leverage when it came her way.

Macus simply smiled and followed her into the senator's office, enjoying the view of her ass as she walked in front of him.

"Faith, Macus," Palmutter said, standing up from behind his desk. "Come in. Sit down."

Macus and the young woman both took a seat. Palmutter paced back and forth in front of them as he spoke. "Faith, I want you to distract Dirkson. So stay on your feet, stay close to the man, smile at him a lot, let him look at that nice derriere of yours, and let's see if he's got a dick to go with all those brains. Macus, you stay seated. Stay in the background and remain silent. I want you to observe and take notes."

Macus had used the senator's clearances to access academy records. After quite a bit of digging, he had uncovered the fact that Dirkson had provided extracurricular tutoring in Kelk language and customs to John Mathius. Palmutter had been quite pleased to learn of that, and Macus's standing with the senator had ratcheted up another notch.

The senator stopped pacing and faced them squarely. "I have sources that tell me the Kelk refer to John Mathius and one of their young women as brushkuda, or something like that."

Sources, Macus wondered. What kind of sources did the senator have inside the Kelk Supremacy?

Palmutter continued. "It's got the Kelk all bent out of shape, and I and my colleagues want to know why. Though, if the young fellow's now dead, I suppose it's a moot point. Oh, and I almost forgot. Jenine Catarvin is going to join us for this. She'll be here shortly."

Macus managed to not wince. He could never fathom how that imbecile of a woman managed to get elected to the senate, and then reelected again every term.

As if on cue the door opened, and in walked the plump little airhead. Faith and Macus both stood.

"Silas," she said breathlessly. She crossed the room eagerly, holding her arms out. They grasped hands and did a double air-kiss to both cheeks.

Macus decided he should revise his opinion. The woman was actually quite pretty in a jiggly-breast sort of way. And she certainly went out of her way to expose plenty of cleavage, as if advertising her assets. He thought she might be quite fun in bed, certainly more fun than the not-so-pretty aide presently servicing his needs.

Catarvin turned away from greeting Palmutter to look at Macus and Faith. "And these are two of your young aides, are they not?"

Macus wanted to slap the stupid little bitch. They'd already been introduced a dozen times, but there just weren't enough neurons firing in that vacant head of hers to remember such details.

Palmutter reintroduced them. Faith and Macus both shook the woman's hand, then the three of them sat down. The Catarvin woman drew Faith into a conversation about makeup. Palmutter rolled his eyes in a way that only Macus saw, and Macus smiled sympathetically man to man.

After a few minutes of makeup conversation Palmutter stiffened for a moment, probably getting a message from his receptionist through his implants. They all noticed it and the two women paused in their conversation.

Palmutter relaxed and his eyes focused again on them. "Our guest is here. Showtime."

A few seconds later a wiry little man entered the room. He probably weighed only a little more than a small woman, constantly vibrated with energy, and gestured with short, jerky motions. The rumpled business suit he wore hung on him like the shroud on a cadaver. He demanded, "Which one of you is Senator what's-his-name?"

"That would be me," Palmutter said as he crossed the room to greet the fellow. He reached out, took the little man's hand, and shook it vigorously. "Senator Silas Palmutter at your service, Professor. Thank you for joining us."

"I didn't have much choice," Dirkson said, "did I? You political types control all the funding."

When Palmutter released his hand, the little fellow examined it as if it had been smeared with shit. At least he didn't sniff at it to see if it smelled like shit. "What do you want?"

Faith stood and crossed the room. She introduced herself and shook his hand. When she released his hand, he again examined it for contamination.

Faith said, "I've heard so much about you, Professor."

He scrunched up his nose and squinted at her. "Really, what have you heard?"

"That you're an expert on the Kelk."

Dirkson shook his head. "As much as anyone is an expert on them, I suppose."

If Dirkson *had a dick*, he didn't respond to a good-looking young woman the way Macus would have expected, and Faith seemed a little insulted by that. Macus enjoyed her discomfort.

Palmutter threw an arm around Dirkson's shoulders. "Come now, Professor, you're one of the great experts on the Kelk."

Palmutter escorted him to a comfortable chair and tried to get him to sit down, but the little man would have none of that. He insisted on standing and vibrating in place, which clearly frustrated Palmutter. "You're tutoring a young cadet, aren't you?"

"Yes, until recently. And that Blacksword woman too."

Faith asked, "Blacksword woman?"

"Yah, the redhead. She's prettier than you."

Palmutter's eyes widened with interest. "Colonel Primatov?"

"Yes, that's the one."

"The young man," Palmutter said. "I've heard the Kelk call him a brushkuda, or something like that. He and a young Kelk woman are both brushkuda. What does that mean?"

Dirkson squinted and shook his head. "Brushkuda? Brushkuda?" His eyes widened. "Do you mean breschkada?"

Macus found it interesting to see the senator at a loss for words. "I suppose. I've heard through confidential sources he and the young woman are this . . . breshakuda thing." Unlike Dirkson, Palmutter hadn't rolled his r's when speaking the Kelk word.

Dirkson paused and for the first time seemed to stop vibrating. "They are breschkada, are they? He didn't tell me that. I wish I had known. That puts a whole different light on his interactions with them."

"Yes," Palmutter said. "I've been told he and a young Kelk woman are this breshakuda thing, whatever that is. Tell me what that means."

Dirkson spoke almost reverently. "It's very rare."

He now had the senator's undivided attention. "How rare?"

"I don't know. It's not spoken of much."

Palmutter's frustration boiled to the surface. "Just tell me what it means."

As Dirkson spoke he sounded like a different person. They heard a confusing and disjointed description of two enemies finding a higher cause in the heat of lethal combat.

When Dirkson finished, Palmutter asked, "So the Kelk actually revere them?"

Dirkson shrugged. "They might. They might also hate them, and hunt them down like dangerous animals."

Macus liked that last part.

They questioned Dirkson further, but never got a truly clear picture of what breschkada meant to the Kelk. After the professor left, Palmutter stood in the center of the room for a moment, rubbing his chin and lost in quiet thought.

Jenine Catarvin broke the silence. "I suppose that was interesting, though I'm not sure why."

Macus agreed with the stupid little woman on that.

Palmutter perked up, looked at Faith, then at Macus. "Thank you for helping, both of you. Now, if you don't mind, Senator Catarvin and I have something we need to discuss in private."

At the obvious dismissal, Macus stood and followed Faith to the door. But Palmutter stopped them by saying, "Oh, one more thing."

Macus and Faith turned to face him.

"Macus," he said. "You're no longer an aide. I'm making you my Chief Military Adviser, effective immediately."

Macus suppressed his excitement, and made sure he did not smile or appear smug. "Thank you, sir."

Palmutter smiled. "You earned it, especially with this Dirkson info. That'll be all."

Macus followed Faith out of the room, leaving Palmutter with Catarvin. But as he closed the door he heard that disgusting imbecile of a woman giggle like a pubescent schoolgirl, and he hesitated with the door still open a crack.

"Silas, don't be such a devil, you naughty man."

Palmutter grumbled deep in his throat, and Catarvin giggled again.

"Oh Silas," she said breathlessly. "At least . . . wait until . . . we're alone."

Macus had just learned another piece of information that might come in handy. He closed the door and turned away from it, but almost ran into Faith standing there waiting for him. She smiled at him pleasantly and said, "That was certainly interesting."

Wondering where this was going, he said, "Yes, it was."

"I was thinking," she said, batting her eyelashes at him. "Perhaps we should get a drink and discuss the ramifications in more detail."

Macus wanted to see her play her hand completely. "That's an excellent idea. I know a small place just down the street."

She stepped in a little closer. "I can mix up a couple drinks at my place. Why don't we go there?"

Yes, things were definitely looking up. Finagling an appointment as an aide to Palmutter had been a stroke of pure genius. He just hadn't realized it at the time.

4

Foul Play

NIKAELA STARTED AWAKE. A quick query to her implants told her she had been asleep for a little over six hours.

With the exception of the faint vibration of the ship's drive, her stateroom remained eerily silent. But something had brought her to full wakefulness, and she wondered what had done so. She tried to access shipnet through her implants, but she got only interference, which meant something had gone seriously wrong.

A thump against the door startled her. Another thump followed that, and then another.

With her heart pounding, she swung her legs off the bed and stood, scanning the room for some sort of weapon. Nothing obvious came to mind, so out of desperation she crossed the room and gripped the back of one of the chairs at the table. It was small, and light enough that she thought she could swing it like a club, though she wasn't foolish enough to believe that would do any good against an armed and trained opponent. But it was better than nothing.

She lifted the chair, crossed to the door and stopped a pace short of it, then set the chair down in front of her. She didn't lift it and hold it in a static position while she waited. If they took too long coming for her, she'd weaken, and not be able to swing the chair with any real force. She did hope she was being foolishly paranoid.

The door burst open and Geltkarl staggered into the room, carrying a heavy grav pistol in one hand. Blood stained the front of her tunic, and she held her left arm clutched close to her body, a grimace of pain on her face.

She put her back to the door and slammed it shut, then extended the pistol toward Nikaela and spoke through gritted teeth. "Take the weapon."

Nikaela shoved the chair to one side, took the pistol from the wounded NCO, checked the safety, but didn't take precious seconds to check the load and charge. Geltkarl would not have handed her a useless weapon.

Nikaela spun about, grabbed the edge of the table, tipped it onto its side, and slid it in front of the bed. She helped Geltkarl stagger across the room, and they both took cover behind the bed. The table wouldn't stop a heavy grav slug, but it would slow it down, and hopefully the bed could do the rest.

A thought jammed itself into Nikaela's brain like a hot poker. "John," she said. "They'll be going after him too."

Geltkarl shook her head. "Nothing we can do about it. They're jamming shipnet. Just try to stay alive and hope he and his guards can do the same."

Shipnet wasn't the only way Nikaela could call for help. "Fucked them. Fucked them all."

With a quick scan of the room she spotted a hard-wired intercom recessed in the bulkhead to one side. She stood, held the pistol in both hands and kept it aimed at the door. Without taking her eyes off the entrance, she remained in a crouch, kept her back to the bulkhead and shuffled sideways toward the intercom. When she reached it, she took her left hand off the weapon and slapped the transmit switch. "Bridge, code red emergency, priority access."

"Bridge here," a male voice acknowledged. "Clarify immediately."

Nikaela kept her eyes focused on the door. "Vreekande here. We're under assault down here. And if they're coming after me, then they're going after my breschkada too."

There came only the briefest of pauses. "We're scrambling a response team now. Try to maintain your perimeter, and do not move."

Nikaela remained in a crouch as she rushed back to the bed, and hunkered down behind it with Geltkarl. She could only hope they'd get to John in time.

••••

After Primatov and Vagle left John alone, he sat down at the table to eat. There were a few items on the tray new to his taste buds, and he was thankful for that, though there was a slimy, yellow thing he found impossible to choke down. He hoped his Kelk hosts wouldn't be insulted that he passed on that one.

He was chewing on a spicy red thing he thought might be some sort of meat, when he heard a noise like that of a spring uncoiling rapidly. The bulkhead separating him from the passageway had muffled the sound, and it had almost been below the threshold of hearing—almost. It could be the kind of sound a grav pistol might make.

His thoughts raced. The closest thing he had to weapons were the knife and fork on the tray. The knife ended in a rounded point, and a quick test of the edge proved it wasn't that sharp; it didn't need to be to slice through properly cooked food. But the fork ended in three long, sharp prongs. It wasn't much, but if he had to fight for his life it would have to do.

Behind him he heard the door open slowly. He gripped the handle of the fork tightly in his right hand, stood, and turned to face the open door. A female Kelk officer walked into the room, and as she approached him he kept his right hand pressed tightly against his thigh to conceal the fork. A male oberkrieger walked in behind her, and John caught a momentary glint from something in his right hand, something shiny like polished steel or plast. Both wore a sidearm, and had styled their hair in dreadlocks, which for some Kelk was an open statement of a more martial attitude toward the Commonwealth.

The officer stopped about a pace from John, the male oberkrieger about a pace behind her. She smiled pleasantly, and spoke in Lingua. "Maestra Mathius, our captain wishes to meet you. We're here to escort you to see him."

It sounded reasonable, and could be true. If it was, and he was wrong, and he attacked them, he'd face an entire ship full of pissed-off Kelk. But a small red dot just below her eye on her left cheek caught his attention. He spotted another red dot on the sleeve of her tunic, and another just above her belt line, and two more in the hair of the man standing behind her. John had seen it before, the back-splash that occurred when shooting an opponent at close range with a heavy grav pistol: blood spatter.

It all fell into place. Possibly they were there to protect him, but if they had just repelled an attack and picked up a little blood spatter in the process of doing so, they would tell him that, not feed him some bullshit about meeting the captain. And both the officer and the man standing behind her seemed to be concealing something in their right hands.

John tried to look stupid and unaware as he smiled. "I would consider it an honor to meet your captain. Please, lead the way."

He extended his left hand in a polite gesture toward the door, but in that moment she stabbed upward with her right fist, something bright glinting in her hand as it shot toward John's face. He deflected her arm with his extended left hand and hammer-fisted the fork into her throat, aiming for the carotid artery. He charged forward as a white-hot lance of pain stabbed into his chest just below his left armpit. He plowed into her and slammed her into the man behind her, trying to keep both of them off balance so he didn't have to face two unimpeded opponents. His momentum rammed the two Kelk into the bulkhead near the door, sandwiching the woman between John and the oberkrieger behind her.

John had pinned the man between the woman and the bulkhead, and he tried to stab the fellow in the eyes with the fork as blood arced out of the woman's throat, though all he accomplished was to open several puncture wounds in the fellow's face. Every breath brought an agony of sharp, intense pain, and John knew he didn't have a lot of time to finish this. The fellow pinned against the bulkhead kept stabbing out at him with some sort of blade, while the woman struggled to reach for her sidearm, all three of them sticky with her blood.

John coughed up blood and staggered. The male Kelk took that opportunity to push off from the bulkhead, shoving the woman forward as she fumbled at her sidearm. John staggered back a step, and knowing he couldn't let the woman draw her pistol, he stabbed the fork upward into her throat just beneath her chin. She cried out and reflexively reached up to her throat, clearing her hands from her sidearm. John reached out with his left hand and snapped the weapon out of her thigh clips just as the man behind her swung out with his blade and caught John under the chin.

Pain radiated out from his jaw and he fell back stumbling over his own feet like a drunkard, the woman's grav pistol held in his left hand. Some sort of steel spike locked his jaw immovably in place, and with his own blood pouring down his chest he struggled to simply stay on his feet.

Behind the woman the male Kelk reached for his sidearm. John staggered sideways and certainly couldn't aim a weapon accurately. So he raised the grav pistol, pointed it in the general direction of the man and woman, and started pulling the trigger. The weapon kicked in his hand, the force of each recoil knocking him back a step. He fired round after round, until he finally backed into the medical bed.

He almost lost consciousness, but fought to hold onto some remnant of reality, of sanity. Someone groaned.

John managed to focus on the room for a moment. The woman lay on her back, her eyes glazed over in death and staring at the deck above her. The man lay on his side, blood leaking from a couple of wounds in his chest. His sidearm lay on the floor just out of reach. He struggled to get to it, so John pushed off from the bed, staggered the short distance to the fellow, pressed the muzzle of the grav pistol against the side of his head, and pulled the trigger. Backsplash hit John in the face and arms, and he remembered it had all begun with blood spatter.

John staggered to the bulkhead near the door and leaned against it to stay on his feet. He looked down toward the pain in his chest, but couldn't bend his head forward without intensifying the pain in his throat. The handle of some sort of blade protruded from his ribs below his left armpit. He reached up and gently touched his face. The handle of another blade protruded at an angle from just below his chin. He reached across to the right side of his face where he found the point and the last few inches of the blade protruding from his cheek. The blade had entered under his chin, bisected his tongue, and exited through the side of his face. His implants tried to suppress the pain radiating from his wounds, and perhaps they succeeded to some degree, but it sure didn't feel like it.

Somewhere in the ship alarms blared, and he wondered if it had anything to do with him.

He needed help, so he staggered to the door, opened it and staggered out into the passageway, ready to shoot at anything that moved. Two dead guards lay sprawled on the deck at his feet. Not far down the corridor he spotted a Kelk officer walking briskly toward him. At the sight of John the man froze, a pistol in his right hand, the muzzle aimed at the deck beneath him. John raised the grav pistol, intending to use the same technique he'd used earlier: pull the trigger until he finally hit something.

"No, John, don't."

He recognized that voice and hesitated. Nikaela!

••••

"Mistress Primatov, you mustn't be late for your appointment with Vice Skalde Nygaard."

Katrine looked up from unpacking her duffle and smiled at Vagle. The young woman had not spoken with any reproach in her voice, but from the look on her face she probably wanted to adopt a parental tone and say something like, *It would not be proper to keep a member of the Larscom Executive Council waiting.* Katrine had been fully conscious of the time, and did not need to be coached on the etiquette required for such a powerful woman, but she kept her thoughts to herself.

She abandoned the unpacking and turned toward the door of their small stateroom, but Vagle extended an arm, blocking her path. "Please allow me to do my job, Mistress."

Katrine nodded her acquiescence. "My apologies, Mistress Vagle. I'm not used to operating under such extreme circumstances." She didn't add that she thought it unlikely anything would happen so soon after John and Nikaela's rescue.

Vagle rested her hand on the butt of the pistol strapped to her side, then unlocked and opened the stateroom door a crack. She peered out into the passageway beyond, then glanced over her shoulder at Katrine. "It's clear."

Katrine followed Vagle out of the stateroom, and as they walked down the passageway a couple of enlisted personnel passed them going the other direction. It was a busy day on a big ship driving hard to up-transit out of the Sarkovie system. There would be harried crew members everywhere, and they encountered several on their way, all moving hastily to accomplish some task.

They climbed a ladder up to another deck and headed toward mid-ship where the large and luxurious staterooms for flag officers were located. Up ahead, as Vagle approached an intersection, a female NCO carrying some sort of tool kit rounded the corner from a connecting passageway, and headed their way. She was followed by a male officer carrying a similar tool kit. The NCO smiled and nodded politely at Vagle as she passed her, and then the alarms blared.

Katrine and Vagle both froze. The NCO, now a step past Vagle and slightly behind her, reached into her tool kit. Just as the woman lunged at Vagle, Katrine shouted in Kelk, "Behind you," and reached for the small pistol in the shoulder holster beneath her armpit. In the same instant the male officer in front of Vagle reached into his tool kit for something.

Vagle spun and barely cleared her sidearm from her holster as the NCO plowed into her. Katrine heard the report of a grav pistol just as Vagle screamed in pain. The NCO staggered away from her clutching at her gut. Vagle slumped to the deck, the handle of some sort of blade protruding from her side. Just beyond her the male officer pulled a grav pistol out of his tool kit.

Later, Katrine realized they expected her to be unarmed and were focused on killing Vagle. They needed to clear the real threat first, then they could handle an unarmed Commonwealth Blacksword with little difficulty. Their focus on Vagle gave her the fraction of a second she needed. As the male officer stood over Vagle and lowered the muzzle of his pistol toward her head, Katrine crouched, holding her small pistol in both hands, and aimed for a quick body-shot.

She pulled the trigger, the gun kicked in her hand, and a bright red splotch blossomed on the man's chest. He staggered back, raising the pistol and fired a wild shot in Katrine's direction. The bullet tore a chunk of muscle out of Katrine's left upper arm, she cried out at the pain and dropped her left hand away from the pistol. But she had the presence of mind to keep it gripped tightly in her right hand as she lurched sideways.

As the male officer tried to raise his pistol again, years of training helped Katrine focus on the mission and ignore the pain. She marched forward to shorten the distance between them, raised the pistol and fired another round. The bullet punched a hole high on the right side of the man's chest and he dropped his pistol.

He froze for a moment, a look of surprise on his face. He looked at Katrine, then at Vagle, then at the pistol on the deck in front of him. He bent forward carefully, reaching for the weapon. Katrine marched two more steps forward. By that time he had bent over quite a bit and all she saw was the salt and pepper hair on the top of his head. She raised the pistol, pulled the trigger, and planted a bullet in the middle of his head. He crumpled to the deck in a heap.

Movement from the NCO drew Katrine's attention. The woman had dropped her tool kit and was struggling to reach it. A gut wound could take a long time to kill a person, so Katrine still treated her as a threat. She took one step, stood over the tool kit, and kicked it out of reach of the NCO. She backed up to lean against the bulkhead on the other side of the passageway, and kept her pistol aimed at the woman.

Lying on the deck at her feet, Vagle's breathing came in gasps, a grimace on her face.

Katrine asked, "How bad?"

Vagle spoke through gritted teeth. "Not good, but I'll live. Security team is on its way."

5

Double Insult

WHEN THE DOOR to Nikaela's makeshift stateroom swung open and slammed against the interior bulkhead, she started and almost fired the pistol at nothing. The doorway remained empty, with a clear view of the passageway outside. She saw the legs of someone sprawled on the deck there, smears of blood nearby. She tensed, preparing to fire her pistol the moment anyone appeared in the open door.

Someone out in the passageway shouted, "It's Brynjar here. Don't shoot me. I like staying alive."

Nikaela thought she recognized the Command Superior's voice, but she wasn't going to take any chances. "Move slowly and step into view, hands empty, no weapons."

Brynjar stepped into the open doorway with his hands held out at his sides, empty palms aimed forward. Nikaela recognized him immediately and stood up. She raced around the bed, but at the doorway Brynjar blocked her path. "Where do you think you're going?"

"My breschkada," she shouted. "They'll be going after him too. I'm going with or without you."

He shook his head. "With me, and behind me, or not at all."

He turned away from her and marched up the passageway. Nikaela followed, hindered by a squad of armed troops filing into her stateroom. She called over her shoulder, "Geltkarl's hurt. Help her."

Even though Brynjar didn't run, his long legs and stride forced Nikaela to move quickly to keep up with him. They turned at an intersection, and he marched ahead of her toward John's stateroom. In the passageway near his door, two guards lay in a sprawl unmoving, blood spatter on the door and smears of it on the deck around them.

Brynjar was half way to the door when it burst open and John staggered out into the passageway. Marching in front of Nikaela, Brynjar froze. At the site of John covered in blood from head to foot, Nikaela did the same and her gut clenched with horror.

John swayed drunkenly from side-to-side, a pistol in his left hand. It took Nikaela a moment to understand what she saw. The handle of some sort of blade jutted from the left side of his chest. The handle of another blade protruded at an angle beneath his chin, and some sort of spike extended out of his right cheek a few inches.

When he saw Brynjar he froze and raised the pistol, aiming it at the command superior, the barrel of the weapon wavering unsteadily. Brynjar remained unmoving and didn't raise his own pistol, but held it close to his side, the muzzle pointing at the deck.

Nikaela wanted to kiss the command superior for his presence of mind, wasn't sure she could have squashed her natural reaction to defend herself the way Brynjar had. She shouted, "No, John, don't."

Her breschkada hesitated, tried to say something, but all that came out was a piteous groan. Nikaela tasted the salt of tears as they drizzled down her cheeks and across her lips.

"It's Brynjar, John," Nikaela shouted. "He's a friend. Don't shoot him."

John lowered the pistol just a little, looked over it and squinted at them as if trying to focus. Nikaela carefully placed Geltkarl's pistol on the deck, then stepped around Brynjar and held her hands up with her empty palms out. "Only friends here, John. Only friends now."

John hesitated, swaying unsteadily from side to side. Then he lowered the weapon and his shoulders slumped. He staggered as if he might fall over at any moment.

Nikaela lowered her hands and walked cautiously toward him. She stopped a pace away and held out her hand. "It's over, John. Give me the weapon."

He stared at her, continued to sway back and forth, and his eyes appeared unfocused. She reached out and gently took the weapon out of his hands. "It's over. Only friends here now."

His eyes finally focused on her face. But behind him, a crewwoman striding toward them drew Nikaela's attention. The women held a pistol in one hand, and as she marched toward them she raised it, aiming it at John's back.

Nikaela leaned to one side, raised John's pistol, aimed past him and pulled the trigger. The weapon kicked in her hand, and the woman staggered just as she fired her pistol. The bullet zinged of the bulkhead near John's face. The crewwoman came to a stop, a bright red spot appearing in the middle of her chest, a look of confusion on her face. She tried again to raise her weapon and aim it at John.

This time Nikaela took a fraction of a second to aim carefully. She pulled the trigger, the gun kicked, and a bright red dot appeared in the woman's forehead just above her left eye. The crewwoman dropped her pistol, crumpled to the deck and lay there unmoving.

Nikaela approached the body slowly, keeping the muzzle of her pistol aimed at the woman's head. She kicked the crewwoman's weapon down the passageway toward John, and looked closely at her. The woman's mouth hung open, and her eyes stared blindly at nothing, the back of her head a cratered exit wound.

Nikaela backed away from her, then turned, looked John's way, and gulped back more tears. She tried to sound casual. "Well, I guess *she* wasn't a friend. But we don't have to worry about her anymore."

John swayed and stared at her dumbly as Brynjar approached him. The command superior stopped a pace away from him, his eyes focused on something in John's hand. Brynjar said, "A fork!"

John looked down at his right hand. Nikaela followed his gaze. In his blood soaked fingers he held a fork, gripped so tightly his knuckles had gone white.

John's knees buckled and Brynjar caught him, then lowered him gently to the deck.

••••

When the security team arrived, Katrine slid down the bulkhead and plopped her butt on the deck of the passageway, though she kept her pistol aimed at the wounded NCO. The head of the security team, a tall male command superior, halted a few paces away, a grav pistol in his hand.

Katrine waved her weapon at the NCO. "She tried to kill us." She nodded toward the dead male officer. "So did he."

As two crewmembers of the security detail restrained the NCO, a medic tried to examine Katrine's wound, but she waved the woman off. "Mistress Vagle is worse off than me. Take care of her first."

The medic's eyebrows rose, but she didn't argue and turned her attention to the young Kelk officer.

The command superior called for more medical people, and they arrived in short order. With the NCO no longer a threat, and a medic administering to Vagle, Katrine didn't argue as another medic cut away the uniform surrounding the wound in her upper arm.

Damn, she thought. She didn't have that many serviceable uniforms, and now she would have one less.

The command superior stood over them looking on. The medic looked up at him. "Nasty wound, but nothing life threatening. Let's get a grav stretcher up here and get her to surgery."

"Wait," Katrine said. She addressed the command superior. "What about Maestra Mathius and Mistress Vreekande?"

His eyes defocused as he communicated through his implants. When they focused again on Katrine, he didn't look at all happy. "Mistress Vreekande is unharmed. But Ensign Mathius is seriously wounded."

Katrine knew she could put on a really good bitch-face when she wanted to, and she let the medic see it now. "Just field-prep it, give me something for the pain, and you can do the real work later."

••••

John awoke lying on his back, and he decided he had too many women in his life. An entire circle of female faces stood over him looking down on him: Nikaela, Primatov, Kristdokar, an older woman wearing three four-pointed stars on the collars of her uniform—that must be Nygaard—and a woman he didn't recognize wearing surgical scrubs. Primatov's left arm hung in a sling, and bright red smears of blood stained bandages on her shoulder and the material of her uniform.

Nygaard said, "A fork!"

John had a vague memory of someone else saying the same thing, though he couldn't recall who or when.

The woman in surgical scrubs said something in Kelk, but spoke too rapidly for him to understand her.

Nikaela clutched his right hand like a concerned mother and spoke in Lingua. "She said it's good you didn't try to remove the blades. You could have bled to death. She told me you're going to live. Just don't move. And whatever you do, don't try to talk."

Her cheeks glistened with moisture, and John realized she had been crying.

She looked at the woman in surgical scrubs—probably a doctor—and spoke Kelk slowly. "Speak more slowly so he can understand you. Or better yet, speak Lingua."

They had clearly placed him on a gurney of some sort. The doctor nodded and spoke in Lingua. "We've nerve-blocked the wound sites so you should feel a little less discomfort. And we've paralyzed much of your face. But even then don't move. Don't try to say anything. You'll only cause more damage. The knife in your throat barely missed your carotid artery, and any movement could cause the blade to slice into it."

A couple of med techs moved among them, sticking needles in John and attaching all sorts of wires to him. Primatov leaned forward over him, grimacing with pain as she did so. She carefully examined the blade bisecting his chin and jaw. She pursed her lips and glanced briefly at the one protruding from his chest. Her brow furrowed, an odd look of curiosity formed on her face, and any hint of pain disappeared.

She straightened, frowned, shook her head, and appeared to address John as she said, "Both appear to be bone-handled steel knives. That seems rather odd." She looked at Kristdokar, then at Nygaard. "Or is it symbolic?"

Nikaela's face tightened with anger as she looked into John's eyes. "Fucked them. Fucked them all. They tried to fucked you good, but you fucked them gooder." She hesitated, tears streaming down her cheeks. "Did I say it right?"

The other three Kelk women appeared quite uncomfortable, and for a moment John's senses cleared. The looks on their faces told him he needed to hear the answer to Primatov's question. It took every bit of strength he had, but he forced the confusion of pain and fear out of his mind. His thinking turned diamond hard and crystal clear, though he could maintain that only briefly.

Kristdokar spoke hesitantly. "A double insult. A long time ago, in a more primitive time, by tradition, butchers used a bone-handled steel knife to slaughter livestock. Their blades were quite good and they were highly skilled."

She paused and closed her eyes, as if reluctant to continue the story. When she spoke again, John easily heard the strain in her voice. "It became customary that when someone committed a capital crime, the local head of the butcher's guild acted as executioner, dispatching the offender with a bone-handled steel dagger thrust up through the chin into the brain. More often than not, the butcher's skills did not translate well to the talents needed for a swift execution, and the death was neither quick nor easy."

Nikaela looked into John's face and fed him with her anger. Nygaard and the doctor would not meet John's eyes, but Kristdokar looked at him without hesitation. "I'm sorry, John. It was intended as a double insult. Their message is that you are a criminal, and you deserve to be treated no better than cattle."

Primatov asked, "Is that the same kind of knife they pulled out of Mistress Vagle's side?"

The skin around Kristdokar's eyes had tightened, bringing out a field of small crow's-feet surrounding them. Her voice cracked when she said, "Yes."

Primatov looked really scary at that moment. "Then the same was meant for me. Does the hatred for us run so deep in all Kelk?"

Nygaard said, "Not in all Kelk."

Kristdokar said, "It's complicated."

Nygaard seemed to struggle for words. "It doesn't help that you're Blackswords."

With the blade bisecting his jaw, John couldn't speak, but he pinned Kristdokar with his eyes, tried to give her a predatory and hateful look, and she gave him the satisfaction of flinching.

He couldn't talk, but he could communicate with Primatov directly through their implants. *The blades are mine . . . my property . . . I want them. I own them. Keep them for me.*

Primatov looked into his eyes and nodded, her lips pressed into a tight, straight line. When something made Primatov really angry, she looked like the scariest woman John had ever met. She turned to Nygaard and Kristdokar. "Ensign John Mathius claims these two knives as his property. When you've removed them, please do not clean them, do not remove his blood from them, and deliver them to me. I will hold them in his name."

Kristdokar looked to Nygaard for a decision. The vice skalde's brows rose and her eyes blinked rapidly for a second. She took a deep breath and after several seconds of silence let it out slowly, then spoke in a flat, cold tone of voice. "I suppose we cannot deny such a request."

Still displaying her scary bitch-face, Primatov shook her head. "It's not a request."

••••

The fear that John was close to death, and anger at those who had attacked him so brutally, had clouded Nikaela's thinking. And when the surgeon finished her initial examination and announced that, while his wounds were horrific, he would nevertheless live, the flood of relief had distracted her as much as the fear and anger. Not until Primatov pointed out that the blades were bone-handled steel did Nikaela realize the insult John's attackers had intended, and then her anger blossomed into absolute fury.

It was also rather astute of Primatov to recognize there might be a symbolic element to such weapons. Had she not done so, Nikaela's superiors might have decided to never mention the symbolism meant by the use of butcher's blades. That wouldn't have stopped Nikaela from telling John, though in doing so she would probably have incurred Nygaard's wrath, and possibly that of Kristdokar as well. Fucked them!

When they floated John on the grav gurney into the surgery, leaving Nikaela alone with Nygaard, Kristdokar and Primatov, Nikaela turned to the Blacksword officer and demanded, "I want one of those blades. He's my breschkada. We should both carry one."

Nygaard's eyes immediately hardened with anger and disapproval, while Kristdokar appeared to be simply curious.

Primatov shrugged. "It's a moot point. They belong to John, so I don't have the right to give one away."

Nygaard's anger dissipated, and smug satisfaction replaced the look on her face.

Nikaela considered making her request a demand, but she didn't think the ire of a lowly command boss junior rank would carry any intimidation value for a vice skalde. As she tried to think of another approach, Primatov added, "But I'll relay your request to John, and I have no doubt he'll be happy to comply."

Nygaard's anger returned.

6

One Sided Relationship

NONE OF THE assailants who attacked John or Nikaela had survived. But the NCO who attacked Katrine had suffered only a gut wound; nasty, but not life threatening if treated quickly. When Katrine asked to see the woman, the ship's medical staff informed her that the NCO had died of her wounds. Bullshit!

Katrine worked her way up the chain of command to *Konigsborge*'s Chief Medical Officer, a man who stood a few centimeters shorter than her. To get in to see him she browbeat one of his subordinates, and though she wouldn't admit it, it surprised her that she succeeded. She cornered the CMO in sick-bay.

"Colonel Primatov," he said, "what can I do for you?"

To emphasize her height advantage and any intimidation factor that might provide, she stood fairly close to him. "I want to see the woman who tried to assassinate me."

He shook his head. "I'm sorry, but she died of her wounds."

"Then let me see her body."

He shrugged. "If you wish."

"I do."

They led her into the ship's morgue and to a body draped in a preservation blanket. The Chief Medical Officer peeled the blanket back enough to expose the face of a dead Kelk woman. Perhaps they thought all Kelk looked alike to Katrine, but the woman lying on the gurney in front of her had an oval face, whereas the woman who had attacked her had a long face with high cheek bones.

To confirm her suspicions, Katrine reached out and quickly pulled the blanket down, exposing the woman's naked body down to her waist. The Chief Medical Officer reacted quickly and pulled the edge of the blanket back up to cover the woman completely. "See here," he said. "That was uncalled for."

Katrine merely smiled and walked out of the morgue. She had seen all she needed to see. The dead woman had a bullet hole in her chest, and her abdomen remained undamaged, but the NCO who had attacked Katrine had received only one wound, the gut wound.

She contacted Kristdokar through her implants.

Can it wait for another time? the skalde asked. *I'm quite busy right now.*

No, it can't. I want to see the assassin who survived.

None did.

That's not true. You're lying to me.

Kristdokar answered her with a long moment of silence, then said, *Why do you say that?*

Katrine explained how the CMO had showed her the wrong corpse. *The NCO who attacked me had only one wound, a gut wound, and I know that because I watched Vagle put it there. And I held a gun on her until she was subdued by your people and taken away. Taken away alive, I should add. I'm guessing they showed me the body of one of the other assassins, or perhaps one of the guards killed protecting our breschkada. You're lying to me. You're all lying to me.*

Again, Kristdokar answered her by saying nothing. Katrine waited, allowing the silence to grow pregnant and uncomfortable.

Very well, Kristdokar finally said. *Meet me in sick-bay.*

When Katrine reached sick-bay, she found Kristdokar speaking in hushed tones with the CMO. He saw her approaching and grimaced. Then he led the two women into the ICU, and to a bed occupied by a woman whose face Katrine easily recognized.

The woman lay in a semi-conscious stupor. Gut wounds took a little longer to clean up, but it had been more than a day since the attack, and they still had her heavily sedated. They had also restrained her tightly to the bed, her hands, legs, torso, and forehead strapped down so she couldn't move. She mumbled something incoherent.

Katrine leaned down to hear her better.

"Kill me . . . please . . . headaches . . . Blackswords . . . dying anyway . . . kill me . . . kill me . . . kill me."

Katrine straightened and looked again at the straps holding the woman down. They could be used to keep a dangerous person from harming others, or to keep a delusional woman from taking her own life. Katrine looked at the surgeon who wouldn't meet her eyes, then at Kristdokar.

The older woman grimaced and said, "She's quite superstitious."

Katrine nodded. "How so?"

Kristdokar shook her head. "We don't know. She's delirious."

That had been a lie. Of that, Katrine had no doubt. Katrine threw several questions at Kristdokar and the surgeon, but they answered her with nothing but evasion.

What did they so desperately want to hide from her?

••••

Fran Thealone watched the virtual image of Katrine as she finished reciting her story and her report came to an end. Seated at a fold-down desk in the shipboard office of *Lightspear*'s commanding officer, the younger woman spoke as if the two of them were in the same room. Fran listened to every word with rapt attention.

"So I'm not sure how I did it," Katrine said, "but you're going to get an invitation to send a diplomatic mission to Viktorkinde to, and this is the official line, '. . . initiate preliminary discussions on matters of mutual benefit.' I tried to keep it as vague as possible so it won't piss off too many members of the senate. And I recommend you play down the whole assault and kidnap thing. The hawks will probably call that an act of war by the Kelk, even though a Commonwealth company was originally responsible for John's abduction. And above all, don't say anything about the fact that they gave me no choice when it came to John accompanying them back to Viktorkinde. They'd have a field day with that as well."

Katrine paused for a moment and drummed her fingers on the surface of the small desk. "Maybe you can spin it something like . . .'We were out here in the dark reaches of space and after mutual cooperation against a common enemy, they invited us to return with them to pave the way for more fruitful interactions between the Commonwealth and the Supremacy. And we accepted their invitation because it was an incredible opportunity to gather heretofore unheard-of intelligence on the Kelk.' "

Katrine inhaled carefully. "Go with that, or whatever you think best. But I think it has to be something along those lines. That might satisfy the hawks, especially the stuff about gathering intelligence. And I know I need to keep my name out of this as much as possible, so Nygaard has agreed to issue the invitation officially from the Executive Council to the offices of Senator Gascoigne. You should receive it in the next five to ten days."

She paused again, and rubbed her chin like a man testing the stubble on his face, her eyes focused a thousand yards away. Fran had seen her rub her chin that way a hundred times before. "I recommend you use *Lightspear* to ferry messages between our chain of communications buoys and theirs. In that way you and Kristdokar can communicate with a delay of no more than three or four days. But we're going to be in transit back to Viktorkinde for the next two tendays, so she won't receive anything you send until them. At least that's what they've told me. Stall, Fran. Buy us time."

She paused and rubbed her temples. "On the other hand, if they stop at any of the intermediate buoys on the way there, they could retrieve messages earlier than that, messages going either way, and I won't know about it unless they tell me. So number your messages and start sending them as soon as possible. *Lightspear* has about a four-day round trip between the terminuses of the two relay chains, so it won't do any good to send them any more frequently than four days. But do respond immediately, even if it's nothing more than a simple acknowledgement, and follow that with a new message every four days regardless. If I don't receive your messages, or any are missing out of the numbered sequence, I'll know something is wrong. I'll number mine as well, and this is my message number one."

Primatov leaned back and appeared to be finished. But then she started and said, "Oh yes, one more thing. Get hold of John's O-School roommate, May Forester. She'll be worried about him. Tell her he's okay. Tell her he's alive and healthy."

Fran leaned back in her chair and sighed. She had played the message back in its entirety twice now, and still couldn't believe what she had heard. What was it about John Mathius? Tarsik Obradour had called him a catalyst, and now he had proven to be that in spades. She would need Obradour's help and cooperation on this.

She opened a channel in her implants directly to her secretary. *Find Senator Gascoigne. I don't care where he is or what he's doing. Tell him I need to talk to him yesterday if not sooner. And tell him it has to be here in my office.*

I'm sorry, Colonel, the woman said, *but I know for a fact he's out of town at the moment at some sort of political rally.*

Fran knew exactly what would spur Mani to cut short his trip. *Then tell him I've heard from Katrine Primatov. Tell him I need him back here as soon as possible. And politely contact Tarsik Obradour. They'll probably only put you through to one of his staffers, so tell them to tell him I've just received a report from Katrine Primatov, and ask for a few minutes of his time at his convenience. He'll know what that means.*

••••

Lying on top of Faith, Macus's heart slowly stopped pounding and his breathing slowed. He put his palms down on the bed on either side of her and pushed up off of her. His sweat and saliva glistened on her bare breasts, and that always gave him a bit of a thrill.

"That was good," he said, grinning at her, though the look on her face didn't reflect his own satisfaction.

He licked one of her nipples, then rolled to one side, swung his legs off the bed, and stood. He grabbed a corner of the sheet on her bed and wiped off his penis. When he did that her eyes flashed with anger, but he ignored her and turned toward her bathroom.

Behind him, she spoke calmly and precisely. "Where are you going?"

He stopped and glanced over his shoulder. "Thought I'd grab a shower before going home."

She shook her head. "I'm not done yet."

"Oh," he said, turning to face her squarely. "You didn't get off? I'm sorry about that."

"No you're not."

He chuckled and shrugged. "No, I guess I'm not. But you know how it is. It happens."

She gave him a flat, lifeless grin. "Not anymore it doesn't."

He took great care not to sigh visibly or show any exasperation. That would just piss her off even more. There had been little signs lately that she would be trouble, and he wondered if he should dump her. On the other hand the sex was damn good, and if he could figure out a way, he'd like to keep her around, as long as she didn't make too many demands. And unlike Dog-Face, her looks were up to his standards, so he wouldn't mind appearing in public with her.

"Listen," he said. "You've enjoyed yourself other times. So what if it didn't work for you this time. Big deal."

Faith sat up, swung her long legs off the bed, and sat facing him in a most matter-of-fact way, making no effort to close her legs, and with no pretense at modesty. He liked that about her.

She stood and crossed the short distance between them, stopping with the points of her nipples only an inch or two away from his chest. "It wasn't just this once, darling, and it's not the sex that's the issue here. In fact, the sex has nothing to do with it. Oh, it's nice to take care of that itch with an intelligent, capable, and handsome partner. But if it was just the sex that was lacking, I'd get that taken care of elsewhere. Unfortunately, the sex is symptomatic of the one-sided nature of our entire relationship."

He grimaced, and tried not to sound condescending as he said, "But our relationship *is* rather one-sided. Yah, we fuck each other, and you must admit you have enjoyed it too. But I'm the one on the way up, and you're the one who's still a glorified gofer. You wouldn't give me the time of day until I got that promotion."

She shook her head sadly. "You and I are the two pretty ones on Palmutter's staff, and good looks help with everything. But if we were going to join forces, I needed to see if you had more than that going for you."

He scoffed at her. "Well I'm no longer just a fucking aide, am I?"

She grinned as if he had missed some point. "You and I are also the two smart ones, so stop acting like a moron."

He rolled his eyes, and from the way her eyes again flashed with anger, he realized immediately that had been a mistake.

"No shower," she said, her voice almost a whisper. "Just get dressed and leave. Until you decide you want to have a truly mutually beneficial relationship, you can go back to fucking Dog-Face."

Macus didn't recall telling her his nickname for Palmutter's not-so-pretty aide, but he must have.

Faith sat down on the bed, and again didn't close or cross her legs. She watched him silently as he put on his clothes. He couldn't resist a few surreptitious looks her way, glancing at the shadow between her legs, and he left her apartment with an erection.

7

Move Quickly

JOHN AWOKE LYING on his back in a medical bed with a bank of instruments above his head, which didn't come as any great surprise. His implants told him he'd been out for three days.

His first thought was that they had returned him to his makeshift, private stateroom. But when he raised his head and glanced about, he saw no sign of the table and chairs, there were two other medical beds in the room—both empty—and the place looked more like the ICU of a ship's sick bay.

He carefully probed at the wound in his left side, found a lot of bandages and tenderness there, which struck him as unusual after three days. He reached up and delicately touched his face, was not surprised to find bandages there as well, but was surprised to learn how extensively the dressings covered his neck, jaw, and the right side of his head. Tubes protruded from every orifice he had, and some from surgically implanted holes in his skin. There were enough wires attached to him to light him up like one of the more gaudy establishments on the strip just off the O-School academy campus.

They must have been monitoring him, because the door opened and in walked a male Kelk doctor and a female medical tech, escorted by short, stocky Grandeseergent Matsen, and tall, handsome Unterseergent Kolbeck.

For some reason John felt safe with those two men present, and he relaxed a little, though he didn't know why he should trust them any more than anyone else. Perhaps he had faith in them simply because they had had plenty of opportunities to kill him, and yet he still remained among the living. He thought it ironic that he now limited his friends to those who weren't hell-bent on murdering him.

The med tech helped John sit up, and in doing so he learned that everything hurt. With speed healing, rapid regrowth, and all the other medical technologies available, after three days he should be close to completely healed.

"Hurts, doesn't it?" the doctor said, speaking Lingua. "Your body didn't respond to some of the accelerated healing tech we tried on you, so repair of the punctured lung and reconstruction of your tongue and throat has progressed more slowly than I would have liked. Have you gone through a lot of accelerated healing recently?"

John recalled calm-voice and pissed-off-guy's beatings, and the way the doctor had warned them that repeated use of those technologies would produce side effects like rejection. She had been as much a victim of those two assholes as John, and he did hope she survived.

John nodded, but moving his jaw and lips still hurt quite a bit, so he spoke slowly, and the words came out somewhat garbled. "Yah. A lot." He had trouble pronouncing consonants, so "lot" had sounded more like "loh."

The doctor nodded in an all-knowing, irritating way. "That's what I thought. That means our use of accelerated healing and in-situ rapid regrowth is going to be quite limited. We can still culture new tissue rather quickly in the lab, but we'll have to surgically reconstruct. And you're going to have to do a lot of healing the old-fashioned way."

The man launched into a lecture on the overuse of medical tech and John tuned him out. He noticed Matsen rolling his eyes, and Kolbeck grinning. When the doctor finally finished educating them on his vast knowledge of medical technology, he and the tech left, while the two soldiers remained and approached John's bed.

John scanned the room around him. It appeared to be an ICU on a ship. "Is this the ICU?"

Matsen nodded. "Yah, but we moved you to *Drakan Helgis*. Moved Mistress Vreekande here too." Again, he spoke Kelk slowly and carefully so John could follow him.

Kolbeck said, "And moved that good-looking Blacksword colonel here too."

The tall man nodded and lowered his voice, speaking in a confidential tone. "I sure wouldn't mind getting that woman in—"

"Button it," Matsen snarled, shaking his head sadly. "Higher-ups figure the three of you got a better chance of surviving the journey to Viktorkinde on *Drakan Helgis*."

"Smaller ship, smaller crew," Kolbeck said. "Fewer people want you dead."

Primatov had told John the destroyer's crew had been vetted from the start to limit anti-Commonwealth sentiment, so it was probably a wise move.

Matsen leaned down to look carefully at the bandages covering the side of John's face. "Wouldn't know he had it in him, would you?"

Kolbeck shrugged. "You never know. It's the crazy ones that don't look crazy."

John demanded, "What are you—" He had forgotten to speak slowly and that hurt like hell. "What . . . are you . . . talking . . . about?" It had sounded more like *Wha are ooo awking aowou?* but Matsen seemed to have a basic understanding of what John had tried to say.

Matsen nodded his head up and down, then switched to side-to-side. "Killed 'em with a fork, eh?"

Kolbeck added, "And there was two of 'em. Two to one, with sidearms and butcher's daggers, and you took 'em out with a fork."

Kolbeck leaned down and put his head next to Matsen's to examine John's facial bandages at close range. "And then you bust into the passageway, blades sticking out of you everywhere, bleeding all over the place, waving a fork about, and ready to keep on killing. Scared the shit out of everyone." He nodded and reiterated, "Took 'em out with a fork."

"Not true," John said. "Started . . . fork, but . . . killed with . . . pistol."

The two men stopped examining John's bandaged face and straightened. Matsen looked like he didn't believe a word John said. "You know what they're saying about you?"

John shook his head, his irritation and frustration growing, especially since he had to find a way to communicate with the fewest possible words. "Crazy."

"Yah, they're saying that," Matsen said. "But they're also saying that while one Kelk soldier is worth any two Commonwealth soldiers, the fucking asshole Blacksword just proved he's worth any two Kelk soldiers. That's really pissing some people off, and some of 'em want to prove that ain't true."

The last thing John needed was Kelk hot-heads lining up to challenge John Mathius's standing as the meanest dude within three hundred light-years. He couldn't hide his frustration any longer. "Not true."

Kolbeck shook his head sadly and lifted his eyebrows. "Killed two of 'em, with a fork."

The door opened and Primatov walked into the room accompanied by Vagle, her constant shadow. The Blacksword colonel carried a cloth-wrapped bundle beneath one arm, and as she approached John's bed, Matsen and Kolbeck stepped back a pace. Kolbeck's eyes followed Primatov like radar tracking a target, though he seemed to be focused mostly on her chest until she walked past him, then his eyes concentrated on her butt.

Primatov stopped beside John's bed and placed the cloth-wrapped bundle in his lap. "You claimed these as yours."

John unwrapped the bundle to reveal the two bone-handled steel daggers, both discolored by dark brown stains. He didn't touch either of them, just stared at them lying on the cloth in his lap.

Primatov picked one up and examined it carefully. "What are you going to do with these, John?" John thought he heard a note of disapproval in her voice.

He had not really expected them to honor his demand. "I don't know, ma'am."

She returned the blade to the cloth, laying it next to its companion. "This has become a delicate situation. So when you figure that out, please let me know."

"Yes, ma'am."

"I have a question for you," she said, her tone lightening. "What is it with you and kitchen utensils?"

Kolbeck and Matsen stood in the background nodding knowingly, though Kolbeck's eyes still remained focused on Primatov's ass.

Primatov continued. "I suppose we should now arm all our combatants with forks and paring knives. They can simply snack their way through an enemy engagement."

John prayed that Kolbeck and Matsen's Lingua wasn't good enough to follow that. And to his relief, Kolbeck frowned as if full understanding had eluded him, though that was probably due more to his intent focus on Primatov's ass, than any lack of facility with Lingua. On the other hand, Matsen squinted suspiciously at John, and with a questioning look on his face he silently mouthed the words, *paring knife?*

••••

As Senator Manifort Gascoigne watched Katrine Primatov's report, Fran Thealone sat silently and observed his reaction. When Katrine disclosed she had finagled an invitation from a member of the Larscom Executive Council for a Commonwealth diplomatic mission to Viktorkinde, he sat up straight and said, "Holy mother-fucking shit!"

His reaction had not been terribly different from Fran's own, and was exactly what they could expect from just about everyone else. Fran knew Mani well enough to know his response was merely a display of surprise. On the other hand, when hawks like Palmutter learned of this, they might say the same words, but the emotion behind them would be more akin to anger and fury.

When the report ended, Gascoigne looked at Fran and said, "Shit! Shit! Shit!"

Fran nodded. "Exactly."

"That woman can think on her feet."

"She's one of my best."

"That's obvious," Gascoigne said. "So let's give her a little more rank, bump her up to bird colonel."

Doing that would please Fran no end. "If you can get that past the promotion board, I'll be happy to do so."

Gascoigne gritted his teeth in a grimace. "If the promotion board hears what she's done, some of them are going to want to court-martial her, though they won't say that openly. They have to at least pretend they're in favor of preventing open hostilities with a foreign power. But I think the majority of the board would view her actions favorably and vote for promotion, which is all we need. Still, we're better off if we just don't tell them she's responsible for the invitation."

Gascoigne nodded, his wheels clearly turning. Then he started, as if some thought had occurred to him. "How long has that young Kelk woman been an officer?"

Fran consulted her implants, but they had next to nothing on Command Boss Junior Rank Nikaela Vreekande. "She was an officer on Reisenar, and I think newly commissioned at that time. That would make it a little over a year and a half, maybe more."

Gascoigne appeared none too happy about that answer. "That's what I thought. So if they're anything like us, she's coming due for a time-in-grade promotion."

Fran's thinking caught up with Gascoigne's. "I hadn't thought of that. She'll out-rank him, and we don't want that, do we?"

Gascoigne asked, "But can't Primatov just give him a brevet promotion? And once she's got the rank of bird colonel it'll carry even more weight."

Fran shook her head. "That won't work. A brevet rank doesn't carry the full authority or precedence of the actual rank."

Gascoigne slashed his hand through the air like a knife. "Then we'll cut hard orders Primatov can hold in reserve and promote him as she needs to."

Fran shook her head again. "But he doesn't have time-in-grade."

Gascoigne threw his hands up in frustration. "I don't care if he's still in diapers. I don't care if we have to make him a bird colonel tomorrow, and a fucking admiral the day after that. Just leave it to me, Fran. I'll make it happen, even if I have to do it by an act of congress. We could throw a whole shit-load of medals at the kid and they'll have to promote him."

"Calm down, Mani," she said. "That would draw too much attention to him, and the way things are going right now, that could get him killed."

He took a deep breath and she watched him force an artificial calm upon himself. "You're right. But trust me, I'll still figure out a way to make it happen."

There was one issue that bothered Fran a lot. "You're talking as if this diplomatic mission is actually going to happen. You know as well as I do there are a lot of hawks who'll try to block it."

Gascoigne dismissed her fears with a wave of his hand. "That's a good point, but I figure we can handle that by moving quickly. It doesn't matter if you're a hawk or a dove, after a hundred and fifty years of killing each other, being on a diplomatic mission to the Supremacy will carry a great deal of prestige. So we sit on this without making an official announcement, but we start a few controlled rumors. While the rumors are spreading, and they'll spread like wild fire, behind the scenes we enlist the right people. Then we simultaneously announce that the invitation is real, and who is going to be on the mission. And we tell everyone we've been quietly working on this for months. Then before anyone can get organized, we jump on those ships and get the hell out of here before anyone can stop us."

"So we're going to move fast on this, eh?"

He grinned. "You bet your ass we are."

Fran's thoughts raced as she considered what would be needed to make it happen. "I'm going to start immediately looking into how we can divert two cruisers. And we'll also want to divert a couple of hunter-killers. We'll need them scouting ahead of us, just so we don't run into any unpleasant surprises. We can't bring them with us into sovereign Supremacy space, but they'll stay with us as long as they can. I'll have to bring Ben Harcourt into this. He is Chief of Naval Operations, and thankfully he's a moderate."

Gascoigne stared at the floor and rocked back and forth for a few seconds. Then his eyes focused on Fran. "If you can get away with it, tell him you're sworn to secrecy, so you can't tell him everything, but you thought he should know. You won't have to tell him everything, and that might help feed the rumor mill."

Fran shook her head. "Not with Ben. If he agrees not to talk, he won't."

Fran's implants chimed with a message from her secretary. *I have Tarsik Obradour for you. He's returning your call from yesterday.*

Fran said to the woman, *Hold on a second or two.*

She focused on Gascoigne. "Mani, Obradour is returning my call."

He grimaced. "Do we have to bring him in on this?"

She shrugged. "Without his G-2 we wouldn't have known about *Caliban*, and I do feel we have an implied quid pro quo here. And with recent events, I think his hawkish inclinations are shifting a little bit closer to moderate."

Gascoigne held his hands up in resignation and leaned back in his chair.

When Fran's secretary connected her to Obradour, he appeared standing in front of the floor-to-ceiling windows of his penthouse. Fran had never been there, but Katrine had described the place to her.

"Colonel Blacksword," he said, "it's a pleasure to speak with you. My staff tells me you have late-breaking information from Colonel Primatov. I do hope it's good news."

"It is," she said. "The young man and young woman were both rescued, and at last report are alive and healthy."

He beamed a smile at her. "Excellent! Excellent! I assume Colonel Primatov also filed a full report."

Fran nodded. "She did."

"Then please transmit it to me immediately."

Fran grimaced. "I can't do that, sir." Obradour's eyes hardened as she continued. "It contains some very sensitive information, and it relates . . . some extremely unusual developments. It's not going to leave this building. In fact, I haven't even entered it into the official system. I'm keeping it in a private code block only I have access to, but you're certainly welcome to come here and view it in its entirety."

She had clearly piqued his interest. "Unusual developments?" he asked. "Private code block? Is that legal?"

She ignored his question and asked, "Your end of this line is secure?"

He smiled as if placating a recalcitrant subordinate. "Of course. And quite possibly more secure than yours."

He had an uncanny ability to irritate her, but Fran took great care not to let it show, and she hoped this time she could one-up him just a little. "Vice Skalde Nygaard of the Larscom Executive Council commanded a Kelk strike force that rescued the two young people. She invited us to"—knowing that the wording of the invitation had been carefully crafted, Fran read from a hard copy of the report—"to send a diplomatic mission to Viktorkinde to initiate preliminary discussions on matters of mutual benefit. She further invited Colonel Primatov and Ensign Mathius to accompany them back to Viktorkinde to establish the operating parameters for such discussions. To be honest, Nygaard didn't really give them a choice in the matter, so Katrine is improvising."

Obradour's eyes widened, and Fran thought, *Got you, you little son-of-a-bitch.*

He said, "I knew that young fellow was a catalyst, but I hadn't really realized just how reactive he could be. I agree that you should not release that report to anyone. I'll be at your facility in ten minutes, and I'd like to see the entire thing."

Fran worked hard to conceal any appearance of smugness.

"You said *Nygaard?*" he asked.

She nodded. "Yes, Vice Skalde Nygaard."

He grinned. "That would be Lana Nygaard. Oh, sorry, it's really Earlana Nygaard, but her friends all call her Lana. I haven't seen her in years, and I am most certainly looking forward to speaking with her again."

Fran smiled, and did not say what came to mind.

8

Crewmates

THE ACCOMMODATIONS ON the destroyer *Drakan Helgis* were more Spartan than those on *Konigsborge*. Katrine suspected there was any number of reasons for that. The destroyer, while not a small ship, was still considerably smaller than the cruiser. Furthermore, *Konigsborge* was larger than most cruisers, perhaps because it was intended as a flagship for members of the Larscom Executive Council, with spacious and luxurious staterooms available for flag-rank officers. On a ship-of-the-line like *Drakan Helgis*, the commanding officer occupied the most spacious stateroom, though it was far from luxurious, and just barely large enough to hold a private meeting of four people.

Brynjar had requested a meeting with Primatov, Kristdokar and the destroyer's skipper, Command Hawk Britta Taugrim. As Katrine approached Taugrim's stateroom, she found the door open. Inside stood Taugrim and Brynjar, chatting amiably.

Taugrim stood almost as tall as Katrine, which meant both of them stood just short of eye-to-eye with Brynjar, and a head taller than Kristdokar. The command hawk wore her snow-white hair close-cropped and spiky. Either her hair had prematurely grayed to pure white, or she had altered its color through chemical treatment or gene therapy, which would be quite unusual for a Kelk. Taugrim usually displayed a confident smile, and often walked with a hint of swagger in her step. She struck Katrine as the type of woman who might want to change the color of her hair on a regular basis, no matter how unconventional that might be among the Kelk, so Katrine's guess would be chemical treatment.

Taugrim glanced her way. "Colonel."

Katrine returned the greeting. "Captain."

When Katrine had first boarded *Drakan Helgis*, Brynjar had introduced her to Taugrim. But during the intervening three days their interactions had been limited primarily to polite conversation during meals in the officer's wardroom. Like the Commonwealth, it was customary on Kelk warships that one did not discuss business during meals in the wardroom.

Brynjar smiled at Katrine. "Colonel Primatov. Thank you for joining us. Skalde Kristdokar will be here shortly."

They shared a little small talk for a few minutes, the same kind of polite conversation that occurred during meals. When Kristdokar showed up, Brynjar closed the door and they all sat down at a small table. Once the skalde had served them the traditional tea and taken a seat, she said, "Command Superior Brynjar, you requested this meeting, so what do you wish to discuss?"

Taugrim leaned forward. "And why is my XO not present?"

Brynjar grimaced. "I have an idea, something that might bridge the divide between our two guests"—he glanced Katrine's way—"and the crew of *Drakan Helgis*. But if it's rejected, I don't want my suggestion to reach the gossip mill on ship, so I want to limit knowledge of my proposal to the absolute minimum necessary to make a decision on the matter."

Taugrim leaned back, steepled her fingers in front of her, and stared at him. "I'm intrigued."

"So am I," Kristdokar said. "What is this idea of yours?"

Katrine had come to know Brynjar well enough to see the strain in his face as he spoke. Whatever he intended to propose, he clearly expected a strong reaction from one or all of the three women seated at the table.

"I think . . ." He hesitated. "I think that during our remaining time on *Drakan Helgis*, we should ask our two guests to integrate with the crew and stand regular watches."

Katrine had not expected that, and her thoughts raced.

Kristdokar's eyebrows rose in a rare show of surprise.

Taugrim barked out a laugh. "There'll be nothing regular about that."

Both Kristdokar and Brynjar looked Katrine's way, clearly wanting to hear her reaction. It was a brilliant idea, but she could think of a hundred reasons why it would never work. "My initial reaction is that it's an excellent idea. But even after Ensign Mathius has healed more, he can't stand a regular watch with Matsen and Kolbeck hovering over him. And I don't want him outside the confines of his stateroom without them present."

Brynjar shook his head. "I don't think that's much of an issue on this ship. They can still shadow him, except while he's on duty, and then we'll assign him to bridge watch where he'll be surrounded by people we know we can trust. We'll just have to carefully orchestrate the watch roster for his shifts. He won't stand watch unless Mistress Taugrim or her XO has the conn, and as an extra precaution, we can arm both of them quietly and inconspicuously."

Taugrim slapped the palm of her hand down onto the table. "He's not trained."

Again, they all waited for Katrine's reaction. She shrugged. "He is an experienced combat soldier, and he is trained in many shipboard functions like navigation, helm, and fire-control. He's just lacking in shipboard experience." She toyed with her teacup for a moment. "What would you do with a newly commissioned command boss fresh out of the academy with lots of training and no experience?"

Brynjar and Kristdokar looked to Taugrim.

The command hawk leaned back in her chair, her lips pursed and her brow wrinkled in thought. "I would . . . I'd apprentice her—him—to a more experienced officer. But you say he's an experienced combat soldier?"

Katrine nodded. "Unlike you, we do not have a four-year academy for officers. In the Commonwealth, all officers must rise through the ranks. They start with basic training, then a year of advanced training, then one year of active service. During that year, Ensign Mathius met Mistress Vreekande on the planet Reisenar and they became breschkada, though they almost killed each other doing so."

Taugrim's eyes hardened, but Katrine saw that her interest had been sparked. "Tell me more."

"Following their year of active duty they return for six months of command school. After that, they can apply for admission to O-School, though some who show promise, like then Sergeant Mathius, are actively encouraged to do so. O-School is an additional year of training to hone their leadership skills and turn them into officers."

Taugrim closed her eyes for several seconds, then opened them. "So he actually has quite a bit more experience than one of our newly commissioned command bosses straight out of the academy?"

"Yes," Katrine said. "I believe that to be the case."

They all sat silently and waited for Taugrim to think it through. She frowned and stared at the teacup in front of her as if addressing her remarks to it. "I suppose . . . it could work . . . if we did it properly."

Her eyes focused again and she looked pointedly at Kristdokar.

The skalde nodded slowly and spoke specifically to Taugrim. "The decision is yours"—she looked at Katrine—"and yours. But both of you must approve, or I will not allow it. And even then, if you do approve, I'll have to get Vice Skalde Nygaard's authorization to do something so . . . unusual."

Taugrim gave Katrine an appraising look. "I'm willing to try if you are."

Katrine nodded. "Then let's do it."

Taugrim considered Katrine for a long moment. "As long as you understand I will—I think the expression in Lingua is—fracture his ass."

Katrine shook her head. "No, I think the expression you're looking for is *bust his ass*."

"Bust," Taugrim said. "I thought that meant a statue of a head, or a woman's breasts."

Katrine didn't want to get into the etymology of the word. "It has a third meaning akin to fracture, but it's less formal."

Taugrim smiled and sat up straight. "Then I will bust his ass."

Katrine thought it might be rather unpleasant to be the target of the woman's ass-busting. "And why do you want to do that?"

The command hawk grinned happily. "I bust every newcomer's ass. Especially newly commissioned command bosses." Her eyes flashed happily. "I'm known for it. Part of my reputation. If I didn't, my crew would think he's getting special treatment."

Katrine shrugged. "As long as it's equal treatment, I have no objection." She decided not to complicate the situation by making the woman aware of the phrase *bust his balls*.

Taugrim leaned forward and her eyes narrowed with suspicion. "I heard he asked for the butcher's blades. Did you give them to him?"

Katrine nodded. "I did."

"What does he want with them?"

Katrine thought of the way John had been treated, and she took a deep breath to quell the anger rising in her chest. "I don't know. But he's extremely angry, and I must admit I'm rather angry myself."

Kristdokar said, "I too am angry about those blades. And I too want to know what he intends to do with them."

Katrine held her hands up in a gesture of supplication. "When I learn that, I'll let you know."

"Please do," Kristdokar said and stood. "It appears we're all in agreement."

They all stood, but Taugrim halted them by saying, "I have one further recommendation: We should fit them both with Kelk combat armor." She looked at Katrine and smiled. "I noticed you didn't bring yours, and combat armor is very symbolic to all Kelk, not that you'll have any reason to use it."

"Excellent idea," Kristdokar said. "If I get approval from Vice Skalde Nygaard, then make it happen." She crossed the room, opened the stateroom door and walked out.

As Katrine started to follow her, Taugrim stopped her by saying, "Colonel Primatov, do you know the details of how the two young people became breschkada?"

Brynjar hesitated as well and Katrine glanced at him. "Actually, Maestra Brynjar and I were both there at the time."

Taugrim's eyes brightened. "I have a bottle of kirva here somewhere. Please sit back down. I'll pour us all a drink, and the two of you can tell me the story."

••••

As the car pulled into the circular, covered driveway in front of Obradour's high-rise apartment building, Gascoigne turned to Fran and reluctantly admitted, "Yah, you're right, we couldn't pull this off without him."

Obradour had agreed unequivocally with Gascoigne that the best way to block opposition was to sign up the right people in advance, and get the mission on its way as soon as possible. And he fully concurred with using some carefully placed rumors to speed the process.

When the car came to a stop, security guards waiting at the entrance to the building opened the rear doors of the vehicle. Fran and Gascoigne stepped out, and another guard held the large glass door of the building open as they walked through the entrance. As they crossed the lobby another guard kept the doors of Obradour's private lift open so they could step into it without delay.

In a single heartbeat the lift shot to the top floor. Its doors opened on a large entrance foyer where a dark-haired young man wearing an expensive business suit stood waiting for them. He greeted them as they stepped out of the lift. "Senator Gascoigne, Colonel Blacksword." He gestured toward an arched hallway on the far side of the room. "Mr. Obradour is waiting for you."

Fran had not previously experienced Obradour's penthouse, though she had seen it virtually through her implants from Primatov's perspective. But when she stepped out of the hallway, the view out the tall plast windows took her breath away. The city of Trafalgar extended to the horizon, and Obradour's apartment building appeared to be the tallest structure within sight.

Obradour greeted them warmly, and to Fran's relief they spent very little time on small talk. The little man led them to a richly appointed office, and they sat down at a conference table. A male servant poured them cups of caff, then left the room.

Gascoigne got the ball rolling by asking, "What do we know about *Caliban*?"

Fran consulted the notes provided by Katrine. "Vice Skalde Nygaard provided Colonel Primatov with details on *Konigsborge*'s last scan intercept of *Caliban*. We have the rogue's last known position and transition vector, and we believe the ship was damaged because they weren't driving at their full capability. But they were able to maintain transition, so they could be anywhere. I'd really like to get my hands on them."

Obradour's brow furrowed in thought. "You don't really have any hard evidence upon which to hold them, so if you try to do anything officially, it'll just get bogged down in the courts. To that end, I think it would be best if I handled *Caliban* quietly behind the scenes."

Gascoigne's eyes narrowed with suspicion. "And how would you do that?"

The senator's misgivings reflected Fran's own thoughts on the matter.

Obradour gave them a noncommittal shrug. "Actually, I've already set those wheels in motion. If and when the rogue resurfaces, if it's anywhere within two hundred light-years of Trafalgar, my people will intercept them. Trust me, I'll get a lot more information out of that ship and her crew when not hampered by the complexities of our legal system."

Fran actually preferred Obradour's way of handling it, but she certainly couldn't admit it, and wasn't about to say so. "I didn't hear you say that."

Gascoigne said, "Likewise."

Obradour said, "Say what?"

Fran shrugged. "I don't know. To what are you referring?"

The little man gave her a conspiratorial smile. "To be honest, I don't recall. Probably some trivial matter of no importance."

"About the rumors," Gascoigne said. "I think we should start spreading them immediately."

That worried Fran. "But what if the Executive Council doesn't follow through on Nygaard's agreement with Primatov and we don't get the invitation?"

Gascoigne grinned and held his hands up like a guilty man professing innocence. "They're just rumors. We had nothing to do with them. They'll die down eventually."

"I know Lana Nygaard," Obradour said. "She wouldn't have struck such an agreement with Colonel Primatov if she had any doubts about the backing of her colleagues on the Executive Council."

"Then it's settled," Gascoigne said.

"Colonel Blacksword," Obradour said. "Have you spoken yet with Admiral Harcourt?"

Fran shook her head. "Not about this. But we do speak almost daily about one thing or another."

Obradour reached out, lifted his cup and took a sip of caff. "I think it's time you speak with him. If he gives you any problems, let me know and I'll have a word with him."

Fran had worked with Harcourt for years and knew him well. "That won't be necessary."

Fran addressed both men to ask the big question. "So who are we going to include on this mission?"

Gascoigne rapped his fingers on the table, his eyes staring at an empty spot on its surface. "I've been thinking about that. We need to keep it to a small, select group. And they have to be powerful enough to help us prevent everyone and their kid brother from trying to join the mission. And it'll have to include both hawks and doves."

"I'm concerned about one thing," Fran said. "If Nygaard's ships are in transition, we may not be able to communicate with them until they get to Viktorkinde, and that's something like fourteen days out."

Obradour's eyes narrowed suspiciously. "And how will you then communicate with them? The way you phrased that, it doesn't sound like you'll be hindered by the twenty or so days it'll take a fast courier ship to carry a message across three hundred light-years."

To learn the little man didn't know everything pleased Fran. "After Reisenar, we set up a chain of relay buoys that extends out to the edge of Commonwealth space. If a ship gets within five light years of its terminus and broadcasts a message to the last buoy, it will land on my desk in less than a day. Our Kelk comrades from Reisenar did the same at their end. And right now we have a hunter-killer on station out there ferrying messages between the ends of those two chains. We can communicate with Viktorkinde with a delay of only about two days one way, round trip maybe four or five. As soon as they are within transition com range of Viktorkinde, I expect to hear from Colonel Primatov. Though, if they make stops along the way to connect with intermediate buoys, we could hear from her sooner."

As she spoke, Obradour's look of suspicion slowly morphed into a pleasant smile. "That must have been quite difficult to set up."

Fran didn't try to hide her discomfort. "The biggest difficulty has been concealing the expense from the Appropriations Committee. We shifted some funds around to make it happen, basically borrowed from my left hand to pay my right."

Obradour grinned. "I can help with that."

Fran acknowledged his offer with a nod. "That will be greatly appreciated."

Obradour asked, "Am I correct that right now we three are the only people on Trafalgar who are aware of the details of Miss Primatov's report?"

Fran gave Gascoigne a questioning look and he shook his head. "I haven't told anyone."

Fran nodded. "Nor I, so it's just us three."

"Good," Obradour said. "Let's agree that, other than Admiral Harcourt, we'll keep it that way, at least until the three of us decide to make it public."

They were all in agreement on that. Obradour continued. "And I'm glad to see your Colonel Primatov had the presence of mind to recognize the invitation could not come through her. It would be a career killer if it got out she proposed a diplomatic mission to the Kelk."

Fran had been concerned about how the financier would react to that, and was pleased he had chosen to be pragmatic. "She's quite savvy that way."

"Yes," Obradour said. "I'd hate to lose her. She's a valuable asset."

Fran thought it interesting Obradour counted Katrine as an asset, though he probably considered them all pawns of one sort or another. "That's why the three of us are going to be the only ones who see her message in its entirety. And that's why the invitation is going to come from the Executive Council to the Right Honorable Senator Gascoigne."

"I concur," Gascoigne said. "And in any case, I'm never ashamed to take credit where credit isn't due. And it might help me stay in office another term."

Obradour grinned. "Or get you kicked out prematurely." He leaned back in his chair and regarded Gascoigne for a moment. "Since the invitation will be issued to the Commonwealth through your offices, you should head up the mission. And since I have a number of contacts in the Larscom, I will attend as well. The official reason for my presence will be to explore the possibility of mutually beneficial commercial interactions. But I still want to find out who at Norddansk and Transmarin were responsible for Novalis III and Reisenar."

Obradour's eyes settled on Fran. "What about you, Colonel Blacksword? I assume you will attend?"

Fran had already considered that carefully. "I think my presence would be . . . counterproductive. From Katrine's report, the Kelk harbor some sort of special dislike for Blackswords. And to have *the* Blacksword present . . . I think not."

Obradour regarded Fran with a look she couldn't read. "I'm not sure I agree with you on that. But let's defer discussion on that for a later time."

"In any case," Fran said, "we're going to promote Lieutenant Colonel Primatov to full colonel. She'll represent the Blacksword nicely, so let's focus on who else should be on the list."

Gascoigne's lips stretched into a grimace. "As much as I hate to admit it, I think we have to include Palmutter."

"Really?" Obradour asked. "I would have thought you'd be the last person to propose his name."

Gascoigne shrugged and didn't try to hide his distaste. "I'm somewhat dovish, so we're going to have to include a hawk, and he's one of the most powerful. If we include someone less influential, Palmutter will simply raise a big stink, and we'll have to include him anyway. So let's just go with him and be done with it."

Gascoigne looked pointedly at Obradour. "You're considered a hawk as well. So to be honest, with you and him both present, everyone should consider the hawk ranks nicely represented. That should limit the number of righteous demands we'll get from other hawks."

Obradour's upper lip curled as if he had just tasted something sour. "Doesn't he have some sort of relationship with that Catarvin woman?"

Fran nodded. "There are rumors, but nothing confirmed."

Obradour's look of distaste remained. "In this city, such rumors usually contain some element of truth. Will she cause problems?"

Gascoigne shook his head. "I doubt it, but if so, we'll handle it. And anyway, I think we should include her on the mission."

Obradour winced as if he'd just tasted cheap, stale wine. "Why would you want to include that imbecile?"

Gascoigne leaned forward to make his point. "Precisely because she is an idiot. She's considered a moderate on the Kelk issue, so that'll round out our ranks nicely, and finish off the roster for the mission. And because she is an airhead, she'll be easy for us to handle, easy to manipulate."

It took some convincing, but Gascoigne finally got Obradour to agree Catarvin would be part of the mission. The little financier liked to control everything, and Gascoigne convinced him Catarvin's presence would enhance his ability to do so. Though Fran wondered what devious little plot Mani hoped to hatch with the woman's inclusion.

They discussed a number of other possibilities, but ruled most of them out. When the meeting broke up, Gascoigne invited Fran to join him in his office. The drive to the Senate Office Building took about fifteen minutes. Because of the possibility of eavesdropping, they didn't discuss anything substantive on the way, but once behind the closed doors of his private office, he grinned and said, "That went rather well, didn't it?"

"What?" she asked. "Why do you look so satisfied? And why do you want Catarvin on the mission?"

His grin broadened. "I had an ulterior motive for recommending both Palmutter and Catarvin. At this point it's quite likely he's fucking her. Why don't you approach her and admit Primatov told us about her alternate persona? Ask her if she'd like to be part of the mission. With her in Palmutter's bed, we'd have an insider in his retinue at Viktorkinde."

Fran shook her head. "Mani, you're the sneakiest son-of-a-bitch I know."

He perked up. "What did you expect? I'm an elected official, and the only way you get votes is to lie, cheat, and steal."

9

Recovery

THE MEDICAL FACILITIES on Novalis III had offered only limited access to advanced tech before the unrest there had begun, and none once the troubles started. John had grown up with few of the wonders of modern medical science. He had learned early-on that healing the old-fashioned way could be quite tedious. But *Drakan Helgis*'s medical staff didn't really understand the *old-fashioned way*. Under their care John's wounds still healed a lot faster than what he'd experienced growing up. And as his body's rejection of the advanced medical tech diminished each day, his healing accelerated, and his condition improved rapidly.

Damage to his lower extremities had been limited to a few bruises and strained muscles, so he could walk around the ICU to get some limited exercise. He spent quite a bit of time pacing back and forth, trying to rebuild his strength.

The reconstruction of his tongue and throat had progressed nicely, though he still had to speak carefully. And he could swallow again, so they had removed the tubes feeding nutrients directly into his stomach and started him on real food.

They had moved a small table and chairs into the ICU near his bed. Primatov had requested it so he could continue his studies, telling him, "We need to improve your ability to speak and read Kelk." Kolbeck, Matsen, and all the other Kelk he interacted with were under strict orders to speak only Kelk to him, and to do so slowly. Primatov had also sent him a list of required reading: a selection of novels, stories, news articles and text books, all written in Kelk script. When John wasn't exercising or eating, Primatov required him to spend every waking moment reading from that selected list. John wondered why the sudden interest in his facility with Kelk, and it all made sense when he learned he would soon stand a regular watch as part of *Drakan Helgis*'s crew.

Matsen and Kolbeck had been assigned to stick to John like glue. They even slept in the empty medical beds, while other crewmembers stood guard outside the entrance to the ICU. Six days into his recuperation, John sat at the small table examining the two bone-handled steel daggers. They each ended in a needle-like point, with edges that were quite sharp. Primatov hadn't pressed him on the matter, but John still hadn't come up with an answer as to why he'd wanted the blades in the first place.

Kolbeck dropped into a chair opposite him. "You figure out what you're going to do with them damn blades yet?"

John shook his head as he considered the knives. "No. But when I do, I suppose I'm going to need something to carry them in."

Kolbeck leaned forward to examine the two blades. John picked one up, reversed it and extended the handle to the Kelk soldier. But the man held his hands up and leaned away from it, as if touching it might contaminate him with some sort of bad juju. John shrugged and laid the blade down next to its companion. He wondered if all Kelk were suspicious that way, or was it just the man seated opposite him.

Kolbeck leaned forward again and looked closely at the two knives, his head moving from side to side to examine them from all angles. "We sometimes carry a trench knife, depending upon circumstances and terrain. I suppose I could dig up a few sheaths and modify them so they fit these cattle-stickers."

"Thanks," John said, "I'd really appreciate that."

The next morning Kolbeck presented John with two modified sheaths that fit the butcher's blades nicely. The fellow sat down at the table while John attached one to his belt, but it rode too high on his hip and wasn't terribly comfortable. John paced back and forth in front of Kolbeck as the man examined his handiwork.

Kolbeck shook his head. "Maybe we'll have to go for version two."

Matsen sat down next to the taller man, and seeing the two of them seated together reminded John of a question he had. "Why do I need two of you? Mistresses Primatov and Vreekande only need one shadow, so why do I need two?"

Kolbeck frowned and squinted at John as if he were an idiot. "Ain't it obvious?"

"No," John said. "Spell it out for me?"

Matsen sighed, as if begrudging the need to explain the obvious to a dimwitted fool. "You see, everybody hates you, and only some of them hate the two women."

Kolbeck added, "And them two women are pretty good looking."

Matsen shook his head angrily. "That don't have nothing to do with it." He looked at John and hooked a thumb toward Kolbeck. "Well, with him it has something to do with it. I mean, anyone with tits can try to kill him all they want, and he'll still want to get in bed with them—as long as they got tits. But everybody hates you clean and simple, and there's just fewer of them who hate the two women."

Kolbeck shook his head. "We don't hate him, do we?"

Matsen rolled his eyes. "Of course we do. I said everybody, and we're part of everybody, aren't we? We're just better at controlling our instincts."

Kolbeck shrugged and turned to John, a serious look on his face. "I didn't know we hated you like everybody else, but I guess we do. But don't worry, we ain't gonna let nobody kill you. Like Matsen said, we'll control our instincts."

Kolbeck looked at Matsen and grinned, and that was when John realized they were having a bit of fun with him. Unfortunately, he didn't think they were joking about all the hatred directed his way.

••••

Macus rushed down the hall and into the reception area outside of Palmutter's office. The old man's receptionist looked up as he approached her, and she frowned at him. "Where have you been?"

He shook his head. "I didn't get the message about the meeting."

She raised an eyebrow as if she didn't believe him. "That's not possible."

That had been his initial reaction as well. No one missed messages that way. The system for delivering messages through implants was infallible, and missed deliveries just didn't happen.

"It shouldn't be possible," he said, "but it did happen, and to me."

She clearly still didn't believe him.

He looked toward the closed door to Palmutter's office. "I'll go right in, try to smooth things over."

She shook her head frantically. "I wouldn't if I were you. He was furious when you didn't show up, and the meeting's almost over anyway."

As if on cue, the door to Palmutter's office opened. A ComSecCorps Admiral stepped out and Macus heard the senator say, "I'm glad you both could make it. I really appreciate your input on this matter."

A brigadier general followed the admiral, and the senator emerged behind them, a smile on his face. He glanced Macus's way, and while the smile remained on his lips, his eyes hardened with anger. Chatting amiably, Palmutter escorted the two officers to the outer door of the reception area. They paused there for a moment, and all agreed the meeting had gone well.

When the two men had gone, Palmutter pivoted on his heel and marched back toward his office. As he passed Macus he said, "DeLeon, in my office, now."

Macus followed him into his office, and as soon he had the door closed, the senator exploded. "Where the fuck were you?"

Macus faced him squarely. "I didn't get—"

"I needed you," the senator screamed.

He stepped forward and stopped just short of knocking Macus over, his nose only a few inches from Macus's just like a pissed-off DI. "You're supposed to be my fucking Military Adviser, and here I have a fucking meeting with two fucking high-ranking ComSecCorps officers, and you don't fucking show up."

"I'm sorry, sir, I didn't get the message."

The senator continued his tirade, tiny drops of saliva spattering Macus's face. "Don't make up a fucking lame excuse like that. That's fucking impossible. I'm not a fucking idiot."

Realizing that any excuse he made would only inflame Palmutter's anger all the more, Macus decided to cut his losses. "I'm sorry, sir, it won't happen again."

"You're fucking right it won't happen again, because if it does, your ass is fucking fired. Do you understand me?"

"Yes, sir."

"Now answer me this. Have you heard anything about these fucking rumors?"

"What rumors, sir?"

"The fucking Kelk. And some sort of fucking diplomatic mission. You're supposed to be my fucking Chief Military Adviser. You're supposed to know these fucking things."

Macus thought the senator's presumption was decidedly unfair. A diplomatic mission wouldn't be the responsibility of a military adviser.

Palmutter extended his arm, pointing past Macus's shoulder to the door. "Get out. Get the fuck out, and I don't want to see your fucking face for the rest of the fucking day."

Macus made a hasty exit. Once through the door, he closed it and paused to catch his breath. The receptionist looked his way, a grimace on her face. "How'd it go?"

The walls of Palmutter's office were actively damped for sound proofing, so she couldn't have heard the senator's tirade no matter how loud he screamed. Macus shrugged. "He was upset, but not too much. He's already started to calm down."

He had noticed once before that Palmutter's receptionist was actually rather good looking. Now that Faith had returned to her earlier bitchy self and wouldn't even give him the time of day, he had considered going back to Dog-Face for a quick maintenance fuck. But looking at the young woman seated in front of him now, he reconsidered.

He crossed the room to her desk, and standing over her he got a nice look down her blouse. Yes, she would do just fine, and he wouldn't be embarrassed to be seen in public with her.

"After work today," he said, "why don't you join me for a drink?"

She frowned and shook her head. "I don't think so."

"Come on. It'll be fun. We'll have a good time together."

"No," she said. "I have a policy that I don't date anyone from the office."

He knew for a fact she had dated one of Palmutter's bodyguards for a while, but he decided not to call her out on the lie. "Let me know if you change your mind." He put his hands on her desk and leaned forward, allowing him to get an even better look down her blouse. "Trust me, you really will enjoy yourself."

She grimaced and shook her head, but didn't say anything.

He pushed off her desk and turned to leave, but she said, "By the way."

He turned back to her, not really surprised she had changed her mind so quickly. "Yes?" he asked, expecting to hear her accept his invitation, with some lame excuse for why she had changed her mind in a heartbeat.

She smiled. "I checked with Tech. Their records confirm you did get that message mid-afternoon yesterday."

That just didn't add up. He headed for the office Dog-Face shared with three other low-level staffers and found her alone. When he stopped beside her desk, she looked up and frowned.

"After work today," he said, "why don't you join me for a drink?"

She sneered at him. "You just want a quick fuck, then you'll walk away like you did before."

He shrugged. "It was good before. It could be good again."

She leaned toward him. "The only thing you're going to fuck around here is your own hand."

He held up his hands in surrender. "Can't blame a guy for trying. Just let me know when you change your mind."

He headed back to his office, thinking that one of them would eventually come around, either the receptionist, or Dog-Face, or maybe even Faith.

He sat down at his desk. He needed to pin down these rumors about the Kelk and some sort of diplomatic mission. He did still have some contacts in ComSecCorps. They might be able to help, so he spent the afternoon making calls.

••••

Command Boss Senior Rank Kyrsten Stinar had been assigned to shadow Nikaela. She and Nikaela now shared a stateroom, and Stinar would be her last defense should there be another attempt at assassination. But the woman didn't appear dangerous or imposing, and that gave Nikaela pause. There must have been some hint of doubt in Nikaela's face when they first met, because Stinar leaned close to her and said, "Your breschkada, he can be a very dangerous man, yes?"

"Yes," Nikaela said, not sure what point the woman hoped to make. "He can be."

Stinar smiled. "But he doesn't look it, which can make him even more dangerous."

It occurred to Nikaela she should do a better job of masking her inner thoughts.

Stinar gave her a broad grin. "He's also good looking, for a common-face. I wonder what he's like in bed. Might be kind of fun to take a common-face as a lover. Bit of a novelty, don't you think?"

"I suppose," Nikaela said, trying to keep the look on her face neutral. "I've never really considered it."

Again, there must have been something in her face, because Stinar shook her head sadly. "You need to pay more attention to the way he looks at you, especially when he thinks you don't know he's looking at you."

As she and Stinar walked down a passageway headed for the ship's ICU, Nikaela recalled that brief conversation. She had never thought to pay attention to that kind of thing, and decided she should probably take Stinar's advice. Though she didn't know how she would know when John thought she didn't know he was looking at her.

Primatov was concerned she or John might commit some gaffe during their time on Viktorkinde. To that end they had scheduled the first of several meetings to educate the two Blackswords on some of the more subtle customs of Kelk society. For some reason, John had asked Nikaela to come a few minutes early.

He was now close to full recovery, but as a practical matter, Brynjar had consigned the ICU to him as his stateroom until they reached Viktorkinde. It was reasonably defensible, and large enough to house John and his two shadows: Matsen and Kolbeck.

With Stinar on her heels, Nikaela walked between the rows of beds in the outer sick bay toward the two armed guards standing at the door of the ICU. She stopped between them, knocked on the door, and a moment later Kolbeck answered, opening it just a crack with his hand resting on the butt of his sidearm. Seeing Nikaela and Stinar, he opened it a little further and glanced around. The guard standing on Nikaela's right outside the door gave Kolbeck a nod.

Stinar asked, "How's our patient?"

Kolbeck shook his head. "Stir crazy, and driving us crazy with his stir-craziness."

Apparently satisfied that they weren't accompanied by a horde of assassins, Kolbeck opened the door wide enough to admit them, and Nikaela stepped through.

John stood at the small table with his back to her, examining something on the table and conferring with Matsen. He glanced over his shoulder, and when he saw Nikaela, his eyes brightened. He spun to face her. "Mistress Vreekande."

Nikaela responded with, "Maestra Mathius."

They always began on that formal note. Behind John, Matsen rolled his eyes and shook his head sadly.

"You wanted to see me?" she asked.

"Yes." He turned back to the table, lifted something off it, turned and crossed the room to her. "Colonel Primatov told me you wanted one of these."

He held out a sheathed knife, and Nikaela's breathing quickened when she saw the bone handle on the blade, discolored by dark brown stains.

Behind her Kolbeck said, "Modified a couple of trench knife sheaths. Still could use a little improvement, but they should work fine for them cattle-stickers."

Nikaela reached out and took the sheathed blade from John's hands. At that moment she doubted the wisdom of asking for it.

John leaned close to her and said, "It's just a blade, Nikaela."

"But it almost took your life."

He gave her a predatory grin, a rare look for him, but one she had seen before. "But it didn't."

The sound of the door opening interrupted them. Kristdokar and Primatov entered the room with Vagle close on their heels.

"John," Primatov said, smiling pleasantly. She turned to Nikaela. "And Mistress Vree—"

Her eyes locked on the sheathed knife in Nikaela's hands and the smile disappeared. "Ah, one of the butcher's blades, is it?"

Primatov glanced at Kristdokar and they shared a look. She scanned the room, saw the other knife lying on the table, crossed the room and picked it up. She looked at it carefully for a long moment, then turned to John. "What are you going to do with this, John? You haven't yet answered that question, and now you've had special sheaths made for them. And don't tell me again you don't know, because I think you do."

Nikaela expected to see John wither under Primatov's gaze. The woman could be absolutely frightening when she wanted to intimidate someone. But John didn't flinch or avert his eyes. He didn't puff out his chest either, or try to bluster his way through an answer. He simply looked Primatov in the eyes and said, "I think I'm going to wear it."

Nikaela noticed that all of their shadow-bodyguards—Vagle, Stinar, Matsen, Kolbeck—had miraculously managed to back away from them without obviously doing so. That left Nikaela, John, Primatov, and Kristdokar standing in an isolated group in the center of the room.

Primatov asked, "When exactly do you intend to wear it?"

He didn't hesitate. "Every second I'm on this ship and on Viktorkinde, at least when it's practical to do so. And when I can, I'm going to wear it so it's visible for everyone to see."

Primatov closed her eyes for a long moment, then opened them and said, "I'm not sure that's wise."

John pursed his lips, his anger visible in the strain around his eyes. "I don't care if it's wise."

In the look Primatov gave John, Nikaela saw a small hint of the bitch-face. "I don't think you should do this, John."

John shook his head and spoke in a frighteningly calm voice. "For once, I don't care what you think. They tried to butcher me like livestock. I'm wearing the damn blade whether you like it or not. You can court-martial me, execute me, whatever you want, but I'm wearing the damn blade."

Primatov lifted an eyebrow, her eyes narrowed with anger, and Nikaela expected to see the full-on Primatov bitch face, but instead her lips curled into a hard smile. There was never any question the scary face was just a heartbeat away, but for some reason she suppressed it. "I think I'll hold off on the court-martial . . . at least for the time being. But I can't allow you to wear that blade."

Nikaela needed to speak up, wanted to tell Primatov she was making a mistake. But she really didn't want that look aimed her way.

"Colonel Primatov," Kristdokar said. "May I offer some advice?"

Primatov nodded. "Certainly, Skalde Kristdokar."

Nikaela had never seen the skalde speak with such caution. "What Maestra Mathius proposes is a slap in the face to many Kelk, and an insult to many more."

Primatov's hard expression did not soften as she waited in silence for the skalde to say more.

Kristdokar continued. "But all Kelk recognize that we bear culpability in our failure to protect our breschkada. Under these circumstances, wearing that blade openly here and on Viktorkinde is a very Kelk thing to do."

Primatov's head rotated slowly and her eyes focused intently on John. She cocked her head to one side as if listening to some inner voice, then said, "I stand corrected, John. By all means, wear the blade."

She let them all see the face for just a moment, then finished by looking at Nikaela and smiling. "Young lady, this has been a most excellent day."

10

Blades

"HEY BLACKSWORD."

John wished Kolbeck would stop calling him that. It was one thing to wear the Blacksword patches. At least they were reasonably small, and didn't really stand out that much. John didn't need Kolbeck constantly reminding everyone around him that he was one of the hated Blackswords.

Seated at the small table in his ICU stateroom, John looked up from the Kelk homework Primatov had assigned him. She called it ". . . advanced reading to prepare for continuing career advancement." John knew management bullshit when he heard it, but decided not to call her out on that. When he had told her he was going to wear the butcher's blade regardless of her wishes, for all intents and purposes he had told her to fuck off, and he thought he should probably wait at least a millennium or two before doing that again. But he couldn't resist curling his lip in distaste as he said, "Homework."

Kolbeck dropped into a chair on the other side of the table. "What was that, Blacksword?"

John shook his head. "Nothing."

Kolbeck placed some sort of harness on the table and slid it across to John. "Take a look at that, Blacksword. I think you'll like this one better."

Short, stocky Matsen stood behind him looking on eagerly.

John had taken to keeping the sheathed dagger close at hand. More often than not he placed it on the table next to him while doing Primatov's homework, or beneath his pillow while he slept at night. On the rare occasion when they allowed him to leave the ICU for something other than a shower, he wore it strapped to his belt, but it didn't draw much attention from any of the Kelk they encountered. It wasn't terribly comfortable, and Kolbeck had promised he'd find a better solution. John knew it wouldn't do any good against an opponent armed with real weaponry.

John untangled the harness, a new style of sheath with a couple of extra straps attached to it. "What's this?"

Kolbeck stood and waved his arms at John to do likewise. "Come on. Stand up. Try it on. I think this one'll be a lot more comfortable."

John stood, not sure what to expect. Kolbeck showed him how to attach the harness straps to his belt on his left side. The tall man then retrieved the butcher's dagger from where John had placed it on the table. As always, the fellow lifted it by the sheath, careful to avoid touching any part of the knife itself—probably that bad juju thing again. He extended it to John, with the bone handle forward.

John gripped the handle and pulled the knife from the old sheath, then slid it into the new harness strapped to his side. The added straps positioned the sheath and blade lower on his left hip, almost on his thigh, with the handle angled toward his right. He reached across and pulled the blade, could do so quickly and comfortably.

Kolbeck nodded his approval. "And I don't think it'll get in the way when you sit down. At least not so much."

They experimented. John sat in a chair at the table, then on the edge of his bed, even tried plopping his ass onto the deck with his back to a bulkhead.

"It's a lot better," he said. "How did you figure this out?"

Kolbeck shrugged. "Looked up some old-fashioned, historical stuff."

Matsen leaned down to look closely at the blade resting against John's thigh, but like Kolbeck kept his distance. "According to the history books, this rig is actually called a butcher's harness. It's what the old butchers used to wear."

Once Kristdokar had tacitly approved of John wearing the blade, his two shadow-bodyguards seemed to take it as a challenge to see to it he could do so under any and all circumstances. John wondered at their motives. "Why are you doing this?"

Kolbeck shrugged. "Gotta make sure you can wear that blade properly."

John shook his head. "No, there's more to it than that. You're showing too much enthusiasm for this, too much interest."

Matsen tilted his head to one side and winced. "Lot of us ain't happy at what they tried to do to you."

"You mean that they tried to kill me?"

Kolbeck sighed. "No, trying to kill you is okay. It's the way they tried."

"The butcher's blades?"

"Yah," Matsen said. "Even some of those who'd like to see you dead are angry about that. It was just plain wrong." The man's face hardened for a moment. "And some of us are fucking furious about it."

Kolbeck slapped John on the back. "And then you act like a fucking Kelk and want to wear the damn thing. Can't believe you stood up to that redhead that way." He leaned close to John and lowered his voice. "She's got a nice set of—"

"Focus," Matsen shouted. "You got a one track mind."

Kolbeck rolled his eyes. "Anyway, you gotta deliver the right message. Wearing that harness, it'll look like you're ready to draw that blade on anyone at a moment's notice. Or maybe you ain't about to, but you could if you wanted to. It'll make 'em think twice every time they see you."

Comments like that made John wonder if choosing to wear the blade had been a good idea. But it was now too late to change his mind.

Matsen said, "When you step off this ship wearing that blade, it's gonna be a shit-load more than a fashion statement."

John shrugged. "There's a problem with that."

At their frowns, he said, "I'm supposed to wear my service dress blues when we disembark."

Matsen said, "And that's a problem?"

John retrieved the coat for his blues and put it on. It ended about mid-thigh, leaving only a portion of the sheath visible and covering the blade's handle completely. The coat for Nikaela's dress uniform had an integral, exterior belt from which she could hang her butcher's dagger, especially if Kolbeck made her a harness similar to the one John wore now. They tried wrapping a belt around John's waist outside of the coat, but unlike Nikaela's uniform coat it wasn't cut to accommodate the exterior belt. It destroyed the lines of the uniform and clearly didn't belong there.

Kolbeck put his hands on his hips, examined John carefully and shook his head. "No, the redhead ain't gonna like that."

Matsen's eyes widened and he held up a finger as if a thought had just occurred to him. "I got an idea. We've got lots of time before we reach Viktorkinde, so I'll have this taken care of before then." He grinned and held out his hand. "Give me the coat."

John pulled off the coat and handed it to him.

Matsen held it out in front of him and examined it. "Yah, we're going to make sure you can defend yourself with that blade no matter what. Especially now you gotta stand watch like any Kelk. We ain't gonna be there to protect you, you know?"

John recalled his earlier thought. "I'm not stupid. This blade isn't going to do me any good against someone with a real weapon."

Kolbeck frowned and nodded his agreement. "Well, yah, you've got a point there. You're a dead man if that happens."

Matsen's eyes narrowed in thought. "Maybe we should get rid of the blade and replace it with a real weapon, something we know he can defend himself with."

Kolbeck appeared to be unsure of what Matsen was trying to say. "And what would that be?"

Matsen grinned. "A fork. Let's put a fork in that sheath."

Kolbeck returned his grin and nodded.

••••

When Gascoigne appeared in Thealone's virtual vision, he didn't waste any time with small talk. "Did you get it?"

She smiled and tried to hide her concern. "Yes, I did. But hold on, Mani. Obradour's just coming online now."

A few seconds later Tarsik Obradour appeared in her view as if seated next to Gascoigne, when in fact the three of them were in different parts of the city. As always the little man showed not the slightest hint of stress, and adhered almost religiously to propriety. "Colonel Blacksword, how are you today?"

Like Gascoigne, Fran wanted to cut the bullshit and get to the point, but she played along anyway. "I'm fine, Mr. Obradour."

He glanced slightly to one side. "And you, Senator Gascoigne. I hope all is well."

Gascoigne looked at Fran with his eyes slightly narrowed, as if he suspected she hid something from him. "All is well as long as Fran got the invitation."

Obradour turned his attention to Thealone. "And did you, Colonel?"

She nodded. "Yes, and it was worded exactly as Colonel Primatov described it: diplomatic mission, no diplomatic relations, the purpose being, and I quote, '. . . to initiate preliminary discussions on matters of mutual benefit.' No surprises there. We can bring one civilian vessel escorted by two cruisers, and that's it. No restrictions on who we select to represent us."

Obradour appeared pleased. "I have a private ship that should accommodate the mission principles and their retinues. But as to the escorts, there's no reason we can't bring the biggest and nastiest cruisers we've got, is there?"

Gascoigne clearly approved of Obradour's comment. "I'd feel better that way."

The two men had no idea what they were talking about, and Fran made no attempt to hide her frustration. "It's not like we have a dozen large cruisers just sitting idle here in the Trafalgar system, and we can pick and choose among them. And if the situation does go south on us, and the whole thing comes down to firepower, they'll have us so heavily outgunned, it won't matter how big our cruisers are. We'll be a cloud of thermonuclear vapor."

Obradour grimaced and nodded. "Your point is well taken. I stand corrected. We'll just have to make sure it doesn't go south on us. What are our options when it comes to ships?"

Fran paged through a few screens on her desk. "As we discussed, I brought Ben Harcourt in on this whole thing, and he's been of enormous help. There are three cruisers in the Trafalgar system right now. *Fearless* is undergoing major repair and refit in the low-gravity navy yard on Trafalgar Prime. It won't be space worthy for at least a month. *Endurance* is a medium cruiser so it doesn't fit the bill, but she may be all we've got. *Hellfire* looks like a good candidate. She's docked at Trafalgar Prime for some minor refitting and resupply, and a twenty-day **R&R** for the crew. They're recalling *Hellfire*'s crew now, and Ben is accelerating the refit and resupply. She'll be ready when we need her."

Obradour said, "It looks like it's going to be *Endurance* and *Hellfire*."

"There is one alternative," Fran said. "*Wicked Fury* is a heavy cruiser based out of Miriteen, which is only a slight deviation from a straight line run between here and Viktorkinde. If they're on schedule, then they're docked at Miriteen Prime now for resupply and R&R, and they'll be there for the next fifteen days. We could start with *Endurance* and *Hellfire*, deviate to Miriteen on our way, drop *Endurance* in favor of *Wicked Fury*, and it would only cost us about half a day."

"One question," Obradour said. "You said, '*If* . . . they're on schedule . . .' Why *if?*"

"Miriteen's sixty light-years out," Fran said. "Even for a fast courier ship that's over four days. The last courier update came in from Miriteen two days ago, so our information is over six days old."

"Ah," Obradour said. "Let's keep it simple and go with *Endurance* and *Hellfire*."

Fran said, "I like that better anyway. *Wicked Fury*'s CO is hardline anti-Kelk and could be a problem."

"That works for me," Gascoigne said. "Please keep us posted, Fran."

Fran had noticed something the other two hadn't. "There's something I want to point out about the timing of the invitation from the Executive Council."

Obradour focused his attention on her and waited.

Gascoigne said, "I'm all ears."

Fran paused for a moment to gather her thoughts. "If the Kelk ships left Sarkovie at the same time as *Lightspear*, they would have arrived at the terminus of their relay chain four days ago, at almost the same time *Lightspear* arrived at the terminus of ours. *Lightspear* immediately transmitted Primatov's report to us on our chain, and I must assume Nygaard sent a report to the Executive Council on their chain. Two days later *Lightspear* arrived at their terminus and received the invitation from them. We received it now because it took two more days for *Lightspear* to complete the round trip back to our terminus and transmit it to us. That means that in two days' time the Larscom Executive Council absorbed Nygaard's report, put aside a hundred and fifty years of hostility, and decided to take the initial steps toward opening diplomatic relations with us."

Obradour didn't move, but his eyebrows rose in comprehension. "They must have discussed the possibility long before Nygaard and Kristdokar left Viktorkinde."

Gascoigne nodded and smiled. "They're politicians. I'll bet they discussed several scenarios, and Nygaard came prepared to dance to the sound of whatever tune emerged from the mess with *Caliban* and *Sycorax*."

"No," Obradour said, shaking his head slowly from side to side. "When they left Viktorkinde they had no idea they would find themselves with their interests intertwined with those of the Commonwealth. I'm sure they did discuss several scenarios, but probably long before this situation arose."

"Either way," Gascoigne said, "we have an incredible opportunity." He focused his attention on Fran. "But you say it's a four day round trip for *Lightspear* between the terminuses. So either we respond immediately, or we wait four days, right?"

"Maybe not," Fran said. "The Kelk left the destroyer *Alvilddan* behind to finish mopping up at Sarkovie, with orders that as soon as they completed that, they were to join *Lightspear* ferrying messages between the two terminuses. They've done that now, and that cuts the delay down to two days. I don't know *Alvilddan*'s capabilities, but it's a destroyer so it's probably not as fast as a hunter-killer like *Lightspear*. If its round-trip time is more than four days, the two ships are going to quickly get out of sync, and I have no idea how that's going to play out."

Obradour asked, "Have you considered filling the gap between the two terminuses with additional buoys?"

"I've been looking into that," Fran said. "But I can't do that on short order without raising a lot of red flags here in Trafalgar. And in any case, our ships don't usually carry those kinds of communications buoys, not in sufficient quantities to fill that gap, so we'll have to dispatch something from here. And you can assume about twenty days of travel to get there before they start planting new buoys. So for the time being, we're stuck with what we've got."

Obradour sat quietly for several seconds, his lips pinched in a tight, straight line, his head nodding slightly. "Nevertheless, let's not wait. Please send the specifications for those buoys to me, and if they can be acquired for a price, I'll have a ship dispatched from here within a couple of days."

Fran marveled at how, on a moment's notice, the man could so casually commit large financial outlays and serious shipping resources. "I'll take care of that as soon as we're done here."

Gascoigne appeared quite pleased at the way the situation had developed. "But at least right now we can count on two days. So let's wait two more days, then accept the invitation."

"I concur," Obradour said. "How are the rumors going?"

"They're everywhere," Fran said. "Even my secretary asked me if I knew anything. How did you do that, Mani?"

He grinned like a precocious child. "Two days ago in the cafeteria over lunch I asked a couple of my senatorial buddies if they'd heard any of these wild rumors about a diplomatic mission to the Supremacy. They said they hadn't, and wanted to know what I had heard. But of course I had heard nothing, and that's why I asked. By late that afternoon another colleague asked me if I had heard anything about these rumors. I told him I hadn't heard a thing, and asked what he had heard. Turns out he had heard quite a bit, actually, and filled me in on all sorts of details—all of them wrong, of course."

He sobered. "This is happening faster than I expected, so we need to get the staffing for the mission locked up. I think it's time I approached Palmutter and let the cat out of the bag. At this point he's probably driving his staff nuts trying to pin down the rumors, so I think he'll jump if given the opportunity to act on something more solid than gossip."

Obradour asked, "Can you do that this afternoon?"

Gascoigne nodded. "Most definitely. And I think Fran should approach Catarvin this afternoon as well. If we can get both of them signed up, then we can issue the press release tomorrow, and hopefully be on our way a couple days after that."

The three of them were in agreement on that, though Obradour was still unaware of Catarvin's alternate persona. He assumed Fran would simply approach her to flatter the airhead with an offer to be part of the mission, when in fact Fran needed to break through the woman's subterfuge, and enlist the aid of the real Jenine Catarvin.

Fran thought the meeting might end there. But Gascoigne leaned forward, his eyes pinched with concern. "I've known you a long time, Fran, and I can see there's something bothering you, something you're not telling us."

She shrugged and grimaced. "I won't go into the math, but when *Lightspear* first returned to the Kelk terminus, they were carrying my response to Katrine's initial report. If the Kelk gave it to her, she would have responded immediately, and I would have at least received her reply today, along with the invitation from the Executive Council."

Obradour sat quietly unmoving, and she imagined she saw his natural hawk inclinations battling with the more moderate position he'd adopted lately. "And I take it you received nothing from her?"

"No, nothing," Fran said. "But if they're driving straight to Viktorkinde they might not be in contact with their relay chain."

Obradour gave her a harsh, unpleasant grin. "You don't believe that any more than I do, do you?"

She shook her head. "No. I don't."

11

The Kelk Way

"FOREARM HORIZONTAL AND stiff," Nikaela said, sounding just like an unhappy DI.

John stood with his right hand held rigidly flat and level just above his left breast, his hand precisely positioned half way between his nipple and the top of his shoulder. He kept his eyes locked forward while Nikaela paced around him like a drill sergeant, and Primatov stood in front of him looking on, with Vagle standing behind her.

If he was going to stand watch on a Kelk warship, he desperately wanted to get the basics right. He'd asked Nikaela to teach him things like a proper Kelk salute, and other subtleties of their military etiquette. He could have asked Matsen and Kolbeck. But given their rather twisted senses of humor, they just might purposefully steer him wrong, the way non-coms were sometimes known to haze a newly-commissioned, young officer. And in any case, he'd much rather take lessons from a pretty girl, even if she had temporarily turned into a hardened task-master with demonic red eyes; very attractive demonic red eyes, but still demonic as all hell at the moment.

Matsen and Kolbeck stood in the background looking on and grinning, though as always, with a woman present, Kolbeck's attention seemed to be focused on various parts of the female form. On that day, his biggest problem appeared to be deciding which ass to focus on, Primatov's, or Nikaela's. Thankfully, Nikaela's and Primatov's shadows, Vagle and Stinar, were waiting outside the door in the passageway. John thought it might be pure torture for the man if he tried to take in all four butts at once.

"Eyes forward." Nikaela had stopped behind John. "And heels a hand's breadth apart."

John had quickly learned that, beyond the obvious differences in the way the salute was performed, he had to make a number of subtle alterations to shift from Commonwealth military etiquette to that of the Supremacy. When saluting, a Commonwealth soldier stood at attention with his heels touching, while his Kelk counterpart kept them a hand's breadth apart. Kelk DIs had been known to carefully measure the span of a recruit's hand and compare it with microscopic precision to the space between her heels. It comforted John to learn that DIs were universally evil, malicious, malevolent, calculating, heartless bastards, one and all. There was probably some gene involved, and without it one could never achieve the proper level of malicious and malevolent. Of course, they would test you for that gene before letting you become a DI; no nasty gene, no DI assignment.

Nikaela stopped in front of him and positioned her nose a tiny fraction of a centimeter from his, then barked, "Eyes on my lips."

John wondered if Nikaela had a little of that gene in her. He lowered his eyes to look at her lips, though with her nose parked so close to his, he couldn't really see them. That was another difference: Commonwealth soldiers looked each other in the eyes when saluting, regardless of rank, but in the Supremacy they did that only if their ranks were equal. If not, she with the lower rank lowered her eyes to focus on the other's lips. John thought he might try lowering his eyes to focus on Nikaela's breasts, maybe doing so with a salacious look on his face. That would provide the double pleasure of enjoying the view himself, while pissing her off.

Primatov nodded, her lips a flat, sharp line as if struggling to hide a smile. "Good work, Command Boss Vreekande. But I have a meeting scheduled with Skalde Kristdokar, so I must be going."

She turned and walked out of the room, with Kolbeck's eyes tracking her all the way. He didn't seem at all disappointed at her exit, probably because as soon as the door closed, he swung his head around and focused on Nikaela's butt.

Nikaela drilled John on the Kelk equivalents of *at ease*, though they had four distinct variants, and the Kelk gave the command with the single word *Ease*, sometimes followed by a modifying term. In the most formal they spread their feet and put their fists on their hips, instead of clasping them behind their back. Nikaela was testing John on the four variants when she froze for a second, obviously listening to her implants. Then she turned to Kolbeck and Matsen. "Ensign Mathius has orders to report to the XO's office immediately."

Both men straightened and shifted into professional mode, which for Kolbeck meant he stopped looking at women's asses and paid more attention to his surroundings. Matsen nodded toward the door. "We'll check outside."

The lesson was over, so as the two men turned away from them, John relaxed. But Nikaela spun back to him. "I didn't give you permission to relax."

John stiffened. Like a DI, she again parked her nose a fraction of a centimeter from his, but he refused to lower his eyes to look at her lips. He still hadn't tried the leering-at-her-breasts gambit yet. He thought he'd save that for another day.

Her eyes narrowed. "You're not looking at my lips."

John lifted his eyebrows. "We're of equal rank."

She grinned and said, "You still have a shit-of-bull accent, Mathius breschka-da."

He returned her grin. "But it's getting better."

At that moment he realized they were alone, with her lips only a few centimeters from his. "And in any case, I don't care."

She opened her mouth to say something, but before she could do so, he wrapped his arms around her waist, pulled her tightly against him, and kissed her. Tit for tat, quid pro quo, she had kissed him on that assault boat before their rescue, now he kissed her. And he definitely enjoyed doing so.

She didn't struggle, seemed to enjoy the kiss as much as he did, and appeared to have no qualms about allowing him to once again confirm her tongue was not forked. But she didn't raise her arms and put them around his neck, didn't melt against him the way she had on the boat.

When he ended the kiss, he paused with his lips lightly brushing hers.

"Why did you do that?" she asked, as if she hadn't kissed him on that boat, and his move had taken her completely by surprise.

He grinned. "When you kissed me on that assault boat, that certainly convinced me your tongue wasn't forked. But then the way you've been acting today, I had to make sure that between then and now it hadn't magically split and become forked."

She gave him an all-knowing smile. "That's just an excuse. I think you wanted to kiss me."

"Yah," he said, "there is that."

She stepped out of his arms. "You have to report to the XO."

He shrugged, turned, walked to the door, opened it, and held it for her.

She crossed the room to the open door, stepped half way through it, but paused and turned back to him. "You never know," she said.

"Never know what?" he asked.

She grinned and leaned close to him, her lips lightly brushing against his. She had an absolutely demonic look in her eyes as she ran her tongue across his lower lip. "At any moment my tongue might spontaneously part right down the middle and become forked. One just never knows when, so you may have to check on it quite regularly."

At that moment John wondered if some of the stories about the demonic nature of the Kelk were perhaps true.

She turned and left him standing there, his mouth as wide open as the door.

Standing just beyond the door in the outer sick bay, Matsen asked, "What are we waiting for?"

Kolbeck shook his head. "Something about a tongue. And a fork. It's always a fork with him. You'll have to ask him why there's now a tongue involved."

Matsen looked at John. "Why is there a tongue involved now? We know you're deadly with a fork, but I'm not going to buy it if you try to tell me you can tongue someone to death."

•••

As Nikaela followed Stinar back to her quarters, she couldn't put the thought of that kiss out of her mind. He had taken her completely by surprise because men didn't initiate a kiss like that. That was the woman's prerogative, her right to make the first move. A man never took the first step, not unless a couple had entered into a much closer and longer relationship. And occasionally, though rarely, even some couples who had signed contractual birthing agreements still adhered strictly to the custom of the woman's right to initiate intimacy.

She halted in her tracks as it occurred to her it might be different in the Commonwealth. But how could she confirm that? She could ask Primatov, but that woman would undoubtedly see right through the question to her motive for asking it. Kristdokar might know the answer, but the same was true of her. And she wasn't about to ask John.

Stinar had halted in the passageway in front of her and turned to look at her. "Is something wrong, mistress?"

Perhaps Stinar might know. Nikaela shook her head. "No, nothing."

As Stinar led them along the passageway, another thought occurred to Nikaela. She found it rather thrilling to have no idea if and when he might kiss her again.

•••

The rumors flying around the capital hadn't helped any. At least Palmutter had been furious at everyone, since no one could pin down any solid leads on the sources of the gossip circulating from one end of the city to the other. Macus had watched the old fart rip Faith a new asshole along with everyone else. The senator seemed to think that somehow they'd magically come up with answers where none existed.

That morning when Macus showed up for work, he stopped at the receptionist's desk. At least she had remained neutral regarding his personal predicament. Macus leaned on her desk and got another good look down her blouse as he asked, "What's he like today?"

She rolled her eyes and said, "Livid. Just stay out of sight and keep your head down as much as possible."

Palmutter had scheduled Macus for a meeting in his office at mid-morning. He showed up a few minutes early just to avoid any possibility the senator might use that as an excuse to blow his stack. Faith had arrived before him, sat in a chair showing a lot of nice leg, and when he entered she gave him a neutral smile. Since their split she'd been good about not flashing nasty looks at him in the office. Unfortunately, Dog-Face had not been able to demonstrate the same level of maturity.

Palmutter had a guest in his office, and he introduced him. "This is Mr. Andrew Smith, from Sarkovie."

Smith stood a few inches shorter than Macus and had a rather shifty look to him, as if he didn't trust anyone or anything. Stocky and built like a common laborer, the word *thug* came to mind when Macus looked at him. And the use of such an obviously false name smacked of amateurism. Or perhaps Palmutter wanted them to realize they were not yet important enough to be privy to all the details.

They sat down, got comfortable, and Palmutter continued. "Andrew has certain contacts in the Kelk Supremacy. He has some rather interesting information on recent developments there. Andrew, why don't you tell Macus and Faith what you were just telling me, though do limit it to the edited version."

Smith spoke cautiously. "Are you aware that a cadet named John Mathius was abducted from the academy campus about a month ago?"

Smith did not sound like a common thug, and he hadn't spoken with a Sarkovie accent, which made Macus even more curious.

Faith said, "Yes, we are. It was rather sloppily done, and garnered a lot of press coverage, though the authorities did make some effort to . . . limit the fallout."

Her accusatory tone got a slight reaction from Smith. "Yah," he said. "It was sloppy. Well, the kid's alive and well, and he was taken out of the Trafalgar system to be turned over to the Kelk. Should have happened about twelve days ago. He did something that's got them all bent out of shape, and they really wanted to get their hands on him."

Macus took care to hide his disappointment that the damn fool had survived.

Palmutter slapped his palm down on his desk. "Yah, this breshakuda thing. I still don't understand what that means."

Smith gave an uncaring shrug. "From what little we can get out of the Kelk, a lot of them ain't too happy about him, so he may not live long anyway."

That gave Macus some hope that justice would prevail.

Smith looked carefully at Macus. "Senator Palmutter tells me you knew this Mathius fellow personally, were platoon mates at Miriteen?"

Macus nodded. "Yes, that's true. But your story surprises me. That mess on campus, he isn't good enough to have been responsible for that. He must have had help."

Smith pursed his lips and spoke through gritted teeth. "The extraction team that came for him, all Special Forces and heavily armed, he killed five of them with a fucking knife, and—"

"Enough," Palmutter shouted.

He pointed a finger at Smith. "No more from you."

He pointed the same finger at Macus and Faith. "And everything you just heard, it all stays in this room."

At that point Palmutter dismissed Macus and Faith. As they stepped out into the reception area, Macus waited until they had walked down the hall a short distance before he turned to Faith and said, "If you don't mind, could I have a private word with you?"

"Of course," she said. "Lead the way."

As Palmutter's Chief Military Adviser, Macus had been given a private office, while Faith still occupied a desk in the bullpen with the other aides. He led her to his office, closed the door and said, "Did you hear what I think I heard in there?"

She nodded. "I definitely got the impression our dear senator may be involved in certain recent events that many might consider unlawful. But how deeply is he involved? If he's crossed the line, we might use that to our advantage, though to do so might be to his disadvantage."

Macus shrugged. "I'm not going to shed any tears for the man."

She had said *our* advantage. Did that mean she wanted to work together again? She hadn't moved beyond aide, still a glorified gofer, so Macus decided to ignore that hint, if hint it had been. "Well, thank you for your time."

"Certainly," she said, smiling pleasantly. She turned and walked out of his office.

12

Suspicious People

SEVERAL PACES FROM Senior Command Superior Eberta Falkenberg's stateroom, Matsen and Kolbeck halted to wait in the passageway while John continued on. Just short of the executive officer's stateroom John noticed the door hung open. He stopped out of sight a few paces from it and took a moment to make sure everything about his uniform was proper and in place. Nervous tension fluttered in his gut, and he suspected his isolation from the ship's crew for the past six days might now prove to be an impediment.

He marched forward and stopped in the passageway in front of the open door. Inside, a female Kelk officer sat in profile at a small desk built out from an interior bulkhead. Her chin-length hair appeared to be solid pepper with no salt whatsoever, and even though she was seated, he got the impression she wasn't terribly tall.

At that moment it occurred to John he hadn't thought to ask Nikaela about the Kelk formula for entering an officer's stateroom. He'd have to use the good old Commonwealth way and hope for the best.

He knocked on the open door, she glanced his way and he snapped to attention, his hand held in front of him in a Kelk salute. "Ensign John Mathius reporting as ordered, ma'am—mistress."

For a tiny fraction of a second her eyes glanced down toward his feet. The Kelk were probably all aware Commonwealth soldiers stood at attention with their heels touching, and he prayed his were the required hand's breadth apart. He hoped she wouldn't go all DI on him and actually measure the breadth of his hand.

She spun in the chair to face him, casually returned the salute and said, "Enter."

He walked forward, and her stateroom was small enough that a single step put him one pace away from her. She glanced again at his feet, and he realized to his horror he had forgotten Nikaela's lessons and stood at attention with his heels touching.

She grinned slightly and said, "You may correct your stance, Ensign."

He shifted his left foot.

"That's better," she said. "But don't do that in front of Command Hawk Taugrim. She won't be as lenient as me."

The Kelk didn't use "Aye, aye," to acknowledge an order given. "Yes, mistress."

"Ease."

John spread his feet to shoulder width, squared them off and put his hands on his hips, his chest out, his shoulders as stiff as if standing at attention.

"Ease down."

John clasped his hands behind his back, but still didn't relax his shoulders.

"Ease complete."

John relaxed his shoulders and let his hands drop casually to his sides.

"Ease and relax."

That meant he could drop all formalities, even sit down if he chose, but there wasn't a place to sit, and in any case he wasn't about to go that far.

She reached over to the bulkhead near her, touched a switch, and a simple chair extruded from the wall. "Sit down, Ensign."

John carefully put his butt in the seat, but sat on the edge of it.

Falkenberg leaned back and regarded him for a long moment. "I see Mistress Vreekande has taught you well. And your accent isn't bad, either."

John thought it wouldn't hurt to be frank. "I think you're being kind about the accent, mistress."

She smiled. "I am, a little. But other than Colonel Primatov, you're the only Commonwealth soldier I've ever met who actually speaks our language." She frowned, and laughed at some thought. "Actually, you two are the only Commonwealth soldiers I've ever met. I assume I shouldn't take that as a statistical indication of the probability I'll encounter other Commonwealth officers who speak Kelk."

He tried to hide his discomfort. "Actually, there might not be any others."

She frowned, though he didn't see any anger in the look she gave him. "Really!"

He explained about Professor Dirkson, and how his extracurricular tutoring hadn't counted toward the O-School requirements. "I guess they went to quite a bit of trouble just to get me a tutor."

She leaned back in her chair and regarded him as if examining an unusual and curious object. "I spoke with Colonel Primatov, and learned you asked to be given tutoring in our language and customs during your O-School year. I didn't realize until now how unusual such a request had been. Why did you do that?"

John didn't know the answer to that. "After Reisenar, I was . . . curious."

Her eyebrows rose and she nodded. "Curious about the demonic, blue-skinned monsters, eh?"

He didn't know how to answer that either. "I . . . ah . . ."

She held up a hand to stop him. "Don't answer that. That was unfair of me."

They sat there saying nothing for several seconds. John desperately tried to think of a way to break the silence, but couldn't. And then she said, "You know, some believe you Blackswords can kill with a thought."

"Wow!" John said. "That would sure make combat a lot easier."

She shook her head. "It doesn't work that way. The victim doesn't feel anything at first. But some days later, lesions form in their brain, just one or two at first, accompanied by mild headaches. The lesions are caused by some sort of parasitic growth. As more form, the victim slowly loses touch with reality, organs shut down, and they die in their own shit."

All John could think to say was, "Nasty way to go."

With her eyes unfocused, staring at nothing on the top of her desk, she continued. "It is said that in the latter stages some victims turn homicidal, so it's best to kill them at the first sign of a headache. Kelk who have recently encountered Blackswords have actually been killed, or killed themselves, because of a headache. Those who are most fearful have been known to kill themselves before the first symptoms appear."

John wasn't sure he understood her. "You mean simply because they've encountered a Blacksword, and lived to tell about it?"

She nodded. "They fear they'll harm their friends or family."

She breathed in, let out a slow sigh and looked into his eyes. "The Kelk who attacked you and Mistress Primatov, they probably did so believing they would die some days later, either from the lesions, or by their own hand, or that of a trusted friend. They were very superstitious people. The most superstitious of all call it the Curse of the Blacksword, and a few believe that if they carry something inherited from an ancestor, an object hand-made by that ancestor before the Blacksword existed, it will protect them from the Curse."

She shook her head. "Absolutely ridiculous!"

They sat in silence again for several seconds, and John decided to take a chance. "Did you know you Kelk have scaled lizard tails?"

She glanced over her shoulder as if looking at her own butt, then gave John a faint smile. "I hide it well, don't I?"

"Yes, mistress. And you kidnap and eat our children."

She shrugged. "I had heard we like to eat babies. They're more tender than adults."

John cringed. "They even publish cooking recipes, supposedly taken off dead Kelk combatants."

Her eyebrows rose, and her lips puckered as if suppressing a laugh. "Quite tasty, huh?"

John shook his head. "Haven't tried it myself."

She gave him a serious look. "We prefer them properly tenderized by marinating them for at least a day or two."

He had a difficult time not laughing, but he managed.

She leaned back in her chair and regarded him for a long moment. "Tell me about Reisenar."

She questioned him thoroughly on that, walked him through the entire story piece by piece. He didn't think Primatov would want him to hold back and only give Falkenberg the edited version, so he answered every question truthfully and tried to tell her the full story as he recalled it.

When he finished and she had asked her last question, she sat for a long moment, her eyes focused in a thousand-yard stare, nodding her head slowly up and down. Then she abruptly focused on him. "I questioned Mistress Vreekande as well, and you are truly breschkada-sa. She told me your upbringing on Novalis III had something to do with it. Tell me about that."

He took a moment to decide how to answer that. "No, mistress. I will not discuss Novalis III . . . not with anyone."

She smiled pleasantly. "I thought you might say something like that. Do you blame us for that tragedy?"

He again noticed that the Kelk called Novalis III a *tragedy*, while, with few exceptions, his Commonwealth superiors called it an *incident*. And to simply say, "No," would be a lie, so John chose his words carefully. "I didn't blame anyone at first. I think I was too numb. But since then I've learned there are superstitious and greedy Kelk people who are to blame. And there are also superstitious and greedy Commonwealth people who are to blame."

Her eyes narrowed, as if his words had affected her in some way. "That's fair. I won't press you further on the matter."

Another thought occurred to John, one he hadn't really considered before. Falkenberg clearly wanted to understand the true John Mathius. "I should add that if I ever learn who they are, I'm going to kill them, Kelk or not."

She smiled again, but this time it was not a pleasant look. "If you ever do identify them, let me know, and if I can, I'll help."

At that point she dismissed him, and as he walked down the passageway toward Matsen and Kolbeck, the butcher's harness strapped to his belt dangled against his thigh, the blade contained within it lending it extra weight. He stopped and stared at it for a moment.

He had completely forgotten about it, and she hadn't mentioned it, hadn't commented on it, hadn't asked about it, hadn't even taken a surreptitious glance at it. She had treated the blade as if it hadn't been there at all, as if it had never existed.

••••

When Fran stepped into the reception area outside Jenine Catarvin's office, the senator's receptionist looked at her and smiled warmly. "Good afternoon, Colonel Blacksword. Senator Catarvin is expecting you. Please go right in."

Fran opened the door to the inner office and stepped into it. Catarvin looked up from some papers on her desk as Fran closed the door. The senator stood, came around from behind her desk and greeted Fran warmly.

"Colonel Blacksword," she said, a vapid look on her face. "How nice to see you, and you look so smart in that uniform. Would you like something to drink? Tea, caff, or perhaps you military types like something stronger?"

Fran wondered how to broach the subject of the airhead persona. "Nothing for me, thank you."

Catarvin took her by the arm. "Then let's get comfortable." She led her to a plush couch against one wall, and they both sat down.

"You know," the plump little woman said, "I've had a chance to have some one-on-one girl-talk with your Colonel Primatov. She's such a lovely young woman."

Wondering if that had been some sort of hint, Fran nodded. "She is, and extremely intelligent too."

Catarvin clapped her hands together. "And now you and I have a chance to get to know one another a little better, don't we? I've hoped we might have an opportunity like this."

Fran didn't want to have girl-talk with Catarvin, though that thought made her realize that since she hadn't yet met the other Jenine Catarvin, she was still thinking of the woman as an imbecile. Curious to see what would happen, she decided to drop a piece of information almost no one knew. "You know, as we sit here talking, Katrine is on her way to Viktorkinde."

"Oh really," Catarvin said, smiling vacantly. She hadn't missed a beat. "Does that have something to do with these rumors about a diplomatic mission? The entire capital is abuzz with excitement. And of course, everyone's jockeying for position, though they're not quite sure what position they're jockeying for."

"Yes, it does have something to do with that."

Fran decided to simply approach the woman head on. "She told me about the confidential conversation you and she had about a month ago. She said you spoke quite candidly with her before and after you two met with Silas Palmutter."

One of Catarvin's eyebrows lifted. "She did, did she?"

"Yes. She told me none of us really understand you, not the real you."

Catarvin's expression didn't alter in the slightest. "And you're here to see if that's true?"

Fran carefully shook her head. "No. I know it's true, because if Katrine said it, then it must be."

The vapid look disappeared from the woman's face, and her eyes held a diamond-hard clarity. "Then why are you here?"

"To enlist your aid."

"How so?"

Up to that point Catarvin had not revealed anything, had not stepped out of character in the slightest. But they had now moved into an area that required a great deal of delicacy. "There are rumors drifting about regarding you and Silas Palmutter . . ."

Catarvin remained as still as a statue and didn't respond for the longest moment. Then her lips curled upward into a grin. "Oh dear, you're wondering if I'm fucking good old Silas."

"I . . ." Fran said. "I didn't mean to pry. I—"

Catarvin threw her head back and laughed. "Of course you meant to pry. This is, after all, Trafalgar. Nothing is sacrosanct in this city. And to answer your question, of course I'm fucking him. It turns out he's had quite a bit of gene therapy to . . . shall we say . . . *enhance* his assets in that department. And he can keep his performance *up*, as it were, for quite some time. The encounters are rather pleasing physically, if you can get past his atrocious personality. But what the hell, a good fuck is a good fuck, though, after I fuck him, I usually have to fuck one of my husband's mistresses just to get Si-las's asinine misogyny out of my head. I really do need to find someone besides my husband and Silas for a good hetero fuck."

The little woman sat staring into Fran's eyes with a look one could interpret as in-anely vacant, or quite piercing, depending upon one's knowledge of the woman behind the look. A laugh bubbled up into Fran's throat and she couldn't resist it. She threw her head back and let it out. "I didn't think I would like you."

Catarvin grinned. "And I knew for a certainty I wasn't going to like you. It just shows you how stupid both of us are. Now why did you come here? Certainly you must have some other reason than to simply verify what Katrine told you about me, or to inquire about Silas's artificially enhanced stamina in the bedroom."

"Yes, I do, though I must swear you to secrecy."

Catarvin leaned back and used her finger to make a big X across her chest just above the neckline of her dress. "Cross my heart, and all that."

Fran had her doubts, but Catarvin leaned forward and said, "I may seem flippant, dear, but you can trust me, perhaps more so than most."

Fran decided to go for broke. "I can't tell you everything, but we have received an invitation from the Larscom Executive Council to send a diplomatic mission to Viktorkinde."

The little woman's eyes narrowed with anger. "Why can't you tell me everything? Afraid the airhead can't keep her mouth shut?"

"No," Fran said, hardening her voice. "And yes. We're treating this as need-to-know. Under those circumstances, I don't tell my most trusted assets everything, even people like Katrine Primatov, whom I trust with my life."

The look on Catarvin's face softened. "My apologies. It sometimes rankles to be dismissed out of hand." She brightened. "But I'm an asset, am I? That's rather exciting."

"Actually," Fran said, "you're probably going to find it rather mundane. I will tell you to keep your ears open for any references to Transmarin Industries or Norddansk Weapons Systems, a Kelk manufacturing company. We suspect they've worked together behind the scenes, and if you find any indication of that, I need to know about it right away. And keep in mind that Norddansk is a name you should not have heard before, so I caution you to never mention it."

"You see," Catarvin said triumphantly. "I knew this would be exciting."

Fran described how she, Gascoigne, and Obradour were attempting to staff the upcoming mission to Viktorkinde.

Catarvin's lips hardened into a thin straight line. "You did not reveal my alternate persona to Obradour, did you?"

"No," Fran said. "Katrine was quite clear that you gave her permission to reveal that only to Mani and me, then she swore us to secrecy. No, definitely not Obradour, or anyone else for that matter. Again, need-to-know."

The anger disappeared from Catarvin's face. "I should remember to have more faith in that girl."

Fran nodded. "We all should."

Catarvin perked up. "So what do you need from me? Something to do with the diplomatic mission to Viktorkinde, right?"

"Yes, exactly," Fran said. "As I said, Mani will head up the mission because the invitation came through his office. Obradour will represent commercial interests, and Palmutter's presence will satisfy the hawks. Mani and I were thinking that if the rumors about you and Palmutter were true, it could be helpful if you were part of the mission as well. As a sitting senator, no one would question your presence, and you're a moderate, which balances out the agenda nicely."

Catarvin's eyes brightened. "And while Silas is revealing all his secrets during the throes of ecstasy, I could give you an inside track on his thinking throughout the whole thing."

"Yes," Fran said, still a little concerned. "I hadn't really thought of it in those terms. I hope you're not insulted by such a request."

Catarvin gave Fran a sly grin. "And I hope you're not too surprised to learn I've already set that in motion. Silas has been fuming about all the rumors. And you say Mani is going to enlist him for the mission and insist I be included?"

Fran frowned, not sure where the woman wanted to go with this. "I'm not sure if *insist* is the right word, but he's certainly going to try to make it happen."

Catarvin held up her hands as if trying to stop an approaching car. "Tell him to not even mention me, because Silas is going to do all the insisting. Just offer him the job, and he'll demand I be included. Of course, his desire to have me along is purely lascivious. Someone has to give him the occasional blow job, since that pretty aide of his won't give him the time of day. But do pretend to be surprised when he makes his demands, and do me a favor: argue with him. You can throw out terms like 'that stupid airhead,' or 'that imbecile of a woman.' I have no doubt he'll agree with you on that. Make him sweat a little, then after arguing a bit, you can capitulate."

The woman's eyes brightened. "Oh, and as long as we're passing along secrets, Silas recently learned young Mr. Mathius survived the assault on campus and was turned over to the Kelk. I think he has some connections with the people who abducted the poor young man. I suspect he might be an accomplice to some illegal activities, and I intend to find out more."

The woman paused as if out of breath, and Fran wondered what would come out of her mouth next. She leaned toward Fran, a conspiratorial look on her face. "Do you know what this breschkada thing is?"

Fran tried to hide her surprise as she asked, "Where did you hear that word?"

Catarvin wrinkled her nose with distaste. "Silas has an aide, a rather unpleasant young man named Macus DeLeon. Silas gave him a promotion because he did some digging and learned your Mr. Mathius took Kelk language lessons from a Professor Dirkson. Silas had Dirkson come out to his office to question him on the matter, but I thought it rather telling Silas was only interested in this breschkada thing."

Fran gave Catarvin a brief explanation of the breschkada relationship as she understood it. "There aren't more than a half dozen people in the Commonwealth who know that word exists, let alone what it means, or that it applies to that young man. Be careful."

Catarvin smiled and dismissed Fran's concerns with a casual wave of her hand. "Don't worry, dear. I'm well aware Silas didn't get that information from anyone in the Commonwealth. If you haven't figured it out by now, our dear Silas and his hawk friends are working closely with some very dangerous people, some of whom have blue-tinted pale-white skin and bright red irises."

Katrine had warned Fran about Catarvin, telling her the woman would likely prove to be a most surprising character. Fran left the senator's office thinking she had underestimated both Katrine and Catarvin. But she put those thoughts aside and called Gascoigne.

He immediately asked, "How'd it go with Catarvin?"

"You're not going to believe me when I tell you. Have you met with Palmutter yet?"

"No. I purposefully set it up for later today so we could confer after your meeting with her."

Fran couldn't help but laugh. "Hold onto your seat, Mani. Have I got an earful for you!"

13

Just One of the Crew

THE KNOCK ON her stateroom door startled Katrine. Seated at a small desk built into a bulkhead of her stateroom, the fact that she hadn't received any kind of answer from Fran Thealone to her initial report had haunted her. She had specifically asked Thealone to respond immediately with at least an acknowledgment, if nothing more. And she had no doubt the woman had done so. But Katrine had received nothing.

A second knock on her stateroom door forced her to put those thoughts aside. Vagle stood near the door waiting for her to surface from her musing. Katrine had wrapped the shoulder harness around her grav pistol and placed it on the desk in front of her. She retrieved it and put her hand on the butt of the pistol, then gave Vagle a nod. "Go ahead."

Vagle reached for the sidearm strapped to her side and pulled it out of the holster, then lowered her hand to hide it behind her thigh. She unlocked the door a crack and glanced out. She immediately stepped aside and opened it fully. John Mathius stood in the passageway, a frown on his face.

Katrine waved him in. "Come on in, John, and don't waste time with the formalities."

He stepped into the small stateroom and she asked, "What can I do for you?"

He glanced uncertainly at Vagle as he said, "I wanted to talk to you about something."

Katrine took the hint and said to Vagle, "Can you wait out in the passageway?"

Vagle nodded. "Of course, mistress."

Once the woman had left the room and closed the door, Katrine said, "Okay, John, what's bothering you."

Even with Vagle out of the room, his unease remained. "Command Superior Falkenberg just interviewed me, a standard XO kind of interview. You know, new junior officer assigned to the crew and all that."

Katrine would have to pull it out of him. "And?"

He spoke cautiously. "Have you heard about us killing them with a thought?"

She didn't need to ask who he meant by *them*. "Killing them with a thought. No, I hadn't heard of anything like that."

She reached over, hit a switch and extruded a chair out of the bulkhead. "Sit down."

She got him seated, and wished she had some of that fiery Kelk alcohol. A shot of that might get him to open up more. "Tell me more."

"During the interview," he said, "for several seconds we both got a little candid. She told me they believe Blackswords can kill with a thought."

That frightened Katrine. "They all believe this?"

He shook his head. "No, a small minority, just really superstitious people."

He described a scenario in which Blackswords induced parasitic lesions in the brains of Kelk victims, and did so with no more than a thought. "It doesn't affect them at first, but it starts with headaches, and then they die slowly. She told me the people who attacked us believed they would die that way."

"She used the word *superstitious*?"

He nodded. "Yes." He told her of the Curse of the Blacksword, and how some believed that an inherited amulet might protect them. "She said they're the most superstitious of all."

Katrine recalled the NCO who had attacked her. Vagle had gut-shot the woman, and Katrine saw her afterwards in *Konigsborge*'s ICU. She'd been delirious, muttering something about headaches, and repeatedly begging to be killed. Kristdokar had labeled the woman *superstitious*.

Katrine questioned John further, and learned he and Falkenberg had had a few lighter moments during the interview. They had joked about Kelk with scaled lizard tails, and recipes for cooking Commonwealth babies. When he left her stateroom his unease had abated, but Katrine had trouble sleeping that night.

••••

Nerves prevented John from getting a good night's sleep, and he awoke fearing he might function poorly that day, his first day standing watch on *Drakan Helgis*. As he pulled on his uniform he felt like an actor about to step on stage, ill-prepared for the part he must play. He didn't try to pretend this day would be anything like a newly commissioned officer's first day of active duty on a ship. Under ordinary circumstances most would not care one way or another if a new officer succeeded or failed, but not on that ship, not on that day. Everyone would be watching him, some hoping he botched it badly, some wanting him to shine, but many of them probably fearing he just wasn't up to the task. John would bet good money there wasn't a single person on that ship without a strong opinion one way or the other. They would all be watching the fork-wielding Blacksword.

For a moment he wished he could wear a Kelk uniform so his Commonwealth uniform didn't make him stand out so much. And then he realized how ridiculous that thought had been. He was one of only two people on the ship who didn't have salt-and-pepper hair, pale blue skin, and demon-red eyes.

Someone knocked on the door. Kolbeck answered it and admitted Primatov. John turned to face her as she crossed the room and stopped a pace away from him, with Kolbeck and Matsen standing behind her.

"Nervous?" she asked.

He couldn't hide a grimace. "Scared shitless, ma'am."

She nodded sympathetically. "You'll do fine, John. You've certainly overcome worse."

"Like when?"

A flash of anger momentarily clouded her features. "Like when they tried to murder you with those butcher's blades."

"But that was easy," he pleaded. "All I did was kill the assholes."

Behind her, Kolbeck said, "I don't think it was too easy killing 'em with a fork."

John gave him a nasty look and he grinned.

Primatov rolled her eyes and put a hand on John's shoulder. "Today, as long as they don't try to kill you first, do you think you could refrain from killing anyone?"

John shook his head. "I'll try."

She smiled. "Good man."

Matsen said, "We better move out, or you're going to be late, and you don't want to be late on Captain Taugrim's watch."

To John's relief, Primatov remained behind while Matsen and Kolbeck escorted him to the bridge. He didn't think it would look good if she shepherded him to his first day on watch like a fearful mother, and Matsen and Kolbeck would probably have had something to say about that. The two men waited one deck below while John climbed up a ladder to the bridge.

During John's year of active duty, he had spent a couple of tendays on the bridge of the ComSecCorps destroyer *Defiant*. He had learned quite a bit about interstellar navigation from Lieutenant Commander Forcis, a small woman whose strong personality belied her diminutive stature. They had played cat-and-mouse with an armed Kelk frigate, a dangerous game of ego and wills that lasted for hours.

He was not surprised to see that *Drakan Helgis*'s bridge appeared little different from that of *Defiant*: cramped and claustrophobic, with instrument clusters hanging from above and jutting out from all sides. As he stepped forward he tried not to make a show of it, did not puff his chest out or march like a Stormtrooper. Instead, he walked calmly to the command console and stopped beside Taugrim, standing at attention and saluting her in the Kelk style, his eyes focused on her lips.

Her head pivoted slowly toward him as if controlled by mechanical gears, not the flesh and blood of muscles in her neck. And while she looked at him without expression, and his eyes remained focused on her lips, he thought he saw a message in her face: *Prove to me I should regard you with something other than contempt.*

He had thought long and hard about how he would refer to himself when reporting, and the intimidation he felt pushed him to a little defiance. "Ensign John Mathius, ComSecCorps, Blacksword Regiment, reporting for duty, Mistress Taugrim."

Her eyes hardened, and one eyebrow rose higher than he had ever seen a single eyebrow rise without its companion. She glanced down at his feet, didn't return his salute, looked him in the eyes and said, "I believe your stance is incorrect. Extend your right hand."

He abandoned the salute and extended his arm, his palm flat and aimed downward.

"Mistress Falkenberg," she said. "How incorrect is his stance?"

Drakan Helgis's XO appeared beside him, extended a pair of calipers and measured the breadth of his hand. Then Falkenberg bent down as he kept his eyes locked on Taugrim's lips, and he heard her sigh. "He's off by more than a millimeter."

Taugrim nodded. "As I thought. Maestra Mathius, do it again."

John lowered his arm to his side, pivoted, walked back to the entrance, turned around, walked back to the command console, and repeated the salute. "Ensign John Mathius, ComSecCorps, Blacksword Regiment, reporting for duty, Mistress Taugrim."

The second time, one side of her mouth curled upward in a half-hearted smile.

If the measure of the distance between his heels had to be accurate to better than a millimeter, he'd be marching back and forth between the entrance and the command console all day. She made him repeat the performance over and over, and on the sixth try he either hit the mark purely by random chance, or Falkenberg decided to show him some mercy. She announced, "He's good."

Taugrim returned his salute. "Welcome aboard, Maestra Mathius. Take a seat at Fire Control. You'll be working under Command Superior Dahlborg."

Dahlborg was a slightly plump woman of average height. When John sat down next to her at the Fire Control console, she leaned close to him and whispered, "Did you have to make such a point of being a Blacksword?"

John didn't have an answer to that. He simply grimaced and shrugged.

Her eyes narrowed. "You have the brains of a miere drakan."

John shook his head. "I don't know what that is."

She gave him a cheesy smile. "It's a mythical half-primate, half-lizard creature. During mating season the testicles of the male grow to four times their normal size and turn bright red. Then he struts around showing off his balls to attract a mate. We say that a mating miere drakan male has his brains in his testicles." She glanced down at John's crotch. "You have the brains of a miere drakan."

Dahlborg walked him through the functions and operations of the Fire-Control console. It was quite similar to that on *Defiant*. John was thankful Primatov had forced him to improve his ability to read Kelk, though he still struggled with it.

As the watch proceeded, Taugrim found fault with everything John did. Several times she made him stand up from Fire Control, march over to stand in front of her, and listen to a loud lecture on his failings, a lecture everyone else on the bridge got to listen to as well.

Near the middle of the watch the tech at the com console announced, "Captain, I just received a course correction from *Eldekarl*. And they've included another data packet from Viktorkinde."

To John's relief, Taugrim and most of the crew on the bridge focused on implementing the course correction, and for a time he was not the center of attention. As Fire Control Officer, Dahlborg had nothing to do with navigating the ship, so with a few moments of breathing room, John asked her, "*Eldekarl*, that's a hunter-killer, right?"

"Yes," she said. "They can do over four thousand lights, so they run ahead of us, then down-transit for a nav fix and feed that data back to us."

Something didn't add up. "But how can they be in contact with Viktorkinde. We're too far out, aren't we?"

She grinned and gave him a knowing wink, a Commonwealth kind of expression. "We're running parallel to a relay chain of communications buoys. *Eldekarl* times its down-transition to be near one of the buoys, and by the time we catch up with them, they've sent and received updates to and from Viktorkinde."

When they completed the course correction, Taugrim returned to harassing John.

Near the end of the watch they ran a simulated engagement with an enemy warship of unspecified origin, though it was clear to everyone their target was a Commonwealth cruiser. "Maestra Mathius," Taugrim announced loudly, signaling another round of harassment for the new guy. "How would you handle this difficult situation?"

By that time, large sweat stains discolored the back and armpits of John's tunic, and he had learned there would be no right answer. No matter what he said, she'd find fault with it, and he'd end up standing in front of the command console for another lecture. All he could do was play it straight and take whatever shit she threw his way.

"They have us badly outgunned," he said. "We'd be foolish to engage in any conventional fashion."

Taugrim pursed her lips and nodded. "Then let me hear how a Blacksword might engage them in an unconventional way, Maestra Blacksword."

He had been about to say he would not engage, would withdraw in a conventional way. But her question triggered a flood of defiant thoughts.

"Well," he said. "It's not what any other Blacksword would do. But if it were up to me, I guess I'd give one of the transition launcher crews a fork, tell them to load that into the launcher, and we could fork the hell out of the assholes." He paused for a moment, then added, "Forks are my specialty."

The bridge went eerily silent, the only sound a background of beeps and ticks from the instruments. Seated next to him, Dahlborg's eyes had widened considerably. Without breaking the silence she mouthed the words *miere drakan*.

John watched Taugrim, waiting for her to call him before her for the loudest lecture yet. She and Falkenberg had locked eyes with one another, and John thought he saw a lot of demon-eyed Kelk in both faces. They sat silent and still for the longest moment, then Taugrim exploded, threw her head back and roared with laughter, while Falkenberg gulped air and wiped tears from her eyes.

"No, no," the XO said, "that'll never work. They're too heavily armed. We'll have to launch at least two forks at them."

That produced another round of wild laughter, and before it was done the entire bridge crew had joined in. John didn't really get the joke, and decided it must be some quirk in the collective Kelk sense of humor.

The watch ended a short time later. John walked off the bridge and met his two shadows waiting for him on the deck below.

Kolbeck demanded, "What was all the laughing and shouting about?"

John shook his head. "We forked the hell out of an enemy warship."

As the two men escorted him back to his stateroom, he realized that once again no one had paid the slightest bit of attention to the butcher's blade strapped to his side. They had ignored it completely, as if it didn't exist at all.

14

The Money Guy

SOMETHING HAD GONE sour and Macus struggled to understand what. It had started with that missed message. It still irked him the tech people had confirmed he had gotten it, when in fact he hadn't. Then Palmutter's receptionist had turned him down, so he'd tried to go back to Dog-Face. The main advantage of fucking the ugly cow was that she was handy when he needed her, and she didn't make any demands. But she too had turned him down, and with a fair amount of vehemence. And she kept throwing nasty looks his way, then she'd turn and make a visible show of walking away from him in a huff.

Shortly after that, some of his internal sources of information dried up. It started with a young delivery boy from the cafeteria with whom Macus had carefully nurtured a relationship. He had hinted that as Chief Military Adviser to an influential senator, he might be able to help the fellow with a little upward mobility, perhaps even snare a position for him as an aide to the senator. Macus would never endanger his own standing with the senator by recommending a cafeteria delivery boy to such a position, but the stupid schmuck didn't know that.

Palmutter always started the day early, and ate breakfast alone in his office while reviewing briefings from various staffers. The same young nobody from the cafeteria always delivered his breakfast, then stopped by Macus's desk to fill him in on the senator's mood, and what might interest the senator most that day. But that had ended abruptly. It hadn't been a monumental loss, but several such minor relationships had gone sour, and the effect added up.

That morning when Macus showed up for work, he again stopped by the receptionist's desk. As he'd done the day before, he leaned on her desk, got another good look down her blouse, and asked, "What's he like today?"

Palmutter had continued to harass his staff about the rumors circulating through the capital, and everyone had been on edge for several days now. But instead of rolling her eyes and telling him to keep his head down, she sighed and gave him a look of vast relief. "He's happy as a kitten. I don't know what's going on. It's like night and day."

Macus thought about that all the way to his office. When he sat down at his desk, the message at the top of his queue was an announcement that Faith Carlton had been promoted to Director of Communications. And with the promotion came a private office. At that moment it all clicked into place. His recent problems had begun immediately after he and Faith had ended their relationship.

Palmutter had scheduled Macus and Faith for a meeting in his office later that morning, so Macus left a little early and stopped by Faith's new office. The door was open. He leaned in and said, "Mind if I come in?"

She nodded. "You're always welcome."

He had expected a little rancor, or perhaps a smug look of victory, and her pleasant attitude surprised him. He stepped through the door and said, "Congratulations."

She gave him a warm smile. "Thank you."

He closed the door. "How did you do it?"

She tried to look innocent. "Get the promotion? I worked quite hard for it."

"Come on," he said. "You know exactly what I'm talking about."

She grinned. "I've been here longer than you, and like you I nurtured certain relationships. Sometimes you simply let someone cry on your shoulder and give them a little dating advice."

"The receptionist?"

She shook her head. "No, she turned you down on her own, which I must say, speaks well of her character."

"Dog-Face?"

Her grin broadened and she acknowledged his guess with lifted eyebrows. "Then there's the guy in Tech who makes sure nothing goes wrong with our messaging system. If he has a horrible crush on you . . ." She left that hanging.

"You're fucking him?"

Still grinning, she shook her head. "Not at all. If you fuck someone who's all gaga on you, he might want to get serious, and you can end up with all sorts of nasty complications. The last thing I need is some whiny asshole telling me we're in love." She gave him a shy, virginal look, batted her eyelashes at him, and spoke as if close to tears. "But he's a very sympathetic fellow, and when a girl's had her heart broken by a really heartless bad guy, well, who knows what Mr. Tech might do if he got all angry at Mr. Heartless."

"And the delivery boy from the cafeteria?"

Her grin didn't falter. "Sometimes you do have to fuck someone."

"You're fucking the delivery boy?"

She shook her head. "No, his boss, but it was strictly a one-shot deal. I gave him what he wanted, once only, and in return he gave me what I wanted. It was rather mercenary, I might add, for both of us. But we did have a good time. He was an entertaining fuck, and I really enjoyed the look on your face when the delivery boy started ignoring you."

"One more question," he said, "if you don't mind."

She clearly enjoyed telling him how she had one-upped him.

"Why didn't you fuck Palmutter? He was all over you for a while."

She pursed her lips in thought for a moment. "Because if I let him in my pants, I'd gain some advantage, but only for a short time. And I know his type. After about six months he'd tire of me, stop fucking me, and at that point I'd become a liability. Then a few months later I'd be out the door. I did get him to grab my ass and make a couple of passes at me, though I was quite upset when he did." She displayed a big grin. "And now I'm Communications Director."

He shrugged and shook his head sadly. "I'm impressed."

She didn't gloat or throw a smug look his way. "Macus, to get what you want sometimes you have to fuck someone and make them happy. And sometimes you have to fuck someone and make their life unpleasant, the way I'm fucking you right now."

She stood and said, "I believe we have a meeting with the senator."

He opened the door and held it for her. "After you."

Again, Palmutter had a guest in his office. But where Andrew Smith had been a little rough around the edges, the fellow seated on a couch against the wall wore a business suit that probably cost a year of Macus's salary. He stood as Macus and Faith entered the room. Palmutter also stood, then came around from behind his desk. He didn't do that for just anyone.

"Faith, Macus," the senator said, clearly in a good mood. "Let me introduce you to Lawrence Strikland, Executive Vice President and head of Transmarin Missile Systems."

Strikland stood average height, and was trim with an athletic build. He had a pleasant smile and carried himself with confidence. They shook hands, exchanged a few pleasantries, then Strikland sat down on the couch.

Palmutter pointed Faith and Macus to a couple of chairs in front of his desk, then walked around it and sat down, saying, "Lawrence and I don't have long, but this is important."

Strikland's presence intrigued Macus no end.

Palmutter said, "I had a meeting yesterday with Mani Gascoigne, and he laid to rest all the rumors. He has received an invitation from the Larscom Executive Council to send a diplomatic delegation to Viktorkinde. They've apparently worked on it quietly for months. We now have an opportunity, and we have to move quickly."

Faith perked up and leaned forward. "They want to open diplomatic relations?"

Palmutter shook his head and waved his hands. "No, they didn't go that far. The official line is to, '. . . initiate preliminary discussions on matters of mutual benefit.' Completely noncommittal. I called you in here because I'm going to be part of that diplomatic mission, and you two are coming with me."

Faith said, "I'm honored, sir."

Palmutter shook his head. "It's not an honor. You earned the position, and you're going to work your ass off. Gascoigne's office is going to issue a press release sometime today. So both of you pack your bags and be ready to move quickly. I don't have a departure date, but it's not going to be far off."

He looked Strikland's way and smiled. "Lawrence has agreed to join us as well. He's taken a leave from Transmarin to serve the Commonwealth as my Commercial Adviser. Very generous of him, I might add."

At that point Palmutter dismissed Macus and Faith. Macus stood, opened the door and held it for Faith. As she stepped out of the office, Palmutter called out, "Macus, a private word with you. Close the door." The senator rose and stepped around his desk.

Macus closed the door as Palmutter approached him, leaving Strikland still seated on the couch at the other end of the office, and Faith on the other side of the door. Palmutter leaned close to Macus and lowered his voice to a whisper. "Office scuttlebutt has it there is some difficulty between you and Faith."

Macus started to say he would take care of it, but the senator raised a finger, silencing him. "I need you two working closely together, especially now. Please mend any rift between you."

Macus was impressed. Faith had covered all the bases. She had even set him up so he had to come begging to her. "Yes, sir, I'll do so immediately."

Palmutter slapped him on the back. "Good lad."

Macus found Faith waiting out in the reception area. "What was that about?" she asked, as if she didn't know.

"Nothing," Macus said. "Mind if we go back to your office?"

She raised an eyebrow. "Lead the way."

Once they were in her office Macus closed the door and said, "Yesterday, when we spoke in my office, you gave me the impression you might want to work together again?"

She sat down in the chair behind her desk. "We didn't work together before. We just fucked each other, and sometimes I enjoyed it. But I'm still talking to you because I think we can both go further working as a team of equals, much further than we can working separately. On the other hand, if you can't work with me that way, I'll do fine without you."

Recalling Palmutter's admonition, Macus said, "You seem open to repairing our relationship if I ensure that in the future it is . . . mutually beneficial."

She eyed him with a look of distrust for a long moment. "Don't forget it's not about the sex, except when it becomes symptomatic of other deficiencies in our relationship."

At that moment it occurred to Macus he may have finally met a woman who was his equal. She had bested him, and realizing that, he felt an erection coming on. "I understand that fully."

She nodded. "Okay, then I'm willing to try again."

Macus understood now that sex meant nothing to her, except as a physical need that required regular attention, no love, no emotional attachment. In that they were well matched. He smiled. "Then why don't we go to your place tonight and start over?"

She looked at him for a long moment of silence, then stood. She walked over to the door, locked it, then returned to the chair behind her desk. "No," she said, "let's start over right now."

He grinned, walked around the desk and stood over her, thinking maybe she wasn't his equal, not if she capitulated so easily. He didn't try to hide the visible bulge in his pants.

She wore a pencil skirt, and seated in the chair she reached out, gripped the hem, and slid it all the way up to the top of her thighs, revealing that she wore nothing beneath it. She must have planned this.

He reached for his belt and started to unbuckle it, but she shook her head. "We're not at the mutually beneficial stage yet. Right now you need to make up for not making me happy the last time we were together. We'll start the mutually beneficial part of our relationship at your place tonight."

He nodded, carefully knelt on both knees in front of her, placed his hands on her knees and parted her legs. He leaned forward, but hesitated, a thought boiling to the surface. "You said *my* place tonight. Why not your place as usual?"

She grinned. "Because tonight, after we have a mutually beneficial time making each other happy, I get to wipe myself off on your sheets."

No, he thought, *it's definitely not about the sex.*

••••

In the Commonwealth, since anyone in ComSecCorps was expected to be able to ". . . put on plast and do boots-on-the-ground . . . ," with few exceptions, every member of a ship's crew had a personalized set of combat armor hanging in a locker in their quarters. From Matsen and Kolbeck, John learned the Supremacy operated differently, and only some of them qualified in full armor.

Drakan Helgis had a marine contingent of thirty-two combatants, though a literal translation of the Kelk word for marine, dregkraag, meant something like *dirt fighter.*

Those crew members who had qualified for armored combat operations had a full suit of armor in their quarters. Those who had not, had a simple vac suit available should an emergency arise, or if they were needed to work in a vacuum environment. As such, issuance of a suit of armor elevated its owner to a certain level of enhanced status. And the fact that all ComSecCorps personnel had qualified for such status, lent them a certain mystique among John's new Kelk friends. He didn't mention that he'd seen a few high-ranking Commonwealth officers whose waist-lines gave the distinct impression they could no longer fit into their armor. In all likelihood, ComSecCorps probably made adjustments to accommodate them.

Now that John had become a member of *Drakan Helgis*'s crew, and since he had qualified in armor, he needed to be fitted for a set of Kelk armor. Matsen and Kolbeck were both dregkraag, and for his fitting they escorted him down to the dregkraag Ready-Room.

Inside they found Nikaela and a mixed group of male and female Kelk *dirt fighters* dressed in fatigues, all working carefully on one female in full combat armor. There was no question as to the armored person's gender since the plast fit rather tightly to the wearer's body, including a thin waist with slightly broader hips, and a couple of extra bumps on the breast plate to accommodate a pair of breasts. Commonwealth armor tended toward the androgynous, whereas the Kelk liked theirs tightly fitting. John hoped it wouldn't be so tight as to be uncomfortable.

As John and his two shadows stepped into the Ready-Room, the armored woman turned her head and looked their way. "John," she said, and even with her words slightly distorted by the helmet speakers, he recognized Primatov's voice.

She crossed the room with Nikaela and a few of the Kelk following her, and stopped a couple of paces short of John. She held her hands out to her sides as if modeling the armor for him. "This armor's a lot more comfortable than it looks." She moved her arms up and down experimentally. "They do a better job with the joints than we do."

Behind her, a male Kelk officer said, "If you please, Mistress."

Without turning to look his way, she said, "Of course, Maestra."

He reached up and gripped the reactor pack on her back. He shook her slightly side to side, checking something. "We need to adjust the fit on the back plate, and modify your underpadding. That'll make it even more comfortable. Let's remove the suit."

She reached up and popped the neck seals on her helmet. The Kelk marines surrounded her, popping seals and helping her out of the armor. They stripped her down to her underpadding, then removed that, and in short order she stood among them in skimpy underwear. Like Carla and John's other Commonwealth friends, Primatov didn't think twice about it.

Any healthy heterosexual man would enjoy looking at her that way, John included, but his parochial Novalis III mores kicked in and he felt more comfortable studying the floor. Kolbeck had no compunctions whatsoever about taking in an eyeful, though since he stood behind Primatov she didn't see the look on his face. If she turned about quickly and did see it, she'd probably punch his lights out.

"Your turn," Nikaela said, and it took John a moment to realize she meant him.

"Me?" he said.

"Yes, you. Of course."

John reached down to unbuckle the butcher's harness, and he noticed that at that moment everyone but Nikaela and Primatov had found something to look at that drew their eyes away from him. That angered him, so with a little bit of extra force, he tossed the harness onto a workbench, and it made a clattering racket as it landed. A couple of them flinched, which satisfied him immensely.

He had wondered if the Kelk were as casual about the unclothed human body as his platoon mates on Miriteen, and at that point he got his answer. He tried to act casual as he stripped down, which became even more difficult because Primatov approached him wearing her next-to-nothing outfit. "How'd your first watch go, John?"

He shrugged. "About as good as you could expect. Taugrim busted my ass big time."

Primatov smiled. "Yah, she has a reputation for that. But she'll probably let up after the new-guy syndrome wears off."

He tossed his tunic onto the workbench next to the butcher's harness. "Was it the new-guy syndrome, or the he's-not-Kelk syndrome?"

She grinned and gave him a wry look. "Probably a little of both. Don't let it get to you. From what I've heard, she didn't give you any worse than any other newcomer."

As he pulled off his boots, Nikaela said, "I heard you made a joke."

John recalled them laughing at him, but didn't remember sharing in any of their humor with a joke of his own.

Kolbeck's eyes narrowed with curiosity. "What kind of joke?"

Primatov said, "I heard it was something about forking a ship."

"Oh yah, that," John said. "Taugrim asked me how I would defeat an enemy ship that had us badly outgunned. I told her I'd transition launch a fork at them."

Matsen threw his head back and laughed much the way Taugrim had.

John still didn't find any humor in it. "At the time I didn't think of it as much of a joke."

"You sure you ain't Kelk?" Kolbeck asked. "That was really Kelk of you."

Primatov gave John a friendly pat on the back. "I'm glad you found some humor in the situation. Did you learn anything about a Kelk warship?"

He shook his head. "Not much. Seems to operate pretty much like a Commonwealth warship. And the only time they weren't riding me was when *Eldekarl* sent us a course correction and some data packets."

All the humor disappeared from Primatov's face. "Course correction . . . and data packets?"

Something about his words clearly upset her, and that bothered John. "Yes, ma'am. *Eldekarl's* running ahead of us, down-transiting near the relay buoys, updating Viktorkinde, and getting updates in return."

Her face clouded over, and he wasn't sure if what he saw there was fear, or anger, or both.

It took more than an hour to properly fit John with a suit of Kelk armor. As Primatov had said, it was quite comfortable, even though more tightly fitting than Commonwealth armor. They still had to make some modifications, so it wouldn't be ready for a couple of days. But that really didn't matter since he would never have a need to wear it. Oddly enough, one thing they had anticipated was special clips on the left thigh plate to hold the butcher's dagger, even though none of them but Nikaela would acknowledge its presence.

Through that whole afternoon, one thing stuck in John's mind: the look on Primatov's face when she had learned *Eldekarl* was running ahead of them to communicate with Viktorkinde. She had not been at all happy to hear that, and John wondered why.

15

A Delicate Alliance

TARSIK OBRADOUR PROVED to be an invaluable asset, not simply because he was wealthy, influential, and maintained a rather extensive network of confidential informants. He repeatedly demonstrated a sophisticated understanding of the prominent personalities involved in Commonwealth government, and a savvy knowledge of the way politicians and bureaucrats conducted business. Gascoigne put it succinctly when he said, "The little fellow knows which arms to twist, and how to twist them without pissing off the twistee, at least not too much." Obradour still irritated Fran, but she could overlook that.

Gascoigne's office issued the press release about the upcoming diplomatic mission to Viktorkinde shortly after noon, and as Fran had predicted, the shit hit the fan in every governmental office in Trafalgar City. By mid-afternoon, every bureaucrat, politician, lobbyist, low-level functionary, administrator, janitor, cafeteria cook, waiter, busboy, and bottle-washer had made it clear they wanted their fingers in that pie. Since the release stated the invitation had been extended to the government through the offices of the Right Honorable Senator Manifort Gascoigne, most of the shit fell on Mani's shoulders, for which Fran was most thankful. But Obradour worked tirelessly behind the scenes, and shouldered a lot of the crap.

The hawks all immediately decried such a mission and righteously demanded the invitation be refused. They also each lobbied to be included in the mission, most insisting they should be the one to lead it. The doves all felt the hawks should be excluded, that the team should be comprised of only those who could go with peaceful intent toward the Kelk, and each of them thought they should be the one to lead it. The hawks countered that if the mission were led by doves, they would invariably sell out to the demon-eyed monsters, so even more hawks would have to be included to keep the soft-hearted doves from giving away the store. Fran didn't think they had enough ships in the Commonwealth to carry everyone who insisted on going.

Early in the afternoon on the day of the press release, Gascoigne called her. She hadn't spoken with him after briefing him on her meeting with Catarvin.

"How'd it go with Palmutter?" she asked.

"You're not going to believe it," he said. "Just before our meeting I got a call from Obradour. Palmutter called him, as one hawk to another, and wanted him to put pressure on me. Then when we actually met I resisted mightily. We argued for more than an hour, but he pointed out how I needed to balance out the mission, so I capitulated. Then he made his play for Catarvin. I still haven't agreed to it yet, told him I'd think about it, maybe consult with Obradour. That shut him up. I'll call him in a few minutes and tell him she's in."

••••

Kristdokar looked at the virtual image of Nygaard in her implants, and tried to sound calm and unperturbed as she said, "I must protest, Vice Skalde Nygaard." They had already had this discussion once before, but this time Kristdokar had prepared a much more convincing argument, and she hoped she could convince Nygaard to change her mind.

Nygaard didn't roll her eyes, but still gave the impression of a parent impatiently suffering the whims of a stubbornly recalcitrant child. "You may protest all you want, Brigadier. I've made my decision."

Disagreeing with such a powerful woman could prove to be a mistake, but Kristdokar took the chance. "This is the second data packet we've received from Colonel Primatov's superiors. And the second one we have not transferred to her."

Nygaard made no attempt to hide her impatience. "And until we can decode them, and review them to our satisfaction, you will not transfer them."

Kristdokar knew she must not sound argumentative. "Our top tech people tell me there is no reason to believe their encryption algorithms are any less robust than ours. As such, it will take a lifetime to decode these, if we can decode them at all."

Nygaard shrugged and smiled. "Then we just won't deliver them. That is a direct order from me, and if you don't like it, you can go over my head and put the question before the entire Executive Council."

Kristdokar shook her head slowly. "I have no intention of doing that. I would never jump the chain of command, but please hear me out."

Nygaard waved a hand impatiently. "I'm listening."

Kristdokar doubted that, but dare not say so. "Imagine, if you will, that our situations were reversed. Imagine that at Sarkovie, Colonel Primatov held the upper hand when it came to firepower, you remained on Viktorkinde, and she insisted the two breschkada return with her to Trafalgar. I would choose to accompany them, and just as you allowed her, she would probably allow me to send you a report. In that report I would propose some method of determining if they did not deliver subsequent messages from you to me, or from me to you."

Nygaard's eyes narrowed, and she appeared lost in thought for several seconds. "How might she have done that?"

Kristdokar finally had the woman's full attention. "I could think of any number of ways. First, with our situations reversed, I'd probably ask you to send an immediate message back to me, even if it were of no substance. I might ask you to send a message every day, regardless if one was needed, or every two days. Then when we finally made contact, I could count the days and know if any messages were held back. She will not believe that her superiors did not respond in some way, and if we wait too long, or hold any messages back, it will bode ill for any further cooperation we might have with her and them."

Kristdokar paused for effect, then added, "Two days ago she gave me another message to transmit to her superiors, which would be in line with that kind of scenario."

Nygaard closed her eyes for a long moment, and did not open them when she finally spoke. "How do we correct this situation?"

Kristdokar exhaled slowly as relief washed through her. "With your permission, I'll tell her we just established our first contact with Viktorkinde since leaving Sarkovie, and give her the two data packets we've received for her. She'll still be suspicious, but hopefully her doubts will dim with time."

"I'll think on it," Nygaard said, "and I'll let you know when I've made a decision."

Kristdokar knew better than to ask for more, at least for the moment.

••••

Ten days ago they had left the destroyer *Alvilddan* behind to finish mopping up the mess near Sarkovie. Two days after that *Eldekarl*, *Drakan Helgis* and *Konigsborge* had down-transited at the terminus of the chain of communications buoys set up by Thordahl. They stayed only long enough for Nygaard to send a report that the chain transmitted to Viktorkinde, then up-transited to continue the journey back to the Supremacy. And now, about half way to Viktorkinde, from John's offhand remark while being fitted for armor, Katrine had learned that *Eldekarl* had maintained communications with the Executive Council through intermediate buoys on the relay chain.

Any communications for her from Trafalgar would land first on Kristdokar's desk. Each would contain an unencrypted header asking the skalde to deliver the encrypted portion of the message to Katrine. Katrine would have no way of knowing if the skalde chose to simply ignore the request and not deliver it. She trusted Kristdokar, but it never hurt to be cautious. And that trust had been badly damaged when she had learned from John that they were already in contact with Viktorkinde through *Eldekarl*. If they had been in contact all along, assuming her report had taken two or three days to reach Thealone, she should have received at least two messages by now: Thealone's immediate response, plus one more four days later.

It was certainly possible they had only just reestablished contact. But had Katrine been in charge, with *Eldekarl* at her disposal she certainly would not have waited eight days. She would have immediately sent the hunter-killer forward to keep them in almost continuous contact. It had been two days since John had stood his first watch on *Drakan Helgis*'s bridge, two days since Katrine had learned of their deception, two days during which her trust coefficient had declined to near zero. If Katrine didn't receive those two messages in a fairly short time frame, she would know for a certainty she could not trust her Kelk hosts, which would mean she and John were really just prisoners, regardless of appearances. Trust, but verify.

During the last two days, Katrine's nerves had frayed considerably. Kristdokar was a busy woman, or she might not have the priority to retrieve her messages right away, but she didn't believe any of that. Kristdokar had to know she and Thealone would set up some way of determining if their messages weren't delivered. Katrine would expect no less of the skalde if their situations were reversed.

Katrine's implants chimed with a call from Kristdokar. "*Eldekarl* is scouting ahead of us, and recently made contact with Viktorkinde through the relay chain. I have two messages for you from your superiors." She paused as if considering her next words carefully. "I apologize for the delay in routing them to you. This entire situation is . . . unprecedented and . . . complicated."

Katrine thought it telling Kristdokar would reveal that to her. Perhaps the woman suspected Katrine had some doubts about the skalde's veracity. Or possibly she had learned Katrine had heard they were in contact with Viktorkinde. But it sounded more like a hint that she had difficulty managing her own superiors, Nygaard in particular.

Katrine uploaded the messages into a secure block in her implants, ran them through several malware and subvert-ware tests, decrypted them, ran them through more tests, then sat back and viewed them one at a time. The first message didn't contain any real information.

"Holy shit," Thealone said, sounding breathless. "When this gets out the shit is going to hit the fan. I'm going to bring Mani Gascoigne and Tarsik Obradour in on this. But I'm going to swear them to secrecy, though I'm not sure we can sit on this until you reach Viktorkinde. We may have to blow this open before then. That's all I've got for now. This is message one. I think I'll have a lot more to tell you in four days after I've had a chance to talk with Gascoigne and Obradour."

Thealone had received Katrine's report and recorded her response three days after they had departed Sarkovie, so the numbers added up. She would not have transmitted a third message yet, and knowing that, Katrine's fears began to subside, but only a little.

From the second message it surprised her to learn they had put Obradour's name on the roster for the mission. She understood the logic of including Gascoigne and Palmutter, and she thought it wise to enlist Catarvin's aid in keeping an eye on Palmutter, but she wondered about the little financier.

The virtual image of Thealone said, "Interestingly enough, Mani thought of something I completely overlooked. And maybe you did too."

She told Katrine of their concern that Mistress Vreekande might soon be promoted and outrank John.

"First," Thealone said. "We're promoting you to full colonel, effective immediately. Congratulations, Katrine. Second, I don't know how Mani pulled it off, but this message contains sealed orders authorizing you to promote John at your own discretion. We don't want a discrepancy between his rank and Mistress Vreekande's. You can promote him twice, up to full naval lieutenant or Infantry Ops captain, if need be. And these are full promotions, not warrant or brevet advancements. Sit on them as long as you want, or execute them whenever you feel it's necessary."

Katrine sat in silence for several seconds and considered what she had just learned. Then she prepared a reply, which consisted mainly of a detailed report on the assassination attempts on her and the two young people, including the double insult intended by the use of butcher's daggers. She finished it with, "With that level of animosity in so many Kelk, I'm not sure we can keep John alive. The situation's much improved with him isolated here on *Drakan Helgis*, but once we get to Viktorkinde that's going to change. He does appear to have a hyperawareness of his surroundings, probably something he developed on Novalis III, and that certainly helps. But I just don't know."

She described how he now wore one of the blades as a slap in the face to the Kelk. "You'll be happy to hear he politely told me to fuck off when I forbade it. Not with that kind of language, of course, but the message was clear." Thealone had also expressed her hope that John would learn to assert himself more.

When Katrine finished her updated report, she contacted Kristdokar and requested a meeting. Kristdokar's virtual image smiled. "I've been expecting your call. Please join me at your convenience."

Kristdokar's stateroom on *Drakan Helgis* was a bit confining, but with both of them seated at a small table extruded from a bulkhead, the woman again served them tea, then sat down and sipped delicately at hers. She put the cup on the table in front of her and gave Katrine a strained smile. "I should tell you some members of the Larscom are not happy at the prospect of a diplomatic mission from the Commonwealth. Vice Skalde Nygaard is facing a certain amount of discontent at having extended the invitation, at least publicly, though privately Skalde Supreme Dornmier and Skalde of the Supremacy Veskarson support her fully."

The woman had been candid with Katrine, and she owed her the same candor in return. "When my superiors announce the formation of the diplomatic mission, I have no doubt they will face discontent on a number of fronts. But we'll deal with it."

Kristdokar's smile softened. "As will we."

Katrine placed a comp chip on the table between them. "That's my latest update for my superiors. As we speak *Lightspear* should be on station at the terminus of your relay chain. If you transmit it immediately, they'll deliver it in a . . . timely fashion."

Katrine had chosen her words carefully, hoping that *timely fashion* would hit Kristdokar as something of a barb. One of the older woman's eyebrows rose, accompanying a momentary flash of anger in her eyes. "It will be taken care of immediately."

Time to broach the subject of John and Nikaela's rank. "I have something I need to discuss with you. In the Commonwealth, after a certain amount of time in any of the lower ranks, if a junior officer's record remains unblemished, they receive a promotion as a matter of course. Though, promotions to more senior ranks beyond that are more complicated."

Kristdokar nodded. "We do something similar here."

Katrine picked up her teacup, but didn't taste it. "Our Mr. Mathius was commissioned a little over a month ago, while Mistress Vreekande has been at her present rank for some time now. Might she be due for such a promotion?"

Kristdokar's eyebrows lifted. "Ah, yes, I hadn't considered that. We are of the opinion it's good for all concerned if our breschkada do not face the barriers of unequal rank. Are you and your superiors of a similar mind?"

Katrine sipped at her tea. "Yes, we are. And I have been authorized to elevate Mr. Mathius's rank, should the need arise. However, it would be helpful if I didn't have to exercise that option too soon. He needs a little more time in grade, say, two months."

Kristdokar nodded. "I'll double check on Mistress Vreekande's status. I'll make sure nothing happens right away, and I'll warn you before it does."

Katrine laid her teacup on the table. "I'm glad we see eye to eye on this."

"Colonel Primatov," the skalde said, smiling, "I think we see eye to eye on many things."

Yes, Katrine thought. *But can I trust you? And do you wonder every second of the day if you can trust me?*

16

Interference

BRYNJAR HAD WARNED Anders his lifeboat might have inherited a little too much velocity from the derelict piece of *Sycorax*. He'd decelerated at the boat's maximum drive now for nine days, and unfortunately that wasn't enough to bring it to a stop as he approached Sarkovie. It did mean he arrived in the vicinity of the planet a little sooner than expected, and he would have loved to take advantage of that to end the unending boredom. But the only way he could do that now would be to provide the locals with a brilliant light show as the boat burned up on reentry. Though on second thought, his velocity was so high, it would be a very brief and quite dramatic moment of entertainment for them.

A hundred million kilometers out he was still travelling at over four thousand kilometers a second. He didn't want to come too close to the planet at those speeds, so he tweaked his vector slightly, continued to decelerate, and several hours later passed within ten million kilometers of Sarkovie as he shot past it. A half day after that he came to a stop ninety million kilometers beyond the planet. It then took the better part of a day to reverse course, accelerate toward the planet, turn over half way there, then decelerate and park in a high orbit well above its atmosphere.

Sarkovie was a backwater planet, and sparsely populated. It could not boast of any serious strategic or commercial resources, and its outer crust did not contain sufficient quantities of heavy metals or rare-earth elements to justify serious mining operations. It did have a livable atmosphere and reasonable gravity with large landmasses. And it was part of a larger cluster of nearby independent systems with which it conducted some trade, though not in sufficient quantities to warrant a big prime station. It had a loosely run central government that provided some limited social services, but left most day-to-day administrative tasks to local entities. Its customs and import-export regulations were nonexistent. And the central government had made it quite clear it did not want to hinder open and free trade, as long as the proper duties were paid in a timely fashion. It was that environment that had proven so attractive to Anders's new employers.

Before attempting reentry, Anders carefully reviewed the data he had on the planet. Most of Sarkovie's population was concentrated in three cities on one continent. The four addresses from which Anders's employers were operating were all located in Calconna, the largest of the three. The other two cities farther to the north had large agrarian populations dispersed throughout the countryside around them. But the terrain in the vicinity of Calconna was quite arid with little vegetation and a low population density, which made it ideal for his purposes. Perhaps that was why his employers had selected the city of Calconna for their base of operations.

The lifeboat's designers had taken into consideration the possibility that the survivors from a warship might be operating in hostile territory. They had equipped the boat with some reasonable stealth capabilities, though nothing as sophisticated as one of the big assault boats. Anywhere in the vicinity of planets like Viktorkinde or Trafalgar, he would have been detected immediately.

Anders set up the reentry burn, then killed his orbital velocity and dropped toward the planet's surface with the boat's stealth capabilities fully activated. He didn't want to announce his arrival with a sonic boom so he carefully controlled the boat's drop velocity to keep it under Mach one.

He set the lifeboat down in a deep canyon about ten kilometers from the city. It would never lift again so he stripped it of everything useful, including simple, civilian clothing that would allow him to remain reasonably anonymous. The boat included a standard selection of makeup, contacts and wigs, which he carefully applied to produce the appearance of a local common-face. He made up a small pack, stuffed it with some ration packs and a careful selection of drugs from the medical cabinet. He didn't need them, but that would support his story of selling drugs to acquire some of the local currency. He was looking forward to eating something other than rations.

He could have done the ten-klick hike to Calconna in a single day, but he moved cautiously and stayed out of sight. Half way there he detoured and buried some of the drugs he had pilfered from the lifeboat. If his employers inventoried the boat's supplies, and compared that to the drugs in his makeshift pack, he would need the numbers to come up a little short, since he had supposedly sold some of drugs on the street. They probably couldn't tally the numbers that accurately, but he'd learned long ago to take nothing for granted if he wanted to stay alive.

He took a total of three days to reach Calconna. He timed his entry into the city to take advantage of the anonymous hours of early evening. As he walked into the streets on the outskirts of the city, a young couple walking the other way caught his attention. They both looked like prostitutes.

Anders had gone to some effort to study the local customs, and had learned prostitution was the only inviolable industry on Sarkovie. Sarkovie had originally been a penal colony where the Heraclean Hegemony dumped what they called *misfits*, mostly prostitutes male and female. It had been a hard life for the early settlers, but once freed from the yoke of Hegemony rule, they institutionalized sex-for-money in their constitution. They had a saying: clients paid, and servers—as they called themselves—delivered. Free sex—sex without money changing hands—was only legal between couples who had entered into a marriage contract or a birthing agreement. If a couple didn't qualify in that respect, and wanted to have a good time, they were in violation of the law if money didn't change hands. Couples, young or old, who saw each other regularly, took turns acting as client and server. That wasn't exactly legal, but tolerated, and in that way, neither of them went bankrupt.

Anders's implants detected Calconna's citynet, which was quite rudimentary compared to what he'd been accustomed to. Back on Viktorkinde, he and his colleagues had shipped product to four addresses on Sarkovie, one of which was listed as the headquarters of a shell company they used to cover their activities there. He connected to citynet anonymously, selected that address, and began walking. A few times he passed undisguised Kelk walking openly on the streets, which intrigued him. An hour later he approached the address he sought, a small warehouse on the outskirts of the city.

He considered the place for a moment, wondering how he should approach them, then decided to simply walk up and knock on the front door. He knocked several times, and waited about ten minutes before anything happened.

The door opened just a crack and a woman with pale blue skin, red irises, and salt and pepper hair peered out at him. His makeup wasn't intended to withstand close scrutiny, and she would know enough to see through it easily.

"Who are you?" she asked.

"Anders Eindride. I come from Viktorkinde."

She didn't move, or open the door further. "Eindride, eh? I need verification of that."

His implants received a query from someone in the building, and he responded with a secure identity sequence.

"Okay," she said. "So you're Eindride. Why the disguise?"

He shrugged. "I really didn't know what I was getting into here."

"Why are you alone, and on foot? When anyone comes from Viktorkinde they usually arrive in a boat, with others."

"The ship I was on no longer exists. I got here in a lifeboat."

She nodded slowly, then stepped back and opened the door a little wider, just enough for him to step through. "Come in."

The faint light of early evening had darkened the streets, but from outside, the interior of the warehouse appeared even darker. He stepped blindly through the opening, and was not surprised when someone pressed the barrel of a gun against the back of his head.

••••

Captain Taugrim and the crew of *Drakan Helgis* had apparently satisfied their need to make John's life unpleasant. His next bridge watch proved to be quite routine, and the next. She rotated him through the stations on the bridge, and he never served at the same one twice. Taugrim had obviously assigned Command Superior Dahlborg to assess John's knowledge and skills, because she rotated with him. When he took his turn at Nav, Dahlborg complemented him. "You're better at navigation. In fact you're doing quite well." John had oddly mixed feelings at receiving praise from a Kelk officer.

Serving under Lieutenant Commander Forcis at the navigation console on the destroyer *Defiant*, he had learned a few things beyond text book exercises. "During my year of active duty, I trained at the Nav Console on a ComSecCorps destroyer."

"That would account for it," she said. "Any real experience at any of the other bridge stations?"

"Just helm."

She smiled and nodded. "Well then, maybe we'll see how you do on Helm at the next watch."

Taugrim also had John and Nikaela take their turn at the conn, saying, "You're officers on a warship, in the chain of command, so you'd better be prepared to take command if the need arises."

It felt strange to sit at the command console and command an entire warship, though with Taugrim standing over him watching every move, John had no delusions as to how much authority he exerted over the crew. Taugrim orchestrated a number of simulations, everything from mundane docking maneuvers to full-combat drills. John got a lot of them killed in one simulation. In another the ship took a direct hit from a large warhead, and went out with all hands. It was all part of the training for a young officer on a fighting ship. In that, the Commonwealth and the Supremacy were very much alike.

"Captain," the scan tech said. John thought he heard a slight note of tension in her voice, which the other crewmembers confirmed when the bridge went silent. "*Eldekarl* has detected some unusual transition activity about eight light-years off our bow."

Eldekarl scouted ahead of *Drakan Helgis*. Dahlborg brought up a scan summary in the corner of one of the Nav screens. It showed the hunter-killer coasting in sublight three light-years in front of them. Eight light-years off *Drakan Helgis*'s position would put the activity *Eldekarl* had spotted at the limit of the hunter-killer's detectable range, and well beyond that of *Drakan Helgis*. John and Dahlborg carefully examined the raw data stream *Eldekarl* fed them.

"What do you see?" Dahlborg asked.

The unidentified ship had down-transited briefly, then up-transited and drove toward them. The data was quite straight-forward, but from the tone of the woman's voice, John thought he must be missing something. "Another hunter-killer, Kelk emissions profile. Looks like they down-transited for a nav fix, then up-transited to continue on their way. Seems rather obvious, doesn't it? What am I missing?"

Dahlborg nodded, though her eyes remained focused on the data on the screen. "You might not be missing anything. But they could also be scouting ahead for someone else, just like *Eldekarl* is scouting ahead for us. Either scenario works."

The pieces fell into place. "And we wouldn't yet detect who they're scouting for because they're beyond the limit of *Eldekarl*'s scan range."

"Exactly," Dahlborg said. "Best to assume the worst and be prepared. Pure luck *Eldekarl* happened to be coasting in sublight before that hunter-killer down-transited."

That was the last piece. "They don't know we're here, but we do know they're coming our way."

Dahlborg shook her head. "You could be right about that, but they might have picked up some of our transmitter splash when we communicated with *Eldekarl*. If they did, they're too far out to get a good reading on our position, but they might know we're here somewhere behind *Eldekarl*, or at least suspect it."

The com tech spoke up. "Captain, I just picked up some transmitter splash. Too weak to get anything from it, but that hunter-killer is communicating with other ships in its vicinity. *Eldekarl*'s closer, and they report they've picked up another transition wake, off to the side of the unknown hunter-killer's course by about five light years, probably running parallel with them. Again, too far out to be sure, but they think it's another hunter-killer, Kelk origin. If so, they're in a sweep-and-search configuration."

Dahlborg leaned close to John and spoke softly. "Multiple hunter-killers sweeping forward in parallel like that, they're probably running ahead of a larger force and searching for something, searching for us most likely."

Taugrim and Falkenberg put their heads together for a hushed conversation, probably consulting with Kristdokar and Nygaard. When they finished, Taugrim announced, "Okay, people, let's start dumping lights. We need to down-transit as soon as possible."

Taugrim stood. "Mistress Falkenberg, you have the conn. I have an urgent meeting, but I'll be back shortly."

••••

Listening to Primatov's second report, Fran's gut tightened with anger and fear. Katrine had included 3D scans and photos of John Mathius taken shortly before they floated him into surgery. The assassination attempts had been beyond brutal. And the butcher's blades had been just plain vicious, symbolic of the abject hatred with which many Kelk regarded Commonwealth citizens. When the report ended, Fran sat in stunned silence for a long moment, wondering if they could ever overcome the enmity they had fostered between their two races.

In her report Katrine had worn the bitch-face she sometimes consciously used to good effect, but this time Fran thought it purely a subconscious reflection of her internal feelings. "For a moment or two, I wanted to annihilate the Supremacy, to murder and destroy everything Kelk, to completely obliterate any last vestige of them from the galaxy." She closed her eyes, lowered her head, and spoke without looking into the pickup. "But I . . . came to my senses. It's only some of them, and we have our own superstitious, ignorant hardliners, don't we? And now that I've had a chance to think about it, I'll bet they're driven more by fear than ideology. Fear can drive people to do unpleasant things."

Fran had had similar feelings when looking at the poor kid's butchered neck and face, and like Katrine, had quickly come to her senses. But while they weren't going to start a war of annihilation against the Kelk, she could damn well do something. She opened a channel through her implants to her secretary.

What can I do for you, Colonel?

The mission to Viktorkinde was scheduled to depart late that day, so Fran didn't have a lot of time. *Contact Senator Gascoigne and Mr. Obradour. Tell them I have another report from Colonel Primatov, and I need them to come here as soon as possible to view it. Also, cancel all my appointments for the foreseeable future. I'm going on that mission to Viktorkinde, along with a select group of soldiers I'll hand-pick. When you contact Obradour and Gascoigne, tell them that as well. And get me the last known location of every one of John Mathius's platoon mates from basic training on Miriteen. In fact, drop everything and do that first.*

The woman sounded a little breathless when she said, *Yes, Colonel, right away. Anything else?*

Another thought hit Fran. *Yes. Check on the location of Mathius's O-School roommate. I don't recall her name.*

I believe her name was May Forester.

Fran's secretary had proven her value a hundred times by coming up with little obscure bits of information like that at just the right moment. *That's right. Find out if she's still in-system. And give that the same priority as the locations of his platoon mates.*

While Fran waited for her secretary to deliver the requested information, she dug up every one of Katrine's reports regarding Reisenar and John Mathius, scanning them carefully for any mention of John's old platoon mates. She also scanned Primatov's report on John's abduction from campus, and one short note caught her attention. Katrine reported that May Forester's lover was a news hype named Karya Chemina. Katrine had run a full security check on Chemina, given her a clean bill of health, and confirmed that she was a dove on the Kelk issue. Primatov had also contacted the young woman's editor, and Fran played the recording of his praise for the girl. "She's one of my best, young and inexperienced, but tenacious as all hell. If someone's trying to hide anything from her, she'll find out what it is."

Katrine finished by saying, "I like her. My gut tells me I can trust her."

That was all Fran needed. She placed a call to her secretary. *One more thing. There's a news hype name of Karya Chemina.*

Her secretary said, *Miss Forester's lover?*

The woman never failed to amaze Fran. *Yes. Get hold of her and tell her I'm going to personally give her a scoop. But if she wants it she's got to be in my office in twenty minutes. And isolate her when she gets here. I don't want her running into anyone else.*

Yes, ma'am, and I've got those names and locations for you.

The woman uploaded the locations of John's old platoon mates into Fran's implants. There were several in the Trafalgar system, including Macus DeLeon—she didn't need anyone to tell her to scratch his name off the list. One name stood out: Sergeant Carla Nigurski, presently assigned to *Fearless*, which was docked at Trafalgar Prime.

Fran went back to Primatov's reports and searched out the young woman's name, found it several times, but in one reference Katrine had noted that Nigurski and John Mathius were close friends. She suspected they had been lovers as well, but couldn't verify that.

Fran punched a high-priority call through to *Fearless*. She got a com tech. The young woman's eyes widened when she saw Fran, and she started to say something, but Fran cut her off. "Give me the OOD, now."

A few seconds later, a young male lieutenant j. g. appeared in her virtual vision. "Colonel Blacksword," he said, "What can I—"

Fran cut him off too. "Where's Carla Nigurski?"

"Uh," he said. "I'll have to look that up. Please give me a moment."

Fearless was a big ship. He'd have to check his crew roster. She wanted to browbeat the poor fellow and make him hurry, but that would buy her nothing, so Fran bit her lip and kept her mouth shut.

"She's on leave," he said. "I'm not sure if she's on Trafalgar Prime, or down on the planet somewhere. I'll have to—"

"Forget that," Fran said. "I'm authorizing a high-priority military override of normal privacy restrictions. Find her, now, and when you do, call me back and put me through to her."

When she ended the call, her secretary came online. *May Forester is still in the city.*

Fran was about to bark orders at the woman, but before she could speak her secretary said, *I've contacted her and sent a car for her. She'll be in your office in twenty minutes.*

Not for the first time, the woman had left Fran speechless. *When I get back from Viktorkinde, remind me to give you a big bonus.*

She smiled. *I definitely won't forget that, Colonel.*

You never forget anything.

Her smile widened. *I know.*

17

Good Times Interruptus

"IS THAT TOO tight, Mistress?"

Encased in her new Kelk combat armor, Katrine flexed her right arm and bent it at the elbow, then at the wrist. "No, it feels quite good, in fact."

There had been no surprises during her final fitting, but as she stripped out of the armor, the marine CO hesitated and froze, the way most people did when getting an urgent call through their implants. It only lasted a second, but when the CO again moved, a certain tension hung in the air. She had spent enough time on ships to know when something was up, though since they had not interfaced her own implants with shipnet, she didn't know what.

She and Vagle were half way back to their stateroom when she got the call from Kristdokar. *Something has come up. Please meet me in the captain's stateroom.*

I'll be right there, Katrine said.

She turned to Vagle. "You got that?"

The young woman nodded.

Katrine found Kristdokar, Taugrim, and Brynjar waiting for her in the CO's stateroom. Taugrim had changed the color of her hair to coal black. They sat down at a small table, and after Kristdokar served them the customary tea, and each of them had taken a sip, she immediately said to Taugrim, "Please tell the colonel what you've detected."

Taugrim laid out the situation with multiple hunter-killers sweeping forward in parallel, possibly running ahead of a larger force and searching for something. "*Eldekarl* has confirmed two hunter-killers and picked up weak transmitter splash from a third. We have not been informed of any scheduled movements in this area, which makes us wary. It's fairly certain they suspect we're here. They were headed more in a direction that would take them straight to Sarkovie, but they're maneuvering now toward us. They're definitely on an intercept course, probably picked up some of our transmitter splash, though we doubt they have a hard fix on our position."

Kristdokar said, "Vice Skalde Nygaard and I have discussed this carefully. We're not taking any chances. I'm transferring back to *Konigsborge*, and we're going to proceed alone with *Eldekarl* and *Drakan Helgis* both coasting in sublight, and running silent."

Taugrim slapped her hand on the table. "I object. I and my ship do not hide from danger."

Kristdokar gave her a withering look. "Your objection is duly noted, but our decision is final."

Taugrim leaned forward, clearly intent on arguing further, but Kristdokar cut her off. "Enough. That is a direct order from Nygaard and me. Your job is not to fight, your job is to protect our guests and Mistress Vreekande. I'm leaving our breschkada in your hands, and if you have to run to protect them, you'll run, and hide, and do whatever it takes. That . . . is your mission."

Taugrim leaned back in her chair, her jaw muscles clenched.

Katrine tried not to be paranoid. With both Kristdokar and Nygaard on board *Konigsborge*, they wouldn't lose anyone terribly important if something happened to *Drakan Helgis*. They might even find themselves relieved of an inconvenient complication. "Why are you returning to *Konigsborge*? Why not stay here with us?"

The older woman must have sensed Katrine's distrust because her eyes narrowed with suspicion. It occurred to Katrine that distrust only fostered more distrust, but at that moment she had to assume the worst and be prepared for it.

Kristdokar nodded slowly, as if recognizing the uncomfortable wall separating them. "It is no secret that I left with Nygaard aboard *Konigsborge*, whereas we sent *Drakan Helgis* out here in a highly clandestine way. There are few who know she is present in this sector, so with me on *Konigsborge*, we're simply returning from a minor engagement near Sarkovie that yielded no results other than the destruction of a rogue ship. You and our two breschkada are the cargo we must protect."

"If you don't mind," Katrine said, "one last question, though it's a bit off topic."

Kristdokar cocked her head slightly to one side, her face expressionless. "Ask away, Colonel."

Katrine wondered if Kristdokar would lie to her. "The woman who tried to kill me, the NCO, the one who survived, what's her condition?"

Kristdokar spoke without hesitation. "She's dead."

Katrine asked, "The gut wound?"

Kristdokar shook her head. "No."

"Then by her own hand?"

At that moment Taugrim and Brynjar found their teacups of abiding interest and would not meet Katrine's eyes. Kristdokar sat silently staring at Katrine for several seconds, then she said, "No, by another's."

Katrine tried to suppress her distrust, and tried even harder not to let it show in her face as she nodded.

••••

With the barrel of one gun pressed to the back of his head, and that of another jabbed against his spine, Anders didn't move a muscle. The woman who had opened the door and admitted him stood in front of him. She nodded toward his makeshift pack. "Drop that."

He released the pack and it thudded on the floor.

"Arms out to your sides."

He extended his arms straight out from his shoulders. She frisked him so thoroughly that, if they ever became lovers, she would already know what to expect. But he didn't think that would happen.

She carefully emptied his pockets, and when she came across the local currency, she asked, "How'd you get this?"

He sometimes wondered if he'd grown too paranoid, but that question validated all his precautions. "How do you think? Pilfered the lifeboat's med units for drugs and sold some on the street. Didn't know how long I would have to provide for myself."

She looked at the wad of script in her hand. "This isn't much."

He shrugged. "I don't know the local going rate. Didn't want to push too hard the first time. Only sold a little of what I had. Figured I'd get it right with a little practice, if I had to."

She carefully counted out the money, one note at a time. "Who'd you sell it to?"

"Some young fellow and his girlfriend." He knew something about the style of dress in vogue among young people on Sarkovie. "They both looked like prostitutes."

She looked him in the face and rolled her eyes. "Probably not. That's just the style here."

It would be good to play a little dumb. "Young and old alike?"

Behind him someone chuckled. The woman in front of him shook her head. "No, thank all the gods of space. Can you imagine old people walking around dressed like that?"

Behind him, a male voice said, "Depends on what you're into."

By that time Anders's eyes had adjusted to the dim lighting of the room. He, the woman, and whoever stood behind him pressing weapons barrels into his head and spine, still stood near the door. A desk had been shoved against one wall, with a table and chairs in front of it. The woman lifted his pack off the floor, then emptied its contents on the table. She examined the grav pistol, its extra loads and power cells. She carefully went through every item on the table, then turned back to face him. "Okay, lock him up."

Anders didn't resist as someone grabbed his elbows and pinned them behind his back. Using the barrels of the guns to push him forward and guide him, they walked him across the room to another door. They opened it, walked him into another room, then through another door, and down a flight of stairs into a basement that smelled a little of damp mold. They unlocked and opened a heavy metal door, released him and told him to walk forward. He stepped into a room with four concrete walls, no windows, a cot with blankets and a pillow, a sink, a toilet, a small table, and two chairs.

Behind him a man said, "Walk to the far wall and turn around."

Anders crossed the concrete cell, turned and pressed his back to the wall.

Two men stood just within the doorway, both holding grav pistols aimed at him. One appeared to be about Anders's age, the other quite a bit younger. The older of the two sported a neatly trimmed goatee, with unusually dark hair and no signs of graying.

The woman entered the cell carrying a bundle, which she dumped on the cot. She turned and walked out of the cell. The two men back stepped out through the door, closed it, and Anders heard the rattle of its lock mechanism as they engaged it.

He crossed to the cot and unwrapped the bundle. It contained simple soap, towels, toiletries, and shaving tools

Anders sat down on the cot. He had a fair amount of experience living in a cell, and apparently he would now gain more. Living in a cell was preferable to some of the alternatives.

••••

"Down-transition," the helmsman announced. "Coasting at point three lights. Time dilation factor five percent."

In a corner of one of John's screens, a scan summary showed *Eldekarl* running silent three light-years off *Drakan Helgis*'s bow. The data feed from *Eldekarl* placed the line of unidentified Kelk hunter-killers eight light-years distant and driving hard toward them, most likely still unaware of their presence. And they still had no proof the hunter-killers were running ahead of a larger force. They would only know the answer to that if other ships drove within range of *Eldekarl*'s scan systems, or several hours passed and no more ships appeared on her screens.

"Captain on the bridge."

Taugrim returned from some sort of urgent meeting. She had only been gone for a few minutes.

John's first experience with Taugrim had left him with the idea she was a hard woman, and at times almost demonic, the way Kelkies liked to appear. But once she had stopped hazing him that impression had dwindled with time. And had they been of a similar rank he might actually find her attractive, but to acknowledge that now would be like finding a DI appealing—not gonna happen.

John glanced her way, and at that moment she appeared almost childlike as she concentrated intently on the displays in front of her. "Well done, people. Steady as she goes."

Konigsborge had down-transited not far from them.

"Navigation," Taugrim said. "We've got to transfer Skalde Kristdokar to *Konigsborge*. I want a sublight course correction that'll match *Konigsborge*'s velocity and put us ten thousand kilometers off her starboard bow."

John worked frantically to compute the vectors and drive sequence. Working in parallel, Dahlborg did the same. When John finished she reviewed his solution carefully. "Not exactly the same as mine, but it'll do the job nicely. Upload it to the captain's console."

John transferred the data to Taugrim.

Dahlborg looked Taugrim's way, a smile on her face. "Captain, the Blacksword has a solution for you and is uploading it now."

They all now referred to him as *the Blacksword*. It was probably Kolbeck's doing, and he wished they would back off on that.

Taugrim said, "So the Blacksword can navigate, eh?"

Taugrim reviewed John's numbers, then gave the helmsman orders to execute his plan. Five minutes later they matched velocity with *Konigsborge*. Shortly after that the scan summary showed the blip of an assault boat accelerating away from *Drakan Helgis*. It rendezvoused with the big cruiser and was swallowed into her hangar bay.

Taugrim said, "Navigation, while we're waiting for them to return, I need a transition plan to backtrack to the nearest relay buoy."

Again, John and Dahlborg did their computations in parallel. The woman looked at John's work, nodded, and announced, "The Blacksword got it right again."

He really wished she would stop calling him that.

John kept his eyes glued to the scan summary, watching for any change in the disposition of the unidentified hunter-killers. After the assault boat returned from *Konigsborge*, Taugrim instructed the helm to execute his transition plan, a short hop of a little over a light-year. Three hours later, they down-transited two hundred million kilometers from the buoy, and pushed the sublight drive hard to kill their velocity.

Dahlborg leaned close to John and lowered her voice. "That buoy's close enough now we can communicate with the relay chain using standard EM transmissions. Less chance of being detected that way."

Taugrim said, "Drones out. Position them at a million klicks, cut power feed and run them static."

The hull of the ship echoed as she launched her six combat drones. They guided them out to a million kilometers and killed their velocity. They now had a baseline for their scan systems of two million kilometers. It wasn't as effective as circulating the drones around them, but it still gave them enormously improved resolution.

Once the drones were in position, the look on Taugrim's face soured as she said, "All stations rig for silent running."

John pulled up a summary of the ship's systems and parked it in the corner of a screen. They cut gravity, and without the harness strapping him to his seat, he would have floated away. Engineering shut down all power to shields and weapons stations, and cut life-support back to a bare minimum.

At that point the only sounds John heard were pops and groans from the ship's hull as thermal variations in its mass caused it to expand in some places, and contract in others. But it was not the silence of sound that mattered; it was the silence of their emission profile that hid them from any danger.

John leaned toward Dahlborg and whispered, "I've never before been on a ship running silent. It's kind of weird."

She grinned and whispered. "If there's an enemy out there, they can't hear you talk, so you don't have to whisper. But don't worry, the silence gets to us all that way, and we all do it."

Taugrim walked them through a thorough review of all ship's systems. With their shields and weaponry shut down, they were extremely vulnerable. The hardest part of running silent fell to Engineering. To avoid detection they kept the power plant operating at an extremely low level, but high enough for them to quickly bring it up to full combat status if the need arose. Ships had been lost to enemy fire when Engineering took too long to execute a power-up ramp.

Dahlborg took the opportunity to drill John on various maneuvers, and the rest of the watch proved to be routine. By the time it ended, *Eldekarl* had verified the existence of a third hunter-killer in the line sweeping toward them, but had yet to find anything following in their wakes. With the watch over, John joined Kolbeck and Matsen, who were waiting on the deck below near the ladder that led to the bridge. The three of them floated down eerily silent passageways, moving from handhold to handhold, and like John the two men spoke in hushed whispers.

••••

Carla's implants woke her from a sound sleep. "What the fuck is going on?" she asked no one in particular.

In the other bed in the room, Leeze Caputto, her closest friend, said, "Waa . . . huh."

Carla glanced around the bunk room, but it wasn't the bunk room on *Fearless*. As her implants kept jabbering something unintelligible at her, it took her a moment to overcome the disorientation of waking up in a strange place.

She and Leeze had rented a small bungalow on the other side of the planet. They had spent the last two days getting a little buzzed by drinking fancy, fruity drinks while walking along the beach in extremely skimpy and revealing swimming suits. They thoroughly enjoyed the sun, and the eyeball action they got from quite a number of handsome guys lounging on the beach and watching them walk by. She and Leeze made sure they walked by them repeatedly.

Her implants kept trying to hammer a message into her head, and it finally got through to her. *Incoming call from ComSecCorps Command, code red, high priority. If you do not respond in twenty seconds, the data stream will revert to active push.*

It started to repeat, but she said. *Nigurski here, acknowledged.*

A woman appeared in her virtual vision seated behind a desk. She had narrow cheeks, blue eyes, and short white hair. Wiry thin and athletic, she didn't appear to carry any extra weight on her. She wore a military uniform with colonel's eagles on her collars, and the stencil above her left breast pocket read . . . BLACKSWORD.

There was only one person in the Commonwealth who could wear that name, and Carla's heart raced. Out of reflex she jumped to her feet. "Colonel Blacksword."

The colonel didn't waste time with pleasantries. "You were one of John Mathius's platoon mates on Miriteen, and a friend of his, right?"

"Yes, ma'am."

"Good friend?"

"Yes, ma'am."

"How good?"

"Uhhh . . ." Carla didn't think the woman was asking about her love life, but she still needed to think about her answer before . . .

The colonel leaned forward, and was clearly angry about something. "Were you lovers, or was it purely platonic?"

"Ah . . . well . . ."

"God dammit, young woman, start acting like a soldier and answer my questions."

Carla's heart pounded up into her throat. "Yes, ma'am."

The colonel's anger seemed to blossom. "Was that *Yes, you were lovers*, or just *Yes, you'll start answering my fucking questions?*"

"Yes . . . lovers . . . for a while."

"Did it end well?"

Carla wanted to ask what this was all about, but bird-colonels did all the asking, especially one named Blacksword. "Yes, ma'am. From the beginning we both knew we'd probably get assignments light-years apart, and we were always more like friends than lovers. The sex was just . . . a bonus. He's a nice guy, never did anything wrong to me, never treated me with anything but—"

The colonel slashed her hand through the air like a knife. "I'm not talking about that kind of shit. I have a question for you. If you had to risk your life to save his, would you?"

Carla didn't have to think about that. "Of course. He'd do the same for me."

That seemed to calm the colonel a little. "That's what I thought. I'm going to read you a list of names. They were all in your training platoon on Miriteen, and they're all in the Trafalgar system right now. I want to know which of them you'd trust with your life and John's."

The colonel read a list of eight names one at a time, and Carla gave five of them a thumbs-up. The colonel finished by asking, "Same thing, they'd risk their life for John and he'd risk his life for them?"

"Yes, ma'am. No doubt about it."

The colonel had now calmed considerably. "That's what I wanted to hear. Pack your bags, young lady. I'm sending an assault boat for you. It's going to land on that beach within the hour. You and your five friends are coming with me, and don't make that assault boat wait for you."

The colonel cut the line. Carla glanced out a window. It looked like it was the middle of the night, so she checked her implants; it was.

"Wassa going on?"

Leeze sat up, rubbing at her eyes.

"Something to do with John," Carla said.

"What John?"

Carla had the feeling she would soon see John again. "John Mathius."

"What'd good ole Johnny-boy do now?"

Carla shook her head. "I don't know. But we gotta pack our bags. You and me and a couple others are going somewhere."

"Where?"

"I have no fucking idea."

18

Connecting the Dots

TO JOHN'S SURPRISE they finally moved him out of the ICU and into a stateroom that he shared with another junior officer. It would be less defensible against an assassination attempt, but that didn't really bother him, and he had to think about why. His crewmates on *Drakan Helgis* still gave him the occasional surreptitious glance, but there wasn't any animosity in the way they looked at him, just simple curiosity. He was just the new guy, and different, quite different actually.

He was still under orders to never go anywhere alone, but it could be Matsen, or Kolbeck, or any other crewmember he trusted, and that list grew daily. Primatov had told him, "You're one of their crewmates now. You're no longer an unknown, mysterious, alien entity. And Kristdokar spent a year vetting the crew of this ship, so we're confident you're safe."

With Matsen and Kolbeck floating on either side of him, John gripped a handhold near Primatov's stateroom door and knocked once. Now that they had interfaced their implants with shipnet, she would know it was him through their implants. She said, *Enter.*

He opened the door and saw Primatov strapped into the seat of a small desk built into a bulkhead, Vagle floating nearby and hanging on precariously to a handhold. As he pulled himself through the door, the Kelk woman shoved off and drifted past him out into the passageway. She joined Matsen and Kolbeck there, and closed the door.

The traditional formula of snapping to attention was always suspended under weightless conditions. "Ensign Mathius reporting as ordered, ma'am."

Primatov said, "At ease and relax."

She pointed to a handhold next to the desk. "And grab on to that."

As he pushed off the door and floated across the cabin, she said, "You should assume we're being monitored."

He had operated under that supposition for some time now. "Yes, ma'am."

She glanced down at the butcher's harness buckled to his side. "How do our Kelk friends react to that?"

"They don't," he said. "They don't look at it at all."

He had tried a few times to catch one of them off guard. "I haven't even caught them looking at it when they think I'm not looking."

"You've tried?"

"Oh yes. It's weird. Other than Mistress Vreekande, it's like it doesn't exist at all."

She nodded. "Interesting!" She pursed her lips for a silent moment, then added, "Perhaps it's more that they wish it never existed in the first place."

She held up a small comp chip. "I just received this. It's an update from Colonel Blacksword."

She opened a direct link between their implants. *The rest of our conversation here is going to be on an encrypted link, so don't say anything out loud.*

Yes, ma'am.

I have a few things I need to tell you.

John knew Trafalgar would be sending a diplomatic mission to Viktorkinde. But now Primatov told him the circumstances under which she had negotiated that outcome. He had not been aware Nygaard had refused to let her take him back to Trafalgar on *Lightspear*. Though, when she told him that now, it didn't surprise him.

He shrugged. *From what little interaction I've had with Skalde Nygaard, she strikes me as the type of person who likes to be in control and pull strings.*

She smiled as if at some joke. *That's rather astute of you, John. Just never forget that regardless of the uniform, she's still a politician.*

Primatov filled him in on the makeup of the Commonwealth mission. He had met Gascoigne and Palmutter, but had never heard of Obradour.

He's a financier, she told him, *and a bit of a hawk, though he seems to be immune to much of the more irrational thinking that spreads among many of the hardliners. Extremely wealthy, donates a lot to various political causes and organizations, and can at times be a king maker.*

She leaned forward, clearly wanting to make a point. *If you meet him, and you most likely will when they get to Viktorkinde, be cautious around him.*

Yes, ma'am.

Senator Jenine Catarvin will also be part of the mission.

He had heard Catarvin's name in the news feeds a few times, but hadn't paid much attention. *I don't really know anything about her.*

Primatov smiled at some inner thought. *She's a nice enough woman. I think you'll like her. And they're all bringing rather large retinues.* She hesitated. *I should warn you Macus DeLeon will be accompanying Silas Palmutter.*

John decided he would not let that bit of news ruin his day. *I can handle DeLeon.*

She grinned. *Of course you can. Just don't kill him.*

He returned her grin. *I won't. But can I at least break his arms?*

She chuckled and grimaced, but the grin didn't go away. *There's something else I need to tell you. We have information from a reliable source that Silas Palmutter knows just a little bit too much about your abduction, and the people behind it, and what they intended to do with you.*

For a moment John's memories of the beatings aboard *Caliban* flashed through his thoughts. *He's dirty?*

Maybe? But we don't know for certain. We're not sure if he's crossed the line into illegal activity or not. Just be cautious around him.

She gave him a list of the supporting staff accompanying the four members of the mission, uploading it into his implants. It contained about sixty names. *When you have a moment, please go through that list carefully and let me know if you recognize any names.*

At that point she dismissed him. He pushed off, crossed the small stateroom and reached out to open the door, doing a quick once-over on the list of names as he did so. But one particular name brought him up short.

He turned back to Primatov. "Strikland. Lawrence Strikland."

She raised a finger to her lips, reminding him he should be speaking through the encrypted link between their implants. *Strikland's name is familiar somehow. He's listed as a Commercial Adviser to Palmutter. For some reason his name is ringing alarms in my head.*

She closed her eyes, probably consulting her implants. *Interesting! Strikland is the Executive Vice President in charge of Transmarin Missile Systems. He's taken a leave of absence to—*

That information hit John like a punch in the gut, and he recalled then how he'd come across Strikland's name when searching for information on Transmarin.

What's wrong, John?

He struggled to focus as a flood of memories pushed his thoughts in a hundred different directions. *Back on Trafalgar, when you asked me to dig up information on Transmarin, I came across his name. His division had some indirect connections to the Supremacy, and he donated heavily to Palmutter's reelection. But he did so through some sort of shell advocacy group that supports hawkish hardliners, like he didn't want anyone to know about it.*

Primatov steepled her fingers in front of her. *How did you dig up this information?*

The look on her face worried him. *A woman at an investment brokerage registered me with Transmarin so I could dig through their databases.*

You got that connection from Transmarin's databases?

Not directly. What I found in their system was that a whole lot of managers in his division had donated to Palmutter's reelection. And that led me to a public database that tracks political donations by big-shot corporate officers. That's where I found out about the advocacy group.

Oh, John! Primatov closed her eyes, rubbed her temples and sighed. When she once again looked at him, he saw sorrow and regret in her face. *They want you to use their database so they can track what you're looking for. If Strikland's dirty, your digging raised red flags all over the place. And if he saw that you were making the right connections, he might have panicked, and that may be why they abducted you.*

John took slow, steady breaths to calm his racing heart. He recalled the excruciating pain of the gut wound he took during the abduction on campus, and calm-voice's and pissed-off-guy's beatings, and the torment at the hands of his Kelk jailers on *Sycorax*. He decided then and there that if Strikland was responsible for any of that, if he ever got the chance, he'd kill the asshole with no more hesitation than when he'd killed Cranoch and Mercier.

Primatov interrupted his thoughts. *So there's a possibility Palmutter is dirty. And there's a possibility Strikland is dirty. And now they're working together.*

John's eyes met hers. He didn't think she realized the bitch-face had come to the fore.

John's implants chimed with an incoming message from Captain Taugrim. Primatov's eyebrows lifted, telling him her implants had also activated. *Taugrim here. Eldekarl just detected some weak transmitter splash coming from behind those hunter-killers. It's too weak to pin down anything hard, but it confirms they're running ahead of something.*

••••

May Forester marched into Fran's office in text-book fashion, snapped to attention and saluted. "Lieutenant May Forester reporting as ordered, ma'am."

The young woman had chin-length, brownish-blond hair, and bright-brown eyes.

Fran abhorred the way some senior officers saluted their juniors sloppily. She snapped her arm up and returned the salute properly. "At ease, Lieutenant."

Primatov had reported that after Mathius's abduction, Forester had been concerned about his wellbeing. Fran asked, "Can you guess what this is about?"

The young woman didn't hesitate. "John Mathius."

"And how did you come to that conclusion?"

Forester almost shrugged, but caught herself at the last instant and kept her eyes locked straight forward. "Ma'am, he's a Blacksword, and I'm here talking to you, so it's got to be a Blacksword thing. And there haven't been too many cadets who disappeared from campus shortly after a firefight that resulted in multiple fatalities."

A touch of sarcasm, but just the right amount so it had come out as humor, not disrespect. "You have a relationship with a young woman here, am I correct?"

"Yes, ma'am, I do."

"Is it serious?"

"I hadn't thought about it, but I guess it is."

"Well, I'm sorry, but you're going to have to put it on hold for the time being, perhaps indefinitely."

Forester nodded. "We always knew it would probably end that way. After all, I am a ComSecCorps officer."

The right answer, and that's what Fran had looked for. "Relax, Miss Forester. Grab a chair and sit down."

The young woman retrieved a chair, positioned it in front of Fran's desk and sat down on the edge of it, her back straight and rigid in a very prim position.

"I said relax, and I meant it."

Forester relaxed a little, but not completely. "May I ask a question, ma'am?"

Fran nodded. "By all means."

"Is John all right?"

Fran thought carefully about her answer. Primatov had questioned John at length about the night of his abduction, and the events that followed, right up to the moment he awoke in the makeshift stateroom on *Konigsborge*. He had given her detailed descriptions of the men he referred to as *calm-voice* and *pissed-off-guy*, and the poor surgeon they had forced to repeatedly heal him. Primatov had pressed him a little to get him to be candid about his treatment at the hands of his Kelk captors on board *Sycorax*. Interestingly enough, inside that cell he had finally learned from the young Vreekande girl how she had saved his life on that subway platform on Reisenar.

At that moment, Fran didn't have the time to go into that kind of detail. "Yes and no. He was okay when you last saw him, and then he wasn't, and then he was again, and then he wasn't again, and apparently he is now. Unfortunately, there are some bad people who want to kill him, both Kelk and common-faces, as they refer to us. I need you to help me make sure they don't succeed. Would you risk your life to keep him alive?"

Forester hesitated for a moment. "I would. I'd do the same for him as I'd do for any comrade on the battlefield."

Fran leaned forward and placed a hand flat on her desk to make a point. "This won't be on the battlefield. And you may find it necessary to kill someone who you thought was an ally or comrade only moments earlier."

Forester didn't react in the slightest to that. "I'll do my duty, ma'am. But I think you're really trying to understand how I personally regard John." She shrugged. "He's a good friend. I like him, though he's a little naïve at times."

That got Fran's attention because she and Primatov shared that opinion. "How so?"

The young woman grimaced. "There was this dirt bag on campus named Nash Wakeland. John fell for his crap completely. I thought the guy was nothing but trouble, but I could've been wrong about that."

Fran smiled and shook her head. "You weren't. In any case, Mr. Wakeland won't be a problem anymore, because he's no longer with us."

"Really?" Forester asked. "What happened to him?"

At that point Fran had made up her mind about the young woman. "John tore out his femoral artery with a paring knife."

"A paring knife?" Forester's eyes narrowed. "So John left that restaurant with Wakeland, and a short time later there's a big firefight on campus. Then the next morning both of them are missing. And now you tell me Wakeland is dead and John killed him. And you haven't mentioned anything about charges or a court-martial for John . . ."

She didn't finish, but left the thought hanging. Smart girl.

Fran stood. Catching Forester by surprise, the young woman shot to her feet.

"Go pack your bags," Fran said. "You're coming with me to Viktorkinde."

That got a reaction out of the young woman, and her eyebrows rose. "One more question, ma'am, if you please."

Fran nodded. "I'm listening."

Forester grinned. "If I know John, when whatever happened on campus that night happened, he fucked 'em up pretty good, didn't he?"

Fran decided she liked May Forester. She returned the grin. "That, he did, young lady. That, he did."

••••

The night before their scheduled departure from Trafalgar, Macus spent the night with Faith at her place. They didn't know what the accommodations would be like on Obradour's yacht—if yacht was the right term. Certainly the four members of the mission would travel in some sort of style, but they had no idea what kind of quarters would be assigned to staffers like Faith and Macus. For all they knew, they'd end up sharing some large barracks with dozens of aides and assistants. Faith seemed especially energetic that night, probably because she feared there would be little opportunity to satisfy her needs for some time to come. Macus was careful to not wipe his penis off on her sheets.

They split up in the morning. Macus returned to his apartment, showered, grabbed his luggage, and headed for the airport. Obradour had a couple of private shuttles ferrying people up to his ship. When Macus stepped into the waiting room he spotted Faith talking with Lawrence Strikland, both standing in the middle of the crowd that had assembled for the next shuttle flight up. Faith saw Macus enter, looked his way, raised her hand and waved. It was at that moment, with Faith's attention drawn away from Strikland, that the man's eyes settled hungrily on her breasts. Macus waved back, and when Faith returned her attention to Strikland, the man reluctantly looked away from her chest.

Interesting, Macus thought. Until that moment, for all the interest Strikland had shown in Faith, he could have been gay. Macus had even considered attempting to seduce the man himself. He could do gay if it bought him something like the kind of information a man like Strikland could provide. But with this new bit of evidence, that was now a moot point, unless the fellow was bi, in which case he and Faith might have to double-team the fellow.

Strikland had been quite careful, probably because a man in his position would have to be discreet regarding any non-professional relationships. The man couldn't have risen to his present position if he were sloppy about such things. He was probably a lot smarter than Palmutter, and wasn't about to get entangled in a situation where Faith could put the screws to him. Yes, a man like Strikland would be careful about any relationship he might enter into.

Macus crossed the room and the three of them greeted each other. They chatted about the upcoming trip, and the mission, and the excitement of actually seeing the capital and home world of the Kelk Supremacy. But Macus couldn't put the thought of what he'd seen out of his mind.

He spotted a casual acquaintance across the room. He didn't know the fellow well, couldn't even remember his name, but to confirm his suspicions he needed to step away from Faith and Strikland. "I have to go touch bases with a fellow I know. Sorry, but I shouldn't be long."

Strikland nodded politely. "No need to apologize, young man. I understand you have your responsibilities." He seemed pleased that Macus would now leave him alone with Faith, or perhaps Macus was simply imagining that.

Macus eased his way through the crowd to the fellow in question, but only spoke to him for a few minutes. Then he stepped back to the edge of the crowd to observe Strikland. He watched the fellow for several minutes, and every time something drew Faith's attention away from him, his eyes settled on her breasts. If nothing else, Strikland had exceptionally good taste.

When Palmutter arrived and approached them, Faith turned away from Strikland to greet the senator. And now with her back to him, Strikland's eyes settled on her butt, and remained there until she turned around to face him again. With Palmutter present, Strikland stopped stealing glances at Faith's boobs and butt. Macus eased his way back through the crowd and rejoined them.

Ten minutes later one of Obradour's people announced that they were ready to board the shuttle for the ride up to Obradour's ship. The shuttle would make three trips: bigshots first, then mid-level staffers like Faith and Macus, then last of all, low-level staffers like aides. Each succeeding shuttle flight would be more crowded than the last.

Three young men and a young woman joined Strikland for the ride up. All four of them were athletically trim, non-descript and unimposing. They wore business suits, and the woman had opted for pants, not a skirt. Everything about them cried *security*. Strikland had brought his own retinue, and included among them were four body-guards that rode with him and the bigshots. Apparently, the money guy got just about anything he wanted.

Lady Victorious was officially a yacht, but with a crew of over a hundred, many of whom were really just servants. It had no trouble accommodating the four members of the mission and their staffers. Macus and an aide for one of the other senators were assigned to a stateroom that could have slept four in a pinch, and he realized he and Faith would have no problem finding privacy to accommodate their physical needs.

When he finished unpacking, he checked the passenger manifest for Faith's state-room, then headed there, though he needed a little help from a crewman to find it. When he knocked on the door she answered it.

"Come on in," she said. "I'm just about finished unpacking."

He stepped in and closed the door. Glancing around, he saw no roommate. "Got the stateroom to yourself?"

"No," she said, as she stuffed some underwear into a drawer. "I've got a room-mate, but she's off exploring." She glanced around the stateroom. "I have to admit, this is a lot better than I expected."

Time to broach the subject of Strikland. "About Strikland, are you going to fuck him?"

She froze and gave him a hard look. "I think I would if I could. He's too valuable to pass up. But if I did, are you going to go all jealous and bitchy on me?"

Macus shook his head and felt a momentary flash of anger at her accusation. "Of course not. In fact, I was going to encourage you to give the old guy a ride. He'd clear-ly like to."

She continued unpacking, but the hard look had softened. "Really? I didn't get that from him, and I've certainly tried to get some reaction out of him. I've been won-dering if he's gay."

"I wondered the same thing," Macus said. "Was considering seducing him myself, but I just learned he's definitely not gay. When you're facing away from him, his eyes are locked on your ass, and when you're facing toward him, he can't look at anything but your tits. He's just careful about it, only does so when he's sure no one will spot him look-fucking you."

Macus described how he'd slipped away from them in the waiting room at the air-port. "Did it just so I could watch him when he didn't know I was watching him. Trust me, he's working up a real hard-on for you."

She had a curious look on her face. She abandoned the unpacking, crossed the small stateroom and stopped at an intimately close distance, her breasts pressing against his chest. "So you don't mind if I fuck his brains out."

"No, not at all. But I think you're going to have to approach him a lot differently than the delivery boy's boss in the cafeteria in the Senate Office Building."

She grinned and licked her lips. "Now that's the kind of mature attitude that bodes well for our continuing relationship."

Not sure where she wanted to go with this, he said, "As you pointed out, it's not about the sex. Strikland could be a wealth of information, if you can tap him."

Her eyes brightened. "Oh, I'll tap him, in more ways than one. Just give me time to do it right."

"Good," he said. "And while you're fucking him, I'll find someone else to scratch my itch. What's your roommate like?"

She raised a hand and ran a finger along his lip. "Not bad looking. You can fuck her if you want, but you don't need to. I can keep both you and Strikland happy, though if you want to, you can fuck her as well. In fact, speaking of scratching itches, this new maturity you're demonstrating is making me all itchy at the moment, and I definitely need some scratching in all the right places."

Macus was learning to really appreciate the relationship they had developed. "Here?" he asked, looking at the closed stateroom door. "Now?"

She gave him a chaste kiss on the cheek. "No. But once we're on our way, let's find an opportunity."

19

To Viktorkinde

STANDING ON THE beach in the middle of the night, both of them holding their packed duffels and waiting for the assault boat to arrive, Leeze asked, "You spoke to the Blacksword, *the* Blacksword?"

"Yes," Carla said for the tenth time.

They had packed in a rush, frantically jamming their clothing and gear into their duffels, then hurried down to the beach. They had arrived there less than five minutes after Thealone had ended the call.

"I mean . . . *the* Blacksword, you spoke to the one and only Blacksword?"

"Yes," Carla said for the eleventh time.

"And we're going somewhere, but you don't know where?"

Carla had lost track of how many times she had answered that one.

"And I'm going with you. Why am I going with you?"

Carla tried not to sound short and impatient with her friend. "Because you and I both knew John on Miriteen, and because I told her you'd risk your life for him and he'd risk his for you?"

"Yah, so, what does that have to do with anything?"

Carla threw her hands up as if to pray to some great god of space farers. "I have no fucking idea. She didn't tell me shit. She just told me to get our bags packed and stand out here on this fucking beach."

Carla dropped her duffle onto the sand, then sat down on top of it. Leeze did the same, saying, "Completely ruined our fucking leave."

They sat in silence for a while, listening to the soft rush of the surf as it gently caressed the beach. Then Carla noticed a bright light about forty-five degrees above the horizon. It was just barely larger and brighter than the stars around it, and far in the distance. Its size and intensity grew as she looked on.

Leeze spoke softly and kicked some sand. "Fucking wasted R and R. I was really looking forward to this. And those guys were really hot."

"Be quiet," Carla snapped.

A luminous ionization tail trailed the bright light, and for a moment she thought it might be a meteor entering the atmosphere. Then Carla's ears picked up a faint rumble in the distance. It was a sound she knew but couldn't really place at that moment.

In just a few seconds the faint rumble grew to a roar and its volume now drowned out the sounds of the surf. The noise included an accompanying shriek, and she now recognized the sound as the roar of hypersonic reentry. Just beneath that she heard the grating whine of heavy-duty grav field generators pushed to the limit. The boat was still too far away to resolve, but it now lit up the night sky with about thirty kilometers of ionization trail behind it.

Carla stood. "They're doing a mid-G drop."

Leeze stood up next to her. "Yah. It looks like they dropped straight down from Trafalgar Prime. Must have just dropped below Mach one?"

Carla nodded, and now had to shout to be heard. "Braking hard, probably cranking ten or twenty G's."

Leeze shouted back. "Gonna wake up the neighborhood. I guess something got that Blacksword woman really excited."

"No," Carla shouted. "Excited's the wrong word. What I saw was more like she's really pissed-off about something."

Carla felt the sound waves slamming into her face and chest, and then the noise peaked and began to diminish. Lights in bungalows up and down the beach flicked on one by one. And then the assault boat came to a stop directly overhead. It hovered for a moment, then slid to the side and settled on the beach about thirty meters away. A large hatch in its side dilated, and a squad of ComSecCorps soldiers fanned out of it, all wearing light combat armor and carrying assault rifles.

"Yah," Leeze said. "Something's got that woman mad as hell."

Carla and Leeze both shouldered their duffels and marched toward the boat. The squad leader marched toward them and opened up a direct link between his implants and theirs. *Nigurski? Caputto?*

Carla transmitted an authentication code, Leeze did the same, and he responded with, *Good, follow me.*

Carla noticed everyone from the boat wore Blacksword patches. They hustled her and Leeze aboard and sat them in the midst of the squad, sealed the hatch, and the boat lifted off the beach.

Carla turned to the man sitting next to her. "Where are we going?"

He shrugged. "All we know is we're supposed to deliver you to *Hellfire*."

"The cruiser?"

"Yah."

"Why *Hellfire*? Where's *Hellfire* going?"

He turned his head slowly and looked at her as if she were an idiot. "Where the hell have you been?"

Blacksword or no Blacksword, she didn't care if she threw a couple of megatons of attitude in his face. "I've been on the beach, enjoying some R and R, and having a good time. And my leave just got cut short, and I'm not happy about it."

"The beach?" he asked. He grinned and his eyes tracked slowly down the length of her body, taking in every inch of her. He stripped her naked with his eyes and look-fucked the hell out of her. "Bet you'd look good on the beach."

She put on some DI attitude and parked her nose a fraction of an inch from his. "Don't even think about going there, asshole."

He shrugged and his grin broadened. "Can't blame a guy for trying."

She didn't budge. "God damn it, would somebody tell me where the hell *Hellfire* is going?"

One of his buddies said, "When you get back, you'll have to tell us what the beaches are like on Viktorkinde."

Carla worked hard to keep from producing what Sergeant Major Prescott called a full-on pant-load, and somehow she managed to avoid shitting all her attitude right into her pants.

••••

"Colonel," Fran's secretary said. "Miss Chemina is here."

"Send her right in."

"Don't forget," her secretary said. "She's a civilian, so don't scare her too much."

Fran felt like a grumpy old woman as she said, "I want her scared."

Her secretary rolled her eyes.

A few seconds later the door opened and a young woman stepped into the room. She had brown hair, though light enough to be almost blond. It ended several inches below her shoulders and was a little tousled, as if she didn't spend too much time in front of a mirror. She stopped just inside the door and carried herself rather timidly for a pushy, tenacious news hype. "Colonel Blacksword?"

Fran's patience had run thin. "That is me, young woman, so close the door, come in here, and get to the point."

Chemina closed the door, crossed the room and stopped a few paces in front of Fran's desk. "Since you sent for me, I don't know what the point is, so I can't really get to it. I guess it's you who should get to the point."

That's better, Fran thought, finally seeing a little attitude from the girl. She pointed to a large wingback chair to one side. "Pull up a chair and sit down."

The young woman dragged the chair across the room, parked it in front of Fran's desk, then sat down and crossed her legs. "What can I do for you, Colonel?"

"I may need your help," Fran said. "Your boss says you're quite good at digging up information and uncovering secrets."

Chemina raised a questioning eyebrow. "What information and secrets do you want me to dig up and uncover?"

"I don't know."

"Then who do you want me to dig it up and uncover it from?"

"I don't know."

"Then where do I have to go to do this digging up and uncovering?"

Fran stood and walked around her desk. Chemina rose out of the chair to face her, and stood a little taller than her. Fran decided to cut to the chase. "Colonel Katrine Primatov trusts you."

Chemina pursed her lips as if uncertain of what she should say. "At this moment I fear you're going to ask me to do something I can't. Please understand that I can't compromise my sources, or shade the news the way you want it written, or . . ." She grimaced. "I think you already know what I'm going to say."

Fran made a point of carefully shaking her head. "I'm not going to ask you to do any of those things." It was time to shake the girl up. "But if you agree to help me, before the day is out you'll be on that ship with the diplomatic mission to Viktorkinde."

Fran had just offered Chemina a young reporter's dream scoop, a real career maker. The girl's eyes widened and she took a step back. "I . . . uh . . ."

"Exactly," Fran said. "There's going to be some unpleasant people on that ship, with a lot of nasty secrets. All I need from you is to help me dig up any secrets that might be used to harm certain people, like May Forester or John Mathius. You can do that, can't you?"

"I . . . uh . . . suppose so."

Fran had her where she wanted her. "I'm glad we see eye to eye on that. You can cover the mission from the inside, and write your stories as you see fit. I won't ask you to change them, or compromise your sources, but I may redact them as I see fit. I may also slap a serious classification lock on some or all of those stories and you won't be able to publish them at all. Does that scenario violate your journalistic principles?"

Chemina's eyes blinked rapidly. "No . . . I don't suppose it does."

"Do you accept?"

The young woman managed to calm down a little. "Yes, as long as you understand the limits beyond which I cannot go."

Fran smiled and nodded. "I think I do. So we have a deal." She extended her hand.

The young woman shook it and said, "You mentioned May, that I might need to help protect her as well. Is she coming also?"

"Yes, she is," Fran said. "But you won't see her. She's going to be stationed on the cruiser *Hellfire*, while you're going to be with the diplomatic mission on Tarsik Obradour's yacht, *Lady Victorious*. You might see her on Viktorkinde, but don't count on it."

"I won't."

"We don't have a lot of time. You should go pack."

From the look on her face, the young woman had only now begun to comprehend what she had stumbled into. "We're leaving this afternoon, right? I guess I . . . don't have much time, do I?"

"No," Fran said, "you don't. But don't worry, I have a little pull around here. They're going to wait for me . . . and for you, because I'll tell them to."

Chemina frowned. "Where do I go after I pack my bags? The airport?"

"No," Fran said, shaking her head. "It's all taken care of. As of this moment, you're not going anywhere without a couple of my people at your side. They'll get you to your apartment, and then up to that ship."

"A couple of your people?"

"Exactly. Two young women I think you'll rather like." Fran leaned close to her. "They look rather ordinary and unassuming. But if anyone gets in the way, they can turn real mean real fast."

••••

Macus wanted to take a chance and tried to convince Faith to give him a quickie right then and there in her stateroom. The sex had been good, and she was always drop-dead gorgeous, but before they had broken up, the sex had been just plain old sex: she laid down, spread her legs and he climbed on top of her. But once they had begun working together again to their mutual benefit, and he had demonstrated what she now called his *new maturity*, she had become much more creative in that department, and even sometimes quite inventive.

"No," she said, shaking her head carefully. "Later."

As she turned back to unpacking her clothing, his implants chimed with a call from Palmutter. Macus froze. That asshole had the worst timing.

Macus, where are you?

He spoke out loud. "I'm unpacking, sir."

Faith gave him a questioning look. He pointed to the side of his head and silently mouthed, *Palmutter.*

Her eyes widened, and she nodded to indicate she understood.

Do you know what's going on?

"Uh, no, sir. I wasn't aware anything was happening other than that we're about to depart."

There's been some delay. Something to do with our military escort. You know about that stuff. What's going on?

"I'm no longer in that loop, sir. I do have a few sources, but they're not travelling with us. I could try to contact them before we depart."

No, don't worry about it. I guess we just have to put up with it. Go back to whatever it was you were doing.

Macus looked at Faith and rolled his eyes. "It was Palmutter. He's gone."

"What was that about?"

Macus shrugged. "Some sort of delay. Has something to do with the military, so he thought I could help, but I can't."

The door opened and Faith's new roommate walked in. Faith introduced them, and as she had told him, the young woman wasn't bad looking. Maybe he would give her a shot.

With Faith busy unpacking, and chatting with her new roommate, Macus had nothing to do at the moment, so he decided to kill time and wandered down to the lounge. There were quite a number of aides and staffers gathered there, clustered in small groups and speculating excitedly about what they would find on Viktorkinde. He recognized them all, but was acquainted with only some of them. And then he spotted someone new, a good-looking young woman seated alone at the bar. She had light-brown hair a little tousled in an attractive way. Her eyes were focused on a small access terminal on the bar in front of her, with what appeared to be a glass of water next to it.

He approached her from behind, and heard her subvocalizing into her implants. He paused, hoping to learn something, and heard, ". . . last minute . . . no warning . . . chance . . . lifetime."

She hesitated, stiffened and went silent, then glanced over her shoulder at him. She smiled, and her eyes narrowed with suspicion. "Were you trying to listen in on my conversation?"

Macus needed to think quickly. "No, of course not. I was approaching you, then I thought I heard you talk, but I wasn't sure, so I hesitated, trying to figure out if I would be interrupting you or not. Just trying to be polite." She seemed a little familiar, but he couldn't place her.

He extended his hand. "Macus DeLeon, Chief Military Adviser to Senator Palmutter."

She held up a finger and touched it to her ear, indicating her implants. She spoke aloud so Macus could hear her. "Mike, I've got to run. I'll try to contact you again before we're too far out to communicate."

That pleased Macus. Palmutter's status and Macus's position carried quite a bit of weight, and might help him get her in bed all the sooner.

With the call ended, she extended her hand and shook his. "I'm Karya Chemina, with Capital Politico."

"A news hype," he said as he sat down at the bar, thinking she had nice tits, nice everything. He would definitely enjoy a little fun-time with her.

She pursed her lips unhappily. "We prefer the term *journalist*."

"Buy you a drink?"

"You can't buy me a drink. They're all free."

They talked for several minutes. Like all hypes, she tried to pump him for info, but he had had plenty of experience handling her type. Maybe he could get her under the sheets if he hinted she might learn something, but for the time being he struck out with her.

20

More Suspicious People

THE ASSAULT BOAT lifted straight up from the beach.

Leeze turned to Carla and whispered. "I sure hope we're not in trouble."

Carla shook her head, still thinking how close she had come to Prescott's full-on pant-load. "I don't think we are. But Colonel Blacksword seems a little irritated about something, so she might be a bit short with us when we get there."

The pilot angled the boat's nose up and aimed it at a point about forty-five degrees above the horizon, then poured on the coals. Less than a minute later they were about half way to orbital velocity when they cleared atmosphere. The pilot drove them straight to Trafalgar Prime with a lot of drive and a considerable disregard for orbital mechanics, but traffic control slowed them down as they approached the big station.

Carla feared Thealone would hold it against her if they were late, though she didn't know what constituted late, and wasn't about to ask the Blacksword asshole who had look-fucked her when she'd boarded the boat. He'd probably look-fuck her again, but this time it would involve all sorts of disgusting, deviant acts, at least in his twisted mind. The jerk probably went to Kelkie parties when he got some time off.

At Trafalgar Prime, *Hellfire* was coupled to one of the main docks. Its hangar bay doors were open, and one of its assault boats floated nearby clearing a slot for the Blacksword boat, which coupled to the personnel hatch in its docking bay.

Carla and Leeze stood and shouldered their duffels. Their Blacksword escorts didn't stand with them. Look-fuck-guy waved goodbye with a leering grin on his face, and said, "I know it breaks your heart, honey, but we ain't going with you." Then he look-fucked her one last time as she walked out through the personnel hatch.

In the passageway they were met by a female second looie with chin-length, brownish-blond hair, and the name FORESTER stenciled on the tag above her left breast pocket. "Carla Nigurski, Leezil Caputto, I'm May Forester. I'm your new squad leader."

They shook hands, then Forester said, "I'll show you to your bunks."

As she led the way, Leeze asked the question Carla wanted to ask. "Shouldn't Carla and I head to *Fearless* and get our gear?"

Forester threw the answer over her shoulder. "You don't have time. You're the last to arrive, so we're departing now."

She stopped, turned to face them, and spoke to Carla. "You spoke to Colonel Blacksword, right?"

Carla answered carefully. "Yah."

Forester lifted an eyebrow. "That woman told someone to make sure your gear got transferred to *Hellfire*. It's already here."

Allship blared, "Initiating cast-off sequence."

Forester continued. "When we get to the bunkroom, check your gear. If anything is missing or damaged, personal or otherwise, it'll get replaced, but you're not going back to *Fearless* for a long time."

Something loud and heavy clanged through the hull. Allship blared, "Cast-off sequence complete."

Carla asked, "This has something to do with John Mathius, doesn't it?"

Forester looked a little perplexed. "I don't know the details, but someone wants him dead. And Colonel Blacksword is putting together a special detail of people who know him, and who she can trust to keep him alive. We're part of it."

Leeze said, "Fucking right we'll keep him alive. Where is he?"

Forester shrugged and shook her head. "Somewhere between here and Viktorkinde."

Carla asked, "How did you know him?"

"I was his O-School roomie in the dorm."

When they got to the bunk room, it turned into a little mini-reunion between Carla, Leeze and four guys from their training platoon. Leeze and one of them, a fellow named Matty, had had a relationship on Miriteen during advanced training. But they had been assigned to different ships so it had ended when they went their separate ways. The guys asked Leeze and Carla what was going on, and they told what little they knew. Forester probably knew more than any of them, but she held back and stayed out of the conversation, while they speculated on what John Mathius had done to piss off the Blacksword.

••••

Nygaard paced back and forth on the bridge of *Konigsborge*, though there wasn't a lot of room for pacing, but she managed it anyway. For the benefit of the crew, Kristdokar took care to appear calm. And as captain of the ship, a composed demeanor was almost mandatory for Command Eagle Holverzon.

The opposing hunter-killers advanced at a speed obviously slower than their capabilities, and more commensurate with that of a larger ship. They came forward one light-year, then one of them down-transited briefly. It didn't stay in sublight long, but quickly up-transited and raced forward, using its greater hunter-killer speed to catch up with its comrades. At each one-light-year interval, one of the three took its turn doing that, a classic gambit that allowed it to acquire more accurate scan data and see things they couldn't see while in transition. They could then feed that data to the rest of the advancing force.

Eldekarl continued to run silent, and when any of the oncoming force had down-transited, no matter how briefly, she also remained transmitter silent. They didn't want to take the chance she might be detected by even a faint vestige of transmitter splash, which could only be picked up by a ship in sublight. But when all of them were in transition and blind, she fed updates to *Konigsborge* and *Drakan Helgis* on the developing situation. If worse came to worst, they needed something to even the odds a little.

The oncoming force could have been sent from Viktorkinde as an escort for the diplomatic mission coming from the Commonwealth. But they were early for that, and their original vector had been aimed more for Sarkovie. When *Konigsborge* had left Sarkovie, they had first deviated to the terminus of the relay chain so Nygaard could file a report. That put them on a vector more in line with the Commonwealth, and the oncoming force had diverted only when evidence indicated *Konigsborge* was returning from a slightly different direction. And in any case, if they had been officially sanctioned, Viktorkinde would have warned Nygaard to expect them. No, all the data indicated with high probability that this was not a chance encounter. They were facing warships that had come out looking specifically for them.

Four hours after leaving *Drakan Helgis* behind, with *Konigsborge* and the opposing hunter-killers advancing toward each other, they had closed the distance between them to about five light-years. It would be the first time any of the hunter-killers could acquire solid positional data on them and assemble a proper emissions profile. If they were looking for *Konigsborge*, they were probably still too far out for the data to be good enough to compare to known spectra and confirm her identity, but that would soon change.

An hour and a half later *Eldekarl* reported a large ship had come within range of its detection systems. It was running about two light-years behind the hunter-killers, and was still two distant to acquire a detailed profile. It was big, but that was about all they could tell at that range.

A little over eight hours after leaving *Drakan Helgis* behind, Holverzon ordered his helmswoman to start dumping lights, and they down-transited near *Eldekarl*. If the oncoming force proved to be hostile, and *Eldekarl* had managed to remain undetected, the hunter-killer could even the odds a little against the overwhelming firepower they faced. Hopefully, they would think *Konigsborge* had simply down-transited for a nav fix, spotted them, and decided to wait for them to come their way.

"Captain," the scan tech said. "At this point I've acquired a pretty good emissions profile on that big ship. It's definitely a large cruiser, and of Kelk origin, but I can't find anything to match its profile in our registry. I have matched profiles on two of the hunter-killers, but they're not operating in this sector, or at least they're not supposed to be."

Nygaard leaned close to Kristdokar and lowered her voice. "Interesting! It occurs to me that if we had nothing to hide, and this was merely a chance encounter, we would hail them."

Kristdokar considered that carefully. "And it occurs to me that if they had nothing to hide, they would have hailed us by now."

Nygaard's eyes narrowed with thought. "That is true. What do you think?"

Kristdokar shrugged. "We have nothing to lose. I think we should play it straight and contact them."

Nygaard instructed Holverzon to do so, and he gave orders to the com tech to open a channel to the oncoming ships. But when the young woman tried, the force coming their way remained silent and kept advancing. Holverzon maneuvered *Konigsborge* to get closer to *Eldekarl* so they could support each other with firepower if the need arose.

Three hours later, with the hunter-killers only one light-year distant, the three of them down-transited and held their positions. They had been sweeping two light-years ahead of the cruiser, and in five more hours it caught up with them. They then up-transited to join it, and together they drove toward *Konigsborge*.

Holverzon said, "They're amassing so they can concentrate firepower." As captain it was his job to think first of the safety of his ship and crew, with no regard for the politics in play.

Nygaard met Kristdokar's eyes and said, "Let us hope that is not their intention, but at the same time we should assume it is."

"Engineering," Holverzon said, "stand by and be prepared to provide full combat status on my order. And power the shields, with priority to defensive stations. We may take fire."

Nygaard continued to hold Kristdokar's eyes as she said, "Captain Holverzon, contact *Eldekarl* and tell her captain I authorize her to fire upon Kelk assets if she must do so to defend us or her ship. Also, pass the same message to Captain Taugrim on *Drakan Helgis*. And I authorize you to do the same."

Holverzon's face remained completely expressionless as he nodded, his eyes locked on Nygaard. In the history of the Supremacy, never before had two Kelk warships fired upon one another. "That's a message I should deliver personally. Com, open up a channel and put me through to the captains of *Eldekarl* and *Drakan Helgis*. And sound general quarters."

A horn burped once, issuing a grating note throughout the ship, a sound guaranteed to wake even the most hungover spacer after a tenday leave. The steady clang of the alert Klaxon immediately followed it. As a flag officer, Kristdokar's responsibility during combat operations was to keep her mouth shut and let Holverzon and his people do their jobs.

Three hours later, the four oncoming ships down-transited just before reaching *Konigsborge*.

"Captain," the scan tech said. "They're ranging at three hundred million kilometers."

Kristdokar couldn't stop from thinking they had chosen a good distance for accurately targeting the torpedoes of the hunter-killers, and the transition batteries of the cruiser.

"Captain," the com tech said. "I have a transmission from the cruiser identifying it as *Valhaukr*. Vice Skalde Haugrund wishes to speak with Vice Skalde Nygaard."

Holverzon looked at Nygaard. "*Valhaukr*? Never heard of it."

Kristdokar had heard the name somewhere, but knew nothing of the ship.

Nygaard sighed and nodded. "When we left Viktorkinde, *Valhaukr* was nearing completion in the Norddansk Navy Yard. It wasn't scheduled for christening for several months. They must have considerably compressed its schedule."

Haugrund's presence bothered Kristdokar. "I thought Haugrund was somewhat sympathetic. Didn't you tell me she felt manipulated by whoever is cooperating clandestinely with the Commonwealth?"

Nygaard's lips tightened into a straight line as she said, "Perhaps she's changed her mind, or maybe that's just what she wanted us to believe. She knows you diverted *Drakan Helgis* to Sarkovie, so we're going to have to make this up as we go. I want you in on this conversation, but be careful. I don't want them to know we have survivors from *Sycorax* on board."

Kristdokar nodded once, and opened up her implants.

Nygaard turned to Holverzon. "Captain, I want you to listen in as well, but not participate. Just observe. And be prepared to act, if need be."

"As you wish," he said.

A few seconds later Haugrund appeared in Kristdokar's virtual vision. On her left stood Command Eagle Aubrecht Machtberg. He appeared to be in late middle age and had an even mix of salt and pepper in his hair. On Haugrund's right stood a woman who looked absolutely ancient. She wore no uniform, but Kristdokar knew her well: Brigadier Skalde Marta Nvalheim, retired. Machtberg and Nvalheim were both members of the Larscom General Secretariat, and like Haugrund, well-known, hardline, anti-Commonwealth hawks. Kristdokar thought it telling that Nvalheim was also a member of Norddansk's board, and a significant shareholder.

Haugrund nodded politely. "Vice Skalde Nygaard, and Brigadier Skalde Kristdokar. It's always a pleasure to see both of you."

Nygaard greeted them in turn. "Secretary Machtberg, Secretary Nvalheim, and Counselor Haugrund. What brings you out to these far reaches of space?"

Kristdokar saw something unpleasant in the smile Haugrund gave them. "Norddansk is conducting qualification and compliance trials on *Valhaukr* before transferring ownership to the Supremacy. And Marta was kind enough to invite me and Aubrecht to come along and observe, purely in an unofficial capacity, of course. Imagine the likelihood of encountering you out here purely by chance."

"Yes," Nygaard said. "Imagine that. Purely by chance."

Qualification and compliance, Kristdokar thought, a good way to fund and hide a rogue operation.

Haugrund leaned forward. "I should ask how your mission to Sarkovie went. Did you rescue the missing young woman?"

Nygaard shrugged. "Unfortunately, no. We did encounter two rogue commercial vessels that rendezvoused off Sarkovie. One had apparently suffered some unexplained internal damage, because when they tried to escape it broke up. There were no survivors, and to our chagrin, the other rogue did manage to evade us."

"And *Drakan Helgis*?" Haugrund asked. "Skalde Kristdokar diverted the destroyer to Sarkovie before you left Viktorkinde, did she not?"

Nygaard shook her head. "It wasn't in the vicinity, must have been drawn away by something of interest."

At that point Haugrund made no attempt to hide her insincerity as she frowned. "But what of *Alvilddan* and *Eldekarl*?"

Nygaard played it straight. "We left them at Sarkovie to clean up the mess precipitated by the breakup of the rogue. I'm afraid we're returning rather empty handed."

"Really," Haugrund said. "That's a shame. I was—"

Her image froze in mid word, not as if she hesitated, but because she had clearly stopped transmitting anything for their implants to display. At the same moment, *Konigsborge*'s com tech spoke excitedly. "Captain, there's been some sort of unauthorized transmission from the lower decks."

"Engineering," Holverzon barked. "Full combat status, now."

Haugrund's image reanimated and she smiled, a look of triumph on her face. "So, you have the breschkada, both of them, on board *Drakan Helgis*. And she's only a few light-years behind you."

"Captain," *Konigsborge*'s scan tech said. "Those three hunter-killers just up-transited and are driving—"

Konigsborge's hull shrieked as her shields deflected a salvo from *Valhaukr*'s transition batteries.

21

Time to Run

STRAPPED INTO A seat at *Drakan Helgis*'s scan console, Katrine watched the three hunter-killers up-transit and head their way. In almost the same instant *Valhaukr* fired on *Konigsborge*, and the two cruisers lit up space around them with their transition batteries.

Taugrim had allowed Katrine to sit at the scan console and observe the encounter between *Konigsborge* and the unknown force. Unlike the hunter-killer *Lightspear*, *Drakan Helgis* had two seats at each console, so she didn't have to stand and look over the tech's shoulder, which would be rather difficult under weightless conditions while running silent.

"Captain," *Drakan Helgis*'s com tech said, her voice straining with fear. "Vice Skalde Nygaard orders us to run and take evasive action."

Taugrim shook her head. "Everyone hold, take a deep breath, and calm down. They're four light-years out. Scan, how many lights are they pushing?"

The scan tech said, "Just over thirty-nine hundred, mistress."

"Exactly," Taugrim said. "They have to stay together, because if they come at us one at a time, we've got them outgunned. So they're limited to the maximum drive of the slowest of the three."

She looked at John, manning a post at the navigation console. "Isn't that right, Blacksword?"

He nodded. "Yes, mistress."

"So how much time do we have, Blacksword?"

Katrine thought it interesting they called John *the Blacksword*, or simply addressed him as *Blacksword*. She was thankful they didn't do that to her.

John didn't consult his console or pause to run some calculations, so he must have done a quick tally in his head. "About nine hours, mistress."

"Exactly," Taugrim said. "We've got plenty of time to decide what we're going to do, and where we're going to go, before we do the doing and go the going. Isn't that right, Blacksword?"

"Yes, mistress," he said.

Katrine sensed that the mild hazing in their banter now sounded more like friendly ribbing. They teased the young Vreekande girl the same way. In the Commonwealth all junior officers had to put up with that when fresh out of O-School, and it appeared to be the same among the Kelk. The crew now regarded the two young people as crewmates. Tarsik Obradour would find it most interesting that once again, John Mathius had proven to be a catalyst.

"Mistress Vreekande," Taugrim said. "What do you think we should do?"

Nikaela was training at the com console. "I don't know, mistress."

Taugrim shook her head sadly. "Well, Mistress Vreekande, you're going to be in command someday, so don't you think you should figure these things out?"

Nikaela looked stricken as she said, "Maybe we should go back to Sarkovie."

Taugrim nodded. "That's a possibility. What about you, Blacksword? What do you think we should do?"

John shrugged uncertainly. "Head toward the Commonwealth?"

Taugrim grimaced. "A bunch of Kelk warships driving hard into Commonwealth sovereign space. That's a good way to get our butts vaporized by several big warheads. But it doesn't matter. Sarkovie or the Commonwealth, we won't make it. We can only push about thirty-four hundred lights. With the extra five-hundred lights they're pushing, they're going to catch up to us in three days. How far can we get in three days, Blacksword?"

John's eyes narrowed in thought, and there was no uncertainty in his voice when he said, "Just over twenty-seven light-years."

Interestingly enough, Nikaela's timid indecision had also disappeared. Taugrim had given them a problem, and the two young people were now focused on that.

Taugrim said, "We actually have a little more time than that, because they're going to skip-jump." She pointed at John, then at Nikaela. "We'll save that lesson for later. But if we just sit here and think about it, those assholes are going to nuke us in about nine hours. So, at this point, we simply run, and it would be preferably to run *away* from them. That puts us headed toward Trafalgar, at least for now. That'll buy us time, and we'll figure out something before *those* assholes shove a warhead up *our* asshole."

She looked at John. "Give me a transition plan, Blacksword."

He nodded. "Yes, mistress."

"Nav, get out your charts. We're on a direct line between Viktorkinde and Trafalgar, so this part of space ought to be fairly well mapped. Scan, work with Nav, and before we up-transit, I want to know about every piece of rock that's ahead of us, every piece that's bigger than my tits, and every piece that's within fifty light-years of where my tits are right now."

John and Dahlborg worked closely with the scan tech. Quick work confirmed that the available charts were fairly complete, so a short time later they up-transited and headed toward the Commonwealth.

••••

Anders awoke lying on the cot in the concrete cell in the basement of that warehouse. The room was cool and comfortable, and he had enough blankets to keep warm when he slept. He threw the blankets off, swung his legs off the cot and stood, wearing nothing but underwear. The previous night he had stripped out of his clothing, carefully folded it, and placed it beneath the cot.

He stripped out of his underwear then bathed standing at the sink, washing down with a cloth and the soap they had provided, then rinsing off with the same cloth. He toweled off, put on his underwear and clothing, then shaved. If his incarceration lasted much longer, he would start exercising just before he bathed. It was certainly better than SecureMax, though since his implants no longer included the enhanced programming that zoned him out and made him not care, it was also going to be a lot more boring.

He sat down on the cot and wondered what they intended to do with him. He tried not to think of the story he would tell them, because if he thought on it too much, he'd sound overly rehearsed when he did tell it.

The metal door had a small window embedded in it about head high. Shortly after he finished shaving, a face appeared behind the transparent plast, the door opened a crack, and the fellow with the goatee stuck his head in the room. "Move to the far wall."

Anders stood, walked across the cell, and put his back to the wall. The door opened and the fellow walked in carrying a grav pistol aimed at Anders. He stepped to one side and put his back to the wall next to the door, then said, "It's clear."

The woman who had searched Anders walked through the door carrying a tray of food. She crossed the cell and placed it on the table. Then she walked out, the man followed, the door closed, and Anders heard the clank of the lock mechanism.

He sat down at the table and ate. The food was good, plentiful, nourishing, and reasonably enjoyable, a welcome respite from the ration packs that had been his only source of food in the lifeboat. They had provided a healthy shot of kirva as well, and he sipped at it slowly to make it last.

An hour later the man and woman returned, repeating the process where the man covered Anders with a grav pistol while the woman retrieved the tray and dirty dishes. At the end of the day they followed the same procedure when they brought his evening meal, and again an hour later when they retrieved the tray after he had eaten.

On his second day in the concrete cell, he bathed as usual, wondering if he should point out to them he needed a change of clothing, or at least ask for some way of laundering what he had. Then he went through the routine of the morning meal, followed an hour later by retrieval of the tray and dirty dishes.

About mid-morning the fellow sporting a goatee appeared in the window in the door, it opened a crack, and the man said, "Move to the far wall."

The previous day they had left him completely to his own devices between the two meals. Wondering at the change in routine, Anders crossed the room as usual, then turned and put his back against the wall. The door swung open and the fellow with the pistol stepped in. He shifted to one side and put his back against the wall near the door. This time he held the weapon casually against his thigh, the barrel aimed at the floor. "It's clear," he said.

The woman who stepped through the open door was not the woman who had searched him. She was a little older, looked at him with bright red irises, had very little salt in her hair, and smiled pleasantly. He thought he recognized her, but wasn't sure from where, and then realized she had been one of the many faces he'd seen in passing on *Sycorax*. Now, as then, she wore civilian clothing, but all appearances indicated she was in charge here, though from her he didn't sense the impending threat that had colored his interactions with his last interrogator.

She pointed to a chair at the table. "Sit down, please."

He crossed the cell, selected the chair that would put him facing her and the door, and sat down. The fellow holding the pistol stepped farther into the room, obviously making sure he had a clear line of fire to Anders. The woman crossed the short distance to the table and sat down opposite him. "Tell me what happened to *Sycorax*."

Anders grimaced. "I can only guess."

"Then tell me what you know, and what you can guess at, but make it clear which is which."

She had probably been the reason *Sycorax* had first stopped at the planet before moving to the rendezvous point with the other ship. "When did you leave the ship? I'll start from there."

Her eyebrows rose in surprise. "You recognize me?"

"I must have seen you in passing, but I don't recall exactly when or where. And it could only have been on *Sycorax*. I would remember you if we had met on Viktorkinde."

She considered his answer in silence for several seconds. "They shuttled me down to the surface of Sarkovic immediately upon arriving here, then moved to a position well off planet. Do you know where?"

"Not exactly," he said, "but it was something like two hundred light-hours out."

She nodded. "Then start from there."

He tried to think carefully to recall the sequence of events. "Two or three days after they dropped you here, a Commonwealth ship arrived and made rendezvous with us. I think it was named *Caliban*. I think that was when they transferred the breschka-da-sa over to *Sycorax*."

Her upper lip curled in distaste. "The Blacksword."

"Yah," he said. "I didn't have much to do with the two breschkada, but a couple days after that, Command Hawk Eskildsen had me observe while she interrogated them."

"What did she learn?"

He gritted his teeth. "I think she learned they are truly breschkada, which clearly disappointed her." Anders didn't tell her he suspected Eskildsen had hoped he would lose control and kill the two young people, eliminating the problem for them all.

The woman seated opposite him closed her eyes and rubbed her temples. The news that the young people were truly breschkada clearly disappointed her as well.

Anders then described how the day after the interrogation he had accompanied Eskildsen to the personnel airlock of the assault boat. "They were going to transfer me and the two breschkada down here. But the airlock was closed and locked. The pilot had left his post, and arrived outside the airlock just a few moments after we did. And then the boat launched without him. And then everything went crazy." He didn't tell her how he'd set a few fires on *Sycorax* and triggered false alarms to help the two young people.

"They sounded general quarters, for which I had no assignment. So I grabbed an all-purpose vac suit, put it on and hunkered down in my bunk. I heard a lot of crap echo through the hull of that ship, so I'm guessing we were hit with something big. I think someone fired on us, and there were casualty and damage alarms sounding all over the ship. Then a gravity spike hit me like nothing I've ever felt and I blacked out. When I woke up it was all silent, no lights, no gravity, no power. I rapped on the hull a bunch of times to see if I could locate anyone else, but got no answering pings. So I made my way to a lifeboat, and then made my way here. By the way, from the lifeboat, I saw that what I had survived in was only a piece of *Sycorax*. I think the ship broke up for some reason."

Her distrust was quite visible in her face. "Why are you the only one who made it out alive?"

That was an interesting piece of information. He was quite certain others survived as well. He was just the only one who wasn't in custody. He shook his head. "I'm the only one who didn't have a duty station. I ended up on a derelict piece of that ship that was pretty much deserted except for me. And don't assume I'm the only one who made it out alive. You'll have to tell me if I'm the only one who escaped, but there might have been others in the other pieces of that ship." He shrugged. "Might have been some in the piece I was in too, but I wasn't going to search the whole thing compartment by compartment. We lost, they won, and I wasn't going to stick around to be rescued just so I could get thrown into another cell."

She asked for, and he gave her, the location of the canyon where he'd hidden the lifeboat. He hoped he had covered his tracks enough that they wouldn't find anything to fuel their suspicions.

She questioned him for two more hours then left, and he returned to his daily routine. But she returned again the next morning and questioned him for most of the day, made him repeat everything two or three times. He tried not to sound rehearsed, and was careful to make insignificant little mistakes here and there, just as a normal person might.

Again, he returned to the daily routine of life in a cell.

22

No Help for the Hunted

"FIRE CONTROL," HOLVERZON said. "All main batteries target *Valhaukr* and stand by for my command. Helm, stand by to retreat."

Konigsborge's defensive stations intercepted much of *Valhaukr*'s fire, but some got through and her hull echoed with a cacophony of sounds as her shields deflected transition shells from the other ship's main batteries. The fire from *Valhaukr* was not as effective as Kristdokar would have expected. It was not well coordinated, and it took her a few seconds to realize Haugrund, Machtberg and Nvalheim must have cobbled together a crew in a hasty rush. They had not had the time to properly shake down the ship and its crew, nor to run space trials on a newly commissioned warship.

"One salvo," Holverzon said. "Fire."

With all of *Konigsborge*'s main batteries firing at once, the hull thrummed like a massive drum, and a gravity spike punched Kristdokar in the gut.

"Fire Control, return fire at will. Helm, retreat away from them, all ahead full."

Kristdokar had a scan summary displayed in her virtual vision. *Konigsborge*'s helmsman firewalled the ship's sublight drive and they accelerated away from *Valhaukr* at more than ten thousand gravities. Haugrund must have taken their retreat as a sign that their bombardment had been effective against *Konigsborge*. *Valhaukr* followed, and as they passed the still silent and undetected *Eldekarl*, the hunter-killer threw a warhead in their way. A new sun of thermonuclear fire blossomed just off *Valhaukr*'s bow, and the scan summary in Kristdokar's vision went blank as *Konigsborge* instantly shut down its sensors to protect them from the nearby detonation.

Valhaukr had ceased firing on *Konigsborge*, and the ship's hull no longer thrummed with shells slamming into its shields. *Konigsborge*'s main batteries continued to spit transition shells at the other ship's last known position. Kristdokar hoped the other ship hadn't disengaged merely to take on *Eldekarl*, because the hunter-killer wouldn't stand a chance.

Holverzon glanced briefly at Kristdokar and Nygaard. "Stand by all defensive stations. Be prepared—"

Their sensors came back online. Fire Control adjusted their targeting to track *Valhaukr*.

"Maestra," the com tech said. "*Eldekarl* reports *Valhaukr* is retreating. It appears they have sustained heavy damage to the bow and some minor damage amidships. Their drive appears to be undamaged."

Holverzon barked, "All stop."

He turned to Nygaard. "Do we give chase? Or do we try to help *Drakan Helgis*?"

Nygaard looked at Kristdokar as she said, "What do you think, Brigadier?"

Kristdokar tried not to rush as she hurriedly did the math. "*Drakan Helgis* can outdrive us by a couple hundred lights. And those hunter-killers can outdrive her. If we chase after them the distance between us will only increase until they catch her. Whatever is going to happen will be over long before we can provide aid."

There had been a number of reasons she had originally selected *Drakan Helgis* for Brynjar's covert mission to Sarkovie: one, she could divert the ship without drawing attention to her actions; two, the destroyer's commanding officer did not exhibit overtly anti-Commonwealth sentiments; and three, Command Hawk Taugrim was one of the best.

"No," Kristdokar said. "We really have no choice. *Drakan Helgis*'s fate rests solely in the hands of Captain Taugrim. And we have an obligation to get to the bottom of what Haugrund, Machtberg and Nvalheim have been up to."

"I concur," Nygaard said. "So we'll have to hope for the best with *Drakan Helgis* while we clean this mess up. Captain Holverzon, instruct *Eldekarl* to join us as we pursue *Valhaukr*."

Holverzon issued orders and *Konigsborge*'s hull groaned with the sound of its drive pushed to the limit.

In her virtual vision Kristdokar watched the stream of data coming in from *Eldekarl*. *Valhaukr* had sustained serious damage and there would be loss of life.

Nygaard must have looked at the same data, because she leaned close to Kristdokar and lowered her voice. "Such a hastily prepared attack was foolish of them. Haugrund is not normally a foolish woman."

"Perhaps it was not so much foolishness," Kristdokar said, "as desperation."

Nygaard's face saddened. "Your point is well taken."

"Yes, they grow more desperate the closer we get to Viktorkinde."

Nygaard shook her head slowly. "No, they grow more desperate the closer *he* gets to Viktorkinde."

Kristdokar turned her head to look squarely into Nygaard's eyes. "A subtle distinction, but probably correct. Our breschkada-sa frightens them no end."

Nygaard kept her voice low and spoke as if thinking out loud. "We could look the other way, let the assassins have the Blacksword, then execute them for killing him. It would rid us of a difficult problem."

The worst thing Kristdokar could do at that moment would be to react strongly and display an emotional response to the woman's idea. "At best, we would revert to the status quo, which in all probability will eventually lead to an interstellar war we cannot win. At worst, it might precipitate that interstellar war sooner rather than later."

Nygaard leaned away from Kristdokar and gave her a piercing look for several seconds. Then slowly she smiled, but it was a smile only of her lips. Her eyes remained sad. "Again, your point is well taken."

"Captain," *Konigsborge*'s scan tech said. "I've detected a warhead detonation. Its location coincides with that of the nearest relay buoy back toward Trafalgar. It appears one of those hunter-killers chasing *Drakan Helgis* targeted it intentionally as they passed it. I pinged the relay chain, and they've broken it. We can still communicate with Viktorkinde, but nothing's going to make it through to Trafalgar."

That also meant they couldn't communicate with *Drakan Helgis*.

••••

The only thing Carla and her friends from Miriteen knew about their new assignment was that Fran Thealone had formed them into a squad under the command of May Forester, and they were going to Viktorkinde with the diplomatic mission. From her brief conversation with the Blacksword, Carla knew it had something to do with John Mathius, and she had blabbed that to Leeze back in the bungalow on the beach. Then Leeze blabbed it to the rest of the squad within five minutes of joining them on *Hellfire*.

She and Leeze were still unpacking their gear and speculating with the guys about the mission, when Fran Thealone appeared in Carla's virtual vision. From the way her squad mates tensed and froze all at once, she guessed they were getting the same message. Thealone appeared to have calmed considerably, "Your mission is going to be top secret, so you don't talk about it with anyone other than me or your squad mates. If anyone asks, you don't know anything. You're just a bunch of grunts in a squad who are going to do what you're told, and no one's told you what that is. You people are not cleared for highly classified operations, so let me give you the following caution. If any of you blab anything to anyone, I'm going to cut off your balls and hang them on my wall. And don't any of you women think you're getting a pass on that just because you don't have balls. I'll use gene therapy to grow balls on you, then cut them off so I can hang them up there with the men's. I wouldn't want anyone to think I showed any favoritism to one sex over the other." She smiled, and the look she gave them made the whole concept of demonic Kelk seem rather benign.

Without another word, she disappeared from Carla's virtual vision. Everyone, including Forester, had the same look on their face. Forester said, "Did all of you get the same balls message I just got?"

Matty said, "You said she's tough, but I had no idea."

Leeze asked him, "Getting our balls cut off is really going to hurt, right?"

A fellow named Digger rolled his eyes and Matty just shook his head.

For the next two days they didn't discuss anything about the mission. Carla found it amazing that grunts didn't speculate about the job. Normal grunts would come up with all kinds of wild guesses and make up all sorts stuff. It was just not in the grunt DNA to keep one's mouth shut like that. They spent their time drilling together, working out in the gym, performing maintenance on their gear—especially their combat armor—reading, playing cards, watching vids, but no one talked about the mission. May Forester summed it up for all of them when she said, "It's the balls thing."

Two days out from Trafalgar they received orders to report to a conference room in officer's country. Forester led the way, and when they got there she opened the door a crack and stuck her head in the room. She looked over her shoulder and said, "It's empty."

They filed into the room, which contained a large plast table welded to the deck.

Forester said, "We might as well sit down."

They selected places around the table at random, extruded chairs up from the deck and sat down. Carla noted that no one sat at the head of the table. They sat there for a good minute in silence, and then Thealone walked into the room.

Forester barked, "Attention."

"At ease," Thealone said as she walked to the head of the table. "Sit down and relax."

She didn't sit down with them, but stood there and looked them over. Carla managed not to fidget as the woman's eyes settled on her for a moment. Leeze and Digger cringed a little when their turn came.

"I don't bite," Thealone said, and she grinned with none of the demonic look she had displayed previously. "We did get off to a tough start, didn't we? But until a few hours before this mission was scheduled to depart, I didn't know I would be on this ship. And I didn't know until then that I needed your help, so I had to move quickly. I brought you here today so I can tell you the why and wherefore of it all."

She smiled, demonstrating to Carla's surprise she could look pleasant and unintimidating. "First, how many of you were on Reisenar with John Mathius?"

Carla, Leeze and Matty raised a hand.

Thealone nodded. "I'm pretty sure even those of you who were there didn't get the whole story. We clamped down quite hard on the details. But I'm going to tell it to you now, though keep in mind you should treat everything you here in this room as highly classified."

She looked at Forester. "Miss Forester, are your people clear on that?"

"Yes, ma'am," she said, smiling uncomfortably. "We're all quite conscious of the balls thing."

"Good," Thealone said. "You'll probably find it difficult to believe, but I have more confidence in each of you than you may realize. I'm sure you're all aware John Mathius has something to do with why you're here. But you wouldn't be here if each of you didn't also have an excellent record and good recommendations from your superiors."

She paused for a moment as if gathering her thoughts. "Now, regarding Reisenar."

Thealone launched into a detailed description of what had happened to John on Reisenar. Carla and Leeze had been in the assault boat with him when it had taken a hit from ground fire, and she had been ejected from it with John when the pilot executed the abandon-ship sequence. Using the gravity fields in her armor, Carla had landed with some of her squad mates in the middle of a busy street. She knew John hadn't been so lucky, but had no idea of the details Thealone fed them now. The colonel told them of the damage to his armor that isolated him from his squad, and the running firefight with a couple of squads of Kelk that ended on a subway platform deep beneath the city.

Thealone leaned forward and placed her palms flat on the table. "Mr. Mathius recognized that there was a third party involved, so instead of killing that young Kelk officer on that subway platform, he saved her life and gave her the coordinates of one of the mercenary outposts. The Kelk investigated and learned we weren't responsible for the mess we both found ourselves in. That led to a joint effort by our forces and theirs to get to the bottom of the situation."

Thealone carefully explained the Kelk concept of breschkada, and how the young woman had saved John's life in return. She told them of the Kelk hatred for Blackswords, and of the insults intended by the use of the butcher's blades. Then she showed them recordings of John's injuries, detailed footage taken shortly before they took him into surgery.

Carla almost broke into tears when she saw that. One of the men slammed his fist on the table and stood. "Those mother-fuckers. We'll kill all those fucking Kelk."

Thealone looked calmly at the man and didn't say anything in response to his outburst. At that moment she looked more like a concerned mother, and he lowered his eyes and sat down.

She nodded and said. "Along with Mr. Mathius, they tried to kill another of our people: Colonel Katrine Primatov. A young Kelk officer took a bullet in the side to protect her. There were two Kelk guards outside John's stateroom door. Both died trying to stop the people who did that to him. Your job is going to be to keep John Mathius alive, but it's not going to be that easy. You're going to have to discriminate. There are good people and bad people in both the Commonwealth and the Supremacy. You may find yourself fighting beside a Kelk comrade to kill a Commonwealth soldier. Make sure you don't harm any of the good guys—on either side."

She paused and let them absorb that for a few seconds. "Now do you understand why this is so hush-hush?"

Everyone seated at that table either nodded, or said, "Yes," or, "Yah," or something to that effect.

At that point Thealone dismissed them and they stood. But before they filed out of the room she added, "Let me emphasize one final point. It's not your job to die for John Mathius. It's your job to keep both you and him alive. He needs friends, the kind where he can close his eyes, go to sleep, and not worry that someone in the room is going to kill him. And just to be clear on all points, I'm not asking any of you ladies to fuck him."

Again, they all agreed to that. Carla wasn't sure if they were agreeing that they wouldn't kill John, or that they wouldn't fuck him, or maybe both. She'd have to think about the latter.

Again, Thealone hesitated. "I need you to do one more thing." For that one moment she seemed as unsure as the greenest recruit. "I need you . . . John needs you . . . to help him stay sane. Because if I was him . . . I'd probably be going bug-fuck nuts right now. And you people are probably the only friends he has who can keep him . . . who can keep him . . . who can keep him *him*."

23

Intransigence

"ANOTHER DETONATION, MISTRESS. It appears they've taken out another relay buoy."

"Bloody hell," Taugrim swore. "I should have anticipated that. And they're timing them with their skip-jumps. Let's get away from that relay chain. No sense in making it easy for them. And make a hard turn. Give 'em lots of signal so they can follow us."

Ships in transition were virtually blind and could detect only the strongest of transition phenomena, like the detonation of a warhead, or another ship nearby maneuvering hard, or up-transiting, or down-transiting. Thankfully they could also detect stellar masses and avoid them. On the other hand, if *Drakan Helgis* changed course in a long, slow turn, it didn't generate enough transition noise for her three pursuers to see the slow, steady change in her track, and correct their courses to match. If they didn't do something to update their data on a regular basis, they could lose their prey. But the captains of warships had long ago learned to be creative.

Eight hours later, *Drakan Helgis*'s scan tech announced, "Another down-transition, mistress. And right on schedule."

Every eight hours one of the three hunter-killers following *Drakan Helgis* down-transited in what Taugrim called a skip-jump maneuver. They decelerated hard down to about five hundred lights, then forced the down-transition, which lit up nearby space with a healthy flare and dropped them into sublight running just under one light. They released their drones to increase their scan accuracy, spent about a half hour gathering data, then pushed their sublight drive hard and up-transited again about an hour behind their comrades.

In that way they acquired accurate and up-to-date data on *Drakan Helgis*'s position and vector, but it put that one ship an hour behind the other two. They didn't make an effort to correct that, because eight hours later one of the other two took its turn at the skip-jump maneuver, and lost an hour of drive time, which dropped it back near the first ship. And when all three ships had taken their turn, they were once again clustered closely together. They then repeated the process.

The main disadvantage of the skip-jump was that they lost about one hour of drive time every day. That slowed their effective drive advantage, which meant that instead of converging with *Drakan Helgis* in three days and twenty-seven light years, it would be a little over four days and forty light-years. Another disadvantage for them was that every time they down-transited and up-transited, their transition flare gave *Drakan Helgis* an extremely good fix on their position, even while in transition. That didn't matter so much as long as they weren't within targeting range, but that would soon change.

"This is the one I want," Taugrim said, startling Nikaela.

Falkenberg had assigned her to train at Nav that shift, with John at Helm. They had raced ahead of the hunter-killers for over a day, and Nikaela couldn't stop computing and re-computing the ever narrowing gap between them. If they didn't do something to change the equation, they'd converge in another thirty light-years and start slinging warheads at each other. *Drakan Helgis* didn't stand a chance against the massed torpedoes of three hunter-killers.

Primatov stood beside Taugrim's console looking over the captain's shoulder as she pointed at something on one of her screens.

"Mistress Vreekande," Taugrim said, sounding quite pleased, "and you too, Blacksword. Take a look at this."

She uploaded an excerpt from one of the charts to Nikaela's screens. She had selected a binary star system with a main-sequence white star of two solar masses, and a white dwarf of one solar mass. The two stars danced around each other in an elliptical orbit with a period of about fifty years, and a separation that varied from eight to about forty astronomical units.

Taugrim stood. "I couldn't have asked for better. Two stars with plenty of mass, and we don't have one sucking material off the other, so we don't have to worry about a flood of nasty radiation frying our asses. And they're not far off our present vector. Nav, what have we got on planets?"

Taugrim had the data in front of her on her own screens and in her virtual vision, but Nikaela knew the woman was testing her. "There are a half dozen in stable orbits close to one or the other star, none of them habitable. Last survey reports fifteen more of varying sizes in highly eccentric, unstable orbits strongly influenced by both stars. It's quite possible some or all of those have been ejected from the system, so we can't rely on the data we have on them."

Staring at her screens, Taugrim nodded. "Very good, Mistress Vreekande. Nav, Helm, adjust our vector so we're headed for that binary system, but do it slow and easy."

She looked at Primatov standing next to her. "The gravitational gradients in that system are going to be a fucking mess. That's exactly what we need."

Primatov appeared skeptical. "That system's thirty-nine light-years out. Those hunter-killers are going to catch us long before then."

Nikaela watched Taugrim closely to see her answer. The woman grinned and winked. "I have a few tricks up my sleeve."

••••

"We're not catching them," Holverzon said. "Their maximum transition velocity gives them an advantage of a few lights."

Twelve hours into their pursuit of *Valhaukr*, Kristdokar had come to that conclusion long ago. Nygaard was accustomed to having things her way; when a member of the Executive Council gave an order, people usually jumped to comply. The women eyed the screens in front of her carefully, making no attempt to hide her displeasure with the situation. "Is there any possibility that will change, perhaps damage to their drive or something like that?"

Holverzon passed the question on to his scan tech. "Scan?"

The young man shook his head. "Nothing showing up in their emissions profile, mistress. It's possible, but unlikely."

They had begun their pursuit less than a light-hour behind *Valhaukr*. And after twelve hours the other ship had extended that separation to over two hundred light hours. The two ships were similar in size and capability, but *Valhaukr* had a slight advantage in transition velocity. *Eldekarl* would be outmatched by *Valhaukr*'s weaponry, so no one considered ordering the hunter killer to race ahead of them and intercept the cruiser.

Nygaard sighed. "It angers me to let them get away so easily, but we have no choice. Captain, let's reverse course, and please instruct *Eldekarl* to do the same."

Holverzon gave orders and a half hour later they and the hunter-killer down-transited. It would take time to reverse course. Kristdokar and Nygaard were about to leave *Konigsborge*'s bridge, when the scan tech spoke excitedly. "Captain, *Valhaukr* just down-transited."

An instant later the com tech spoke. "Captain, *Valhaukr* is hailing us. Skalde Haugrund wishes to speak with Skalde's Nygaard and Kristdokar."

Nygaard looked Kristdokar's way and their eyes met as she spoke. "Captain, Skalde Kristdokar and I will take the call in the conference room. While we do so, please remain vigilant and watch for any treachery."

••••

Two days out from Trafalgar, Faith's cabin mate approached her to propose they work out a means of accommodating each other when one of them needed the stateroom for something requiring privacy. Lea Osterman was one of Catarvin's aides, and she was in love with, and engaged to, one of her other aides. Faith didn't want to reveal anything about her own relationships, so she simply said, "Sure. Just let me know a little in advance and I can spend a couple hours in the lounge."

The young woman hesitated. "You don't have any needs . . . like that . . . yourself?"

Macus and his roommate had already worked out a similar accommodation, so Faith could always find time alone with Macus in his stateroom. She shook her head. "Not at the moment."

Osterman gave her a sly look. "What about that Chief Military Advisor of Palmutter's. You two work pretty closely together, don't you? And he's awfully good looking."

It pleased Faith to learn that so far she and Macus had managed to keep their relationship out of the rumor mill. "I prefer to avoid office relationships. With other members of the staff, I think it's best to keep it all business, no play."

They were in the lounge, and Osterman glanced over her shoulder, then leaned close and lowered her voice. "I heard Palmutter made a pass at you and you raked his balls over the coals."

Faith shrugged. "You really pay too much attention to what's in the rumor mill. Personally, I don't give much credence to that bullshit."

Faith stood. "Just let me know when you need our stateroom alone. I'm pretty flexible."

She walked out of the lounge, thinking Osterman now owed her a big favor. It was always good to have people around who owed you favors. She decided to never ask Osterman to return the favor, at least not for something as mundane as alone-time in their stateroom so she could fuck Macus or some other fellow. No, she'd let the favor build, then ask for something much more important than that. She just didn't yet know what.

Those first days out from Trafalgar she and Macus were kept quite busy attending meetings with Palmutter and Strikland, or Palmutter and Catarvin, or Palmutter and just about anyone else. Faith noticed that one or more of Strikland's security people always accompanied him. Faith and Macus didn't get any alone-time themselves, but among their peers it quickly became obvious who was fucking who. There wasn't a lot of that going on, but the few liaisons in play suffered from a slight bit of indiscretion by the parties involved, magnified by the restricted confines of Obradour's yacht. It occurred to Faith it might be wise for her and Macus to refrain from satisfying their physical needs until she understood the situation a little better.

After Macus had pointed out Strikland's interest in her, she had taken care to be a little more observant, and she now knew there was no question she could seduce him, or rather, she would succumb to his charm and he would seduce her. But if her name got into the rumor mill for fucking someone else, it could destroy any chance she might have with the man.

••••

In *Konigsborge*'s conference room, as Kristdokar sat down, Nygaard sat across from her at the large table and said, "This is going to be unpleasant."

Nygaard closed her eyes and spoke aloud for Kristdokar's benefit. "Captain, please put the call through."

Haugrund, Machtberg, and Nvalheim appeared in her vision as if seated at the table with the two of them. Haugrund openly radiated distrust. Aubrecht Machtberg greeted them with a polite nod and a pleasant smile, his left arm bandaged and cradled in a sling. The old crone Nvalheim appeared ready to chew nails and spit the pieces at them.

Nvalheim slapped a hand down on the table, startling Kristdokar. "You betray us all to these common-faces."

Machtberg snapped his head in her direction. "By the gods, Marta, at least pretend to be civil."

She spit at him, "Give me one reason why I should."

He closed his eyes and shook his head. "Because we took a chance and lost."

He turned his attention to Nygaard. "It's clear you can't catch us."

Nygaard shrugged. "It's only clear that your ship is badly damaged. Even if you can maintain your drive advantage back to Viktorkinde, there are many members of the Larscom who will be unhappy with what you've done."

Nvalheim growled, "And many who will support us."

Haugrund had yet to speak. Nygaard glanced at her briefly, but focused on Nvalheim when she said, "Your support shrinks every day. And no one supports what you did on Novalis III."

Haugrund's eyes widened, but Machtberg frowned in a thoughtful way, which Kristdokar found odd.

Nvalheim shrieked. "You can't prove anything."

Haugrund's brows narrowed, and Kristdokar wondered if she too had noticed Nvalheim hadn't denied the accusation.

Nygaard smiled unpleasantly. "The evidence mounts every day. And when we can prove your involvement, you and your accomplices in that travesty are going to take a trip to a low-gravity gallows."

Nvalheim's lips puckered. "I have nothing to fear from you."

Nygaard shook her head sadly. "As you now know, we're parked next to a chain of relay buoys that stretches back to Viktorkinde. I've been in constant contact with the other three members of the Executive Council—"

Haugrund started.

Nygaard nodded. "Yes, Dortea. There are only four of us now. We four voted unanimously to expel you from the Larscom, and we haven't selected your replacement yet."

That was news to Kristdokar, and she tried not to let the surprise show on her face.

Haugrund started to say something, but Nygaard cut her off. "And don't say we can't do that, because it's done."

A majority vote of the Larscom General Secretariat was requited to elevate one of their members to the Executive Council. And they could be removed only by death, resignation, or a two-thirds vote of the General Secretariat. Kristdokar vaguely remembered reading long ago that they could also be removed by a unanimous vote of the other four members of the Executive Council.

Haugrund did not sound at all confident as she said, "But I can appeal, and be reinstated by a two-thirds vote of the General Secretariat."

Nygaard radiated the confidence Haugrund lacked. "Dortea, do you think we're stupid enough to have removed you when we didn't have the votes to keep you removed? However, we have decided you will be given one opportunity to present your case to the remaining four members of the Executive Council, and if you can convince all four of us, unanimously, then we will endorse your reinstatement."

"We're done here," Nvalheim said, standing. "Our hunter-killers will hunt down *Drakan Helgis*, and then your breschkada will be no more."

Machtberg and Haugrund both stood, though without the bravado or the vitriol Nvalheim had shown.

"Perhaps," Nygaard said. "Then again, did you know our breschkada-sa grew up on Novalis III? If the young man can survive the annihilation of all twenty million of his countrymen, do you really think you and a few hunter-killers are enough to bring him down?"

Nygaard's words surprised Kristdokar. Only a completely irrational person would take seriously the premise that young Maestra Mathius had some sort of super-human ability to survive almost anything. But then Nvalheim was just the kind of fanatic to believe Blackswords killed with a thought.

Machtberg and Haugrund hesitated as if considering Nygaard's words carefully, while Nvalheim, for the first time, appeared doubtful. Their images winked out of existence.

Alone again with Nygaard, Kristdokar said. "They're desperate and angry."

Nygaard closed her eyes, pinching them tightly shut, bringing out faint lines of crow's feet around them. "They're frightened." She opened her eyes and sucked in a quick breath. "I'm frightened too. Aren't you?"

Kristdokar had not been prepared for such a question, and to answer truthfully she considered it carefully. "Yes. But I don't fear what they fear."

Nygaard cocked her head slightly. "Then what do you fear?"

Kristdokar needed to answer that question indirectly. "I do fear interstellar war with the Commonwealth, because with their superior numbers they'd overwhelm us and destroy us. But I don't fear that as much as you might think, because there are enough of us who understand we cannot win such a war, and I think we have a critical mass in that respect. I don't fear peace with the Commonwealth. I don't fear that they will absorb us, and we will cease to exist as an independent race and a sovereign state. I don't fear that our customs and ethos will be lost. We're too strong for that. Don't get me wrong. Unfettered interaction with the Commonwealth will change us, but not in ways that really count. In fact, I think we'll change them more than they change us."

The strain in the muscles around Nygaard's eyes seemed to soften, as if Kristdokar's words had affected her in some positive way. "Now I know what you don't fear. Tell me what you do fear."

Kristdokar didn't have to think carefully to answer that. "Assuming we're smart enough to avoid an interstellar war in which we're outgunned ten to one, we are our own greatest enemy, and I fear we will tear ourselves apart from within."

Nygaard smiled, and where a moment earlier she appeared lost in fearful introspection, now she perked up. "Then you and I must make sure that doesn't happen."

Kristdokar returned to her cabin. She opened a communication she had received from Fran Thealone earlier that morning. It had been sent shortly before the diplomatic mission left Viktorkinde, and ferried to the terminus of their relay chain by the Commonwealth hunter-killer *Lightspear*. She reread it carefully. By now the diplomatic mission from Trafalgar was well on its way. She was almost thankful the rogue hunter-killers had broken the relay chain, thankful she didn't have to report they had lost the breschkada. If Colonel Primatov and young Ensign Mathius were now dead, she hoped their Commonwealth comrades could put that aside, and not retaliate with interstellar war.

24

A Sordid Request

BIGSHOTS LIKE PALMUTTER and Strikland had been assigned spacious suites on *Lady Victorious*. Palmutter's suite included a bedroom, a small lounge, and a private office, which was probably typical for all the senior members of the mission. It occurred to Faith that Catarvin could probably do without a separate suite of her own, since she spent most nights in Palmutter's bed. Interestingly enough, their relationship had not leaked into the rumor mill.

Faith knocked on the door to Palmutter's suite, and her implants responded in his voice, *Come in, Faith. I'm in the office.*

She opened the door and stepped into the lounge that was part of his suite. On the other side of the room, she saw two doors, one open and one closed. She crossed the room, and through the open door saw Palmutter seated behind a small desk. He pointed to a chair in front of it. "Sit down and relax."

Faith sat down, and noticed Palmutter checking out her legs as she crossed them. She didn't mind men like Strikland taking notice of her attributes, because he did everything carefully and discreetly, whereas Palmutter had obviously just spread her legs with his eyes. She took great care to make sure he didn't know she had caught him look-fucking her. She had put him in his place once, and from that they had developed a good working relationship. If she called him out every time he did that, that kind of friction on an on-going basis would only sour their rapport. He knew damn well to keep his hands off, so she didn't begrudge him his lascivious little glances, and could pretend she didn't notice.

They were about to issue a press release, and Faith had come prepared for a working session to massage its wording. "I assume you wanted to see me regarding the press release. I've made a few changes to the last draft."

She went into detail on the changes she had made, but Palmutter's mind seemed to be elsewhere. He and Catarvin sometimes boffed a quickie in the afternoon, and his thoughts had probably gone to something like that. The man was utterly predictable.

"Yes, yes," he said. "I think that all sounds excellent. That'll work just fine."

Yes, his mind was definitely not on work. Faith started to rise out of the chair. "Well, if there's nothing else then—"

He stopped her. "No, no, stay seated."

She lowered her butt back into the chair and relaxed. He stood, and came around from behind the desk. "Lawrence Strikland, as you know, is an important man."

Faith wondered why Palmutter had chosen to bring up Strikland at that moment. In Palmutter's limited view, the only thing that made Strikland important was his money, and how much he donated to Palmutter's reelection fund.

"Yes, sir," she said. "He certainly is."

Palmutter walked around behind her, which always made her uncomfortable. If he were true to form, the only reason he walked behind her was to look over her shoulder and get a good view down her blouse. To follow him she would have to twist her head about to an impossible angle, so she didn't bother.

"He's an invaluable addition to this diplomatic mission."

Faith had yet to see how Strikland might contribute anything other than money. "Yes, sir, I have no doubt of that."

Palmutter completed the circuit of her chair and stopped in front of her. "I've tried to gain further insight into his thinking. He asked about you, you know?"

Now that was an odd thing to say. "He did, did he?"

Palmutter leaned back and rested his butt against the front of his desk. "Yes, he did. He was concerned he'd done something to offend you because he felt you were . . . avoiding him."

With Strikland, Faith had taken care to be all business, though she had been careful to not go too far. She didn't want him to feel slighted, or think of her as uncomfortable in his presence, but coming on to him in an overt way would likely have the opposite effect she hoped for. And Palmutter had just confirmed her strategy was working nicely. Strikland was just the kind of man to find her indifference all the more intriguing.

Palmutter gave her a smarmy smile. "When he pays attention to you, I think you should be a little more . . . receptive to him. Perhaps even encourage him."

Faith's thoughts came to a grinding halt.

Palmutter's eyes widened just a little. "I can see you . . . understand me. Gaining some insight into his inner thinking could be extremely helpful to me . . . and I would be very grateful for that."

Faith struggled to keep her anger from showing. "Gain insight?"

Palmutter pushed off from his perch on the edge of the desk and leaned over her, his excitement obvious. "If you . . . nurtured a close relationship with him, as your relationship developed, it might naturally become . . . very close. And when you . . .

found yourself alone with him, you could probe his thinking on certain matters, especially if your relationship grew . . . intimate."

Faith's anger had turned to fury, but she clamped down on that hard. "And what matters would I probe him on, sir?"

Palmutter tried to look innocent, but came off more like a guilty school boy caught masturbating. "I don't have anything specific in mind at the moment. But once your relationship with Strikland becomes . . . extremely close . . . well, I could give you more specifics, and while you're alone together . . . you could try to gain some insight into his thinking, catch him at a . . . vulnerable moment, as it were. It would help me greatly if you could help me understand him better. And of course, I would be most grateful, and that could open many more doors for your own career advancement."

Faith nodded politely and managed not to stand up and kick the asshole in the balls. Outwardly she remained calm, but inside she wanted to scream.

••••

Life in a cell, just plain boring. After three more days in the concrete cell, Anders had developed a routine. Based on his own experience, he knew from the beginning he'd have to find some way of killing time. He could use his implants to zone out on stim-sleep, but too much of that might produce nasty side effects. He didn't have anything to read, and considered pounding on the door to ask for a deck of cards, or something, anything. But someone decided to show him some kindness, and they gave him a small terminal about the size of both of his hands laid side by side. It had very limited read-only access.

Each morning he awoke, exercised for about an hour, then bathed at the sink, and a short time later they brought him breakfast. Then he used the terminal to check the news feeds and watch some vids, or read a novel from the library. The Sarkovites had a weird idea of fiction. With plenty of time to kill, he exercised again in the afternoon, bathed again at the sink, ate dinner, watched some vids, then went to bed early.

The bad-guys in many of the Sarkovie stories were frequently guilty of trying to deny a young man or woman the right to prostitute themselves, if they chose. And then there were assholes who tried to exploit them as prostitutes, and take their profits from them. Apparently, when they had established their independence, the Sarkovites had hard coded into their constitution the inalienable right to be a prostitute, and to enjoy the profits of one's labors, without exploitation. And in the stories, anyone who tried to force someone else to be a prostitute, or who tried to force them to not be a prostitute, always suffered an unpleasant demise.

On his fourth day in the cell, he had just finished breakfast when the door to his concrete box opened, and in walked the woman with bright red irises and dark hair.

She had his makeshift pack tucked under one arm. Behind her the fellow with the goatee stepped into the room, but this time he appeared unarmed. The fellow hadn't made him stand against the far wall before he and the woman entered, and Anders wasn't sure what to make of their change in security procedures.

Anders started to rise but the woman waved him back down. "No, finish your breakfast."

He dropped his butt into his chair.

She sat down opposite him and placed the pack on the table between them. "I have a couple more questions; in fact, just two. First, no one on *Sycorax* but me knew the location of this address. How did you find us?"

He shook his head. "For about a year now I've shipped stuff to this address and three others here on Sarkovie. Fill an address into a shipping form enough times and it does stick with you."

She smiled. "I thought it must be something like that."

She seemed nice, didn't exhibit the sharp edges that hatred had sculpted into the psyches of so many of their colleagues, and he felt a twinge of sadness that she and he must be enemies. Eventually he must betray her, or she might unmask him and put a bullet in the back of his head. "You said two questions. What's the other one?"

"Why didn't they send you down here with me? Why keep you up there on *Sycorax*?"

Anders shook his head tiredly. "If you really want to know the answer to that, you're going to have to ask them, if there are any survivors who aren't in custody. My guess is the breschkada. Mistress Vreekande was my subordinate on Novalis III."

Her eyes widened at that, and he continued. "We were friends of a sort, not intimate, just acquaintances. Maybe they thought my presence would help when they interrogated the two of them." He wasn't about to tell them that Eskildsen seemed to hope he'd do something rash and rid them of the two young people.

"That adds up," she said. "I knew you were on Novalis III, and I had heard the Vreekande girl was there as well, but I didn't realize you were there together."

He thought it wouldn't hurt to tell them a little of the truth. He shrugged. "She felt sorry for me. Even looked me up when they paroled me, approached me outside my apartment and apologized. I think she thought it was unfair they convicted me and not her. Stupid young girl!"

He decided to press the woman a little. "So where does this leave me?"

She shrugged. "I was given a full dossier on you before I left Viktorkinde, and your superiors there thought highly of you."

"So, am I allowed out of this cell now?"

"Yes," she said. "We've got a room upstairs you can take until you find something better. But don't go more than a few kilometers from this building without letting me know."

"I'm on probation, eh?"

"Exactly," she said. "At least until we have a chance to check out your story. I'm not sure why Viktorkinde sent you here. We don't really need your help."

Anders knew why they had sent him. "I think they just wanted me on *Sycorax* with the breschkada. But why don't you show me the ropes, and I'll help where I can."

She stood. "I'm Tia Lorenson." She nodded toward the fellow with the goatee standing near the door. "That's Torsten Hohlman. Welcome to Sarkovie, Maestra Eindride."

••••

Four days out from Trafalgar Macus's implants chimed with an urgent message from Faith. *I need to speak with you alone, immediately.*

What's wrong?

He wants me to fuck Strikland.

Who wants you to fuck Strikland?

Palmutter. He wants me to be his whore. He wants me to fuck Strikland and feed what I learn to him. Where can we meet, now?

Macus decided it was even more imperative he not be seen entering Faith's stateroom to be alone with her. *Meet me in the lounge.*

That's too public.

I have my reasons. We'll talk over a secure link.

Macus found a small table in the lounge, ordered a couple of drinks, and a few minutes later Faith walked into the room. Every heterosexual male there glanced her way for at least a brief instant, which confirmed Macus's resolve. As she crossed the room to join him, he put a small access terminal on the table and turned it on. She stopped nearby, standing over him. She had a pleasant smile on her face, but he knew her well enough, and saw by little signs that she was absolutely livid.

He kept his voice low. "Sit down next to me, and look at the terminal in front of us. You and I are busy working together for the senator's benefit, and we're going to be so focused on that screen that no one will feel comfortable interrupting us."

Curiosity replaced the strain in the look on her face, and her eyes narrowed. He watched her get a grip on herself and calm down, then she sat down next to him, focused her eyes on the terminal, and opened a secure link between their implants.

You start, she said. *Why all the drama?*

He looked at her and smiled, then for show, pointed at a blob of nothing on the screen in front of them. *First, you tell me who on this ship is fucking who.*

She frowned and gave him a curious look, then shrugged. *Well, my roommate's fucking her fiancé.*

Who else?

She rattled off a short list of names, none of which were news to Macus. When she finished, he said, *How do you know all this?*

She gave him a sharp look. *You know the answer to that as well as me. The rumor mill, the same way I learned about all the rest, though I knew about my roommate because she's my roommate.*

Exactly, he said. *But I knew about your roommate and her fiancé because they're in the rumor mill as well. Don't you find it interesting we know Palmutter is fucking Catarvin, and yet that's not in the rumor mill? Whereas, when it comes to staffers fucking each other, everyone knows all about it.*

She leaned back, and he saw her thoughts racing. He let her chew on that for several seconds, then he continued. *There's no grand conspiracy here. We're in a closed environment, and staffers don't have the wherewithal to keep their indiscretions from leaking out, but the bigshots do. So what does that tell you?*

To any passerby she appeared to be looking at the screen, but Macus saw that her eyes were focused in a thousand-yard stare, while she nodded her head slowly up and down. *It tells me I can fuck Strikland and get away with it, but you and I have to be careful regarding our relationship, at least until we know more.*

He leaned back and met her eyes. *So Palmutter asked you to be his little spy girl, fuck Strikland, and feed what you learn to him?*

Yah. Apparently Strikland asked him a few questions about me, was discreet, but Palmutter concluded he was interested.

And it really pissed you off Palmutter wants you to whore yourself out for him?

Yah.

Macus gave her a big smile. *I think I know how you can get even with Palmutter.*

She smiled back at him. *I'm listening.*

Macus shrugged. *Do exactly what he asked you to do, and what we had planned you would do anyway: fuck Strikland, and mine him for info. Then we'll feed Palmutter a subtly modified, but incorrect version of that information. We'll have to do it in such a way we can use the information to our benefit. Then when Palmutter plays his hand, he'll look like a jackass. Or better yet, he steps on a real big pile of nasty legal shit.*

Faith sat without moving, staring at the terminal screen for several seconds, her head nodding slowly up and down. Then she abruptly stood, turned to face Macus, smiled and leaned down close to him. She stopped using the link between their implants and spoke, but kept her voice to a faint whisper. "When we finally figure out how you and I can be alone, I'm going to make you a very happy man."

Macus felt an erection coming on.

She turned and walked out of the room, and again every heterosexual man glanced her way, even if only briefly. One young woman did as well, and Macus thought the look she gave Faith was much like that of a man undressing a woman with his eyes. He decided to check up on her. Maybe he could use that to some advantage.

25

A Kelk Invitation

KRISTDOKAR WATCHED THE virtual image of Skalde Supreme Dornmier pour virtual tea into virtual cups placed on the table in front of Skalde of the Supremacy Veskarson and Vice Skalde Tiegnordan. A second later Nygaard poured real tea into the cup in front of Kristdokar. A wisp of steam wafted upward from the cup as the vice skalde then poured tea in her own cup. Once Dornmier and Nygaard were seated, all five of them reached forward, lifted their cups and sipped.

Two days ago, when *Konigsborge* had returned to the relay chain from the confrontation with *Valhaukr*, Nygaard had sent a carefully worded report to the Executive Council. They had remained silent on the matter until that morning, and then Nygaard informed Kristdokar she would sit in on a special meeting of the Council.

By custom, the second most senior of the councilmembers chaired meetings of the Council. Hence, it was Veskarson who spoke first. "This is not an official meeting of the Council, and as such no records will be kept. And in the interest of expediency, we're also waving other formalities."

That was a polite way of saying Kristdokar would not be required to *stand* before the Council.

Veskarson glanced back and forth between Nygaard and Kristdokar as he spoke. "We have cleared all traffic from the space lanes near the relay chain, so if you encounter another ship, and you haven't received prior warning to expect it, assume it is a rogue, and be prepared to defend yourselves."

Nygaard pursed her lips. "We've operated under a rather paranoid set of assumptions for some time now, so we'll continue with that."

Veskarson smiled. "We had hoped to send an armed escort for your protection, and had selected a couple of ships for the task. But given the rogue attack by *Valhaukr*, we decided to take a closer look at them before doing so. We're having trouble finding ships we can be confident will actually protect you."

"Really!" Nygaard said. "What's been the difficulty?"

Kristdokar thought she might already know the answer to that question, but decided to remain silent and just listen.

Veskarson looked toward Tiegnordan. "Vice Skalde Tiegnordan is heading up that effort. I'm confident she can answer your question better than I."

Tiegnordan did not look happy. "We've never before vetted crews based on their attitude toward . . . the Commonwealth. In many ships I literally need to replace half the crew."

Nygaard looked at Kristdokar. "Vice Skalde Kristdokar appears to have been quite successful with *Drakan Helgis*. Perhaps you can offer some advice."

Tiegnordan's eyes hardened as she looked at Kristdokar. Did Nygaard understand the untenable shit she had just dumped on Kristdokar's shoulders? Kristdokar now needed to appease Tiegnordan's ego.

"I had a significant advantage over Vice Skalde Tiegnordan. I was not under time pressure, and was able to take almost an entire year to make adjustments in *Drakan Helgis*'s crew."

The look on Tiegnordan's face softened. "Any guidance you can offer will be appreciated."

Kristdokar spoke carefully. "It took some trial and error, but I noticed that if I found a ship whose captain and XO were already open-minded regarding our new allies, and if they had been in command of that ship for more than a year, most of their senior crew reflected their attitudes. At that point I reassigned a few NCOs and junior officers, and didn't worry about the enlisted personnel. I think it's not coincidental every one of the assassination attempts on *Konigsborge* was led by either a senior NCO or an officer."

They discussed the situation for a good hour, and during that time Tiegnordan's attitude toward Kristdokar eased considerably. They ended the meeting with a caution from Dornmier. "We'll expedite assembling an escort, but until then, remember you cannot trust any ship you encounter along the relay chain."

••••

One of the difficulties of top-secret need-to-know was remembering to whom you told something, and to whom you didn't tell it. Fran kept meticulous notes on all her conversations, revelations, and discussions, but it still got complicated. Jenine Catarvin's alternate persona was an easy one: only Fran, Primatov, and Gascoigne were privy to that secret. But that wasn't really an officially classified piece of information. It was just their sneaky, little subterfuge.

Fran had revealed certain information to the troika of Chemina, Forester and Nigurski, but that was complicated by bits she had disclosed to each of the three, but not to the others. And then there was Jenine Catarvin, Mani Gascoigne, Tarsik

Obradour, and Katrine Primatov. That's where it got rather complicated. Thankfully, her interactions so far with Palmutter had all been in larger groups where no classified information was discussed. Strangely enough, disclosing classified information was not a lie, but it felt a lot like being a pathological liar. At a certain point, it became hard to remember which lies you told, and which you didn't, and to whom you told them, and to whom you didn't.

Fran's implants chimed with a message from her AI secretary. *Senator Gascoigne and Mr. Obradour are ready for your call now.* She dearly wished she could have brought her real secretary.

Fran said, *Connect me.*

Gascoigne and Obradour appeared in her vision as if seated across a table from her. As always, Obradour began with a polite greeting to which Fran would have to respond with something equally polite and meaningless.

Fran decided not to play along. "Gentlemen, we have a problem."

Her abruptness startled both of them, and they waited for her to say more. "I haven't heard anything from Primatov or Kristdokar in several days now. There was a lack of response in the beginning, but that ended rather quickly. After that I received a couple of reports from each of them, though delayed by the gap between the two relay chains, but still spaced in a predictable fashion. Then they went silent, and now they're both long overdue. I have to believe something has happened."

Both men sat in silence for several seconds, then Obradour leaned forward and spoke. "In her reports, Colonel Primatov told us the Kelk have the same problems we have with dogmatic hard-liners. Do you think their hawks might have interfered in some way?"

Fran drummed her fingers on the table in front of her. "Your guess is as good as mine."

Gascoigne asked, "When did you get the last report?"

"Four days ago, one each from Primatov and Kristdokar."

Of the two men, Fran's news had clearly disturbed Obradour more than Gascoigne. The little financier shook his head side to side, as if denying reality. "How many reports would you have expected to receive by now?"

"Something from each of them about every two days. They've both missed two reporting cycles."

Obradour had always seemed unshakeable, but now he made no attempt to hide his distrust. "Should we cancel this mission?"

Gascoigne shook his head vehemently. "We have nothing to gain, and everything to lose by a knee-jerk reaction. Let's stay the course, and if we haven't heard anything by the time we cross the gap and reach the terminus of Viktorkinde's relay chain, we'll revisit the issue before entering sovereign Supremacy space."

Fran had to make the two civilians see the military aspects of the situation. "I should warn the captains of our ships, including Commander Neilosse of *Lightspear*. Something's not right, and they need to be extra vigilant."

"Agreed," Gascoigne said.

Obradour signaled his agreement by nodding his head once.

Fran would have to swear the COs of their ships to silence, though each would want to brief his or her XO as well. Another subset of information carefully revealed to a small group of people. She'd have to make note of that.

••••

"Up transition, mistress," the scan tech said, her voice cracking with tension. "They're a thousand light-hours behind us."

Nikaela tried to calm the flutter of fear in her gut. Four days of running, four days standing watch with the three hunter-killers following them, four days constantly recomputing when the three would catch up to them. The numbers always came out the same: they now had about three hours before the shooting started. Four days eating and sleeping, though sleep didn't come easy now. She had resorted to using her implants to induce stim-sleep. The medical people warned them stim-sleep had its own side-effects if used on an ongoing basis for more than a few nights.

She had tried killing time by working out in the gym, but everyone else had the same idea and the place was always crowded. She spent more time standing and waiting for the equipment to be free, than actually using it. To get some sort of reasonable exercise, she had resorted to doing simple calisthenics in her stateroom each morning before showering.

In other times of such stress, she had sometimes used a lover to help her pass the hours, and she considered taking one now from among the crew. A couple of the younger crewmen closer to her age had given her the impression they might be open to her advances, if she chose to initiate something. The thought of John Mathius flashed briefly through her mind, but she rejected that in an instant. Taking a common-face as a lover; she and he would become the hottest subject grinding through the ship's gossip-mill. And since they were breschkada, it would be even worse.

Seated at the nav console, Nikaela watched Taugrim stare at her screens, her eyes narrow and pinched with thought. After several seconds the captain looked up and scanned the bridge.

"Mistress Vreekande," she said, "and Maestra Blacksword, please come here."

Seated at the helm, John stood at the same instant as Nikaela. Primatov occupied one of the seats at Fire Control. She didn't look up from her screens as Nikaela and

John edged their way between the instrument clusters. They arrived on opposite sides of Taugrim's Command Console at almost the same moment.

After the customary hazing for a newly commissioned junior officer, Taugrim had taken her role as a mentor quite seriously, and almost everything turned into a lesson for Nikaela and John. The captain pointed to the developing situation on one of her screens. "Notice how they're now amassed. That was the last skip-jump they'll make. Did you see how they adjusted their velocities and timings so they could come at us with their strength combined? If they hadn't, they would have had to make an extra skip-jump, and one of them would be an hour behind the other two."

Taugrim looked Nikaela's way for a response and she nodded. "Yes, mistress. I did see that."

The captain looked at John, and his eyes narrowed thoughtfully. "I noticed they tweaked their timing, but I didn't understand why . . . not until now. They're going to come for us now, aren't they, mistress?"

She grinned and nodded. "Very good, Blacksword. We've got about three hours. During that time they'll move slowly to spread out and put a little space between them. They don't want to give us an easy target. And to move off our present vector enough to elude them during that time, we'd have to maneuver hard, and they'd detect that, defeating the whole purpose of maneuvering."

Taugrim looked away from John and Nikaela, and barked orders. "Nav, Helm, shift our vector, and do it slowly so they can't detect it."

At the questioning look Nikaela gave her, Taugrim smiled. "We're still going to maneuver, and do it slowly so they won't know exactly where we are. When they're within range, they'll force a crash stop and down-transit, do a quick re-compute on our position, get a targeting solution, and nail us."

She looked at John and gave him a cheesy grin.

John grinned back at her and said, "But I'll bet you're not going to let them get away with that, are you . . . mistress?"

She maintained the grin as she nodded. "I like a man with brains. Perhaps I'll take you as a lover."

It was an old tease women sometimes threw at men to make them uncomfortable, or conversely, to begin the negotiations for an intimate relationship. None of the other Kelk on the bridge paid the slightest bit of attention to Taugrim's quip. But behind John, Nikaela saw Primatov cock her head slightly at the captain's words. She probably didn't understand it was a common joke. At least Nikaela hoped it was a joke.

On Reisenar, Nikaela had said the same thing purely as a jest to tease John, and he had become quite flustered. An outright rejection would be an unpardonable insult, but a Kelk man could indicate his lack of interest by ignoring the remark, or saying something like, "Perhaps another time." On the other hand, if he wanted to know if the woman was serious, he might say, "And perhaps I'll let you." At that point they could both let the relationship progress from there. But John proved he wasn't Kelk by morphing his grin into a pleasant smile. He looked Taugrim up and down carefully, as if considering her proposition, then finished by looking her in the eyes and raising one eyebrow. Nikaela couldn't tell if he meant it as a question, or an invitation, and it bothered her that he didn't react with some aversion to the idea.

Taugrim barked out a laugh. "Fire Control," she said, her eyes still locked with John's. "What's our stock of big warheads like?"

The Fire Control officer must have known she would ask that, because he responded without taking a moment to consult his inventory. "We've got two we can dial up as high as one gigaton, and four we can push to half that, maybe a little better."

Taugrim broke eye contact with John, pointed to her screens and looked at Nikaela. "If they haven't already done so, our friends out there are going to spread out. They'll want to make it hard for us, make sure we can't track their movements, so they'll move slowly, no hard, fast maneuvering. But their transition wakes are still a couple of light-hours wide. All we have to do is slow them down, buy us time to get to that binary. And we don't need a direct hit for that."

Taugrim turned her attention back to John, and slowly examined him from head to foot, as if anticipating a pleasant meal. He didn't flinch and met her eyes squarely, but Nikaela thought she knew him well enough to see his discomfort in the strain around his eyes.

Nikaela started when Taugrim snapped out, "Back to your stations, you two. And watch closely. You'll learn a thing or two."

As Nikaela returned to the Nav console she noticed Primatov watching John carefully. He returned to the helm, sat down and focused on his screens.

"Okay, helm," Taugrim said. "Put us into a zig-zag pattern, but keep the turns light and sweet. I don't want them tracking us. Fire Control, arm those warheads and set them to trigger when they encounter a strong transition wake."

Taugrim must have seen the curious look on Nikaela's face, because she looked her in the eyes as she barked out orders. "We're not going to launch them. We're going to release them like mines, and the zig-zag pattern helps us spread them out. Disrupt their transition wake hard enough, and it'll ripple right back to the ship."

She looked away from Nikaela toward Fire Control. "And set those warheads to detonate after one hour regardless." She grinned, which seemed to be her favorite expression. "Bad form to leave several gigatons armed and floating about in a busy shipping lane."

26

A Change of Strategy

"NUMBER ONE IS clear," Primatov said as they ejected the first of the big warheads. Hearing her voice reminded John she manned one of the stations at Fire Control. But he was on a Kelk ship. They might not say *manned*. Would they say she womanned a station?

John did a quick mental calculation. Racing toward them at close to four thousand lights, the three hunter-killers would catch up to the warhead in a quarter of an hour. He took a few seconds to calculate the delay more accurately, then set a timer in the corner of one of his screens. He tried not to think of Taugrim's joke about taking him as a lover. At least he hoped it was a joke.

"Number two is away."

That day Taugrim had chosen to have white hair with dark streaks in it. She was actually quite good-looking, trim, athletic, nice figure, pretty face, though she did seem to foster a look more toward the demonic side of Kelk appearances. But the last thing he wanted to do was have an affair with that woman. On the other hand, he feared his life might become rather difficult if he displayed open distaste at the thought of such a liaison. He had tried to play it neutral, but against Taugrim, he was damn well out of his league. It occurred to him that if he did take her up on the offer, he'd probably wake up sore all over the next morning.

"Number three away."

The timer John had set pinged. Their enemy had passed the first warhead without difficulty. He tried to suppress his disappointment as he set another timer for the second warhead. At the moment he didn't have any real responsibilities as a helmsman. Seated next to him, Dahlborg handled the complex maneuver of the zig-zag pattern.

"Number four away."

John recalled that Nikaela had teased him the same way on Reisenar. Was it a common joke among them? Or did they just bait poor Commonwealth schmucks that way? He glanced surreptitiously around the bridge. No one paid him the least bit of attention. Had they shrugged off Taugrim's proposition—joke—whatever—with complete indifference?

"Detonation," the scan tech said. "Yield strength six hundred megatons."

Seated next to her at the scan console, her crewmate said, "And I picked up a down-transition flare. A big one, clearly forced."

Taugrim fist pumped and said, "Got 'em."

The scan tech said, "Another flare."

"Yah," Taugrim said, flashing a mouth full of white teeth. "They don't want to continue without their comrade. Don't want to take us on without all three of them on hand."

"Another flare," the scan tech said. "All three are down."

Taugrim nodded while staring at her screens, her eyes bright and alive. "That just bought us the time we needed. Helm, Nav, I want a course straight for that binary system."

••••

A pencil skirt that ended just above the knee, a tasteful blouse that exposed her long neck but no cleavage, and a form-fitting sport coat that would emphasize her figure nicely, Faith chose her outfit carefully. To seduce a man like Strikland, she needed to look attractive, a little bit sexy, but business-like. She put on everything but the sport coat and applied her makeup carefully, then donned the coat, grabbed a small access terminal, and walked out of her stateroom.

She took the lift up two decks, then walked down a narrow passageway and stopped at the door to Strikland's suite. She knocked, and he didn't respond immediately through her implants. She waited a few seconds, and was about to knock again, when the door opened and Strikland stood in the doorway. Good! Instead of telling her through her implants to enter, he had come to the door to greet her.

"Miss Carlton," he said, smiling. Unlike Palmutter, there were no surreptitious looks at her breasts, no examining her from head to foot like some piece of meat, or some prostitute he wanted to fuck. "Come in. Come in. I'm glad you could make time for me."

He stepped aside and she walked into the lounge that was part of his suite. Like Palmutter's suite, a door on the opposite side of the room led into the bedroom, and another into the office. Faith knew that a third door connected the bedroom directly to the office.

One of Strikland's bodyguards stood nearby. Strikland turned to the fellow and said, "Since it's late afternoon, we'll probably work through dinner and into the evening. You're free for the rest of the day."

That was exactly what Faith wanted to hear.

Once they were alone, Strikland indicated his office door with a wave of his hand. She walked in, stopped near his desk and turned to face him. "You said you wanted to review some of the senator's staff." She held up the small access terminal. "I have complete personnel files on all his staffers here."

"Excellent," he said. "I was allowed to bring only the most limited staff, so Silas has offered to lend me a little time from some of his people."

Faith thought it interesting that he had filled his quota of staff exclusively with four bodyguards.

"Would you like a drink?" he asked, indicating a small wet bar.

She smiled. "Thank you. Just water, please." It was imperative that she come across as all business.

For the next hour Strikland didn't make a single move that wasn't both proper and professional. They reviewed most of Palmutter's staff, and he had a number of questions about each of them. When they got to Macus, Strikland said, "You and Mr. DeLeon work together quite a bit, don't you?"

Faith wondered if he was getting at something. "Yes, we're two of the senator's most senior staffers."

He grinned at her in a way that felt intimate. "Silas is a bit of a handful at times, isn't he?"

Faith didn't want to take that bait. "He has his difficult moments, but any man in his position would."

They moved on to discuss each of the senior members of the diplomatic mission. Strikland didn't say anything overt, but it was quite clear Palmutter's well-known relationship with Catarvin bothered him. That, and a number of subtle comments he made, gave Faith the distinct impression he had some doubts about Palmutter.

At one point they were seated side-by-side at a small table in his office. He had leaned back, with the terminal held in his left hand while concentrating on it intently. He let his right hand absentmindedly drop, and it landed on Faith's thigh.

She had thought carefully what she would do at that moment, and had decided she should react, but not over react. "Oh," she said.

He started as if surprised and said, "Oh, I'm terribly sorry, Miss Carlton."

His spoke with such sincerity, she could only say, "Think nothing of it. It was an accident."

He stood, and she stood to face him. "A beautiful young woman like you, you must have to deal with little subterfuges like that from men all the time?"

She shrugged. "It does happen."

He raised an eyebrow. "In Silas's office I'll bet it happens more often than you'd like."

There it was again, another little crack at Palmutter. He had made several references like that.

In that moment, Faith's thoughts were so focused on his obvious doubts about the senator, that she wasn't prepared when he put his arm around her waist, pulled her against him, and kissed her. He surprised her so much she responded stiffly at first, and then she understood it was time for a change of strategy. If she played this right, she could milk his doubts about Palmutter to the limit.

She melted against him. He was, after all, a handsome, distinguished older man, and she could enjoy him like any other. But her new strategy meant she must not allow anything more to happen that night.

She put the palms of her hands against his chest and pushed him away, and like a gentleman he didn't resist. "No," she said, rather pleased at how she managed to sound just like a reluctant virgin. "No, we can't do this."

He shook his head. "I can see that you're attracted to me. And I've kissed a few women in my time, and you clearly enjoyed that."

She put her hands over her ears and shook her head. "No, we can't, there's too much in the way."

"In the way?" he asked. "What's in the way?"

She took her hands off her ears and looked into his eyes. She even managed to come up with a faint glistening of tears in her eyes, and hoped she wasn't overdoing it. "Nothing," she said. "It's nothing. I can't talk about it."

She slipped past and around him, moving so quickly she caught him off guard. Earlier she had thrown her coat over the back of a chair, and as she marched out of the room she grabbed it without stopping. She moved so quickly she made it to the outer door of the lounge, and had it open before he caught up with her.

She had stepped out into the corridor outside, but he gripped the edge of the door, preventing her from closing it.

"What is it?" he demanded. "There's something you're not telling me."

She looked into his eyes for a long moment, as if she were about to tell him a dark secret. Then she shook her head, turned, and marched up the hallway.

As a last little touch, she had purposefully left the access terminal in his office. He would interpret that as a sign of how deeply distressed she had been, and he would want to know what had upset her so.

••••

Carla's first impression of Fran Thealone was that she was a raving bitch. But after the briefing on what they had done to John, she sympathized with the woman's frustration and anger. Five days after leaving Trafalgar she and May Forester received orders to report to Thealone's office in midafternoon. They found the door open, with Thealone seated at a small table in a surprisingly small office. *Hellfire* was a big ship, with a compliment of more than a thousand officers and crew, and Carla would have thought *the* Blacksword would warrant something more spacious.

Forester knocked on the open door. She and Carla both announced themselves using the standard formula, saluted, and received a crisp, sharp salute in return. Carla had come to understand Fran Thealone did nothing in a sloppy or offhand fashion.

Thealone pointed to a couple of chairs at the small table. "At ease, ladies. Come in, sit down, and relax."

Thealone gave them a few seconds to get comfortable. "I'm going to conference in Karya Chemina."

At the mention of that name Forester started and her eyes widened. "Ma'am, aren't we too far out to communicate with Trafalgar."

Thealone smiled. "She's not on Trafalgar."

She looked pointedly at Carla. "As you know, Lieutenant Forester was Ensign Mathius's roommate at O-School. Miss Chemina is a close friend of Lieutenant Forester's. Ensign Mathius met her through Miss Forester, and the three of them became good friends. Miss Chemina is a news hype." Thealone leaned back in her chair, and now aimed her remarks at both Carla and Forester. "She's covering the mission for one of the feeds, and she's on board *Lady Victorious* because I put her there. I also gave Miss Chemina the same briefing I gave you two on the assassination attempt on Ensign Mathius."

Thealone smiled and her eyebrows rose. "When she saw the images of what they did to him, I think she was even more pissed-off than you two."

As far as Carla was concerned, the balls thing was still in play, so she tried to keep her thoughts neutral.

Thealone set up the conference call, and in Carla's virtual vision a young woman appeared seated across the table from them. She had light-brown hair cut several inches below her shoulders.

Thealone said, "Thank you for joining us, Miss Chemina."

Chemina nodded. "Happy to, Colonel."

She looked at Forester. "Hello, May."

Forester simply nodded, and Carla thought she now understood the relationship between the two women.

Chemina said to Carla. "You must be Carla Nigurski. John mentioned you a few times."

Carla kept it simple. "Nice to meet you."

Thealone took over. "We're running parallel to a chain of relay buoys, with a hunter-killer driving ahead of us and down-transiting to communicate through them.

Through the hunter-killer and those buoys we are in almost constant contact with Trafalgar. Before we left Trafalgar I contacted ComSec Investigative Services and asked them to run full security checks on the three of you,"—she looked at Carla—"and your comrades from Miriteen. I've now received those results and I'm upping the security clearances of you three to Top Secret. I'm also uploading to your implants guidelines and strictures regarding that. Read through them carefully. It's basically a lot of legal bullshit, but it means that if you violate any of those strictures or regulations, you're going to do a lot of prison time."

It occurred to Carla she might need to resurrect the raving-bitch opinion.

Thealone looked pointedly at May and Carla. "I'm bumping you two because, for various reasons, you're closer to John than the rest of your squad, you're the ranking officer and non-com, and this is all highly classified and need-to-know. If, at a later time, I need to elevate the status of any of your squad mates, I'll do so on a case-by-case basis. So be very careful what you say to any of them about this. At this time, they're not cleared for any of this information."

She turned her attention to Chemina. "I'm bumping you because you're on *Lady Victorious* and I may need your assistance on a few things."

Chemina gave her a dubious look, but didn't say anything.

Thealone continued. "Everything you hear in this room today, including the existence of that relay chain, is Top Secret. When I'm done here, one of my people will take over, brief you carefully on your responsibilities when handling classified information, and answer any questions you might have. Everyone with me so far?"

She looked at each of them one at a time, and required each to respond to that question verbally before moving on. "Good," she said, then she leaned back in her chair and steepled her fingers in front of her. "The first thing we're going to discuss is how twenty million people were murdered on Novalis III."

Over the next hour Carla heard a story of how mutual hatred and simple greed had helped mortal enemies overcome their shared antipathy. Thealone told them of Primatov's forensic investigation into the tragedy on Novalis III, and the slim, but telling, evidence she had gathered. Carla and the other two young women learned of Prime Minister Benkamil's duplicity in the incident on Reisenar, and she noticed how Thealone seemed unable to hide her distaste when she mentioned the man's name. They had lost good ComSecCorps people because of the bastard's double-dealing. And Carla now recalled with some satisfaction that a few months after the incident there, Benkamil had died in some sort of transport accident.

Thealone told them of the clandestine cooperation they had established through Primatov and two Kelk command superiors named Thordahl and Brynjar. For the first time in her life Carla heard of Norddansk Weapons Systems, and their suspicions regarding possible collusion with Transmarin Industries. Transmarin was a big outfit that everyone had heard of, but something about that name triggered some sort of memory. Carla lost track of Thealone's narrative for a moment as she tried to recover it, and then she had it.

"Ma'am," she said, and only then realized she had just interrupted a bird-colonel with the name BLACKSWORD stenciled above her left breast pocket.

Forester gave Carla a look that said, *Don't be fucking stupid, you idiot.*

Carla cringed as Thealone paused and looked her way. "Yes, Miss Nigurski. Do you have a question?"

"Ma'am . . . uhhh . . ." She had no choice now but to continue. "For the diplomatic mission, isn't there . . . some bigshot . . . from Transmarin on Senator Palmutter's staff?"

Thealone nodded, the look on her face unreadable. "How did you learn of that?"

Carla shrugged. "It's public information. I figured . . . since this whole mess has something to do with the mission to Viktorkinde . . . I read up on everything I could about it."

Carla braced for a dressing-down by the raving bitch, but Thealone smiled and gave her a single nod of her head. "Lawrence Strikland, Executive Vice President of Transmarin Missile Systems, presently on leave to support Senator Palmutter as his Commercial Adviser. Very good, Miss Nigurski."

Thealone told them of the evidence John had uncovered that Strikland had surreptitiously contributed quite heavily to Palmutter's election campaign. They had also uncovered hints Palmutter may have known too much about John's abduction from the academy campus. "Palmutter may be dirty," Thealone said, "but we can't prove that."

She addressed her next comment to Chemina. "You might be able to help with that. And if Palmutter is dirty, and you can prove it, I'll see to it you get an exclusive on that."

Chemina leaned forward. "I met his Chief Military Adviser just before we departed. I think he tried to eavesdrop on a private conversation I was having with my boss, did it in a sneaky way. The fellow didn't leave me with a good impression. I also met him briefly once when May, John and I had dinner in a restaurant near the O-School campus, but I don't think he remembered me. He was a real nasty piece of work."

Forrester looked a little confused.

Thealone looked at her and Carla as she said, "Palmutter's Chief Military Adviser; that would be Macus DeLeon."

"Oh yah," Forrester said. "He was a real jerk."

Carla couldn't control herself. "That slime-ball is here?"

Chemina laughed. "Interesting that you would call him that. While sitting in front of me, looking me right in the face, he undressed me with his eyes. I'm not sure if he didn't care to hide it, or just didn't realize he was so obvious about it. And I got the impression what he did to me in his thoughts was certainly disgusting, and probably illegal."

27

Sowing More Doubt

TAUGRIM'S THREATENING TAUNT to take John as a lover had clearly puzzled him. Nikaela had seen that, even if others had not. Seated at a table in the officer's ward room, she stared into her cup of tea and tried to recall his reaction. When Taugrim had grinned and said, "Perhaps I'll take you as a lover," he had merely looked her over and raised an eyebrow. Like any man he could have just brushed it off, but he hadn't. She didn't believe for a moment he seriously considered taking the captain up on the offer, but he certainly hadn't reacted the way a man should.

"Mistress."

Nikaela looked up from the tea.

Command Boss Senior Rank Kyrsten Stinar sat down opposite her. "You look quite thoughtful. Anything serious?"

A young female officer sat at a table on the other side of the ward room, her concentration focused on a small terminal in front of her. For all intents and purposes, Nikaela had Stinar alone. She lowered her voice and said, "I want to ask you a question."

Stinar's eyebrows rose with curiosity. "Ask away."

Nikaela lowered her voice even further. "Do you know anything about how Commonwealth men and women interact?"

Stinar shrugged. "Well, they say mister, miss, and ma'am. They don't say maestra and mistress. I've heard there are more men in their senate than women, and that could make you think women don't have as much power as men. But when I look at that Blacksword colonel—have you seen her when she's pissed? She's got a look that could strip armor plating off an assault boat. Why, what were you thinking of?"

Nikaela considered her words carefully. "I was thinking more along the lines of how . . . they . . . become . . ."

Stinar grinned. "Oh, you mean how they fuck."

The young woman across the room glanced up from her terminal and looked their way.

Nikaela hissed, "Keep your voice down."

Stinar whispered. "I think they fuck pretty much the same way we do. The men have cocks just like our men, and the women have vaginas just like we do. And if they're not hetero, they probably get inventive just like we do. And even if they are hetero, I'll bet they get inventive then too. I have to assume they like a good time just like we do. And we're racially compatible with them, so the mechanics have to be pretty much the same, don't you think?"

Nikaela shook her head. "That's not what I mean. I mean . . . do you think maybe their men . . . are a little more aggressive."

Stinar's eyes narrowed with anger. "Did the Blacksword do something to you? If he did, I'll—"

Nikaela shook her head. "No, no, nothing like that." She lowered her voice to a faint whisper. "Promise you won't tell anyone."

Stinar rolled her eyes. "I promise."

"I mean it," Nikaela said. "I really don't need to be the gossip of the ship."

Stinar gave her a begrudging nod. "I won't say anything. I promise."

Nikaela hissed, "He kissed me."

Stinar's eyes flared with absolute fury. "He kissed you first? Did you rip his balls off, fry them up crispy, then shove them down his throat?"

"No," Nikaela said, knowing she could never explain the circumstances of the kiss on the assault boat. And the last thing she needed was for Stinar to go all vigilante on her. "I kissed him first."

Stinar's anger dissipated in an instant. "So what's the issue?"

Nikaela considered trying to explain the forked-tongue thing, but Stinar would never understand. "Well, he just . . ."

Stinar shook her head. "You kissed him and he kissed you back. There you have it. They're just like us."

The woman grinned and stood. "Let me know what he's like in bed."

••••

In the lounge, Macus spotted Faith seated in a low, plush chair. She had placed a portable access terminal on the small table in front of her. Looking at the terminal and pointing to it, while communicating over a secure link between their implants, had proven to be an effective subterfuge for a private talk without starting tongues wagging.

Macus crossed the room and sat down next to her. "Good evening, Faith."

She smiled. "Hello, Macus."

In the closed environment of Obradour's yacht, Macus and Faith had not found an opportunity to be alone, not in a way she could fulfill her promise to make him a very happy man. To get that privacy, one of their roommates would have to know about it, and they didn't trust either of them to keep such a tidbit out of the rumor mill. They had decided to satisfy their physical needs with other people, though as yet Faith had carefully avoided getting involved with anyone. Strikland was discreet, and if he got the impression she was not, he'd probably avoid her.

As for Macus, that young news hype had proven to be quite aloof, and he had struck out with Faith's roommate. That didn't bother him, because he was simply being careful.

Faith opened the secure link between them. *Strikland invited me to his suite last night.*

Macus raised an eyebrow in question.

She smiled. *It was strictly for professional purposes. He wanted me to brief him on Palmutter's staff, and on the members of the mission.*

To Macus, that didn't add up. *I would think a man with his resources would already know pretty much everything there is to know about . . . well . . . everyone.*

She nodded, leaned forward and lifted the small terminal off the table, as if studying it carefully. *The same thing occurred to me, but we worked quite hard. He had quite a number of questions about everyone on Palmutter's staff, and about the other members of the mission, so I played it straight and did absolutely nothing to encourage him.*

They had hoped to make some progress with the man, and that disappointed Macus. *No luck, huh?*

She grinned, which was nothing like her. *After a good hour with our noses to the grindstone, his hand accidentally brushed across my thigh. I didn't flinch, but I eased myself away from him a little. He apologized most profusely, and while standing and facing each other, he put his arms around my waste and kissed me. He actually startled me and I responded stiffly at first. But then I broke it off and pushed him away from me. He clearly knew I enjoyed the kiss, but I couldn't allow that to happen because there was just too much in the way of having that kind of relationship with him.*

Macus shook his head. *I don't get it. I thought you were going to fuck his brains out.*

She looked away from the terminal, gave him a predatory smile, and spoke out loud. "Change of plans."

She switched back to the secure link, and focused on the terminal again. *Strikland didn't say or do anything overt, but I caught a hint or two here and there. And quite frequently, when I mentioned Palmutter's name, an odd look flashed in his eyes, but only for the briefest of instants. And he definitely doesn't approve of Palmutter's relationship with Catarvin, clearly finds it distasteful.*

She sat there for a long moment nodding her head up and down. *I think Mr. Strikland has serious doubts about our dear senator, so I decided it was time for a change of strategy.*

••••

"Up-transition," the scan tech said, startling John. The atmosphere on the bridge of *Drakan Helgis* had been rather subdued. For the last three hours they had watched the three hunter-killers closely to see how long they remained in sublight, while putting as much distance between them and their pursuers as possible. "There's another . . . and another. They're all in pursuit again."

Three hours had allowed *Drakan Helgis* to open the gap between them to more than a light-year. That should give them enough time to cross the remaining seven light-years to the binary star system. But what would they do when they got there? John wondered at that constantly.

"Something interesting here, captain," the scan tech said, and along with everyone else, John looked her way. "They're driving a little slower than before. Not by much, maybe fifty lights or so."

"Ah ha!" Taugrim crowed. "We damaged one of them. Bet that'll make them a little more cautious." She grinned triumphantly and looked around the bridge. "Every little bit helps."

She snapped her head about to look at Nikaela. "Nav, what's our ETA at that binary system?"

"Eighteen hours, mistress," she said. "And they'll still be a half light-year behind us when we get there."

The muscles in John's shoulders relaxed for the first time in several hours.

Taugrim stood. "Okay, people. We've got nothing to worry about for the next eighteen hours. Let's stand down, get something to eat, get some sleep, then be back here in sixteen."

A young Kelk female spacer took John's place in the apprentice seat at the helm. Given the strain of the last several hours, he thought he'd have no problem finding sleep. But as he walked off the bridge, Taugrim called to him.

"Hey Blacksword."

John turned to face her. "Yes, mistress."

She gave him that evil grin of hers, and without doubt she had something up her sleeve. "Dahlborg gave you good marks, especially at Nav and Helm. You ever done a low-lights hunter-killer down-transition?"

He frowned. "No, mistress. Never."

"Good," she said, her grin broadening even further. "In sixteen hours report back to your station at the helm. And in eighteen hours, you're going to do one."

John ate dinner with the other officers in the ward room. All he could think about was the low-lights hunter-killer approach, something at which he had absolutely no experience. Under the strain of their present circumstances, the normal formality of the ward room had been relaxed considerably, and officers came and went as their schedules dictated. John finished his meal quickly and tried to leave early, thinking he'd spend a couple of hours running simulations. But Taugrim stopped him.

"Where you going, Blacksword?"

John grimaced. "I thought I might put in a little time on some simu ... la-tions . . ."

As he spoke she shook her head slowly from side to side. "No, Blacksword. Go to your bunk and get some sleep. Or better yet, find some pretty, young girl to join you in bed and wear you out, then get some sleep. But no simulations. That's an order." She hesitated. "Well, not the fucking a pretty, young girl part. That's not an order. That's up to you. But the rest is an order."

Seated next to her, Primatov lowered her head, her lip muscles puckered tightly as she tried to suppress a smile.

John's new roommate, a young male Kelk officer, accompanied him back to their stateroom. They both stripped and climbed into their respective bunks.

John wouldn't mind getting a pretty, young girl in bed, but Primatov was the only non-Kelk female on board, and she was so way-off-limits it was a couple billion light-years from being an option. And then he realized what had probably been obvious to everyone else: Taugrim hadn't been thinking of a common-face when she had said, ". . . pretty, young girl."

To find sleep John used his implants to induce stim-sleep.

The next morning, when he took the apprentice's seat at the helm, to his great re-lief, Dahlborg leaned close to him and whispered, "Let's run a few simulations."

As she set up his side of the helm cluster for simulation runs, she glanced his way and said, "Did you find a pretty, young girl?"

She struggled to suppress a laugh as he rolled his eyes and shook his head.

They ran through one simulation and he botched it completely. At that, Dahlborg shrugged. "Don't worry. The skipper's having you do this because you'll get some ex-perience in a situation where it doesn't matter if you botch it."

At the look on his face, she added, "We're going to drive into that system hard, and the gravity gradients will warp our vector in an unpredictable fashion, sending us in a direction they can't predict. And from a half light-year out, those gradients will also distort any tracking data those hunter-killers can get on us. You get us below a hundred lights before we down-transit, and we'll be in great shape. And anything be-yond that will reduce their signal and bury their data even farther in the noise."

John was in the middle of another simulation when *Drakan Helgis*'s most senior navigator announced, "I estimate we just penetrated heliopause, mistress." The fellow was Nikaela's mentor at Nav, and rather average looking—for a Kelk. "I should add: the boundary is somewhat ragged and ill-defined in this binary system. We're some-thing like two hundred AUs out from those two solar masses."

Dahlborg took John's side of the helm cluster out of simulation mode, and passed control to him. At that point he was sweating bullets. He really didn't want to screw this up in front of his new crewmates.

Taugrim seemed pleased. "We're now inside the sphere of influence of those two stars, and that'll really screw up their tracking data. Helm, start dumping lights, and do it hard. Take us down to one thousand."

"Yes, mistress," John said.

An easy maneuver. All John did was reduce the space-time distortion field surrounding the ship, and in a few minutes they had dropped from thirty-four hundred lights to a thousand. Dumping lights that quickly made them flare like a warhead, and John suspected Taugrim was doing that to tease their adversaries.

"Hold steady," she said.

"Yes, mistress."

"I want to penetrate about a hundred AU's before we go for broke."

Less than a minute later they hit that mark, and Taugrim said, "Okay, Maestra Blacksword, start dumping lights and go for it."

The low-lights approach was easy until they got down to a certain transition velocity. It was different for every ship, but Dahlborg had warned John he shouldn't have any problems with *Drakan Helgis* until they hit about two hundred lights. Just below that the first gravity wave rolled through the bridge, a weak one, barely strong enough to be noticed. Dahlborg announced, "One-eighty lights."

John had a smooth stretch down to 130, then a gravity wave hit like a punch in the gut. He backed off and held steady for a moment, then continued on downward. He needed to hit that one-hundred-lights goal Dahlborg gave him. He needed that very much.

"One-ten," she announced.

A drop of sweat tickled John's spine as it rolled down his back.

"One hundred."

"Don't forget, Blacksword," Taugrim said, "hold on to as much sublight as you can. We need to keep our flare to a minimum."

"Ninety . . . Eighty . . ."

At that point everything went unstable, a trio of gravity waves slammed through the bridge, and the distortion field collapsed. John thought he actually felt it in his bones, though that was merely an illusion many helmsmen fell victim to.

"Down-transition at seventy-four lights," Dahlborg announced. "Coasting in sublight at just under point-eight lights."

"Drones out," Taugrim barked, and the hull echoed with the launch of the combat drones. "Scan, I want a system map soonest. We've got about an hour before they get here, and we've got to have everything in place by then. Helm, Nav, I want to get in close to that white dwarf, and use it to swing us around in a static trajectory, get us headed back in the general direction of Viktorkinde. Tell me what we gotta do, and you don't have a lot of time to think about it."

John had so desperately wanted to not screw up in front of his crewmates that his hands were shaking a little. Dahlborg gently placed a hand on his forearm. "Good work, John. You relax. I'll take the helm now."

The navigator and Dahlborg put their heads together while Nikaela and John looked on. They worked frantically for a few moments, then the navigator said, "Captain, we need to do a short transition jump. Gotta get within about five AUs of that white dwarf before we start killing velocity."

Taugrim nodded her head once. "Make it happen."

John had nothing to do for the moment. His heart rate and breathing were elevated, but slowing, as if he'd just jogged a short distance.

John knew Dahlborg had taken the helm because this time it had to be done perfectly. They retrieved the drones, up-transited, pushed the drive to about three hundred lights, then she demonstrated how to do a low-lights down-transition the right way. She got *Drakan Helgis* all the way down to forty-two lights before dropping them into sublight. Then they launched the drones again and decelerated hard. At ten-thousand gravities it took them the better part of an hour to get their velocity below two-hundred kilometers per second. They made a course correction, and the navigator said, "We're about half an AU out, mistress. In nine days we'll hit perigee three million klicks off that dwarf, and after that we'll be on a track thirty-seven degrees off a direct line back to Viktorkinde."

"Excellent!" Taugrim said. "Fire Control, dump a couple of one hundred megaton mines. I want them tracking the same trajectory as us. Put one of them half a million kilometers in front of us, the other half a million behind us, and set them to trigger on a signal from us."

"Yes, mistress," the Fire Control officer said. He worked intently at his console for several seconds, then the hull thrummed twice with the launch of the mines. "Need a few seconds to position them, mistress, and . . . they're on track."

"Okay, people," Taugrim said, "all stations rig for silent running."

There wasn't anything for John or Dahlborg to do. Most of the work fell to Engineering to shut down the drive, kill gravity, and make sure their emissions profile dropped down into the noise of the two nearby stars.

Someone slapped John on the back so hard he grunted, and the sound of the slap echoed across the bridge. He looked up and over his shoulder to find Taugrim standing behind him, that big, flashy grin of hers bisecting her face. She gripped the back of his seat as the deck gravity faded. "Good job, Blacksword. Not the best I've seen, but damn good for a first try. We're going to make a fucking Kelk out of you yet."

28

Turn the Table

ON SARKOVIE, TIA Lorenson owned and operated an independent distribution company that marketed, sold, and maintained products for a number of Kelk manufacturers. She headed up the operation, with Torsten Hohlman functioning as her second in command. To Anders's surprise, they actually did run a legitimate distribution business. It was reasonably profitable, and employed more than one hundred people, several of them Kelk expatriates, with a number of locals thrown into the mix. Anders would guess only about ten percent of the employees were aware of the covert anti-Commonwealth side of the operation, but as yet he had only identified a few, and they were all Kelk.

There were quite a few Kelk on the planet besides those employed by Lorenson's company, which didn't surprise Anders. After all, when he had first entered Calconna he had seen a few of them walking openly on the streets. The Supremacy maintained a small embassy there, and some of the larger Kelk companies ran minimalist commercial operations, though nothing extensive. Sarkovie, even when combined with the independent systems nearby, just wasn't a large enough market to justify more than small liaison operations, which meant more business for Lorenson's company.

As she described the operation to Anders, she confessed, "Sometimes I find the success of the legitimate operation a distraction. It detracts from what we should really be worrying about."

Anders was surprised to learn that back on Viktorkinde, he and his tall, bearded accomplice Thoran had frequently shipped legitimate products to Lorenson's company. He slipped easily into the new routine of receiving incoming product, and shipping it out to various locations, though he never forgot that he must find a way to make contact with Brynjar's friendly assets. But while his new friends now treated him as an accomplice and fellow employee, without doubt they considered him on probation, so he had to move with extreme caution.

Brynjar's contacts were running a dark server buried inside citynet, but he'd be a fool to access it locally. Lorenson and her people most likely had the wherewithal to tap into and monitor local nodes, and Sarkovie was just primitive enough that they could get away with it; the planet even maintained an old-fashioned physical mail system. Anders prepared a report he couldn't yet deliver. It provided some detail on Lorenson's operation, but mainly informed them he had arrived safely, and no one had yet put a bullet in the back of his head. Then he encrypted it, stored it, and waited, hoping to find an opportunity to make contact with Brynjar's friendly assets.

In the middle of the second day after Lorenson had released him from confinement, Anders sat down at a place in the small lunch room to eat a simple meal, and scan citynet ads for an apartment. While he concentrated on the feed from his implants, someone said, "You the new guy?"

He focused on his surroundings. Standing on the other side of the table from him, a young common-face girl smiled at him. She had glistening black hair, and lots of curves that filled the dress she wore to overflowing, with plenty of flesh spilling out of it. The material of her dress was more revealing than concealing, and allowed him to see her areolas almost as well as if she wore nothing at all. He tried not to look at the points of her nipples, which protruded rather visibly. He recalled that prostitution was a highly regarded profession on Sarkovie, and many young people, even if they didn't ply the trade, dressed in that fashion. In his experience, prostitutes usually had a cheap and sordid appearance, but beyond all the exposed flesh, her makeup was properly done—not overdone—and she looked young, fresh and pleasant.

He pulled his eyes away from the exposed flesh and looked into her face. "Ahhh . . . yes, I'm the new guy."

She scrunched her nose up. "I heard you're looking for an apartment. There's one available in my building, and it's within walking distance. I think it's just a small bachelor place like mine, but if you're interested . . ."

"Ahhh . . . yes," he said, trying not to stammer, and trying not to look at the various overexposed parts of her. "Yes, I could be interested." He found it a little difficult to remember that his primary interest was in the apartment.

She smiled happily. "How about tonight, after work, I'll show you where it is."

He nodded. "Let's meet out front. You said we can walk there."

She leaned forward, placing her hands on the table and showing him even more flesh. "Great, tonight, after work, out front."

She hesitated and lowered her voice. "And it's all right to look. That's why we dress this way. Go ahead." She winked at him. "Take it all in, and enjoy."

She straightened and extended her hand. "I'm Neddaline Macree. You can call me Nedda."

When he hesitated she looked at her hand. "Oh that's right. You Kelk don't shake hands."

"Anders Eindride," he said. "Nice to meet you, Miss Macree."

She shook her head. "Like I said, call me Nedda."

She turned around and walked out of the lunch room.

After work he met her out front. It bothered him a little, what people might think seeing him walking down the street with her. She kept up a young-girlish stream of chatter. "Yah. I just got this job like fifteen days ago. It pays pretty good for me."

The building she led him to had a storefront bordello on the ground floor. She pointed it out to him, saying, "All the girls and boys who work there are independent contractors. I do a little part-time work there myself just to make ends meet."

Nedda Macree couldn't be more than eighteen, and Anders suppressed his strait-laced response to that piece of information. She should be in the back room at a party with some boy, horny as hell and groping at each other.

"Come on. I'll introduce you to the building manager."

To one side of the bordello, steps led up to the entrance that gave access to the upper floor apartments. She unlocked the front door and they stepped into a small entrance foyer. Once inside she closed the door, turned toward him, smiled, and opened a secure link between their implants. *Brynjar sends his regards, Maestra Eindride.*

••••

The three hunter-killers down-transited at the edge of the binary system. They didn't do anything for a good hour while they coasted inward with about half a light of residual velocity, probably putting together a detailed system map.

Seated next to Nikaela, the senior navigator said, "They'll probably try to model the gravitational distortions in the system, and attempt to predict what our path was from the data they have on us. I've tried that myself, on occasion. It works well for sublight movements, but we drove quite a ways into the system in transition, so they're stuck with garbage."

After an hour the hunter-killers up-transited and executed a short hop to within about a hundred AUs of the two stars. From there they spread out and swept inward, coasting at a fraction of one light.

The senior navigator nodded his head knowingly. "They're hoping to get lucky, but it ain't gonna happen."

Nikaela did a quick calculation. If the hunter-killers stayed with their present strategy, their closest approach to *Drakan Helgis*'s trajectory track would be about fifty million kilometers. But that would be five days from now, and they'd miss *Drakan Helgis*'s specific position by more than an AU. Taugrim's trick of screwing up their transition wakes with a mine had trashed their plans, and now they were desperate.

A skeleton crew took over the bridge watch, but Nikaela hesitated. She wanted to stay there and track the movement of their enemy. She started when she realized she had just thought of other Kelk as the enemy.

"Mistress Vreekande," the navigator said. "Either we have to bide our time for a couple tendays of sheer boredom, or we're dead. So take a break, get off the bridge, and relax. That's an order."

Nikaela knew better than to argue. "Yes, maestra."

She unstrapped from her seat and floated up in the zero-G of the bridge. But before she could push off toward the exit, the man added, "One more thing."

She turned back to him. "Yes, maestra."

His lips split into a broad grin. "If you need to kill time, maybe you could help the Blacksword find that pretty, young girl the captain prescribed for him. Know of anyone available?"

Nikaela glanced about. Several other crew members were displaying similar cheesy grins. The man outranked her, but she sneered at him anyway and said, "Very funny." She pushed off and floated toward the exit, hoping she wasn't blushing.

Stinar waited at the bottom of the ladder that led to the bridge. At that point they had all concluded the danger of another assassination attempt was minimal, at least on *Drakan Helgis*. It would be quite different on *Konigsborge*, and extremely different if and when they reached Viktorkinde.

••••

Since Faith was terribly upset about something regarding Strikland, it was only natural she would avoid him, and only natural he would try to get to the bottom of the matter. He kept trying to get her alone, and she managed to prevent that for two days. Then he resorted to going through Palmutter, giving the senator some bullshit reason why he needed her to come to his office again. With direct orders from the senator, Faith had no choice.

Again, Strikland greeted her at the door to his suite. And again, once she had stepped into the room, he turned to the bodyguard. "You can go."

The young man nodded, turned and walked to the door. Faith kept her back rigid and stiff as she said, "No, I think you should stay." Yes, that had been perfectly in character for a young woman troubled by a dark secret who didn't want to get involved in anything sordid.

The young man hesitated and looked to Strikland for his cue.

Strikland looked into Faith's eyes and said, "I only want to talk. After we talk, if you wish to leave, I will not hinder you. You have my word on that, as a gentleman."

Faith gave him an angry look and blinked her eyes several times. Then she took a deep breath, let it out slowly, turned to the young man and said, "I won't object if you do as Mr. Strikland wishes."

The young man looked at Strikland, who gave him a quick nod, and he quietly walked out of the room.

As soon as the door closed, Strikland faced her squarely and demanded, "You're not telling me something, and it clearly has you quite upset, as well as frightened. Please tell me. Perhaps I can help."

The room had been furnished with plush chairs and a couch surrounding a low table. Faith took two steps, put the table between them, and almost laughed at how frightened and virginal she managed to act. She turned the laugh into a grimace of distraught pain, thinking she'd have to plan ahead carefully. When the time came for him to pull her passionately into his arms, she'd have to make sure the table didn't get in the way.

She did everything possible to sound like a bad liar as she spoke stiffly and spit her words at him. "It's simply that you and I have to keep our relationship . . . professional. Beyond that, there's nothing to tell."

His eyes narrowed. "Oh yes there is. And whatever it is, it's frightened you badly."

For the first time she saw how he could be a very angry man, and decided to be sure he never directed such anger at her. "I said there's nothing, and I meant it."

"That's a lie." He stepped around the table, taking care of that problem for her. "Whatever there is, tell me, and I can help."

"But you can't."

He spoke slowly. "But I can. Believe me."

She closed her eyes and stood with her chin trembling. It had been a long time since she'd played the frightened young woman gambit, and it pleased her to find she could still pull it off without effort. But the timing did need a couple more beats to be perfect.

He spoke softly. "Faith, trust me."

"There's nothing you can do. I'm out of my depth here."

Two more beats.

She kept her eyes closed as he asked, "Out of your depth?"

She shook her head. "He's too powerful. He'd ruin me."

One more beat.

He spoke in a hard and determined tone. "He'd ruin you? Believe me, I can fix it . . . I can fix him."

She opened her eyes and shouted in his face. "He wants me to seduce you, and spy on you for him. He asked me to fuck you like I'm some whore. That's all I am to him, just a whore to get information for him."

She had a little trouble coming up with tears at that moment, so she turned her back on him and buried her face in her hands. She let her shoulders heave as if she were crying, and rubbed her eyes hard with her fingers to redden them. "I'll not whore myself out for that man, or for any man."

"He?" Strickland said, his voice low, cold and hard. "*He* . . . being Palmutter."

As she pretended to cry, she lowered her voice to a tiny squeak. "Of course, Palmutter."

For several seconds her sobs were the only sound that broke the silence of the room, then she felt his arms gently envelope her from behind.

"Don't worry about Palmutter," he said. "Tell him you did seduce me, and I'll keep you safe."

Remaining within his arms, she turned around and looked into his eyes. He kissed her, and she melted against him. He tasted good, and she would enjoy every aspect of this odd relationship.

She let the kiss linger for several seconds, then opened her eyes abruptly and ended it. She put her hands against his chest and pushed, but not hard enough to break his embrace. "I can't, not with that between us. We just . . . we just can't."

He smiled. "But you just told me all about his asinine little plot, so it's not between us, is it? It's out in the open, at least between you and me. We just won't let Palmutter know that I know. And when I kiss you, I can sense that you're genuinely attracted to me."

She shook her head. "I don't know. It's soured everything."

He shrugged. "Then let's sweeten it up."

He kissed her again, and she pressed her body against his. She felt his excitement growing.

When the kiss ended, he said, "And you don't have to seduce me. Just let me seduce you."

He kissed her again. He moved slowly and carefully, and they undressed each other little by little. Unlike some men of power, he proved he was quite conscious of the pleasure he gave, not just of that he received, and she thoroughly enjoyed the next hour. As her breathing calmed after the intensity of their lovemaking, Faith set her implants to wake her in a few hours, and fell asleep in his arms.

When her implants woke her, she slipped out of bed without waking him. She dressed carefully, checked her makeup, and carefully brushed out her hair. To accommodate her present situation, she wore it a little tousled in the style of a professional business woman.

When she was ready she walked back into the bedroom, bent down over the bed and kissed Strikland gently on the cheek. His eyes opened and he smiled at her.

"I should go," she said. "Working a little late is one thing, but it would not be good if I were seen leaving your suite in the morning." Above all, she needed to reassure him she would be the soul of discretion.

"Smart girl," he said. "And perhaps it's time to reconsider my relationship with a certain senator."

She winced fearfully. "Please leave me out of that."

He smiled. "You needn't worry." His eyes brightened. "Tomorrow night?"

She kissed him again. "Of course, darling."

29

Caliban Again

NEDDA MACREE WAS apparently a lot older than Ander's first impression of her. That had become obvious the moment she dropped the veneer of the chatty young girl and told him, *Brynjar sends his regards, Maestra Eindride.*

He also doubted she had given him, or her new employer, her real name. That first day they met, she told him only that Brynjar had warned her he might contact her. "Oh, and don't worry," she added. "I'm the only one here who knows you exist. I did insert some of my people at the other three addresses, but this is their HQ, so I'm covering it myself."

At moments like that she appeared to be fifteen or twenty years older than . . . what she appeared to be. Little comments like that gave him the impression she carried some amount of authority in whatever covert organization she worked for, at least on Sarkovie. She wouldn't tell him if she worked for Sarkovie Intelligence, or Commonwealth Intelligence, or was just a contract spy of some sort, though he had to believe Brynjar wouldn't have revealed his identity to just anyone. He had concluded with a fair amount of certainty she was a native of Sarkovie, and probably recruited to work for the Commonwealth. When he asked her if she was a Blacksword, she shook her head and said, "If I was a Blacksword, I'd lie and say I'm not. And if I wasn't a Blacksword, I'd tell the truth and say I'm not."

The apartment available in her building turned out to be adequate, and affordable, which was exactly what he needed. He signed a short-term lease, since he didn't know how long he'd be on Sarkovie.

She warned him, "You were wise to stay away from the local citynet, at least for anything you don't want our employer to know about. The nodes are tapped."

At the look on his face, she rubbed her fingers together in the universal sign for money and added, "This is Sarkovie. If you've got the cash, you've got the way."

"If I need to contact you," he asked, "to talk about stuff I don't want our employer to hear, how do I do that? I assume I don't just walk up to you in the lunch room and tell you I want to talk privately."

"The bordello," she said, "on the ground floor of our apartment building. Just go there and ask for my services."

She had told him she worked there, that she *did a little part-time work to make ends meet.* "If I'm not there at the moment, they'll let me know, and I'll be there the next day after work."

"But I'm Kelk and you're—"

She rolled her eyes. "And I'm a common-face. There are lots of Kelk here, and we do it all the time." She scrunched her nose up. "You know, we common-faces do it the same way you Kelk do. You have man parts, and I have woman parts, and you take your man parts and put them in—"

"Enough," he said. "I'm well aware of the details."

"You're not gay, are you?"

"No, I'm not gay."

Those were the last words they had shared, and now two days later, when he reported to work, he received a message in his implants to report directly to Lorenson's office. He found the door open, she saw him approaching and said, "Come on in, close the door,"—she waved him to a comfortable chair—"and sit down."

Once he was seated she said, "I just wanted to let you know you're no longer on probation. Your story checks out."

That sent Anders's curiosity marching in several directions. "How can it check out? There's just you and me, and you haven't had time to communicate with Viktorkinde. It's only been two days."

She pursed her lips as if chagrined that she had revealed something. She hesitated for a long moment, then said, "We compared notes with *Caliban*. The sequence of events as they observed it matches what you told us."

"*Caliban* is here?"

She nodded. "Yes. Their transition drive is damaged. They can only do about a thousand lights, and are worried it might fail out in the middle of interstellar space." She glanced upward toward the heavens. "They're in a parking orbit while we try to help them get repairs. This planet isn't really equipped for that, so it could be a while before they go anywhere." She grimaced. "The two men in charge up there are not very nice people. Makes you wonder if we're on the right side, doesn't it?"

Anders forced his thought to slow down. "Never had anything to do with them, myself."

Anders left Lorenson's office thinking only of Nedda Macree. He needed to pass this information on to her. Since taking the small apartment in the same building as her, he'd worked late each day just to make sure he didn't have to walk home with her. That day he took care to finish right on time, and ran into her out front as they both left the building.

"Anders," she said, greeting him pleasantly. "Are you headed back to your apartment?"

He kept his eyes focused on her face, and not the other parts of her. "Yes."

She smiled. "Then we can walk together."

As they walked, she maintained the persona of the chatty young girl. He waited until they were about a hundred paces down the street, and well clear of any of their fellow employees, then said, "I'd like to employ your professional services."

It was a carefully chosen sequence of words they had agreed he would use only if he needed to speak to her about covert matters.

The chatty young girl didn't miss a beat. "Oh, I'm flattered."

When they reached their building, she started up the steps to the upper floor apartments. He hesitated, pointed to the ground floor bordello, and asked, "Aren't we going in there?"

"Oh no," she said. "Since you approached me outside the establishment, I'm free to take you up to my place, and I don't have to pay them a commission. If I trust someone, then I legally have that option. But you do have to pay."

"Uh, how much?"

She pointed to a window in the bordello where they had posted a complete menu. He said, "I'll just have something normal," and he gave her a couple of bills.

They walked up to her apartment, she opened the door, and he followed her in. It was small, Spartan, and almost identical to his place. She tossed a little clutch bag onto a small table, turned and wrapped her arms around his neck. As she brushed her lips along his chin, he opened up a secure link between their implants and said, *What are you doing?*

She ran her tongue along the edge of his ear. *When we're working, they monitor the room, just to be sure I don't find myself in a bad situation.*

You mean . . . we have to?

Yes, we have to. I know you'll find it difficult, but try to have a good time.

He stood there frozen for the longest moment. She was beautiful, even though she wasn't Kelk, and he decided . . . *Oh, what the hell.*

He tried to impart to her the information about *Caliban*, but other activities, and various parts of her, kept distracting him, so that didn't happen for some time.

Quite a bit later, he lay next to her in her bed, his breathing slowly returning to normal. He reopened the secure link between their implants. *I have news of* Caliban. *It's in a parking orbit here waiting for repairs. It's going to be here at least another fifteen or twenty days.*

Her eyes brightened. *Excellent! That's good news. I'll pass it on.*

She looked at him a little sheepishly, smiled and said, "By the way, I lied. They're not monitoring the room."

He shook his head. "You mean . . . we didn't have to?"

Her eyes flashed angrily. "No. Of course we had to. You paid, and I wouldn't be a good Sarkovite if I didn't deliver. That's the law, and that's just the way it is. And besides—" She leaned over and kissed him on the cheek. "You obviously enjoyed yourself, and I think I made it quite clear I did too."

He closed his eyes. She was so . . . so Sarkovie. He had heard the natives were like that, but until now hadn't really understood just how much that was true.

"I can't believe this," he said. "I suppose, when you have a legislative session, all the congress people fuck each other first, then they pass some laws, then they have another fuck fest, then they call it a day."

She gave him a whimsical look and said, "That's not a bad idea."

••••

I fucked him hard. I bet he's sore all over this morning, though he was quite happy when we parted. He asked me to return tonight.

Macus grinned at Faith. *I'm impressed. You are a real pro.*

Pro, she said. *When that word is applied to fucking someone, it usually implies* whore.

Macus retreated. *No, I didn't mean it that way. I—*

No offense taken, she said, shaking her head. *All I meant was that if I wanted to be a whore, I wouldn't be just one of the girls. I'd be the madam running the show.*

Relieved that he hadn't stepped in something, Macus spoke aloud. "I have no doubt of that, and I'd be your biggest customer."

He switched to the secure link. *And telling Strikland that Palmutter wanted you to spy on him was pure genius. Learn anything?*

She shook her head and looked away from the small access terminal, their ruse for a secure link in the lounge. "Not yet, at least nothing substantive, but I'm sure he'll be a wealth of information in the future."

She switched back to the link. *And right now he's so fucking pissed at Palmutter, I think we've sealed the dear senator's fate.*

••••

Thealone closed the door to her stateroom, and ran a full security scan on every inch of the compartment. Then she sat down at her desk and opened her implants to a prearranged channel and encryption key. Mani Gascoigne appeared as if seated across a table from her. Jenine Catarvin sat next to him, a vacant look on her face.

Since they used the main coms to communicate ship-to-ship, they had decided Catarvin would not attempt to communicate directly with Fran. The com links between the two cruisers, their two hunter-killer escorts, and *Lady Victorious* were open at all times, and anyone could open a channel for a conversation with someone on another ship, but they didn't want to take any chances. When Catarvin had something to report, she came up with an excuse to have a meeting with Gascoigne, and he then set up the call.

"Colonel Blacksword," the little woman said. "You're looking very military in that uniform, though still quite attractive. Have you found a man yet, or if you're into women, well . . . I probably shouldn't go there. We do need to find a man for Colonel Primatov, though. I think she works too hard."

Fran didn't try to hide her impatience. "Mani told me you had some information you wanted to pass along."

Catarvin's eyes brightened. "I've done my job, making good old Silas cry out all sorts of things in the throes of ecstasy. Well he doesn't actually cry out, he grunts them out, and whatever he's saying is usually rather unintelligible."

Sitting beside her, Gascoigne rolled his eyes. Fran had learned that the woman was quite sharp, but it always took her a while to get to the point, as if she had trouble dropping the alternate persona.

Catarvin continued. "He's mentioned a couple of names that sound rather Kelkish, though not in the throes of ecstasy, and none that I'd recognize anyway. But one incident stood out. I spent the night in his bed, and he had to get up early the next morning for a meeting with Lawrence Strikland—he's that fellow from Transmarin. I pretended to be drowsy because—" Her eyes brightened. "Well, let's just say he'd been rather energetic the night before. You'd be amazed what gene therapy can do for a man. I mean he—"

She closed her eyes for a moment, then opened them and shook her head. "Sorry. I've worn that persona so long, it's sometimes difficult to put it aside."

The plump little woman sounded embarrassed, but she didn't really appear to be. "So I pretended to be sleepy and asked him to let me sleep in."

She leaned toward Fran and lowered her voice, as if revealing a dark secret. "The office in his suite, it's next to the bedroom and separated by just a door. So that morning he got up, showered, shaved, and . . . well, he took a quick pause to fit in a few rather energetic moments with me, though it was somewhat hurried. Then he went through that door into his office and closed it."

She lowered her voice to a whisper. "I did a real spy-girl thing. I jumped out of bed, ran to the door and put my ear to it. I couldn't really make out any words, but when I heard Strikland's voice—well, Silas has his nose so far up that man's anus, there was no doubt in my mind he wouldn't just sit behind his desk and shout at the fellow to come on in. No, I was certain he had popped around his desk to meet the man at the door and admit him. I took that moment to release the latch on the door and open it a crack."

The airhead persona seemed to melt and drift away. The change was quite remarkable. "They talked about Transmarin, and some new and improved missiles they've developed. Strikland wanted to hear Silas's thoughts on marketing them to the Supremacy."

It was probably the first time Gascoigne had seen the Jenine Catarvin she kept so well hidden from everyone. He looked a little shell-shocked.

She shrugged. "Of course, that's not really actionable. It's only natural they would speculate on the possibilities that might arise with new and improved relations with the Kelk. But at one point Silas said something like, 'When we get there we'll have to talk it over with Nevelhime.' I might have missed it, but Strikland hissed, 'Be careful with that name, you fool.'"

Catarvin paused, winked at Fran and nodded. "You see it too, don't you?"

"Yes," Fran said. "Palmutter's not the one in the driver's seat."

Catarvin grinned like a schoolgirl who'd been given a compliment by a particularly demanding teacher. "So Silas hissed a quick apology at Strikland, then stood and crossed the office toward the door where I was eavesdropping. I rushed back, slipped between the sheets, and pretended to be asleep. He opened the door, glanced around quickly, then closed it. After that I wasn't able to hear any more."

The woman was not in the least bit stupid, something easy to forget when confronted by her alternate persona.

None of them had ever heard of this *Nevelhime*. Fran ran a quick search, but found nothing. They all agreed Strikland's reaction proved there must be some significance to the name. They decided the best thing they could do was to keep their eyes and ears open for any further references to such a person.

Fran waited for Catarvin to leave, and when she had Gascoigne alone, she said, "Mani, I have something else that's really important. I know where *Caliban* is. Get Obradour."

With that bit of information, it only took Obradour a few minutes to conference in. "You've located *Caliban*?"

Captain Miershall on Sarkovie had immediately recognized the importance of the information she had received from an asset of Brynjar's, and dispatched a fast courier ship to the terminus of their relay chain.

"Yes, we have. It's damaged, in orbit around Sarkovie, and awaiting repairs. According to our sources it could be there for a few tendays, or even longer if they have to wait for parts to be shipped in."

Obradour's eyes narrowed. "How do you know this?"

Fran shook her head. "I'm not going to say."

The anger she saw in Obradour's face did not surprise her, or frighten her. "Why not?"

"I have assets to protect."

To her surprise, Obradour smiled. "Believe it or not, Colonel, I do understand that."

Fran now faced a difficult decision. "Mr. Obradour, the three of us once discussed who among us might take action should *Caliban* resurface."

His eyes narrowed and he spoke carefully. "I do recall that conversation."

Fran acknowledged his statement with a nod. "I have a fast courier ship waiting at the end of our relay chain, which I can put at your disposal. Keeping that in mind, are you capable of acting on this information in a timely fashion?"

He considered that for a long moment, probably needed to do a little mental math on the logistics of communicating and moving resources over distances of light-years. "I'm not sure," he said, "and I'm uncomfortable with my own uncertainty. Are you in a position to act, as you say, in a timely fashion?"

Fran had hoped Obradour had some trick up his sleeve. "We have small destroyers orbiting both Sarkovie and Norandyne. The courier ship can reach Norandyne in two days, and that destroyer can reach Sarkovie four days after that. The two destroyers working together should be able to handle *Caliban* easily."

Obradour clearly didn't like yielding the upper hand. "That's better than I can do. Though it does occur to me that if your people don't get the cooperation you'd like from *Caliban*'s crew, we might want to have some of my people take over the interrogation. I have a few people on Sarkovie who . . . are good at that kind of thing."

Fran smiled. "I'll need information on how to contact them."

Gascoigne leaned forward. "Is this one of those conversations we never had?"

Fran ended the call.

30

Conspirators All

KONIGSBORGE DROVE ALONG the Viktorkinde relay chain in the direction of Trafalgar, looking for any trace of *Drakan Helgis*. But with the possibility they might find three hostile hunter-killers lying in wait, they moved cautiously. To Kristdokar's frustration, *cautiously* equated with *slowly*.

They employed a modified version of the skip-jump maneuver. *Eldekarl* drove ahead of them a few light-years, then down-transited to scan nearby space, though they probably couldn't detect a ship running silent, especially an enemy hunter-killer. When satisfied that the odds of danger were slim, *Konigsborge* followed, with *Eldekarl* in sublight, monitoring their progress and feeding them data. When *Konigsborge* reached the hunter-killer, they down-transited near her position. *Konigsborge* then coasted in sublight and focused its detection equipment forward, while *Eldekarl* drove ahead another couple of light-years. *Konigsborge* watched closely, prepared to warn the hunter-killer if they detected any sign of danger while it was in transition. They then repeated that maneuver. It was a slow and tedious process.

A schedule of short transition jumps with repeated up and down-transitions wore on a crew. Three days after leaving *Valhaukr* behind, they had only covered half the distance to where they estimated the hunter-killers would have caught up with *Drakan Helgis*. So far they had detected no debris field. But that gave them no comfort, because there was little likelihood they would find any until they got farther along the relay chain.

They had now crossed the gap in the Viktorkinde relay chain created by the destruction of the two buoys. At that point the diplomatic mission from Trafalgar had been in transit for more than ten days. They would still be transiting along the Trafalgar relay chain, and suffering the delays caused by the gap between the two chains. Kristdokar and Nygaard agreed silence would be more dangerous than the truth, so Kristdokar prepared a carefully worded report of their encounter with *Valhaukr*.

Kristdokar had learned from Primatov that like the Supremacy, the Commonwealth also suffered from individuals who refused to question the doctrine of their beliefs. She hoped the common experience of dealing with unyielding hatred would help her Commonwealth counterparts see the difficulties she and Nygaard faced. Or would they think she and Nygaard had betrayed them? They might abandon the mission outright, and revert to the prior status-quo. If so, it would be disastrous for both sides, but ultimately the ruin of the Supremacy.

Kristdokar had to believe Thealone and her like-minded colleagues felt the same frustrations as she and Nygaard, and she tried to appeal to that in her report. Nygaard offered to contribute, saying a powerful friend of hers was part of the mission. She would say nothing beyond that, but did provide the closing remarks for the report.

Kristdokar encrypted the report and gave it to *Konigsborge*'s com tech to transmit up the relay chain. She wanted to see that it went out properly, so she stood behind the young woman and looked over her shoulder. As the girl sent the report on its way, Kristdokar chided herself for being paranoid.

The com tech glanced over her shoulder. "It's done, mistress."

At that moment the diplomatic mission would have transited to about ninety-three light-years out from Trafalgar. There would be a delay of at least two days while her report crossed the gap between the two chains. If they responded immediately, there would be another delay of two days while the message crossed the gap in the chains on its way back to Kristdokar. She would have to wait a minimum of four days to see if she had succeeded in saving the Supremacy from annihilation. It would be a long four days.

••••

When Fran finished Kristdokar's report on the attack by *Valhaukr*, she closed her eyes, rubbed her temples, and said what had become a silent prayer of late. "Oh shit! Oh shit! Oh shit!"

She didn't know this Command Hawk Taugrim, and hoped Kristdokar's faith in the woman was justified. Fran would certainly have faith in Katrine Primatov, but that was a moot point.

Of the three conspirators in command of *Valhaukr*, she knew of Haugrund, a member of the Executive Council. But regarding Machtberg and Nvalheim, she had to invoke her clearances to run a search in the classified sections of ComSec's databases. In it she found unconfirmed conjecture that they were both members of the Larscom General Secretariat, and solid information that Nvalheim was retired from her active rank of brigadier skalde. She did not miss the similarity to the name Catarvin had heard Palmutter utter: Nevelhime.

Fran opened a channel through her implants to *Hellfire*'s com tech. The man appeared in her virtual vision. "Yes, Colonel Blacksword, what can I do for you?"

"I need a point-to-point secure link to *Lady Victorious*, with a request for an urgent meeting with Senator Manifort Gascoigne and Mr. Tarsik Obradour. Tell them it's extremely urgent."

"Right away, Colonel."

She waited five minutes, a very long five minutes.

Gascoigne and Obradour appeared as if sitting across a table from her. Gascoigne didn't wait for Obradour to waste their time with polite inquiries regarding Fran's health. "What is it?"

The only thing Fran could think to do was to simply spit it out. "*Konigsborge*, *Eldekarl*, and *Drakan Helgis* were attacked by three rogue, Kelk hunter-killers and a large cruiser christened *Valhaukr*. To protect the breschkada and Colonel Primatov, *Drakan Helgis* was ordered to run and evade capture. The three hunter-killers pursued her, while *Konigsborge* and *Eldekarl* engaged *Valhaukr*. They were victorious against the cruiser, which they originally perceived as the main threat. They drove her off, but as of this report, which was recorded two days ago, they've seen no sign of the three rogue hunter-killers, or *Drakan Helgis*."

Gascoigne closed his eyes and said a prayer similar to Fran's. "Shit! Shit! Shit!"

At the dire news, Obradour's voice remained calm and even. "Can you play the full report for us?"

Fran would have done so without such a request, if for no other reason than that she needed to watch it again. "Certainly," she said, and keyed her implants to transmit the report to the two men. It consisted mostly of Kristdokar relating the facts of their present situation, but Nygaard personally provided the closing statement.

The vice skalde looked at the pickup for a long moment of silence, then spoke without emotion. "Given our history, I would not fault you if you suspected duplicity on our part. But this report is the truth in every detail, with no falsehoods, either by direct misstatement, or by omission. I give you my solemn oath on that, as Vice Skalde of the Supremacy, as a member of the Larscom General Secretariat, and as the third highest ranking member of the Larscom Executive Council."

Fran was again struck by the older woman's beauty, which had diminished very little with age.

Gascoigne said, "I'm at a loss. I don't know whether to believe her or not."

"I believe her," Obradour said.

Gascoigne gave him a questioning look, probably the same look on Fran's face at the moment.

Obradour shrugged and smiled. "I have known Earlana Nygaard for thirty years. She is a savvy politician, and can be a dangerous opponent. She would not have given such an oath to cover a lie. And to you, it may not have sounded like pleading, but to someone who knows her well, she was pleading."

Fran shrugged. "Then I too believe her."

Gascoigne shook his head as if trying to clear his thoughts. "I don't know what I believe, but I'll go with the two of you on this."

He turned to Obradour. "Why would she plead?"

Perhaps it was Obradour's knowledge of Nygaard that helped him remain calm. "Because she knows they cannot win a war with the Commonwealth." He looked into Gascoigne's eyes for a moment, then into Fran's. "And if this mission breaks down, that's where this will go, won't it?"

Above all, Fran did not want to speculate about interstellar war. "There's something else." They both focused intently on her. Gascoigne might not have made the connection, but in any case, she didn't want Obradour to realize she and Mani had a secret the little financier didn't know. "I have an asset who recently heard Senator Palmutter mention the name Nevelhime to Mr. Strikland when discussing the Kelk. Strikland reacted strongly to the use of that name. I can't help but notice the similarity between Nevelhime and Nvalheim, but the only G-2 I have on Marta Nvalheim is that she is a retired brigadier skalde, and possibly a member of the Larscom General Secretariat."

She looked pointedly at Obradour. He seemed to have quite a number of connections in the Supremacy, and she hoped he would come up with something now.

He smiled at her as if he could read her thoughts. "An asset. I venture to guess that would have to be someone in Palmutter's retinue." He looked at Fran for a long moment. "I can confirm that Nvalheim is a member of the General Secretariat. And you might also find it interesting to learn she is a director on Norddansk's board, and a significant shareholder."

Gascoigne slapped his hand on the table in front of him. "Hot damn! The plot thickens. How can we use that?"

"I don't yet know," Obradour said. "But in any case, the dots are beginning to connect."

"You know," Gascoigne said. "We have to show this report to Palmutter and Catarvin."

Fran had already come to that conclusion.

Obradour closed his eyes and shook his head sadly. "I know. But if I have to listen to that imbecile of a woman prattle on, I may just murder her myself."

He opened his eyes and looked at Fran. "But we don't have to show them the whole thing. I think you should edit out any references to Haugrund, Machtberg, or Nvalheim. If Silas is dealing under the table with her, I don't think he should know that we're aware of that name."

Fran nodded her agreement. "I agree for the time being, but at some point we might want to see how he reacts if we let him know she's in deep shit."

Gascoigne said, "I concur. And at the right moment, it might even panic him. You never know what you'll learn when someone's running scared."

For several seconds Obradour sat silently with his eyes narrowed in thought. "If at some point the two of you agree on that, I will not oppose you."

••••

Palmutter shot out of his chair and slammed the flat of his hand down on the table, slapping it so hard it must have hurt. "Those two Kelk women, Kristdokar and Nygaard, they're fucking, lying, double-crossing bitches. They set us up, and this means war. We'll annihilate those fucking blue-skinned demons. We'll throw so many warheads at them, there won't be anything left of Viktorkinde but radioactive vapor. We'll hunt their warships down, take no prisoners, and kill them all. We'll wipe every filthy blue-skinned man, woman and child from the galaxy."

In his rage, Palmutter had spattered the table in front him with tiny drops of spittle. Fran thought now was not the time to point out to him that the simple act of advocating genocide was a criminal offense in the Commonwealth.

Obradour said, "Calm down and sit down."

Catarvin said, "But he's right. I'm not advocating genocide, but I do think this does mean war. We're going to have to take the war to them, and I vote for war."

Gascoigne gave Fran a worried look, and she wondered what the woman was up to. Was she double-crossing them? Was she really their agent inside Palmutter's inner circle, or had she played them for fools?

Obradour rolled his eyes, making no attempt to hide his disdain. "We're not voting."

Catarvin gave him a snitty look. "Why not?"

At that point even Obradour lost control. "Because war isn't on the table."

Palmutter slapped his hand on the table again. "Oh yes it is, big time."

Gascoigne shouted, "Everyone calm down."

Palmutter slashed his hand through the air. "I'm done with this." He turned and stormed out of the room.

Obradour stood. "Let me see what I can do with him." He followed Palmutter out of the room.

Catarvin sat primly and watched the two of them leave with a vacant smile on her face. "That went well, didn't it?"

Gascoigne leaned toward her, making no attempt to hide his anger. "What are you doing, woman?"

The look she gave Gascoigne was so sharp it could have cut him in two. "My name is not *woman*."

Fran decided to intervene. "That was rather patronizing of you, Mani."

To Catarvin she said, "But we are both surprised you so readily agreed with Palmutter."

"Oh posh!" Catarvin said. "When he's out of control like that, he's not going to listen to anything you say, so the best way to handle him is to agree with him while he's hysterical, then change his mind later when he's calmed down. I personally have found that the best time to convince good old Silas to do something he doesn't want to do, is while I'm fucking his brains out. He gets even more energetic if we have an argument right in the middle of coitus. He doesn't have much for brains to begin with, but while I'm fucking them all out of him, he doesn't have any. And there's a brief period of time afterwards when he's quite open to suggestion."

Gascoigne shook his head in bewilderment. "I really didn't need to hear that."

Catarvin reached over and patted him gently on the shoulder. "Just let me handle this, Mani."

Clearly, the little woman did know Palmutter better than any of them. "I trust your judgement. And I have something else to tell you. I edited Kristdokar's report."

She told the woman the names of the three conspirators on *Valhaukr* who had orchestrated the attack. Catarvin immediately made the connection. "Nvalheim . . . Nevelhime, I guess I'm not terribly familiar with Kelk names. Palmutter certainly could have been saying Nvalheim."

Fran added, "Marta Nvalheim sits on Norddansk's board, and is a significant shareholder."

Catarvin's eyes brightened. "Thank you for telling me that."

Fran worried Catarvin might unknowingly do something dangerous. "Be careful with that. If they are culpable, as we suspect, they've demonstrated a penchant for absolute ruthlessness. At this point they're responsible for quite a number of murders."

Gascoigne said, "Don't forget the twenty million people on Novalis III."

Catarvin took in a sharp breath. "Oh!" That had clearly gotten through to her. "I'll heed your warning."

When they ended the meeting, Fran immediately contacted Karya Chemina. "We've had some developments recently that are pointing us at Palmutter and Strikland. You mentioned Macus DeLeon has shown some interest in you. Why don't you cultivate a relationship with him?"

Chemina started and flashed Fran an angry look. "I'm not going to whore myself out to that man for anyone."

Fran couldn't stop her frustration from boiling to the surface. "God damn it, I'm not asking you to whore yourself out. I did not use the word *relationship* as a euphemism for fucking the asshole. Pump him for information. If he wants to get under your skirt, lead him along a little without making any promises. I've known about that man for a long time now. As Miss Nigurski said, he is a real slime-ball, so he doesn't deserve any kind of fair treatment. If he's going to look-fuck you every time you meet, you get to string him along and pump him for information. And by the way, I personally would think less of you if you did fuck him."

That seemed to calm Chemina down a little, and Fran recalled that she was working with an amateur. "And keep your ears open for the name Nvalheim. You shouldn't know that name, so be careful, using it could give you away. Marta Nvalheim is an influential Kelk woman, and we have hints she, Strikland, and Palmutter might be working together on some bad things."

Chemina appeared somewhat chagrined. "Okay."

"And be careful. Whoever's behind this has been responsible for several murders." Fran felt it wouldn't be wise to add the victims of Novalis III to that list.

The young woman's eyes widened even further. "I will. I will."

Fran desperately hoped she had made her point with the girl.

31

Alliances Strained

PALMUTTER WAS ON the warpath. He'd gone to some sort of meeting with the other members of the diplomatic mission, and come out of it absolutely livid. The first thing he did was call Macus into the small office in his suite and rip him a new asshole. At that point the man couldn't utter a coherent word, but Macus learned there had been some sort of battle between two Kelk warships, and somehow Macus should have known about it beforehand.

"You're my fucking Chief Military Adviser. What the hell am I paying you for if I have to learn about this fucking shit from someone else?"

Macus decided it would not work at all well to point out that he was not Palmutter's Chief Military Seer.

In the middle of Palmutter's tirade, Strikland opened the door unannounced and stepped into the office, leaving one of his bodyguards outside the door. It was not the first time Macus had seen the man go wherever he chose without invitation, another advantage of being the money guy.

Strikland tried to calm Palmutter down, but in that he achieved only partial success. He did convince the senator to sit down behind his desk, so at least the old man stopped spattering Macus's face with spittle.

Strikland sat down opposite Palmutter and said, "War is not the answer, Silas. Right now peace is a lot more profitable."

"They fucking double-crossed us." Palmutter started to rise, but thought better of it.

Strikland shook his head. "Perhaps, perhaps not. Right now, you tell me exactly what happened. And when we get there, we'll find out how to fix it."

Palmutter nodded. "Yes, Nvalheim will know what to do."

Nvalheim? Macus had not heard that name before. It sounded Kelkish.

Strikland hesitated, looked over his shoulder, and said to Macus, "You can leave us now."

Macus turned and tried not to slink as he quietly left the room. Outside the door he nodded politely to Strikland's bodyguard, and walked away.

He needed a drink to calm his nerves, so he wandered down to the lounge. He stopped at the bar and ordered a shot of whiskey, neat. He spotted a couple of aides he knew, and when they saw him, they waved him over.

One of them leaned close and hissed, "We heard Palmutter blew his stack about something. What the hell's going on?"

He'd be foolish to be too candid with them—after all they were just aides—but it never hurt to remind them he was higher up the chain of command than them. Yielding little tidbits of information demonstrated that nicely.

Macus sipped at his drink and glanced over his shoulder, as if concerned he might be overheard. He did it more for dramatic effect than anything else. They both leaned closer to hear his words. "Something happened on the Kelk side of the equation."

One fellow's eyes widened, and the other demanded, "What? What happened?"

Macus took another sip of his drink and shook his head. "I'm not at liberty to divulge more than that."

They fired several questions at him, so he downed his drink, looked at his empty glass, and said, "I need another. I'll be back."

He turned, left them standing there and walked over to the bar, ordered another drink—a double—then returned to the two fellows. Macus sipped his drink as one of the two leaned close and asked, "Do the Kelk want to back out of it? Is that what it is?"

Macus shook his head. "As I said, I'm not at liberty to divulge more." He really didn't know much more, but they didn't know that.

They fired speculative questions at him, the kind requiring only a simple *yes* or *no* to acknowledge or deny a guess they had taken. He wasn't going to let them draw him into that kind of trap, so he sipped at his drink and dodged their questions nicely. The alcohol took the edge off and helped him put Palmutter's tirade behind him.

Far behind the two aides, that young news hype entered the lounge. She didn't spot him as she started across the room to the bar. She had on an attractive blouse, cut so it exposed her neck and upper chest, and just a tasteful bit of cleavage. He tried to picture her without it on, or better yet, he tried to picture him and her together while he slowly removed it.

She glanced his way, spotted him, and hesitated. For a moment he thought he saw distaste in the look she gave him. But he must have been mistaken, because her eyes brightened and she gave him an inviting smile. She continued across the lounge to the bar.

Macus downed the rest of his drink, and as an excuse to get away from the two aides, he looked at his empty glass and said, "Need another. Let's continue this some other time."

As he approached the young woman he again tried to picture her fully undressed. He stopped beside her at the bar. She glanced his way, smiled and said, "It's Macus, right? Nice to meet you again."

His confidence swelled. She'd been rather aloof, but now seemed to be coming around nicely.

She looked at the empty drink in his hand. "Why don't you buy me that drink you promised when we first met?"

"I can't buy you a drink. They're all free."

She smiled. "Touché, Mr. DeLeon. I'll have what you're having."

He didn't need another drink, but he couldn't pass up this opportunity. He ordered two doubles. He didn't want a double himself, but he wanted to make sure she got a double to loosen her up a little, and he couldn't order one for her and a single for him. That might be obvious.

When he handed her the drink, she lifted it, they tapped glasses, and both took a sip. As a news hype, she probably wanted information, and he'd happily give her some, if she showed that in return she could be friendly. Perhaps if he steered her in that direction, they'd get there sooner rather than later. "Everyone's pretty upset, aren't they?"

"Yes, they are," she said. "But I wouldn't be surprised if it all blew over in a day or two."

Unlike the two aides, she didn't pump him for information, which pissed him off. How was he going to get her in bed, if it wasn't in exchange for something like information? "I know a lot more than these stupid aides." He had had a little too much to drink and needed to concentrate carefully to articulate his words properly.

"I don't doubt that," she said. "You're not just some gofer like them."

As they chatted he had to repeatedly guide the conversation back to the buzz and gossip that had everyone else so enthralled. At one point he said something about Nvalheim. He struggled to recall what he'd just said, something like, "When we get there, Strikland said they'll get it all straightened out with someone named Nvalheim."

He needed to qualify that. "That's strictly off the record." He leaned close to her. "Why don't you join me in my room? I'll get rid of my roommate, and I can pour you a drink there."

She stood and stepped away from the bar. "Perhaps another time."

"Why? You got something better to do?"

"Yes," she said. "I think I'm going to take a bath. I'm not feeling terribly clean at the moment. It's been a pleasure, Mr. DeLeon."

She turned and walked away.

When Macus stepped away from the bar he noticed his drink was almost empty, and yet she had hardly touched hers.

The next morning he had a bit of a hangover, but nothing really serious. He had an appointment with Palmutter, and he met Faith coming out of the old man's office as he walked in. He lowered his voice and leaned close to her ear. "What's he like? Still out of control?"

"Not at all," she said, shaking her head in obvious disbelief. "War is apparently off the table, at least today, and he's happy as a kitten. In just one night he's completely changed his mind."

••••

It had been a busy morning, and Palmutter had monopolized all of Faith's time. She wasn't responsible for writing press releases and speeches, but the old man had tasked her with carefully vetting the final results of anything that came from his office. She spent the morning in a meeting with Macus, Palmutter, and his speech and copy writers. About mid-morning Strikland joined the meeting, but sat in the background, said nothing, and merely observed.

It fell to Faith and Macus to convince Palmutter it would be a disaster to disclose to the entire Commonwealth the details of the battle between *Konigsborge* and *Valhaukr*. "It was an internal dispute," Macus said, "and I recommend we treat it as such." Whenever Palmutter completely lost control, Macus seemed to have a way of handling the old fellow, and Faith was happy to let him do so. It also meant poor Macus frequently took the brunt of Palmutter's wrath.

Palmutter stood and slammed a fist on the table. "An internal dispute between two members of their Executive Council. That's about as high up as it gets."

Macus remained calm. "But still, an internal dispute."

Palmutter wouldn't listen. "The voters need to know about this."

For about ten minutes Macus calmly rebutted each of Palmutter's outbursts, and slowly brought the senator's blood pressure down to something manageable, though the old man had one final demand. "Those blue-skinned demons double-crossed us. They betrayed this mission, and we should tell the public about it, put those Kelk monsters on notice."

Faith intervened. "Senator, you're getting a lot of good press right now from this mission. Such a statement would probably end the mission, and with it, all that good press."

Palmutter sat down like a petulant child. "We have to do something. We can't let them simply get away with this."

Macus surprised Faith when he said, "I agree, senator." That got the old fellow's attention.

Macus leaned forward to make a point. "If we keep it under wraps, we can quietly use it against them during any negotiations. It could give us a considerable advantage."

When the meeting finally broke up, as everyone filed out of the room, Strikland took Palmutter by the elbow and pulled him aside. As Faith walked past the two men, she couldn't make out what Strikland said, but she heard Palmutter utter the name *Nvalheim*, a Kelk sounding name.

Faith had just reached the door when Strikland called out, "Miss Carlton, might I have a word alone with you?"

She turned back and smiled at him. "Certainly, Mr. Strikland."

They walked down the passageway to Strikland's suite, simply because they couldn't be certain Palmutter hadn't installed listening devices in his. Once Strikland had dismissed his bodyguard and closed the door, standing on the other side of the room he turned to Faith and said, "That was deeply disturbing. He's completely out of control."

Faith thought it interesting that she didn't see the anger in Strikland's face she had seen once before. "He can be quite volatile."

He shook his head in bewilderment. "But he acts without thought, without reason."

If Palmutter's unpredictable nature had shaken Strikland's confidence in the man, Faith was not about to rectify that. "He's always been that way, driven by hatred, by emotion."

Strikland seemed to come to a decision. "My colleagues and I all agree there's no room in either politics or business for blind emotion. And we have a friend on the other side that is just as volatile. I sometimes think the two of them feed off one another."

His colleagues! Clearly he did not include Palmutter among his colleagues. And *a friend on the other side*, would that be a Kelk friend? "We try to mitigate some of the senator's more extreme views, but at times it's quite difficult."

One of his eyebrows lifted as he nodded. "I noticed you and Mr. DeLeon handled him quite deftly. I think I'd like to have a one-on-one talk with Mr. DeLeon."

He crossed the room, took her in his arms, and smiled. "I'm beginning to believe we can no longer count on Silas and some of our Kelk friends to work as part of the team." For the second time she saw anger cloud his features. "And I haven't forgotten he asked you to seduce me and spy on me. Don't worry about him. Whatever happens to Palmutter, I'll see to it you come out of this unscathed."

••••

A beep or ping from one of the consoles occasionally broke the silence of *Drakan Helgis*'s bridge, and in the hush Nikaela subconsciously tried to suppress the sound of her own breathing. Taugrim had the ship operating with a skeleton crew. On the bridge, only the scan console and conn were crewed at all times. That way they'd have warning if the situation with the three hunter-killers changed. Nikaela had requested and received permission to practice at the Nav console.

The radius of the white dwarf was smaller than many planets and less than a hundredth that of Viktorkinde's star, even though it contained greater mass. As *Drakan Helgis* sped through its closest approach, from three million kilometers out, the dwarf appeared to be only about a fifth the size of the star that rose each morning in Viktorkinde's sky. And its true brightness wasn't much, so without magnification it looked like nothing more than a rather large, bluish star in the distance. At the moment the bigger of the two binaries, the hot, white star, was more than twelve astronomical units distant, so it too was just another pinpoint of light in the darkness of space.

It had taken them nine days to approach perigee with the dwarf. Nikaela now understood why Taugrim had chosen to swing around the smaller star. The larger, white star was just too big, and much too hot. If they swung that close to its center of mass they would approach to within two million kilometers of its surface, which would tax the destroyer's cooling systems to the limit. To keep from being fried, they'd have to resort to actively reradiating the energy the star threw their way, lighting them up nicely for the hunter-killers to detect and destroy. All those factors meant that if they wanted to grav-assist around the larger star, they would have to keep to a much greater distance. To get the same change in direction they'd have to slow down considerably, and the flyby would take months. The smaller, less-intense dwarf allowed them to approach quite close to a body of considerable mass without being cooked, swing around it at three hundred kilometers a second, exit with a significant change in direction, and do so in a couple of tendays.

Their enemy could figure that out as well, and were concentrating their search efforts in the greater vicinity of the dwarf.

Movement on the other side of the bridge caught her attention. Floating in zero-G, Kyrsten Stinar pulled herself onto the bridge. Moving from handhold to handhold she crossed to Nikaela's console and frowned. "You shouldn't worry about this so much. What will happen, will happen, and with Captain Taugrim, we have a better chance than most."

Nikaela shook her head. "I'm not as worried as I look. Just practicing. When we get back to Viktorkinde, I have to take the tests for senior rank."

That was only half true. She had practiced navigation, but she had also played with possible solutions to their present dilemma. How was Taugrim going to evade the three hunter-killers and keep them all alive? Nikaela had not come up with anything viable.

Stinar grinned and pulled herself down to get her lips a little closer to Nikaela's ear. "What's he like in bed?"

Nikaela didn't need to ask who the woman meant by *he*. "I don't know."

Stinar shook her head, which made her wobble as she floated there. "Well you'd better stop wasting time, because if you don't, someone else will."

Nikaela didn't try to hide her annoyance as she said, "Meaning you?"

Stinar rolled her eyes and kept her voice low. "No, not me. Don't be an idiot."

"Then who?"

The woman's eyes narrowed with anger, and Nikaela didn't understand why. "I don't know exactly, but there are rumors."

She wouldn't say anything more, but swung around and pulled herself from handhold to handhold, leaving Nikaela there wondering what she had missed.

32

Opportunities Arise

AFTER A MEETING with Palmutter, Macus thought he might go down to the lounge for a drink. Perhaps he'd run into that news hype and finally get her in bed. But Faith pulled him aside, retrieved a small access terminal from her briefcase, and said, "I want to show you the latest poll results we received from Trafalgar."

He pointed his eyes at the face of the terminal, but his focus was on his implants as she opened up a secure link. *What's up?* he asked.

She smiled and said aloud. "The results are looking rather good." Over the link she said, *We have to make this quick. Strikland appears to have run out of patience with Palmutter's volatility, actually openly told me he could no longer count on the senator to work with him . . . as part of the team. Those were his words. He said right now there's a lot more profit to be had with peace than war, and I think he really regrets aligning with the old boy.*

Macus recalled Strikland interrupting Palmutter in the middle of his tirade. The three of them had been alone in Palmutter's office, and to calm the senator down, Strikland had said something to the old fellow about peace being more profitable than war. He told Faith about that now. Then aloud, he said, "That's really quite interesting. How can I help?"

"Here," she said, again indicating the terminal. "I think you'll find these numbers quite telling." *Last night Strikland asked me about you.*

He nodded his head and said, "You're right, that is quite interesting. How should I interpret that?"

Faith smiled like a general after an important victory. *I think Strikland's going to approach you. I'm not sure about what, but be prepared.*

"Yes," Macus said. "Thank you for the information." *Oh, and keep your ears open for the name Nvalheim. I think it's a Kelk name. Strikland used it when trying to calm Palmutter down.*

Her brow wrinkled in thought. *Nvalheim. I heard Palmutter mention that name to Strikland just the other day.*

Really. How so?

She shook her head. *I didn't catch it all. It sounds Kelkish. Do you think it's some sort of Kelk contact of theirs?*

I have no idea. Let's keep our eyes and ears open.

She nodded, smiled, turned and walked away.

Later that afternoon, as Macus stepped out of Palmutter's suite, in the hallway he ran into Strikland and one of his bodyguards.

"Mr. DeLeon," Strikland said, giving Macus a big smile. "I'm glad I happened to run into you. I've been meaning to have a word with you. Could you spare me a few minutes of your time?"

"Certainly, Mr. Strikland."

Macus found Strikland's suite every bit as spacious as Palmutter's; again, probably the money thing. Like Palmutter's, his also contained a small office, and with the bodyguard waiting outside, he led Macus into it and closed the door. He invited Macus to sit in a comfortable chair. Strikland didn't walk around the desk and sit down behind it in the seat of power, but instead sat down in another chair facing Macus. Macus wondered if he should read anything into that.

"You and Miss Carlton," Strikland said. "You make a good team. It's quite clear that, were it not for the two of you, by now Silas would have created any number of problems for the rest of us."

Macus didn't think he and Faith were included in *the rest of us*, and he wondered who might be. "I think that's because Faith and I share a similar world-view." It occurred to him Strikland might not really understand just how much truth that statement carried.

Strikland leaned forward, as if the time had come for a more intimate conversation. "You know, Mr. DeLeon, in the closed environment of this ship, the rumor mill is quite telling, and there's nothing in it about you and Miss Carlton. I would think the two of you would be a natural pairing."

Macus now knew what Strikland wanted to hear. "Faith and I haven't really discussed the matter, but again I think we are of a similar mind. An intimate relationship would only complicate our professional lives, and could at some point prove to be a serious problem. I try to be selective with my relationships, and I suspect Faith is the same way."

"Very wise of both of you," Strikland said. He leaned back in his chair and steepled his fingers in front of him. "It occurs to me Silas is getting on in years, and I would expect him to retire in the not too distant future."

"Really," Macus said. "If you had asked me, I would have said he's going to die in office."

Strikland's eyebrows rose, as if considering the matter. "I suppose that's always a possibility. Tell me, Mr. DeLeon, have you considered entering public service?"

Macus's heart raced, and he took care not to appear too eager. If Strikland were to back him, there was no telling how far he could go. He thought it best to simply lie. "No, sir, not really. I wouldn't know how to begin."

"You're intelligent," Strikland said. "You don't spook easily, and you're quite handsome."

Macus wasn't sure what Strikland was getting at, and he let that show in his face.

Strikland smiled and nodded. "Don't discount good looks. No one likes to admit it, but they can bring in that extra percent or two of votes. On the other hand, the most important quality you possess is your pragmatism."

Strikland had an abiding interest in pragmatic profits, so Macus decided to play that card. "I don't think anyone really profits from hard, unyielding ideology." Macus held up a hand and paused. "And I didn't mean *profit* in a strictly monetary sense, though that's important as well. We can't survive if we're not profitable."

Strikland smiled, and sat there for a long moment, his finger tracing a pattern in the material on the arm of his chair. Then he looked into Macus's eyes and said, "There's really nothing more powerful, or enabling, than enlightened self-interest."

He stood, and Macus stood with him. Strikland extended his hand, and Macus shook it as Strikland said, "I've enjoyed our conversation, Mr. DeLeon."

Macus smiled and nodded. "As did I, sir."

Strikland escorted him to the door. He paused there and said, "Perhaps we can chat again some time."

"I'm at your disposal, sir."

Out in the hallway, Macus wanted to find Faith and tell her every detail of the conversation he had just had. Revealing to Strikland that Palmutter had asked her to spy on him had apparently stoked already present doubts the fellow had about the senator. And Palmutter's unreasoned tirades during the last few days may have put the final nail in the old man's coffin.

Macus recalled that when he had said Palmutter would die in office, Strikland had paused to think on that, almost as if he considered Macus's words a recommendation, rather than an observation. He realized then that they might have already put the final nail in Palmutter's coffin, and not just figuratively.

••••

Military grade implants included software and circuits that could suppress pain, but they did so by blocking nerve impulses to certain sections of the brain. That could produce side-effects like numbness or tingling, and if pushed to the limit, loss of motor function in muscles near the site of the injury. On Miriteen, during advanced training, John and his platoon mates had been given careful instruction in the use of such techniques, and since then John had done a little experimenting on his own. Through trial and error, he had learned he could simply suppress his reaction to the pain, without killing the pain itself. In that way he didn't have to worry about the muscular side-effects, but it did induce a kind of schizophrenic split in his thinking. It produced a part of him that suffered the agony of the pain, and another that ignored all that, made cold, hard decisions, and functioned much like a machine. He didn't like either of those Johns.

Coasting through their trajectory around the white dwarf, everyone on *Drakan Helgis* had a lot of time on their hands. John killed some hours by working with a few of the dregkraag to practice weightless techniques in his new Kelk armor. With the gym almost always full, Matsen and Kolbeck showed him how he could use the armor to get some exercise. They tweaked the gain adjustments so his armor moved the way he wanted it to, but it resisted a little. With his armor tuned that way, an hour moving about stressed every muscle in his body, and gave him a good workout. He also grew quite accustomed to the Kelk armor and learned its eccentricities.

The day after they passed perigee, he spent some time thinking about what Taugrim hoped to accomplish. With the vastness of an entire solar system to search, they could hide from their enemy forever. But if they made a run for it, even if the three hunter-killers were on the opposite side of the system, they'd only have a few hundred AUs head start. They'd drive hard for a couple of hours, with their enemy hot on their tail, and when they up-transited the hunter-killers would do so as well. Their differential velocity would close that gap in a matter of minutes, and it would all be over in short order.

He requested a few minutes of Taugrim's time, and she told him to report to her office. He carefully told her his thinking, and as he spoke her eyebrows rose and the corners of her mouth curled upward in her familiar, toothy grin.

When he finished laying out his thinking, he asked, "Mistress, what am I missing?"

She shook her head. "Nothing, Blacksword. We're just buying time, because that's all we've got."

"So how do we escape?"

She held her hands up in a gesture of supplication. "We bide our time, and maybe we get lucky."

"What if we don't get lucky?"

"Well as long as they don't get lucky, we'll be here until they give up or we run out of necessities. But if they do get lucky, we're fucked." They were speaking Kelk, and John wandered if they had been speaking Lingua, would Taugrim, like Nikaela, have the same difficulty with the tenses of fucked versus fucking.

He tried to think how they might change their luck, but came up empty on that.

She interrupted his thoughts. "Listen, Blacksword. Right now the odds are in our favor. They're the hunters, so they have to zip around the system searching for us, whereas we get to just sit here quiet and still. If they make even the tiniest of mistakes, and they will, we get to pick and choose if it's enough of a mistake to act on, and we get to choose the moment to act."

He considered that, saw the logic of it, but then she might simply be trying to make him feel better.

"By the way, Blacksword," she said, and she had a funny look on her face. "You're thinking like the CO of a warship. Good for you."

She dismissed him, and he thought he might get in a workout in his armor. But he recalled Nikaela in her armor on Reisenar, and that thought, combined with Matsen and Kolbeck's adjustments to his armor, gave him an idea.

He needed Nikaela's help, and found her in the ward room. They had rigged a few tables to generate about a tenth gravity above the table top. It didn't draw enough power to light them up and give their position away, and in zero-G, it allowed them to strap into chairs around the tables, play cards, eat a normal meal instead of the zero-G glop, or sip at some caff. One still had to be careful, because a tenth G wasn't enough to prevent a real mess if someone moved quickly, or thoughtlessly. And if the bridge detected an enemy warship approaching to within a few hundred million kilometers, Engineering might cut even that small bit of power generation, though hopefully they'd give some warning before doing so.

At the far end of the ward room, Primatov and Falkenberg sat strapped into seats at a table, and were talking quietly with their heads together. Three other officers sat at another table, while Nikaela sat at a third, with Stinar seated opposite her, cups of caff in front of them both.

As John floated into the room and approached them, Nikaela said, "Maestra Mathius."

John responded with, "Mistress Vreekande."

Stinar rolled her eyes.

John said, "I need your help. May I join you?"

Stinar pointed to the seat next to her, so John strapped in. He asked Nikaela, "Remember on Reisenar when I blew your foot off with a micro-nuke?"

Every head in the ward room turned to look his way.

He continued, "You did something to your armor to generate a gravity field so you could walk around like you had a peg on your leg. It looked like the stump of your leg floated up off the ground."

"Yes," she said, a curious look on her face. "Why do you ask?"

"Could you show me how to do that?"

She placed her cup of caff down onto the table top, doing so carefully. "I don't know how. A dregkraag medic showed me how to do it."

Stinar said, "Then let's go find a dregkraag medic."

As the three of them unstrapped from their chairs. Falkenberg and Primatov unstrapped as well. Primatov said, "Didn't mean to eavesdrop, but I'm curious to see what you come up with."

Falkenberg introduced them to the command superior in charge of the dregkraag platoon. She took them in hand, and introduced them to her most experienced medic. When John described what they had done to Nikaela's foot on Reisenar, the fellow shook his head. "I've done something like that myself a few times. But that wasn't just her armor. They must have added a small grav plate, with maybe an extra power cell."

"Yes," Nikaela said. "That medic did exactly that, and gave me a single cell reactor pack to power it. And now I recall they had already removed my armor."

She turned to John. "Sorry, John."

The medic asked John, "What were you hoping to do?"

John hadn't really thought it through. "If I was ever in that position, you know, a piece of my leg blown off, and I didn't have a medic to help me, if I could rig up something like that myself, I could still function."

The medic's eyes narrowed in thought. "Interesting idea! The armor would be badly damaged, but most of its circuits and materials are self-healing, to a limited extent. And the fields you could generate would be badly distorted. I can show you a few tricks though, show you how to modify some of the gravity fields coming off your armor. But don't mess around with it too much. You'll really fuck it up, and then we'll have to fix it."

The dregkraag medic showed John a couple of adjustments he could make to his armor, but none of it came close to what he had hoped for.

"Tell you what," the fellow said. "I'll think on it further. Maybe I'll come up with something."

John thanked him, but didn't think anything would come of it.

33

Dodged a Bullet

AFTER SIX MORE days of searching, *Konigsborge* and *Eldekarl* had swept well past the point where the hunter-killers would have caught up with *Drakan Helgis*. Early on they had encountered the debris fields where the hunter-killers had destroyed the two relay buoys. Hunter-killers mounted a couple of small ship's guns, and under normal circumstances they would use those to destroy something like a buoy. But their opponents had not had the time to down-transit and deploy their guns, had instead launched warheads while passing in transition, leaving nothing but an expanding sphere of radioactive vapor in place of each destroyed buoy. On the other hand, the greater mass of a warship, even if destroyed by a direct hit from a large warhead, would leave behind a well-defined debris field, along with a fair amount of radioactive vapor. They had found nothing like that.

Kristdokar and Nygaard decided to turn around, and sweep back along the relay chain, moving down one side of it. With *Eldekarl* running parallel to them, and with a separation between them of five light-years, they could remain in contact with each other and the chain, and cover a swath of space fifteen light-years wide. It was a much more dangerous way of searching than the modified skip-jump approach they had used before, but they could cover a greater area in a shorter period of time, and at that point they felt they had no choice.

Kristdokar had once heard John Mathius use the Lingua phrase *sweating bullets*. She had asked him about it, and he had said it meant, ". . . you're really nervous, or worried, or something like that." She had looked up the two words separately to confirm that she did understand their meaning, and that they didn't have some alternate meaning of which she was unaware. But until two days ago she hadn't really understood the phrase. Two days ago was the earliest she might have heard a response from her Commonwealth colleagues. Two days ago was the earliest she might have learned if they chose to cancel the diplomatic mission and declare war. She had received nothing, and since then, had come to understand intimately what it meant to sweat bullets. And every few hours for the last two days, Nygaard had asked her if she had received a reply. She concluded the vice skalde would also understand the Lingua phrase if she told her about it.

When the com tech told her the reply had finally come in, she contacted Nygaard immediately. They gathered in Nygaard's conference room.

Kristdokar said, "Let's forego the tea ceremony."

"Thank you," Nygaard said. "I didn't feel much like tea anyway."

They both sat down, Kristdokar ran the response through malware and subvertware checks, decrypted it, reran the checks, then cued the message up. Fran Thealone appeared standing before them. "I don't think I need to tell you the difficulties this has caused at this end. Like you, we have individuals who do not think clearly regarding this unprecedented situation we find ourselves in. It has taken us two days to get everyone calmed down, but we now unanimously agree we should continue with the diplomatic mission, though we have to make a few changes to our original agreement."

Kristdokar glanced at Nygaard. The worst case scenario had been averted.

Thealone continued. "There are two hunter-killers that have accompanied us, scouting ahead to make sure we don't encounter something unanticipated. We had originally intended that they would remain behind when we entered sovereign Supremacy space. But given the heightened instabilities in the Supremacy, of which you have now made us aware, that is no longer the case. Those two hunter-killers will accompany us all the way to Viktorkinde. These terms are not negotiable."

Kristdokar paused the recording and looked at Nygaard. The vice skalde winced. "I'll smooth it over with the Executive Council."

Kristdokar started the recording up again, and Thealone continued. "We've also taken steps to fill the gap between the terminuses of the two relay chains with additional buoys. That should be complete in less than a tenday. *Lightspear* will no longer need to ferry messages between the chains, so we're bringing her with us as well and assigning other ships to patrol the chain between Trafalgar and the edge of Supremacy space. We recommend you assign *Alvilddan* the same duty in Supremacy space."

Thealone paused for a moment, then looked at the pickup, her expression hardening. "Ensign Mathius and Colonel Primatov swore an oath to protect the Commonwealth, with their lives if necessary. I hope it hasn't come to that, but please let us know immediately if you hear anything."

The recording ended.

Nygaard looked at Kristdokar and smiled. "There is a Lingua expression that is particularly appropriate at this moment. They say, 'We just dodged a bullet.'"

Kristdokar nodded. "I'm familiar with that expression."

••••

When Gascoigne proposed that they start pushing Palmutter's buttons, to Fran's surprise Obradour concurred without hesitation. He merely said, "Yes, I get the impression he's running a bit scared, so we might learn something." Gascoigne quietly warned Catarvin in advance, then he set up the meeting.

At the prearranged time Fran sat down in her stateroom on *Hellfire* and keyed her implants into the conference room on *Lady Victorious*. She found herself seated alone at the table with Palmutter.

Catarvin had reported that he was now operating in a constant state of foul disposition. At her appearance he spoke in a surly growl and immediately demanded, "What's this about?"

Fran went with the story she, Gascoigne, and Obradour had worked out. "I've received some additional information from our Kelk colleagues."

He leaned forward. "Then spit it out, goddammit, I don't have all day."

He did have all day. Fran had spent many a tenday on a ship in the dark reaches of space, and when they weren't busy dodging warheads, everyone had lots of time on their hands. "Why don't we wait until the others are—"

Thankfully, at that moment, Obradour walked into the conference room. He sat down and greeted both of them in that overly polite way of his. Catarvin arrived a few seconds later, and Gascoigne a heartbeat after that. To Fran's great relief, their presence tempered Palmutter's anger, though that was probably due to Obradour more than anything else. He clearly intimidated the senator.

Gascoigne took control of the meeting. "Colonel Blacksword asked me to arrange this meeting because she has received some new information from *Konigsborge*. So I'm simply going to give her the floor."

Gascoigne, Obradour and Fran had carefully scripted her words. "I received a message from Brigadier Skalde Kristdokar. They have identified those responsible for the attack by *Valhaukr* on *Konigsborge*. The names they gave me are Vice Skalde Haugrund, Command Eagle Aubrecht Machtberg, and Brigadier Skalde Marta Nvalheim, retired."

As she spoke that last name, Fran watched Palmutter closely, but he didn't react in the slightest. "Haugrund is a member of the Larscom Executive Council, but she has been removed from that post by unanimous vote of the other four members of the Council. We know almost nothing about Machtberg, and only a little about Nvalheim, but at this point they are under indictment and are persona non grata in the Supremacy. What further action will be taken against them has yet to be determined."

Palmutter still hadn't reacted in the slightest, and that bothered Fran.

Like actors on a stage, she, Obradour and Gascoigne then pretended to trade the information they had exchanged when they first learned of Machtberg and Nvalheim. Fran related what little there was in ComSec's databases about the two, Obradour confirmed that Nvalheim was a member of the Larscom General Secretariat, but didn't reveal her connections to Norddansk Weapons Systems. If they were right about Palmutter, he already knew those details.

Through it all Palmutter didn't blink, and during the discussion that followed he remained subdued. The meeting ended without incident.

••••

The powers that be sponsored a mixer in the lounge every five days, one at mid-ten and one at ten-end. Attendance was optional for all staffers, but the members of the diplomatic mission were always careful to attend, so Macus would not have missed it for anything. And there were a few beneficial side benefits: He'd met one of Gascoigne's speech writers at the first mixer. She was quite pretty, but so junior there could be no benefit in nurturing a relationship with her. At the time he hadn't paid much attention to her, but when he and Faith decided to put their physical relationship on hold, it didn't take him long to get the girl in bed. She was good for a regular maintenance fuck, though she was a bit of a pain in the ass because he had to pretend more interest in her than that.

Earlier that day they had reached the terminus of the Viktorkinde relay chain and were now in constant contact with *Konigsborge*. The talk at the mixer that evening focused mainly on that, and many of the younger staffers were quite excited.

Holding a drink and standing in front of Macus, Faith met his eyes as she said, "They have no idea, do they?"

The junior staffers were not privy to the situation with *Konigsborge* and the missing destroyer *Drakan Helgis*, nor were they wholly aware of the discord within the Larscom.

Faith wore a low-cut evening gown that clung to her like a coat of paint. "You look outstanding in that dress." Macus used his implants to speak privately with her. *That dress, with you in it, is giving every man in the room an erection.*

She smiled, sipped demurely at her drink, and spoke out loud. "You're being kind, Macus." Through her implants she added, *Tonight I hope to get dear Mr. Strikland to be more candid about some of his Kelk connections. By the way, he seems quite pleased that you're fucking that girl.*

"It's not kindness," Macus said, "to simply acknowledge a fact." *I was careful to let my relationship with her leak into the rumor mill. When Strikland and I spoke, he seemed concerned I might have some personal interest in you, so knowing I'm fucking that girl should alleviate any fears he might have.*

She nodded. "That was most considerate of you."

"Faith, Macus."

At the sound of Strikland's voice, they both turned to face him as he approached them, a broad smile on his face. He gave Faith's dress a sterile glance with no outward indication he might be look-fucking her, and Macus appreciated the man's restraint. "Miss Carlton, as always, you look quite lovely."

She batted her eyelashes like a virginal school girl, and Macus admired her performance. "Thank you, Mr. Strikland."

Strikland leaned close to her. "Forgive me, but I need to steal Mr. DeLeon for a moment or two. You don't mind, do you?"

"Not at all," she said, and gave him a look filled with promise. "I need to freshen my drink anyway."

She turned and walked away, and Strikland didn't succumb to any temptation to stare at her very nice backside, though quite a few of the other men in the room did not show the same restraint.

Strikland leaned close to Macus and lowered his voice. "Let's step aside where we can talk privately."

The man led Macus to the edge of the room where the crowd was thinner. Without being overt about it, Strikland positioned them with his back to the room, and Macus facing him. Then he activated a privacy screen, which would null out his words anywhere beyond a foot or two from his mouth. "Regarding that private conversation we had a few days ago, have you had a chance to think about what we discussed?"

Macus nodded. "Yes, sir, I must confess it has been on my mind. I would certainly relish the opportunity to work with the right kind of people."

Strikland's eyebrows arched up just the faintest bit and he smiled, as if acknowledging the implication in Macus's words. Palmutter might once have been *the right kind of people*, but he had recently become a liability.

"Excellent," Strikland said. "I have access to the relay chain, and after our discussion I contacted some of my colleagues on Trafalgar. Let me put a thought into your head. You should look into the forty-third precinct in Trafalgar City. I have it on good authority the present precinct supervisor might not chose to run again in the next election cycle. It's a rather low-level position, but it is Trafalgar City, not a post on some backwater planet. And just as important, it's an *elected* position. A few years' experience as an elected official, a couple of good speeches, some legislative accomplishments, perhaps an article in the news feeds about a new rising star on the political scene, those things could position a young man nicely for greater things."

Strikland gripped Macus's shoulder in a fatherly way. "Think on it, Macus. Take your time and do some homework. The election is a year away, so we have plenty of time, and nothing's going to happen before we get back to Trafalgar. Think on it."

"I most certainly will, sir."

As Strikland walked away, Macus spotted that young news hype, Karya something. He still hadn't had any success getting up her skirt, but recently his luck had improved on an almost daily basis, so perhaps that might change as well. He decided to give it one more try.

••••

The hunter-killers changed their sweep patterns, and Nikaela and the senior navigator carefully analyzed the new data. They were four days past perigee, and in eight hours, one of the enemy ships would pass about three hundred million kilometers off *Drakan Helgis*'s bow, within range of her main batteries, but still a longshot.

The navigator looked at Nikaela's results and nodded. "Excellent work, Mistress Vreekande. Upload it to the conn."

"Mistress Falkenberg," the navigator said. "Mistress Vreekande is uploading her analysis to the conn. You should look at it immediately." That was his way of telling Falkenberg he had reviewed and approved Nikaela's work.

Nikaela watched Falkenberg as she scanned the data. Her eyes slowly brightened and a smile formed on her face. "Com," she said. "Please ask Mistresses Taugrim and Primatov to report to the bridge immediately."

Nikaela didn't understand the excitement in her voice.

Taugrim arrived, breathing a little heavily as if she'd rushed from handhold to handhold in the weightless passageways of the ship. She didn't relieve Falkenberg of command, but gripped the back of her seat and floated behind her, looking over her shoulder as the XO pointed something out on her screens.

After a few seconds Taugrim shouted, "Yes," startling Nikaela. "That's what we've been hoping for."

By that time Primatov had arrived and hovered next to Taugrim.

"Mistress Vreekande," Taugrim crowed. "Tell me what you see in this data."

Nikaela wasn't sure what answer the women was looking for. "They'll be within range of a longshot."

"Maestra Blacksword, what do you see?"

John sat in the apprentice's seat at Helm, a smile slowly forming on his face. "Their friends are too far out to help them, and they're on the other side of the mass of that white dwarf. It'll get in their way, warp their vectors if they try a short transition hop to come to their aid quickly. We'll have this one all to ourselves."

Reflecting the look on Taugrim's face, Primatov smiled. "Yes, it'll take forty or fifty minutes for the nearest of the other two to get close enough to range on us, unless they're desperate enough to try a short transition jump. And as Maestra Mathius pointed out, the probability of that working is almost nonexistent."

Taugrim shook her head, her grin broadening. "We're going to have that one all to ourselves, one on one, a hunter-killer against *Drakan Helgis*; that's bad news for them. It's dangerous, but this is the bit of luck I've hoped for."

That was the hint Nikaela needed, and it all came together for her. *Drakan Helgis* would have the single hunter-killer heavily outgunned. Even if the other two drove as hard as they could in an attempt come to their comrade's aid, with one of them three AUs out and the other six, *Drakan Helgis* would have more than enough time to even the odds. If they could destroy that one hunter-killer, then *Drakan Helgis*, with her heavy batteries and transition launchers, would be on par with the combined might of the other two. It could drastically change the status quo.

"Okay everyone," Taugrim announced. "We've got eight hours. I want everyone to get a meal and some sleep."

Nikaela unstrapped and saw John doing the same, but Taugrim stopped them all.

"Hey, Blacksword."

John froze and turned to face her, a look of resignation on his face. "Yes, mistress."

Taugrim wore that big grin of hers. "No pretty girl this time. I don't want you all worn out."

Her words implied that John had taken some girl to bed with him. Nikaela didn't think that was the case, and she couldn't suppress a small laugh. John gave Nikaela a dirty look, rolled his eyes and said, "Yes, mistress."

••••

"Mistresses," Captain Holverzon said, "*Eldekarl* is now in position, and we've verified the chain back to Viktorkinde is again working."

It was not uncommon for warships to carry a single com buoy. Before entering a potentially hostile situation in an unfriendly system, they could drop it a few light-years out, which allowed them to communicate with other ships operating beyond the normal transition-com limit of about five light-years. Since hunter-killers frequently operated covertly, they almost always carried one, and *Eldekarl* was no exception. Unfortunately, *Konigsborge* did not. To repair the gap in the relay chain caused by the destruction of two buoys, *Eldekarl* replaced one of them with the buoy she carried, then down-transited and went static in place of the second buoy. The hunter-killer would act as a relay, which left *Konigsborge* operating alone.

Holverzon looked up from his screens at Nygaard. "I don't like it, mistress. This puts you two in even greater danger."

"Come now, Captain," Nygaard said. "With *Valhaukr* out of the picture, it's only three hunter-killers. Wherever they are, they have *Drakan Helgis* outgunned, but *Konigsborge* should handle them easily."

Holverzon shook his head. "Not if they're lying in wait and take us by surprise." He turned his attention to Kristdokar and looked her in the eyes. "It's dangerous, mistress. Can you not convince her?"

Kristdokar appreciated the man's concern. "I would not if I could. It's unlikely we'll encounter any of those hunter-killers. When last seen, they were chasing after *Drakan Helgis*. What little danger exists, is worth the chance, and I concur completely with Vice Skalde Nygaard's decision."

"Captain, mistresses," the com tech said, speaking cautiously, and clearly uncomfortable that duty required her to interrupt an argument between three high-ranking officers. "The diplomatic mission from Trafalgar has entered sovereign Supremacy space. I just received a ping from them on our relay chain."

Holverzon looked her way. "Respond so they know the link is good."

Nygaard said, "Captain, please carry out the orders I've given you."

Holverzon sighed and did not look away from the com tech. In profile Kristdokar saw the displeasure on his face as he said, "Give them our position, and tell them we're coming their way to rendezvous with them."

"Captain," Nygaard said, drawing his attention to her. "Do you not see that this is an historic moment? For the first time in recorded history, Commonwealth government ships have entered sovereign Supremacy space without hostile intent."

His lips stretched into a sharp, straight line, and Kristdokar heard the pain in his voice as he said, "Can you be sure of that?"

34

Time to Move

KATRINE SLAMMED AWAKE, her heart fluttering as she struggled to overcome the disorientation of being yanked abruptly out of a sound sleep.

Allship blared. "Watch condition red. Battle stations, all hands, this is not a drill."

Katrine pulled on a one-piece coverall, her eyes glancing over the colonel's birds on the collar. When Taugrim heard Katrine had been promoted, the woman made the destroyer's machine shop do their best to fabricate metal pins that matched the rank insignia of a bird colonel in the Commonwealth. If one didn't look too close, they had done a pretty good job.

With the coverall on, she pushed her hair back and held it in place with a billed cap. Taugrim had made her people fabricate cloth patches as well.

Katrine hurried up to the bridge, moving from handhold to handhold in the weightless passageways of the ship. She stopped at the command console, gripping one edge of it to steady her motion as she floated nearby, and faced Taugrim.

With her new rank equivalent to that of a Kelk command eagle, Katrine now outranked Taugrim, but there was only one captain on a ship. Under weightless conditions, most situations that normally required a salute were temporarily suspended. But because of the rank discrepancy, Katrine needed to show everyone she understood which of them gave orders aboard *Drakan Helgis*.

She aimed a crisp salute at Taugrim, though she moved carefully in zero-G to make sure she didn't spin like a top. Unlike John Mathius, she presented the Commonwealth style of salute. She did take one thing from John's first time standing watch. "Colonel Katrine Primatov, ComSecCorps, Blacksword Regiment, reporting for duty, Mistress Taugrim."

Taugrim returned her salute in the Kelk style, then pointed at her screens. They had long ago interfaced John's and her implants to shipnet, and Katrine's virtual vision gave added dimension to what she saw there. In about fifteen minutes, the sweep vector of that one hunter-killer would cross *Drakan Helgis*'s static trajectory in its swing around the white dwarf. It was not the situation they had analyzed a few hours ago.

Taugrim tapped her screen. "They changed course again. If they hold to their sweep trajectory, in short order they're going to pass five million kilometers off our bow. If we take a shot at them, we'd have to be bloody incompetent to miss at that range."

Katrine asked, "What about the other two?"

Taugrim flashed that grin of hers. "They changed their course as well, but they're still on the other side of that white dwarf and still three and six AUs out. Just a little bit too far for targeting."

Katrine looked carefully at the new data. The mass of the nearby white dwarf would distort the track of a hunter-killer's transition torpedoes far more than that of the shells from *Drakan Helgis*'s transition batteries. Ranging at two hundred million kilometers would have given them a significant advantage. But at only five million, that advantage had considerably diminished. "It's going to be a lot more dangerous."

Taugrim nodded once, but didn't say anything.

Katrine met her eyes and grinned. "But we're still going to have plenty of time alone with them."

"Exactly," Taugrim said.

Katrine strapped into her seat at Fire Control.

••••

John listened carefully as Taugrim barked orders. "Engineering, stand by for rapid power-ramp on my command. Initially, I want power priority to the shields, then on my command to the main batteries. Fire Control, stand by main batteries, and be prepared to blow those mines we dropped in front and behind us. When I give the command, use a standard EM signal to trigger them, no transition signal."

The scan tech said, "Closest approach in one minute and counting."

John had to think carefully to understand Taugrim's strategy. The two mines were positioned half a million kilometers from *Drakan Helgis*, one in front and one behind them. If they used a transition com signal to trigger them, it would reach the enemy hunter-killer at almost the same instant as the mines, and give them a targeting solution. But a simple electromagnetic signal would take about two seconds to reach the mines, and another fifteen to reach the hunter-killer in front of them. And long before that, the transition noise generated by the expanding fireballs of the two mines, one of which was nicely positioned between them and their enemy, would scramble any scan data they might acquire.

"Closest approach in twenty seconds and counting."

"Fire Control," Taugrim demanded. "Do you have a targeting solution?"

"We do, mistress, and we're constantly updating."

"Warn all defensive stations to be prepared. And when I give the command, trigger the signal for those mines, and one second later fire all main batteries at the same moment. I want that hunter-killer. I want her bad."

John had a combat status summary compressed in the corner of one of his screens and a scan summary in another. Their target coasted in sublight at ten thousand kilometers per second, running on a course almost perpendicular to *Drakan Helgis*'s. That allowed them to make a sweep through the near vicinity of the white dwarf twice a day and cover a lot of territory.

"Closest approach in ten seconds . . . nine . . ."

"Engineering," Taugrim snapped, "full combat status, now."

Drakan Helgis's hull had been silent for thirteen days, but now a low, rumbling whine filled John's ears, growing in pitch with each second.

". . . eight . . ."

"Gravity up. Shields up."

". . . seven . . ."

John's weight settled into his seat.

". . . six . . ."

"Stand by, Helm. Stand by Fire Control."

". . . five . . ."

Seated next to John, Dahlborg gave him a reassuring smile and said, "You've got the helm, Maestra Mathius."

John tried to keep his hands from shaking as he rested them on the controls for the sublight grav drive. If he fucked up, she'd take over in an instant.

". . . four . . ."

The combat status summary showed power at fifty percent. They needed at least eighty to defend themselves and fight back at the same time.

". . . three . . ."

"Fire Control, execute."

Primatov triggered the EM signal for the two mines.

". . . two . . ."

Drakan Helgis's hull thrummed with the coordinated fire from its main batteries.

"Helm, thirty degrees a port and firewall sublight."

John swung the ship's bow to port and pushed the sublight drive to maximum.

". . . one . . ."

When the two mines exploded a new sun appeared off their bow, and another behind them. Many of *Drakan Helgis*'s sensors blanked to prevent damage. And then a third sun blossomed to starboard and astern. Her hull shrieked, and the combat status summary showed the power plant redlining. The sublight drive sputtered and dropped back to five thousand gravities as the ship's shields sucked power to keep the hull intact.

"They tried a Hail Mary," Taugrim said, her voice cracking with strain, "and almost got lucky. Fire Control, do you have a targeting solution?"

"Negative, mistress, standing by."

"When you have one, do not wait for my command. Fire at the earliest possible opportunity."

With the thermonuclear fireballs of three warheads lighting up nearby space, much of their detection capability had been blanked. But power quickly returned to the sublight drive.

The Fire Control officer shouted, "Solution acquired," and *Drakan Helgis*'s hull again thrummed as her main batteries spit transition shells at the enemy.

The scan tech said, "One of the hunter-killers behind us just up-transited."

"That fucking idiot," Taugrim snapped.

The scan summary in the corner of John's screen showed one of the two hunter-killers behind them now in transition, its vector initially aimed their way. But as it passed in close proximity to the white dwarf, gravitational distortions from the mass of the star warped its track badly and it arced to one side. It gave up and down-transited, now even farther away than before, and with a lot of sublight vector they'd have to kill before they could swing around and come back.

"Captain," the com tech said. "Engineering reports we may have some damage to our heat dissipaters. They're assessing it now."

"Shit!" Taugrim growled. "Scan, what's our target look like?"

"It's not moving, mistress. And I'm picking up traces of a debris field. I think we hurt her badly. The two remaining hunter-killers are three and eight AUs behind us, but driving hard in sublight."

"Yah," Taugrim said. "With that dwarf in the way they're not going to try another crazy stunt like that transition jump. Okay, people, let's all take a breath. Helm, Nav, set a course back to the nearest relay buoy. We need to let *Konigsborge* know we're not dead. And let's see how much damage we took. I want a damage report soonest. And keep an eye on those two hunter-killers behind us. They haven't given up yet. And the defensive station that got that warhead before it nailed us, give them an extra kirva ration tonight."

"Mistress," the scan tech said, "another warhead detonation twenty million kilometers off our starboard bow."

One of the hunter-killers behind them had tried a long-shot, but the nearby white-dwarf had distorted the track of its transition torpedoes in the same way it distorted the track of a ship in transition.

The mood on the bridge calmed significantly. They had sustained some minor damage amidships, but nothing they couldn't repair themselves if they could coast in sublight for a few days, and that wasn't going to happen. The damage amidships was limited to a few hulled compartments, nothing that might slow them down, but the jury was still out on the heat dissipaters. Damage there could slow them considerably.

Ordinarily, they would drive hard and build up relativistic velocity until they reached heliopause, then up-transit outside the sphere of influence of the two stars. But apparently Taugrim didn't like to do anything the normal way.

"First," she said. "We keep those assholes honest. Fire Control, arm a one hundred megaton cluster mine and dump it in our wake. Set it for simultaneous proximity detonation."

A clang echoed through the hull as Fire Control jettisoned the mine. The mine immediately bloomed into an expanding cluster of one hundred warheads, each capable of yielding one megaton.

"Probably won't hurt 'em," Taugrim said. "But that'll keep them honest. Helm, Nav, let's get the hell out of here. Helm, all ahead full in sublight, and get us into transition soonest."

John firewalled the sublight drive, while Dahlborg pushed to force an up-transition. The whine of the ship's drive rose in pitch and John felt it vibrating in the deck beneath his feet. Then the sublight drive went dead and the ship's systems diverted all power into the transition drive.

"Up-transition," John said, trying to keep his voice calm and business-like. The last thing he wanted to do was sound like an excited newbie. "Three hundred lights and climbing."

As Dahlborg pushed their transition drive, John kept his implants attuned to a channel from Engineering. "One thousand lights."

In John's implants, an engineering tech said, *We're good down here.*

Dahlborg nodded and pushed the transition drive harder. "Two thousand lights."

The engineering tech said, *Still good, you can keep pushing it.*

John counted the seconds with heartbeats.

"Thirty-four hundred lights," Dahlborg said. "We're at max."

They all waited in silence for the verdict from Engineering. John didn't know the chief engineer, but an icon in his virtual vision identified him when he said, *Captain, I'm not sure we can hold this for long.*

John listened to Taugrim and the chief engineer discuss the situation. Their thermal recycling system couldn't handle the load for long, so they dropped back to three thousand lights, and that stabilized the situation.

John leaned back in his seat and wondered why they had up-transited from so deep within the binary system.

Taugrim must have been watching him at that moment and saw the questioning look on his face. "It's crazy, isn't it Blacksword? We're too deep inside the heliosphere, and we'll squirt off in some crazy, unknown direction." She winked at John. "But we're far enough out from that dwarf we'll still be going *roughly* in the direction I want to go. If they try the same thing, they'll squirt off in their own random direction and they won't be following us anymore, so they've got to get past that star first."

John asked. "But then they'll try a crazy jump, won't they? And they'll be past that star so they'll still be going in roughly the direction they want to go, which is after us."

"You're right, it's not over yet," she said. She pointed a finger at John. "I still may take you as a lover."

At the Nav console, Nikaela gave Taugrim a sharp look.

Taugrim glanced around the bridge, then loudly announced, "I have an unopened bottle of good kirva in my quarters. They've already tried a crazy stunt and it didn't work. I'm betting they play it straight now. The first one will clear the dwarf then up-transit to get outside heliopause, down-transit there and wait for the second one to clear the star and join them."

She looked John's way, and flashed her white teeth in her characteristic grin. "Care to take me up on the bet, Blacksword? Whichever one of us wins, you and me can share that bottle of kirva"—she paused for a moment of dramatic effect—"alone in my quarters."

Next to John, Dahlborg choked back a laugh. John just shook his head.

••••

Taugrim had given them one hour to grab a quick bite and maybe a shower, if time permitted. With the ship at general quarters, the normal formalities of the officer's ward room had been suspended. Nikaela found John there seated alone at a table. She grabbed a plate of food, and as she sat down opposite him, he looked up and smiled. "Mistress Vreekande."

Nikaela leaned forward and hissed. "We have to talk—alone."

His eyes widened and he leaned forward so they were almost ear to ear. Thankfully, he took his cue from her and kept his voice to a faint whisper. "About what?"

Nikaela hoped she could get through to him. "You didn't handle her right."

"Handle who?"

"The captain."

John grimaced and looked completely lost. "I guess you're right. We do need to talk alone."

He stood and glanced down at his tray. "I'm not that hungry anyway."

They bussed their plates and dishes, then stepped out into the passageway. Nikaela had thought this through carefully. "Let's go to my stateroom. Mistress Stinar is on duty in Security."

She led John down the passageway, then up a ladder-well, and along another passageway to her cabin, desperately hoping no one saw him following her there. They slipped into her stateroom, then closed the door and she turned to face him.

Nikaela thought it best to simply blurt it out. "When she offered to take you as a lover you handled it all wrong."

He shook his head uncertainly, and anger clouded his features. "But she didn't really offer. She's just being . . . she's being Taugrim, isn't she?"

Nikaela tried not to come across as angry. "It was an offer . . . but it . . . also wasn't. It was kind of both."

John threw his hands up in exasperation. "You Kelk are all fucking crazy."

She needed to get through to him. "You can turn her down by completely ignoring it. But the way you handled it—a smile, then looking her over and raising an eyebrow as if considering it—that was almost an invitation."

He cringed, clearly completely out of his element. "I thought it was kind of . . . I don't know . . . just banter. No Commonwealth captain would ever say that."

It was time to give him all the bad news. "And you're not supposed to kiss a woman like that."

"Like what?"

"The way you kissed me."

"But you kissed me that way, and you kissed me first."

She didn't know how to respond to that, and in that moment of silence, he marched toward her, his eyes sharp with anger. She backed away from him, and in a single step her spine hit the bulkhead. She knew without a doubt he did not intend violence toward her, but the look on his face frightened her. He stopped with his nose an inch from hers and snarled through gritted teeth, "I'm doing the best I can. Most of the time I don't know what the fuck is going on, and no one here seems inclined to help me, except when someone gives me cryptic, vague, bizarre, Kelk shit-of-bull, like this crap you're feeding me."

The two of them froze that way for the longest moment, him breathing heavily, her frightened for him, but not frightened of him. They had both been on the bridge for several hours, worrying about nuclear warheads being thrown their way. But for some reason kisses now seemed to be more dangerous that warheads.

She spoke carefully. "You're on a Kelk ship among Kelk, so you have to figure out how to handle Kelk ways. And this is the way a Kelk woman kisses a man."

She gripped his shoulders, spun him around, pushed his back against the bulkhead where she had been a moment ago, and kissed him hard. He tasted good, and she tried not to lose herself in the kiss, but she did a little. He wrapped his hands around her waist and pulled her tightly against him, clearly as lost in the kiss as her. She had meant the kiss as a simple demonstration, but she quickly lost control of it, and it went way beyond that. When their lips parted they were both breathing heavily.

"You surprised me," he said, speaking softly. "I thought for sure your tongue had gone all forked on me. But I've now confirmed it hasn't split and turned forked, and I did enjoy doing so." He ran his hands down her back and stopped with them resting just below her waistline on the curve of her butt. "I still haven't checked to make sure there's no scaly lizard tail. I'm definitely going to check on that someday. I suspect I will have to conduct a long and careful tactile examination, just to be sure."

He grinned, a mischievous glint in his eye. "And this . . . is how I kiss a woman."

He planted a soft kiss on her cheek, then ran a line of delicate kisses down her neck, starting at her earlobe. She felt her pulse quickening as he ended with kisses where her tunic was open at the top, planting a line of them across her chest, almost, but not quite, kissing the top of her breasts. Somehow he had gleaned the way a Kelk man was supposed to kiss a woman.

"One more thing," he whispered. "I also kiss a woman this way."

He gripped her by the shoulders, spun her about, pressed her spine against the bulkhead, and kissed her hard. His grip on her shoulders softened and he wrapped his arms around her, both of them completely lost in the kiss. It lasted longer this time, and when it ended they paused for a long moment, staring at each other.

He smiled, didn't say a word and stepped out of her arms. Then he opened the door to her stateroom, walked out into the passageway, and closed the door.

35

Client-Server

MOST OF THE work at the warehouse was routine, much like any company. More often than not, Anders couldn't tell the difference between crates containing *special* supplies, and those that were part of Lorenson's legitimate distribution operations. Sarkovie did not warrant a large prime station, but to support commercial operations, the government had funded the construction and outfitting of several orbiting warehouses. Lorenson had leased one in its entirety, and Anders spent about half his time up there in five-day stints. The accommodations in orbit were Spartan, but adequate.

Crates came in from off planet, and he logged them into the system. Some went down to one of the warehouses on the surface of Sarkovie, then onto grav trucks for delivery locally. Some they transshipped out to one of the nearby star systems, though they no longer shipped anything to Novalis III.

After a hundred or more light-years of shipping and handling, the outer casings of all the crates were marred, scratched, and scored. One day Anders noticed a crate with a particularly serious gouge. He looked at it closely, and confirmed that the damage did not penetrate the outer casing and extend to the contents within. Following standard procedure, he took note of the details on its shipping label, and recorded a couple of pictures of the damage. Then he sent it on its way down to the planet's surface.

A few days later he thought he recognized that same crate sitting on the incoming dock in the orbital warehouse. But the shipping label didn't match what he had recorded earlier. He compared it to the pictures he had taken, and the gouge and a whole field of scratches around it matched perfectly.

After that Anders noticed an unusual pattern with certain shipments. Some crates went down to one of the four addresses on the planet's surface, were then moved by surface transport to one of the other addresses, then shipped back up to the orbital warehouse for transshipment to another star system. And somewhere during that process their labels were altered to give them completely different origins and destinations. Those crates always came originally from Viktorkinde, never from anywhere else, but looking at the altered label, one would not know that. It was certainly possible the crates had been emptied, then reused to ship something else outbound. But the shipping weights going down, and those coming back up, always matched to within a fraction of a gram, and the new point of origin wasn't Sarkovie. He considered opening a few crates before and after to visually verify that their contents remained unchanged. But that might be the kind of mistake that led to that bullet in the back of his head, so he decided to forego that. Somehow he needed to alert Miss Macree to the way they changed the labels.

One afternoon, at the end of his five-day stint in the orbital warehouse, Anders rode a cargo shuttle down to the main warehouse in Calconna. Tia Lorenson met him as he stepped off the shuttle, and she appeared quite stressed. She took him by the elbow, pulled him aside and opened a secure link between their implants. *We're going to be working late tonight, just those of us who work on* special *shipments.*

What happened? he asked. *What's wrong?*

She looked over her shoulder before answering, even though they were on a secure link. *Commonwealth forces attacked* Caliban. *They took quite a number of prisoners. It's unlikely any of them know any details about our operations down here, but we're not taking any chances. Until further notice, we're shutting down all special operations.*

Once all of the other employees had clocked out for the night, Anders, Lorenson, her lieutenant Torsten Hohlman, and three others went to work. Lorenson and Hohlman identified seven special crates, and since Anders was qualified on a heavy grav lifter, he loaded them onto a large grav truck, and the other three muscled them into place. Then Hohlman climbed up into the driver's seat, and with Lorenson seated in the cab next to him, they drove out of the warehouse around midnight. Anders walked back to his apartment and fell into an exhausted sleep.

The next day, work at the warehouse proved to be quite routine. Lorenson said nothing about the previous night's work, and the employees who didn't work on *special operations* seemed none the wiser. When the day ended, Anders didn't linger because he wanted to run into Nedda Macree leaving the warehouse. She raised an eyebrow when she saw him, but didn't say anything, and together they walked back to their apartment building.

Just outside the entrance he said, "I'd like to employ your professional services."

She smiled, nodded, and extended her hand. In it she held some cash.

He shook his head. "What's this?"

She frowned. "I'm just giving your money back."

"Oh," he said, "okay." He took the bills.

She said, "Let's go to your place."

They walked up the stairs, he opened the door to his apartment, followed her in and closed it. She tossed a little clutch bag onto the small table in his tiny kitchenette, turned and wrapped her arms around his neck. As she brushed her lips along his chin, he opened up a secure link between their implants and said, *What are you doing? You said you lied, that they're not really monitoring you.*

She looked him in the eyes and smiled. *But we don't know if Lorenson is monitoring your place.*

He couldn't deny he had enjoyed their last tryst, but he thought it could be dangerous to make it an ongoing thing. *Then let's just go to your place.*

She shook her head. *Can't.*

Why not?

She smiled triumphantly. *I paid you. I'm the client, you're the server. Don't forget, this is Sarkovie. It's illegal to have sex if you don't pay for it, and once the client has paid, it's illegal to not have sex. So, Mr. Server, deliver, or I'll report you to the authorities.*

He closed his eyes, shook his head, opened his eyes, and kissed her. It wasn't until sometime later, lying in bed with her, that he reopened the secure link. He told her about Lorenson's reaction to the successful assault on *Caliban*. And he told her how they switched labels on certain special crates.

Yah, she said. *Shuffling them around to different warehouses helps them cover that up. We need to find out a way that you can identify a crate at the start, and get that info to me so my people can watch for it at all four warehouses. I'd like to follow the whole trail. You never know what might turn up.*

Let me think on it, he said.

She smiled. *I'll think on it too. Then we can meet again.*

She spoke out loud. "Next time, do you want to be the client or the server?"

••••

An hour out from the binary system Taugrim ordered them to down-transit. "We need to get a nav fix, see how badly off track we are. And I want to see what those assholes behind us are doing."

Dahlborg let John handle dumping lights, and ten minutes later they down-transited, holding onto as much sublight as possible.

Since they had up-transited from deep within the gravity well of the white dwarf, their vector could be off by a considerable margin. Nikaela and the chief navigator crunched numbers, but from the scan summary in the corner of one of his screens, John saw that they were off track by a considerable angle, though they were still headed in roughly the right direction.

They had down-transited about three thousand light hours from the white dwarf. Taugrim ordered the combat drones out, and held them in forced orbits around *Drakan Helgis* at a million kilometers. But even with that baseline they couldn't resolve much back in the binary system.

Nikaela and the navigator uploaded a course correction to the captain and the helm. Taugrim quickly reviewed the data. "Helm, this looks good, make it happen."

John swung *Drakan Helgis*'s bow around and loaded the computed vector into the system, then he firewalled the sublight drive.

"Helm," Taugrim said. "Do not up-transit until I give the order. One of our friends back there should be clearing that white dwarf about now, and I want to see what they do when they don't have the star between us and them."

They watched and waited in silence as the minutes ticked by, and then a field of small suns appeared near the white dwarf. John didn't understand what he saw until Dahlborg leaned close to him and whispered, "They triggered the cluster mine."

Distributed over a large volume near the white dwarf, one hundred warheads had detonated, each with a yield strength of one megaton.

"Probably didn't hurt them," Taugrim said. "But it'll keep 'em honest. Hey, Black-sword."

John looked her way, and knew what to expect. She grinned. "I still got that bottle of kirva in my quarters, and the bet's still open."

John shook his head. "I'll pass, mistress."

He had barely finished speaking when the scan tech said, "Up-transition detected in close proximity to that white dwarf. But it looks like they cleared the star first. Their vector's off, but not too far."

The course correction had put *Drakan Helgis* on a vector that would take them back to the nearest relay buoy, and ten minutes later they up-transited. Of the two hunter-killers that remained, one had cleared the white dwarf and up-transited from deep within the system. It would be another hour before the second could clear the star and follow. Like *Drakan Helgis* the two hunter-killers would have to down-transit outside the heliosphere for a course correction. When the first one did so, would they wait for their comrade, or charge ahead alone? If they did, Nav computed they would catch *Drakan Helgis* in about three hours.

An hour later Taugrim ordered, "Crash stop. We need data so get us into sublight soonest. And don't wait for my command. As soon as we down-transit, launch the drones."

With her greater experience, Dahlborg dumped lights while John looked on and monitored other ship's systems. Now was not the time for a training exercise.

"Down-transition," Dahlborg announced.

The hull echoed with the launch of the drones.

Taugrim demanded, "Talk to me scan."

John's heart pounded as they waited for the scan tech to acquire data.

"I've got it." the young woman said. "I'm picking up two transition wakes just outside heliopause and driving away from the binary system. They're widely spread, mistress, about three hundred light-hours apart."

Taugrim nodded. "They didn't want to take us on alone, so they waited for their friend. And just like the first, the second up-transited deep inside the heliosphere, which squirted them off to one side. It was still a smart move, got them beyond heliopause in short order. They'll correct before they catch up with us."

The scan tech said, "You were right, Captain."

"I win the bet, Blacksword," Taugrim crowed.

John tried to keep his face expressionless. "But I didn't take the bet."

She gave him a sad look. "That's a shame."

She considered her screens for a moment. "Scan, drones in. Helm, get us into transition. Fire Control, dump a couple of cluster mines behind us."

Her eyes returned to her screens and she nodded. "Seven hours. We drive hard for seven hours, then we down-transit, and we fight."

••••

Nikaela found the door to the captain's cabin open, with Taugrim seated at a small desk built into a bulkhead. She rapped on the door, and when the woman looked her way she snapped to attention.

"Mistress Taugrim, if you please, a moment of your time?"

Taugrim nodded. "Come in, Command Boss. Ease and relax. Have a seat."

Nikaela stepped into the small stateroom, extruded a seat out of the bulkhead and sat down. Taugrim spun in her seat to face her. "What's on your mind, Mistress Vreekande?"

Taugrim clearly didn't understand that John Mathius didn't know how to reject her advances in a proper Kelk way. "I wanted to . . . speak to you . . . about Ensign Mathius."

Taugrim flashed that grin of hers. "You want him for yourself, eh?"

Nikaela tried not to think about that as she sputtered, "No, it's not that."

Taugrim frowned and her eyes narrowed with disbelief. "Then what is it?"

Nikaela wasn't sure how to broach such a subject with a superior officer. "It's . . . just that . . . well, he doesn't understand our ways."

Taugrim leaned forward and put her elbows on her knees. "How so?"

Nikaela tried not to stumble over her words. "I don't think he knows how to properly . . . say no . . . to your offers."

"Offers?" Taugrim asked. "What offers would that be?" She clearly intended to make this hard for Nikaela.

"Well . . . you've made it clear that—"

"Oh, you're talking about the offers where I offered to fuck him."

Nikaela decided she was way over her head, and probably had a look on her face much like that on John's face when she had tried to explain it to him. She simply nodded.

Taugrim shook her head sadly and leaned back. "I know damn well my conduct with respect to Maestra Mathius, by Commonwealth standards, is atrocious. But I'm testing him, something I wouldn't tell you if he hadn't already passed the test."

"Testing him," Nikaela asked, "for what?"

The woman raised an eyebrow and appraised Nikaela carefully, as if trying to decide what to say. "When we get to Viktorkinde, he's going to be under a microscope with everyone he meets. Once we shake those hunter-killers, we'll go back to briefing him and Mistress Primatov on Kelk customs. But no amount of that will prepare him for that microscope and the myriad of uncomfortable moments he's going to encounter. If he hadn't passed my little test, then I'd sit him and Colonel Primatov down and explain a few things to them the hard way, and even then that wouldn't be enough. But I think we've all learned he's not easily phased, doesn't overreact, and wisely knows he shouldn't pull out his Commonwealth reflexes. He's done rather well on his own, don't you think?"

Nikaela thought she must look like a complete imbecile. "I'm sorry I doubted you."

Taugrim smiled pleasantly. "Apology accepted. And there's another thing. Three young women in this crew are running a little betting pool. They were planning on making a play for him, and the winner would be the one who seduced him first." Taugrim's back stiffened and her eyes hardened with anger. "Do you understand the kind of obligation they would incur if they succeeded? Targeted seduction, no prior relationship, no agreements, no contracts?"

Nikaela had not considered something like that. "I guess . . . it might be a lot more complicated than when . . . a Kelk woman seduces a Kelk man."

"Exactly," Taugrim snarled, almost shouting. "I find it unimaginable those three could be so stupid."

She paused and took a deep breath. "And I can't allow that to happen until he knows our ways a little better. So as long as I'm acting like a horny old broad, they're worried that if any of them make their play, and succeed, I'll be really pissed. And they're right about that, so they're staying away from him for the time being."

Taugrim was anything but an old broad, and the woman would have no problem attracting a man, or woman, if that was her preference. "What if he does accept your offer?"

Taugrim gave her that big, white-toothed grin of hers. "I really do have a bottle of kirva here. It would complicate things, but from the look of him, I think we'd both have a really good time. We might even get around to that bottle of kirva."

Her tone shifted abruptly. "Now, I have work to do, Mistress Vreekande."

Nikaela stood, thanked the captain for her time, and stepped through the state-room door into the passageway.

"One more thing, Mistress Vreekande."

Nikaela turned back to face her.

Taugrim flashed the grin again. "In a little while I'll let up on the young man, and that should give you a better chance with him. But don't wait too long, or one of those three might get to him first."

She closed the door in Nikaela's face.

36

Unstable Alliance

"ONE HUNDRED LIGHTS," John said as he watched Dahlborg tweaking the transition drive, easing them toward a low-lights down-transition. He glanced at Nikaela where she sat at Nav, and she gave him a reassuring smile.

"Eighty lights."

Dahlborg did all the work, while John's only job was to sound the count, and keep his lunch down as gravity waves rolled through the bridge.

"Sixty lights."

Their two pursuers had chosen to skip-jump to track *Drakan Helgis*. That slowed them down, but as Taugrim said, "Unfortunately, that keeps *us* honest."

"Fifty lights."

They had driven hard for seven hours, limited by the damage to their heat dissipation systems. Their best estimate was that the hunter killers were now about five hundred light-hours behind them. At that point, if any of their assumptions were incorrect in the wrong direction, a lucky shot could put a big warhead up their ass. They needed to down-transit and get a hard fix on their pursuers.

"Forty lights."

Once before John had watched Dahlborg get them down to forty-two lights before gravitational instabilities had forced them into sublight.

"Thirty lights."

A nasty series of gravity waves punched John in the gut just as the transition drive went unstable and the space-time distortion field surrounding the ship collapsed.

"Down transition at twenty-eight lights," John announced. "Coasting at just over point nine lights."

Drakan Helgis's hull echoed with the launch of its combat drones.

John leaned close to Dahlborg. "Twenty-eight lights. Is that like a record or something?"

She shook her head. "We're in interstellar space. It's easier without the distortions of a solar mass nearby."

"Scan," Taugrim demanded. "What have you got for me?"

The scan tech's fingers danced over her screens for a few seconds, then she said, "Two wakes, four hundred light-hours out and driving hard this way."

John had another question for Dahlborg, but before he voiced it she spoke as if reading his mind. "No nearby mass also means there's nothing close by to obscure our transition flare. So they probably detected it, even while in transition. Their data just isn't as accurate, which hopefully means they don't have a targeting solution on us. At least not yet."

"Engineering," Taugrim said. "Maintain full power status. At this point hiding isn't the way to win this battle. It's time to fight. Com, any response from those relay buoys?"

"Nothing, mistress. We're a little over five light-years out from the nearest buoy, right at the extreme limit of our transition com. I sent the messages anyway, but I didn't get an acknowledgment ping."

In the hope they could get close enough to one of the buoys in the relay chain, Taugrim had prepared a message for Kristdokar and Nygaard. And if the diplomatic mission had stayed on schedule, by now they would have crossed the gap between the two chains, and would be transiting down the Viktorkinde side not far from *Drakan Helgis*'s present position. Primatov had prepared a message for the mission, and no one needed to tell John both messages were urgent calls for help.

"Captain," the scan tech said. "Both of those hunter-killers just down-transited."

Taugrim nodded, her head rocking slowly up and down. "They can do the math just as well as we can, but their data's not good enough for a targeting solution. For a kill-shot, they need to know exactly where we are. I guess we have to make sure they don't get a kill-shot."

••••

With the Viktorkinde relay chain repaired, the diplomatic mission now had the luxury of almost continuous communications with *Konigsborge*; still no sign of *Drakan Helgis*.

When Fran's implants chimed with a call from *Hellfire*'s com tech, she assumed it would be another message from Kristdokar. She tried not to let her frustration show. "Yes, what is it?"

The young man smiled politely and said, "Sorry to bother you, ma'am. We just received a coded message off the relay chain. We were told if anything came in from Colonel Katrine Primatov, it was to be flagged—"

"You have a message from Primatov?"

That had come out more harshly than she had intended and the fellow winced. He gave her a fearful look, and Fran wanted to kick herself.

"Uh, yes, ma'am. It just came in."

"Upload it to me immediately."

Fran chaffed at the need to run it through malware and subvert-ware checks, but now was not the time to skirt security protocols. When she finally decoded the message and uploaded it into her implants, it was short and to the point. *Drakan Helgis* had used a binary star system to evade the three hunter-killers chasing her, had damaged one badly enough to remove it from play, and the other two were now pursuing her. The three ships had down-transited and *Drakan Helgis* was about to engage the two hunter-killers. Their position put them a little over five light-years from the chain, and more than ten light-years from *Hellfire*'s present position. If *Konigsborge* had stuck to the search pattern they had outlined several days ago, they'd be about thirty light-years from *Drakan Helgis*, so it was up to *Hellfire*, or better yet, the hunter-killers accompanying them. They could reach *Drakan Helgis* in about a day. That was probably not good enough, but Fran had learned long ago to play the cards dealt.

She hastily set up a conference call with the captains of the ships in the diplomatic mission. They agreed unanimously that if the two cruisers weren't enough to protect *Lady Victorious*, then all of their intelligence was badly mistaken, and they were already deep in an interstellar war none of them had anticipated.

She and the ships' captains were discussing deploying *Endurance* a few light-years ahead of them to provide the kind of advance warning they had gotten from the hunter-killers up to that point. During that discussion she received a message from Kristdokar. She scanned Kristdokar's message quickly, then interrupted the discussion.

"Ladies and gentlemen, I'm sorry to interrupt, but I've just received a message from *Konigsborge*. Skalde Kristdokar confirms they are farther out than we are. We can get there long before them, so it's definitely up to our hunter-killers."

Fran decided to brief the rest of the diplomatic mission only after the three ships were under way. There would be a lot of hysteria and invectives thrown about, but at that point it would be a foregone conclusion, and if need be, she would flat-out refuse to recall them. They didn't have the right people present to relieve her of command, so if they wanted to go that far, that would have to wait until they returned to Trafalgar.

••••

Carla's implants woke her with a battle-stations protocol and she slammed awake. In her implants May Forester said, *We're being transferred. All of you pack a couple of uniforms and meet me on Hangar Deck yesterday. Pack light and make it fast.*

Carla selected a couple pairs of fatigues, and didn't bother folding them as she jammed them into a duffel. Next to her Leeze yawned while stuffing a couple of uniforms into her kit. "Where are we going?"

Leeze's yawn triggered a jaw-breaking response in Carla, and she had to get past that before she could answer. "I don't know. You heard as much as me."

As Carla, Leeze and the four guys double-timed it down to Hangar Deck, allship blared, "All hands, stand by for down-transition."

On Hangar Deck a spacer pointed them through a personnel hatch into an assault boat where they found Forester waiting for them.

"Where are we going?" Carla asked Forester.

John's O-School roommate widened her eyes and shook her head. "We're being temporarily assigned to the hunter-killer *Lightspear*. Other than that, I don't know anything."

Carla had noticed that when that Blacksword woman snapped orders, people jumped fast, hard, and high. Carla and her teammates strapped in, *Hellfire* launched the boat, and once they cleared the cruiser's hull, the assault boat pilot firewalled the damn thing in a really hot-shot, showoff, boat-jockey maneuver. Half way to their destination he flipped the boat and firewalled it again, breaking hard. In less than two minutes they crossed the one thousand kilometers to *Lightspear*, and in another minute were mated to her cargo hatch.

A male ensign met them just inside the hunter-killer's small cargo bay. Behind them crewmen unloaded their combat armor while the ensign checked each of them off a list. "Follow me," the young man said.

Carla heard the assault boat decouple from the cargo hatch, and as the ensign led them through the narrow passageways of the hunter-killer, the sound of the ship's drive rose in pitch and vibrated through the deck. Allship blared, "Stand by for up-transition."

The ensign led them to a small bunkroom occupied by six ComSecCorps troopers. Two of them lay in bunks reading, while four of them sat at a small table playing cards. They all wore the patch of Zeta Company on their sleeves, but the Z on their patches rested on its side so it appeared as a distorted N.

A captain stood from the table and approached Forester. She, Carla, Leeze and the guys all snapped to attention.

"At ease," he said. "Relax." He extended his hand to Forester. "I'm Edward Fleming. You're all friends of John Mathius, right?"

As he and Forester shook hands, she asked, "Cap'm, do you know why we're here, sir?"

Carla held her breath, wondering if he'd say some crazy, nullhead bullshit, but he simply smiled pleasantly. "Yah. I don't know the details, but apparently we're going to pull your friend's ass out of some really deep shit."

••••

John had a hundred questions, but now was not the time for a lesson.

The two hunter-killers remained unmoving, in sublight, four hundred light-hours from *Drakan Helgis*, which was way beyond targeting range. When they did chose to close the gap and engage, the destroyer's transition batteries would give them a small advantage at extreme range, but the two hunter-killers could launch a lot of big transition warheads their way; stalemate.

As the seconds ticked by and nothing happened, Taugrim said, "They're waiting to see if we panic and try to run for it. They'd be really happy if I was that stupid. So let's give them reason to think I am. Helm, firewall the sublight drive, but wait for my command before up-transiting."

John pushed *Drakan Helgis*'s grav drive to maximum and the hull groaned with the hum of the power demand.

The scan tech's voice held a hint of excitement. "Captain, one of them just up-transited."

Taugrim spoke in a calm and even tone. "The hunter-killer in sublight is going to feed scan details to their friend, and the one charging straight for us is going to take their best shot as soon as they get within range. Steady as she goes, Helm, and bring the drones in to ten thousand kilometers."

John focused on his controls, but kept glancing at the scan summary in the corner of his screen. The enemy warship in transition raced toward them, closing the distance rapidly.

"Fire Control," Taugrim said, "do you have a targeting solution?"

"We do, mistress, but they're too far out for any accuracy."

"Drop a cluster mine in our wake and keep it tight packed. Warn all defensive stations to stand by. They're gonna throw some nasty shit our way."

Taugrim sat silently waiting, and John wondered if her heart pounded in her chest as hard as his. When the oncoming warship had finally come to within fifty light-hours, she said, "Drones in. Fire Control, fire all main batteries." Fifty light-hours was still beyond any reasonable targeting range.

The kettle-drum sound of the main batteries echoing through the hull did not drown out Taugrim's words. "Helm, up-transition, now."

"Up-transition," Dahlborg said. *Drakan Helgis*'s grav drive stopped drawing power as its systems shifted energy demand to the transition drive. "Three hundred lights and climbing."

"Belay that, Helm," Taugrim shouted, and for the first she sounded excited. "Hold at three hundred lights and stand by for crash stop. Fire Control, warn all defensive stations to stand by for incoming. After we down-transit, the moment you have a targeting solution, fire all main batteries regardless of range, and keep firing."

"Captain," the scan tech shouted, "they just triggered that cluster mine."

Fifty small warheads detonated in close proximity to the enemy warship.

"I picked up a transition flare," the scan tech said. "That cluster mine knocked them into down-transition."

Taugrim bellowed, "Helm, crash stop, now."

From a transition velocity of three hundred lights it only took Dahlborg a few seconds to dump lights. "Down-transition," John shouted, a little embarrassed that he hadn't sounded like a seasoned spacer.

In John's scan summary the enemy warship showed as an icon six hundred million kilometers off their stern, extreme long range for transition batteries. "Solution acquired," Primatov said, and in the same instant the boom of the main batteries filled their ears, repeating again, and again, and again. A large warhead detonated thirty kilometers off their stern. The ship's hull shrieked, and its power plant redlined, diverting power to the shields. *Drakan Helgis*'s main batteries continued to pound transition shells at the enemy.

"Helm, hard-a-port and take evasive action."

John swung the ship's bow to one side, then pulled it up and went into a corkscrew pattern Dahlborg had taught him. He'd spent hours in the simulator drilling on it, and now it came to him without thought.

A million kilometers behind them another warhead blew, then another detonated a hundred kilometers to starboard where they had been only a fraction of a second ago. Again, the hull shrieked and the power plant redlined.

"Captain," the scan tech said, her voice an octave higher than normal, "that warship's emission profile is dirty, and they're not keeping up with us. I think we hit 'em."

"Cease fire," Taugrim said. "Power priority to the shields and tell all defensive stations to stay alert. They hit us too. I want a damage report soonest."

"Captain," the com tech said. "I'm getting a response off the relay chain, but we're at extreme long range and there's a lot of data packet corruption. They're repeatedly transmitting each packet until we get a clean one."

"Okay, Com, let me know when you've got a message I can read."

"Mistress," the scan tech said. "That other hunter-killer just up-transited and they're coming our way."

37

A Desperate Ploy

JENINE CATARVIN STEPPED into Gascoigne's office on *Lady Victorious* and sat down almost primly. Fran had worked with all kinds of covert assets in her time, from turncoats who betrayed their principles to save their own skins, to dedicated case officers, willing to lay their lives on the line to protect the democratic institutions that guaranteed the freedoms they valued so highly. But few compared to Catarvin.

"Colonel Blacksword," she said, smiling happily. "It's always good to see you."

Fran had no problem being sincere as she said, "It's good to see you too, Senator." Only a few months ago she would have cringed at the thought of having to listen to the woman.

Three hours earlier Fran had briefed them all on her decision to divert the mission and send the three hunter-killers ahead. Obradour had expressed displeasure that he hadn't been consulted before the fact, but basically agreed with Fran's decision. Catarvin, bless her soul, had stayed in character to the end. Palmutter had been quite subdued, which was very much out of character.

Gascoigne sat down next to Catarvin. "So, Jenine, you said it's important. What do you have for us?"

Something had upset the woman. "Silas is growing increasingly unstable."

Gascoigne frowned. "Unstable, how so?"

Fran had never before seen Catarvin appear worried. "He really started to go south when you revealed Nvalheim was involved in the attack on *Konigsborge*. I think he was counting on her to support him in some way, and now that she's on the outs with the Executive Council, he's running scared. It all came to a head a couple of days ago."

She fidgeted for a moment before continuing. "Silas and I were chatting and sharing a bottle of wine in the lounge in his suite." She grinned, and for a moment the airhead persona emerged. "We usually do that before he ravishes me. But Strikland showed up and wanted to have a private word with him, so they adjourned to his office and closed the door. I didn't dare try to open the door to listen, but the door into the bedroom was open, and so was the door between the bedroom and the office. They argued, and it grew heated enough to hear a word or two here and there. I got the impression they had had the same argument before, and quite recently."

She hesitated for a moment and seemed to reconsider her words. "Actually, it was less of an argument and more Strikland giving Silas hell for his lack of discretion. I think I heard the name Nvalheim several times, but I can't be sure of that."

Gascoigne frowned, his brow furrowing with thought. "He was rather subdued this morning."

"Yes," Fran said. "I thought he'd blow his stack when I revealed I'd diverted the mission."

"There's something else," Catarvin said. "He failed to perform last night, and that never happens."

Gascoigne cringed. "You mean he couldn't—"

"Exactly," Catarvin said, "and I would think with all his enhancements, he'd have some software in his implants to make it all happen no matter what."

Apparently, Gascoigne took the significance of such failure to heart, and sounded somewhat sympathetic for Palmutter. "So nothing happened, eh?"

Catarvin winked at Fran, then leaned toward Gascoigne and gave him a motherly pat on the wrist. "Don't worry, Mani. It took a couple of hours, but I got him going." She grinned at Fran. "I'm much better at that kind of thing than some stupid lines of code."

Something didn't add up for Fran. "You said he's growing increasingly unstable— your words, not mine. And yet, you seem to have stabilized the situation."

"Just on the surface," Catarvin said. "He's behaving, but only when Strikland is present, or might hear about it. Privately he's fuming with rage. He even said something about cleaning up loose ends when we get to Viktorkinde. I tried to get him to say more, but for once he clammed up. I can't prove this, but it's clear both he and Strikland are dirty. I think Silas is just more exposed in some way we haven't yet figured out. That's got him worried, and the attack on *Konigsborge* and *Drakan Helgis* has him running scared."

Gascoigne leaned back in his chair and nodded. "That would explain it."

"There's one more thing," Catarvin said.

It was a testament to the woman's effectiveness and credibility that Gascoigne now paid careful attention to every word she spoke.

"I can control Silas. I can keep him stable, keep him from going off the deep end, and I will continue to do so. But there might come a time when we do want him to go crackers. If ever we all agree that time has come, I'll inflame his anger at Strikland and stoke his fears, then set him off like a big warhead."

Fran was extremely thankful Catarvin had chosen to be on their side.

••••

"Captain, Engineering reports damage to the transition drive."

John kept his implants tuned to the command circuit and his eyes locked on the scan summary in the corner of one of his screens. The last of the three hunter-killers had up-transited and was pushing a lot of lights headed toward them. *Drakan Helgis*'s emissions profile made it clear to the enemy warships they had been badly hurt, and the hunter-killer moved in to finish the job. Taugrim had a few minutes at most to come up with something.

"Engineering," Taugrim demanded. "Talk to me, dammit."

John recognized the chief engineer's voice. "Sublight drive's in good shape, I think the transition drive's dead."

"You think?"

"We're fighting an overloaded radiation shield. It's leaking shit all over hell down here, and I don't have all the answers for you."

"No transition drive?"

The chief engineer hesitated. "Maybe, maybe not."

"What's the worst case scenario if I try to up-transit? Are we going to turn into a big cloud of vapor?"

Again, he hesitated. "No, I'm pretty sure I can prevent that. But if we do make transition, I doubt we'll hold it for more than a second or two."

"Mistress," the scan tech shouted, "one minute and they'll be able to target on us."

An uncanny calm seemed to settle over Taugrim. She looked at John and spoke in a calm, even voice. "Maestra Mathius, firewall the sublight drive and take evasive action."

John pushed the sublight drive to the maximum and went into the corkscrew maneuver.

Taugrim continued in a strangely peaceful tone. "Mistress Dahlborg, stand by for up-transition on my command. But when I give the command don't actually up-transit, just flare like hell and keep us where we are. Engineering, your job is to keep us from turning into a big ball of radioactive gas. Fire Control, what's your status?"

Primatov answered her. "Main batteries and transition launchers are green and go on all functions."

The scan tech's voice cracked as she said, "Twenty seconds to targeting range."

Taugrim nodded and smiled. "Fire Control, be prepared to fire forward, not aft, all main batteries and forward transition launchers. And fire continuously until one of us is dead."

John saw it in his scan summary before the tech spoke. "They're dumping lights, mistress. Looks like they're decelerating for a hard down-transition."

"Mistress Dahlborg," Taugrim said in a voice as hard as steel. "As soon as they down-transit, do not wait for my command. Make sure they see our flare the instant they hit sublight."

That was the hint John needed, and he thought he understood what Taugrim hoped to do. He noticed her staring at him with a smile on her face.

"They down-transited," the scan tech shouted.

Dahlborg slammed power into the transition drive, the ship's power plant red-lined, the hull groaned, and nothing happened. If the enemy warship didn't respond the way Taugrim hoped, *Drakan Helgis* and her crew were doomed.

The scan tech said, "They just up-transited."

A massive gravity wave slammed through the bridge as the hunter-killer passed nearby in transition. For an instant it sent John's senses reeling, and as the enemy ship receded in front of them, the kettle-drum sound of the main batteries was followed by the thump of the transition launchers spitting torpedoes in its wake. Three warheads detonated simultaneously in close proximity.

The scan tech spoke with a note of awe in her voice. "Direct hit, one megaton yield strength."

"Cease fire," Taugrim said, and silence settled over the bridge of *Drakan Helgis*.

"Hey, Blacksword."

John looked Taugrim's way.

She wagged a finger at him. "I saw that look on your face just before they down-transited. You figured out what I was going to do just before I did it, didn't you?"

Just as the hunter-killer down-transited, their scans picked up what looked like a forced up-transition flare. Their captain had a fraction of a second to make a decision, and concluded *Drakan Helgis* had up-transited to make a run for it. And since even in transition they could track her easily because of her damaged emission signature, the ship's CO chose to up-transit and give chase. A heartbeat later, *Drakan Helgis* had been in sublight when the hunter-killer passed right by them in transition, the ideal situation for a kill-shot.

In answer to Taugrim wagging her finger at him, John said, "I learned a lot today, mistress. Thank you."

Taugrim flashed him that grin. "You could learn a lot more in my cabin with me and that bottle of kirva."

Dahlborg gave John a sympathetic look.

"Okay, people," Taugrim said, "let's see what kind of damage we took."

"Captain," the com tech said. "I've got a readable message off the relay chain."

Taugrim looked her way. "Give me the short version."

The young woman grimaced. "*Konigsborge* is three days out. The diplomatic mission from Trafalgar is closer. They're sending three hunter-killers ahead to provide aid. They'll be here in less than a day."

Taugrim's head turned slowly toward John, her face expressionless, no big flashy grin. "Three Commonwealth hunter-killers. Not sure I like those odds. We've got one day. Let's see if we can get this ship fixed up enough to defend ourselves."

••••

Falkenberg assigned John to work with one of the exterior repair crews. The material of a standard-issue vac suit was self-sealing and self-repairing—to a point. But nothing compared to the durability of power-reinforced combat armor, and its ability to withstand hard radiation, assault weapons, and serious abuse. It could also pressure-clamp and stave off terminal decompression even with one or more limbs blown off. So when Engineering needed bodies for dangerous heavy-duty vacuum work, anyone qualified in armor could be tapped to support them. In that, the Commonwealth and the Supremacy were alike. But on a Kelk ship, since only a small number of crewmembers were actually fitted with armor, everyone who qualified found themselves temporarily assigned to Engineering when exterior repairs were needed.

John had been assigned to work with Matsen and Kolbeck, and a female dregkraag wearing the insignia of an oberseergent: three clawed talons over two lightning bolts. The woman stood only a few inches shorter than John, which made her taller than Matsen, and about the same height as Kolbeck. When Matsen introduced John to Oberseergent Geltkarl, her face triggered a distant memory John couldn't fully recall. "Have we met before, Oberseergent?"

She nodded. "Briefly, on Reisenar. I was in Mistress Vreekande's squad, and we almost killed each other a couple of times." She finished that with a pleasant smile and no accusation.

That was the hint John needed. "Yes, you were there when we agreed to work together, that first time we all met face-to-face."

Matsen elbowed Kolbeck in the ribs. "I win."

Geltkarl frowned and looked at the two men. "You two have a wager of some sort?"

Matsen nodded, giving them a pleased smile. "I bet the Blacksword could tell one Kelk from another. We don't all look the same to him."

She raised one eyebrow and looked Kolbeck's way. "And you bet he couldn't tell us one from the other, eh?"

He grimaced and shrugged. "Seemed like a good bet." He looked John's way. "After all, he is a Blacksword; shoot first, ask questions later, right?"

John carefully kept the look on his face neutral. "Only when it's a blue-skinned, demon-eyed monster in my sights."

The oberseergent shook her head sadly and aimed her question at Kolbeck. "And you, I suppose *you* can tell the difference between common-faces?"

He grinned. "I can certainly tell the difference between him and that read-head colonel."

She gave Matsen a sardonic look. "Am I correct in assuming he can tell the difference only because she has tits?"

Matsen gritted his teeth and looked Kolbeck's way. "That probably has something to do with it."

"No," Geltkarl said, "with him that always has something to do with it."

They helped each other into their armor, John ran a full status check on his, and got a clean bill of health. Then the four of them sealed up, contracted their visors and joined an engineering tech in a large airlock on Hangar Deck. The fellow wore a standard-issue vac suit. As the deck crew pumped down the airlock, Geltkarl opened a channel to John. "His suit can't generate grav fields, so if he falls loose and floats away, nearest one to him snags him and brings him back."

"Acknowledged," John said. "Are we going to be helping them with the drive?"

"Not us," Geltkarl said. "The transition drive is delicate work. The chief engineer won't let us get near it. It's gonna be just his best and most experienced people for that."

When the deck crew popped the hatch, the airlock momentarily filled with a faint mist due to some residual air. Matson and Kolbeck each hooked a forearm under one of the tech's armpits, and using the gravity fields in their armor, took him for a ride. John and Geltkarl followed. John had logged quite a number of hours practicing and drilling in vacuum, but never before had it been real.

Matsen and Kolbeck led them toward the stern, and even with an untrained eye, John didn't need anyone to tell him there was something wrong with the warped and twisted hull plating there. Under the tech's supervision, Matsen and Kolbeck removed one of the damaged plates, and while they started on the next, John and Geltkarl hurriedly maneuvered it into the airlock. One warhead had detonated within thirty kilometers of their position. In the vacuum of space, with no atmosphere to generate a shock wave, the blast had inundated the plating with a flood of atomic particles and hard radiation. The plast was surprisingly light-weight, and yet it could withstand such intense bombardment when powered. John recalled *Drakan Helgis*'s power plant redlining and diverting power to the shielding.

Once John and Geltkarl muscled the damaged plate into the airlock and closed it, they moved quickly to return and retrieve another. As they made their second trip back to the airlock, John realized his Kelk friends shared a sense of urgency clearly fueled by fear.

"Why are we in such a hurry?" he asked.

She paused, and the faceless visor of her helmet turned his way. "We have less than a day, then we're going to be badly outgunned. We need to be ready to defend ourselves."

Perhaps they were concerned one of the hunter-killers they had damaged might effect repairs and come at them again. "Against who?"

She hesitated for a moment. "Your friends."

He could only answer her with silence.

On their next trip, when they opened the airlock, they found a shiny, new plast plate waiting for them. The machine shop had destabilized the plast lattice of the damaged plate, rendering it into its raw materials. They used some sort of molecular sieve to filter out damaged particles and recycled what remained. Then they extruded new plates with filaments and feeds for the power that gave it the strength to withstand the blast of a nearby warhead.

They worked for eight hours, and John couldn't stop thinking that his Kelk friends thought of his Commonwealth friends as their enemy. Engineering determined by some measure that they had made enough progress to take a break. As they waited for the airlock pump-down, Matsen told John, "If Engineering didn't give us the nod, we'd work straight through without food or rest."

To save time, they didn't strip out of their armor. They simply removed their helmets and gauntlets to get a little fresh ship's air and eat a meal. Then they slept for three hours while their reactor pack cells were recharged—maneuvering on gravity fields, even in weightless conditions, quickly consumed their reserves.

When John's implants woke him, he checked and learned that the Commonwealth hunter-killers were now within range of their transition scanners. *Drakan Helgis* was tracking their wakes and monitoring their progress closely. He donned his helmet and gauntlets, they exited through the airlock, and worked for another ten hours.

When they finished, John, Matsen and Kolbeck drifted about thirty meters off *Drakan Helgis*'s hull while Geltkarl and the tech helped Engineering run a series of tests. After about twenty minutes Geltkarl keyed her com. "We're good. Let's go back in."

They returned to the Ready-Room. John had trouble keeping his eyes open as a couple of techs helped him out of his armor. He grabbed a quick shower, gulped down a meal, then fell into his grav bunk, thinking exhaustion would help him find sleep quickly. But he lay awake thinking of his Kelk crewmates, and their fear that they would soon be outgunned by Commonwealth forces. Fear could easily lead to a mistake. Would the arrival of their rescuers precipitate interstellar war?

38

Strained Trust

TAUGRIM CAREFULLY POURED tea for Falkenberg, Brynjar, and Katrine. With all four of them seated at a small table, the captain's office felt somewhat cramped. That morning Taugrim had changed the color of her short-cropped spiky hair to dark brown, a very non-Kelk color.

Taugrim returned the antiquated tea pot to its tray, then retrieved a bottle of kirva from a small locker. She stopped next to Falkenberg, extended the bottle and held it above the XO's teacup, a questioning look on her face. Falkenberg nodded, and the captain added a healthy splash of the clear liquid to her tea. She repeated the gesture with Brynjar, who nodded as well and received his share of kirva. Katrine didn't want any alcohol, but when Taugrim offered, she feared she might violate some tradition by declining. "By all means."

In anticipation of the fiery liquor, Taugrim had not filled the teacups to the brim. She added some to Katrine's tea, then finished by topping off her own. She paused for a moment and looked at the bottle, then raised it to her mouth and took a healthy swig. Katrine wondered if it was the same bottle the woman kept offering to share with John. The captain had warned Katrine that she was testing John with her quips, and told her of the betting pool the three young women had organized. A Commonwealth captain would have simply marched the three into her office, given them hell, and ordered them to cease and desist. It piqued Katrine's curiosity that Taugrim needed to resort to such subterfuge to keep the three young women out of John's bed. For that matter, why bother to keep them out of his bed? Why not just let the young man have a good time for a few nights? It must be some Kelk thing.

Taugrim returned the bottle of kirva to the locker, then sat down, lifted her teacup to her lips, and sipped. Katrine and the others followed the captain's lead. To Katrine's surprise, the liquor actually complimented the tea, flooding her sinuses with the scent of exotic spices in a way the tea alone would not have done.

Taugrim returned the teacup to its saucer, then looked each of them in the eye for a moment. She finished with Katrine. "We are now comrades in arms, Colonel. You are a member of this crew, and I expect you to keep the well-being of your crewmates in mind as you advise us."

Katrine considered her words carefully. "I recognize that obligation, but you must also recognize that I have a higher obligation to the Commonwealth, and to the success of the diplomatic mission. That said, I do believe none of those obligations are in conflict."

Taugrim's eyes narrowed as she considered Katrine. "We have three enemy warships approaching us. They're now within range of our transition scans and we can track their wakes."

"Captain," Brynjar said, "with all due respect, those Commonwealth hunter-killers are not enemies, not in this."

Katrine wanted to thank Brynjar for saying that.

Taugrim's eyes remained locked on Katrine. "That's only true if the captains and crews of those ships believe we are not their enemy."

Katrine knew full well Taugrim was not that narrow-minded. "They are coming to aid us, and in that they are your allies."

Taugrim shrugged and pursed her lips. "Perhaps today, but what of tomorrow, and the day after?"

Katrine carefully sipped her tea, and was glad she had accepted the shot of kirva. "I cannot predict the future, but today we have an opportunity. I know the people who put together the diplomatic mission, know some of them quite well, and they do not want war with the Supremacy."

Falkenberg leaned forward, picked up her teacup and stared at its contents. "But there are those among you who do."

Katrine nodded. "Yes, we have our hawks just as you do. Some are driven by self-interest, and some by fear, like those among you who believe a Blacksword can kill with a thought. I believe you call them superstitious."

The response the com tech had finally received off the relay chain had contained a separate, encrypted message for Katrine. While eluding the three hunter-killers, they had been out of contact for more than twenty days, and only now had she learned that Thealone had added herself to the mission. Given the paranoia she sensed in the Kelk seated at the table with her, it was imperative there be no surprises. "I should tell you Fran Thealone was added to the diplomatic mission at the last moment."

Taugrim's eyes hardened with distrust. Falkenberg's face went flat, like a card player hiding her inner thoughts. Brynjar pursed his lips, forming them into a hard, straight line. Katrine had worked with the man for more than a year, and yet, at the mention of Thealone's name, even he had turned fearful.

Taugrim leaned forward and placed one hand flat on the table. "*The* Colonel Blacksword."

Katrine nodded. "I know her better than anyone else, and she is not a hawk. Both she and I will not hesitate to kill, if that is what we must do to make the diplomatic mission a success."

Taugrim's confident grin slowly returned. "Very well. We will take this one day at a time. But I can't take the chance that there are rogues among them impersonating your friends. So before I'll allow them to approach us, I'm going to demand proof they are who they say they are."

Falkenberg looked at Katrine over the lip of her teacup and smiled. "Do you know the captains of these three hunter-killers?"

The simple mention of Thealone's name had badly strained the trust Katrine had nurtured with Taugrim and Falkenberg. "Only one of them: Captain Neilosse of *Lightspear*. I spent almost thirty days on his ship tracking *Caliban*. I know for a fact he is not superstitious, and Colonel Blacksword has put him in charge of all three warships."

Taugrim drummed her fingers on the table for a few seconds. "Do you know this Neilosse fellow well enough that he could tell you something no one else would know?"

Katrine didn't try to hide her disdain. "Why do you ask?"

Taugrim shrugged. "By your own admission, you have your superstitious people in ComSecCorps. How do I know there hasn't been a mutiny on *Lightspear*, and it's now commanded by some rogue officer who wants to get close enough to shove a warhead up our ass? Electronically replicating Neilosse's appearance and voice is a trivial matter. So how will we know it's truly him? Can he tell you something about you that no one else knows?"

Katrine considered the matter carefully, but she and Neilosse had not been close, had not shared the kind of small talk that produced intimate memories. On the other hand, the recent message she had received from Thealone had included the information that some of John's old platoon mates were on that ship, though she had not had time to get him alone and make him aware of that. "There's a young woman on *Lightspear* name of Carla Nigurski. I'm quite sure she fulfills your requirements nicely."

"And who is she to you?"

Katrine turned the tables on Taugrim and gave her a shit-eating grin. "To me, just another ComSecCorps soldier, but to John Mathius, she's someone quite important."

••••

John's implants woke him, speaking in a calm AI voice. *Ensign Mathius, you're ordered to report to the bridge at your earliest convenience, but no later than one half hour from now.*

If Taugrim wanted to start a shooting war with the diplomatic mission, he assumed she wouldn't want him on the bridge, and his fears eased a little. Then again, she might want him and Primatov there under her thumb if the situation did go bad.

About two hours had passed since he'd dropped into his bunk. It wasn't enough sleep, but it would have to do. John tapped into a feed from the scan console and learned the approaching hunter killers were a little over one hour out. The two cruisers and the civilian vessel containing the diplomatic mission were less than two light-years behind them. He checked the damage control log, and it reported Engineering was still working on the damaged transition drive. Without that they could not defend themselves, which would make Taugrim and all his Kelk crewmates jumpy. It made him a little jumpy as well.

At that thought John hesitated. Like the rest of *Drakan Helgis*'s crew, he had come to fear his Commonwealth comrades, and that troubled him deeply. He had no valid justification to distrust them, especially since Primatov had warned him some of his old platoon mates would be present. John splashed water on his face, and headed for the bridge.

As just another junior flunky, John no longer stopped and formally reported for duty to the captain. But that day, as he stepped onto the bridge and headed for the helm, Taugrim stopped him. "Blacksword, a moment of your time."

John changed course and stopped at the captain's console. "Mistress."

She looked him up and down carefully, but without her usual lascivious grin. "Get enough sleep?"

John shook his head. "Not really, mistress, but I don't think any of us did."

"Yah," she said, "sleep is in rather short supply at the moment. Engineering says you did a good job on the EVA work."

Now that the engineering tech had worked closely with a Blacksword, John wondered if the fellow was monitoring himself for headaches. He shrugged. "All I did was obey orders, do the job, and keep my mouth shut. Isn't that what a soldier's supposed to do?"

She nodded. "Kelk or Commonwealth, that's a soldier's job. Are you prepared to do your job today?"

John had thought long and hard about that. At the Fire Control console Primatov glanced his way as he considered his answer, and her brow furrowed. She had probably struggled with the same issues. His Kelk crewmates had fought and killed other Kelk, and if the circumstances warranted, he might have to fight and kill other Commonwealth soldiers. "Yes, mistress, I am. Though I do hope it doesn't turn into a shooting war."

She considered him for a long moment. "Well, Blacksword, today that may be up to you."

John wondered at such a cryptic comment.

"Mistress," the scan tech said. "Those three hunter-killers just down-transited at a range of a hundred light-hours."

The com tech said, "One of them is hailing us, mistress. Captain Neilosse of the Commonwealth warship *Lightspear* sends his compliments and asks to be put in contact with you."

Taugrim smiled at John. "You may join Mistress Dahlborg at the helm."

John eased his way between instrument clusters and sat down next to Dahlborg.

"Okay, Com," Taugrim said. "Connect me to Captain Neilosse, and put Command Superior Falkenberg, Ensign Mathius, Mistress Vreekande, and Colonel Primatov in the circuit with me. But until I give the word, all but me are receive only."

John's vision shifted and he now stood behind and to one side of Taugrim, who sat at a large table in a virtual conference room. A man seated opposite her wore the uniform of a ComSecCorps Commander. Thin of build, he had dark brown hair, an angular face, and even though seated, John got the impression he might be quite tall. He didn't look John's way, confirming that *Drakan Helgis* was not transmitting his image. Falkenberg, Nikaela, and Primatov were probably also haunting the room as ghosts, like John, though he couldn't see them to verify that.

Neilosse spoke in an unremarkable baritone. "Captain Taugrim, greetings. We are here to render any assistance you may require."

"Captain Neilosse," Taugrim said. John heard the distrust in her voice, and no doubt Neilosse did as well. "Three of you; that's a rather overwhelming amount of assistance, isn't it?"

When Neilosse spoke, his voice now held an extra note of caution. "We were informed by your superiors that three Supremacy hunter-killers were pursuing you. My superiors chose to send what help they could, as rapidly as they could."

John saw Taugrim's face in profile and from behind. She smiled. "We are no longer being pursued."

Neilosse nodded. "Yes, we have detected a debris field not far from your position, as well as radiation plumes from several recent warhead detonations in your vicinity. Again, if you require any assistance, we are at your disposal. Is Colonel Primatov with you?"

"She is."

"May I speak with her?"

Primatov flashed into existence seated on Taugrim's right. She gave Neilosse a polite nod. "Captain Neilosse, it's good to see you again."

Neilosse's smile did not conceal the strain in the crow's feet around his eyes. "Colonel, my orders stipulate I am to place myself and these three ships under your command until higher authority arrives."

Taugrim leaned forward. "Colonel Primatov has spoken highly of you, but are you really you?"

Primatov carefully explained Taugrim's concern that he could be a rogue impersonating the real Neilosse. That was certainly possible, but such fears were probably more indicative of the situation in the Supremacy than in the Commonwealth, though John hoped he wasn't being naive in assuming that.

Neilosse grimaced and shrugged. "I don't know how I can assuage such concerns."

"We think we have a way," Primatov said. "A young ComSecCorps soldier named Carla Nigurski was recently assigned to your crew. Could you bring her into this conversation? And we'll bring one of our people in as well."

In a heartbeat John's perspective shifted, and he now sat at the table on Taugrim's left.

Neilosse looked his way and nodded. "Give me a moment."

Neilosse's image froze as *Lightspear* stopped transmitting. John, Primatov and Taugrim sat in silence and waited for about two minutes. Then Neilosse's image reanimated at the same moment Carla appeared seated next to him, her eyes wide and darting side to side like a caged animal. She had let her dark hair grow a little longer than John remembered, but having her there brought back a lot of good memories. Some of them involved those nice curves of hers.

Primatov introduced John to Neilosse, and Carla to Taugrim. Then she carefully explained the dilemma they faced. During her explanation, Carla visibly calmed down. Primatov finished by saying, "We need you to tell John something no one else would know."

Carla sat there for a long moment frowning in thought. She closed her eyes, squinted and said, "The last time we were together."

She opened her eyes and he saw a world of friendship in them. "You accidentally let it slip you came from Novalis III, said something about me and Roark and Leeze being your first real friends after that. I called you on it, said I always knew there was something. When I asked if you wanted to tell me about it, you said, 'Maybe someday.' "

She smiled, and no imposter could have faked the look she gave him. "We've never had that talk, and we don't ever have to, unless you want to."

John turned to Taugrim and their eyes met. He nodded. "That's Carla."

Taugrim stared at him, judging him, then her head slowly pivoted to Carla. Taugrim gave her a tough-as-nails stare, and Carla had trouble meeting her eyes. "You were platoon mates in basic training?"

Carla nodded once. "Yes, ma'am." No one corrected her on the form of address.

Taugrim stared at Carla, judging her the way she had just judged John. "And you'd die for him?"

Carla shrugged. "Just like he'd die for me."

John thought that would be the end of it, but then Carla leaned forward and slapped her hand on the table. "But first I'd try to kill the bastards so neither of us had to die."

John couldn't stop grinning as he said, "That's definitely Carla."

"Now wait a minute," Carla demanded, turning to Neilosse. "How do we know it's him? Maybe he's an imposter. He should tell me something no one else knows about me."

Carla looked John's way and gave him a snotty grin.

Neilosse said, "She's got a point."

John opened a channel through his implants to Primatov and Taugrim. *She's just being a snot.*

Taugrim asked, *She's being nose mucus?*

Primatov intervened. *Little children always have snot on their noses, and I think hers is quite snotty at the moment.*

Ah, Taugrim said. *I think I understand.* She gave John that big, white-toothed grin of hers. *You two were lovers, weren't you?*

Thankfully, John didn't have to answer that, because Primatov intervened. *Give her something, John. Now that she's brought it up, we have to satisfy Neilosse.*

Oh, I'll give her something all right.

John didn't have to think long to come up with just the right detail for the little snot. He gave her a big, shit-eating grin. "Well, I'm not sure if anyone else knows about this, but . . . you have a small tear shaped birthmark way high up on your inner—"

"Okay," Carla shouted. "Okay."

A ghostly voice said, *Way high up on your inner what? I want to see this birth mark.*

John recognized that voice, and realized it had leaked into the conversation through Carla's implants. "Caputto, is that you?"

Hey, Johnny-boy. Still want to do the obey thing. I'm game if you are. Command me, big boy.

Neilosse shouted like a DI. "That's enough, people. Let's have some discipline here."

Primatov shook her head sadly.

Taugrim grinned at John, making it clear she had gotten an answer to her question.

39

Nikaela's Way

TAUGRIM FINISHED THE virtual meeting with Neilosse and Carla by telling him they didn't need his help, and that she would prefer he hold his present position. She didn't mention that his present position kept them well outside targeting range. And she didn't disclose that Engineering was still desperately working to get the transition drive repaired. After the meeting, the fear and distrust among *Drakan Helgis*'s crew declined considerably, but the trust that replaced it went only so far.

Kolbeck even ribbed John a little. "Heard your Commonwealth girlfriend's a real looker."

Matsen shook his head sadly. "He would focus on that, wouldn't he?"

John said, "And she's not my girlfriend."

Kolbeck's eyebrows rose. "Then she's available?"

Since they hadn't been present at the meeting, John suspected Taugrim had instructed her com tech to record it, or perhaps others had monitored the gathering.

Four hours later *Hellfire*, *Endurance*, and *Lady Victorious* down-transited, then maneuvered to rendezvous with Neilosse's three hunter-killers. Engineering still hadn't completed their repairs, but the Commonwealth ships had them so heavily outgunned at that point, it really didn't matter.

John received orders to report to the officer's ward room, and there he joined Taugrim, Falkenberg, Primatov and Nikaela, all seated at a table.

Taugrim said, "We don't have much time, so we're going to forego tea." She looked Primatov's way. "Colonel, if you please."

Primatov nodded and glanced around the table at each of them. "I've been in contact with Fran Thealone aboard *Hellfire*. We're going to meet virtually with the diplomatic mission from Trafalgar." She looked at John. "They want to see for themselves that you and I are all right."

Again, she addressed the group. "I've given you briefings on those who will be present. Any questions?"

They answered her with silence.

Taugrim must have communicated directly with *Drakan Helgis*'s com tech, because in an instant John now sat at a large conference table with Primatov on his right and Nikaela on his left. The three of them were sandwiched between Falkenberg and Taugrim, which struck John as oddly protective, in a Kelk sort of way. Seated opposite them were Neilosse, Thealone, and Gascoigne, whom John had met, plus Silas Palmutter and Jenine Catarvin, both of whom he knew from news feeds and his briefings. Next to Palmutter sat a fellow in an expensive business suit. His pale-gray hair had been clipped quite short, and while John's briefing made it clear Tarsik Obradour wielded enormous power, the fellow seemed nondescript and anything but intimidating.

Apparently, Primatov was the only one present who knew everyone there. She proceeded to provide introductions. John noticed that Palmutter's eyes kept flitting to Taugrim, Falkenberg and Nikaela. He got the impression the senator didn't like what he saw.

Primatov finished the introductions by saying, "John and I have been treated quite well by our hosts, and we're grateful to them for their courtesy."

Palmutter seemed to be making an effort to hide a sneer, but he failed. "Stabbing the young man in the face with steel knives is what you call being *treated quite well.*"

Obradour gave him a disappointed look and shook his head. "Silas, we've already established that that unfortunate incident was a result of rogue elements in the Supremacy, and I don't think we need to resurrect the issue."

Catarvin smiled at John. "You seem like a nice enough fellow, and I'm glad they fixed up that handsome face of yours. So they're treating you well, are they?"

John nodded. "Yes."

Palmutter shook his head. "How do we know he's not being coerced?"

At that point they digressed into a brief argument. Neilosse described a shortened and edited version of their earlier meeting in which they established there were no imposters involved, though he didn't disclose exactly how John had established his bona fides with a snotty Carla Nigurski. Palmutter would have none of that, and demanded Primatov and John both be transferred to *Hellfire* and into the custody of the Commonwealth. "Only then will we know they're okay and not forced to cooperate."

John had nothing to lose by expressing his opinion, and Primatov had encouraged him to be more assertive. "I'd prefer not to transfer back. At least not yet."

The room went silent for one long second, and John regretted his outburst. Then Palmutter said, "You see, they've brainwashed him."

"No, sir," John said, leaning forward. "They haven't. I'm a member of this crew, and proud of it. I'd like to stay that way, at least until we get to Viktorkinde."

Taugrim looked his way, nodded and grinned. But the look on her face was like nothing John had seen before, more like a silent acknowledgment of unity from one comrade to another. John still had unfinished business aboard *Drakan Helgis*, though he didn't mention that because he thought it might complicate the situation.

Palmutter pointed a finger at him. "It's not up to you, young man."

"Senator," Thealone said, a note of command in her voice that drew everyone's attention. "Nor is it up to you."

"Colonel," Primatov said, and all eyes looked her way. "With your permission, I too would like to remain a part of *Drakan Helgis*'s crew until we get to Viktorkinde."

Thealone looked at Taugrim. "Your thoughts on the matter, Captain."

Taugrim shrugged. "Good crew is good crew. They've both served well, and I and the rest of my crew will be pleased to have them continue with us."

John was thankful Taugrim had chosen to play it straight. Her witty comments would not have gone over at all well, given the present audience.

Thealone aimed her remarks at the other members of the diplomatic mission. "Captain Neilosse has established that we're not dealing with imposters. And I have known and worked with Katrine Primatov for several years. If she were being coerced, she would find a way to let me know. Do any of you object?"

Palmutter grumbled, "I do."

Catarvin's eyes flicked back and forth between John and Nikaela, and a smile slowly formed on her face. "I have no objections."

"Nor I," Gascoigne said.

From the body language in the room, John guessed Tarsik Obradour's opinion carried quite a bit of weight. The man smiled. "So far, working from the ground up has served this mission far more effectively than working from the top down. I think it's an excellent idea."

Primatov leaned forward, and everyone turned their attention to her. "I have a suggestion. You have some of John's old friends with you."

She turned to Taugrim. "They're some of his platoon mates from basic training."

Taugrim nodded carefully, still playing it straight. "Old friends. Close comrades. Like the young girl with the birthmark."

Primatov nodded. "Very close. They could be invaluable on Viktorkinde."

She looked at Thealone and the other members of the mission. "I suggest you transfer them over as well"—she nodded toward Taugrim—"if Captain Taugrim approves."

Taugrim sat in silence for a moment, clearly considering the issue. "Some time spent among my crew might help the young people adjust before we get to Viktorkinde."

Neilosse gritted his teeth. "They can be a little . . . boisterous."

Taugrim's head pivoted slowly toward John, and she gave him that characteristic, big, white-toothed grin. "Ensign Mathius, do you think I can handle your boisterous comrades?"

John flinched and nodded. "Yes, mistress, no question about it."

••••

Engineering reported that they had made some progress and promised to have the transition drive repaired in short order. Taugrim insisted that the new members of her crew be given some orientation training regarding Kelk customs and ways before they transferred over from *Lightspear*. That bought them some time to get the fucking transition drive repaired so they could defend themselves. John tried to be sensitive to the fears of his Kelk crewmates, but he had that unfinished business to take care of.

He carefully checked the roster for fourth watch. Stinar was assigned to Security, so Nikaela would be alone in her stateroom. On fourth watch the ship was as quiet as some legendary ghost ship. He carefully made his way to Nikaela's stateroom, and encountered no one on his way. He knocked on the door and waited. Several seconds passed and no one answered. He knocked again, and still no answer.

••••

Nikaela had some serious unfinished business and it was time to rectify that. John's roommate worked in Engineering, and they were pulling long shifts to finish the repairs on the transition drive, so she'd probably find him alone. If not, she'd figure something out.

She knocked on the door to his stateroom and waited. After several seconds with no answer, she knocked again. When no one responded, she spun on her heel and walked away, a little disappointed and thinking she'd get a few hours' sleep. But as she turned into the passageway a few paces away from her stateroom, she saw John knocking on her door. She didn't miss a step and marched straight toward him, got there just as he turned about, a look of disappointment on his face.

His eyes widened. "Nikaela!"

She almost plowed into him, but slowed at the last instant. He retreated a step, but his back hit her stateroom door just as she reached him. In a single motion she pushed on his chest and keyed the lock on her door with her implants.

He wrapped his arms around her as they both stumbled into her stateroom, and she couldn't say if she kissed him the way a Kelk woman is supposed to, or he kissed her the way a Kelk man is not supposed to. But it didn't really matter because he wasn't Kelk, and at that moment her tongue was having a wonderful time. His hands were also doing a fair amount of exploring, and she enjoyed that as well.

Their lips parted. She kicked a heel back, knocking the stateroom door closed. "Do that thing where you run kisses down my neck."

He grinned. "I think I'm going to kiss a lot more than your neck. And I just confirmed you don't have a scaled lizard tail. It's important I research these things."

She nibbled on his earlobe. "Research away. And I still have to make sure you don't have anything that's forked."

He smiled. "That's an important step in our interstellar relationship, so I intend to cooperate fully."

••••

Carla, Leeze and the guys had been ordered to assemble in the marine Ready-Room.

Carla had enough rank to ask a question or two of Forester, "What's this all about, lieutenant?"

Forrester shook her head. "We're gonna meet with Colonel Blacksword and get some special training. That's all I know."

They positioned a couple of tables and placed chairs at them all facing in one direction, like a classroom. Then they sat down and practiced a few things they had a lot of experience at: waiting, speculating and gossiping.

One of them shouted, "Attention," and they all jumped to their feet as Thealone marched into the room. "At ease, people, and relax. Sit down and pay attention."

Once they were all seated, Thealone stood at the front of the room and said, "I'm going to conference in Colonel Primatov."

A second later the red-hot Blacksword redhead appeared standing next to Thealone. *The* Blacksword said, "It's your show, Colonel."

To Carla's relief, Primatov and Thealone seemed to both be in a good mood, and Primatov actually smiled pleasantly, though Carla had yet to see something like that from Thealone.

Primatov scanned the faces before her. "I'm sure by now Miss Nigurski has let you all know John Mathius is alive and well aboard the Kelk destroyer *Drakan Helgis*. In an effort to foster improved understanding with our Kelk colleagues, he and I have also served as members of her crew under Captain Taugrim. It's kind of like an exchange program, though we haven't actually placed any Kelk on Commonwealth ships, at least not yet. You people are shortly going to join John on *Drakan Helgis*, and like him will be integrated into her crew."

It wasn't Sergeant Major Prescott giving them orders to shit, but at that moment, from the looks on her friends' faces, Carla thought it quite clear they all came fairly close to a full-on pant-load. Prescott liked to refer to all-inclusive, group moments like that as a "pant-load steeplechase." Thealone appeared to be struggling to suppress a smile. Thankfully, everyone did manage to maintain control, and no one blew a big, brown warhead.

Primatov spent the next four hours instructing them on what she had learned during the last couple of tendays about Kelk customs and etiquette. They were highly matriarchal, saluted differently, never shook hands, had four distinct variants of the command *at ease*, and the more superstitious among them believed Blackswords could kill with a thought. Primatov didn't think they'd run into anyone like that because the crew of *Drakan Helgis* had been carefully vetted.

Primatov paused for a moment as if collecting her thoughts. "Sexual relationships between Kelk men and women appear to be more wide open than they are with us, but at the same time more restrictive. We don't fully understand it, so we want you to avoid any complications of that nature at all costs. If you have an opportunity to have a little fun with a good-looking Kelk man or woman, politely walk away from it and don't let it happen. If it doesn't blow up in your face and turn into an interstellar incident,"—she gave them a taste of the scary bitch-face—"you'll still have to face me."

They learned a lot of weird shit that afternoon.

••••

Something woke John, and for a moment he thought he'd fallen asleep in his bunk, though he'd been having a rather nice dream. But his arms were wrapped around a naked, blue-skinned Kelk demon, and he realized it wasn't a dream.

The sounds of someone quietly moving about the stateroom drew his attention. He glanced over his shoulder, and in the dim light saw Stinar, stripped down and climbing into her own bunk.

She glanced his way. "It's about bloody time. I hope you two are done, at least for the night. I don't want you making a lot of noise, because I need to get some sleep."

John and Nikaela had slept for a couple of hours, and John had a few more before he needed to report for duty. "We'll keep it down."

Nikaela stirred next to him and spoke softly. "But maybe we won't."

John still had a lot to learn about Kelk ways, though he had learned quite a bit in the last few years. And in the last couple of hours he'd learned that some Kelk ways were pretty much the same as Commonwealth ways. But he didn't think now was the best time to move on to advanced training, not then and there, not with an audience.

••••

It had been a long day, a tedious day, nothing special, just a lot of incoming and outgoing shipments. Lorenson asked Anders to work late to cover the backlog of manifests that had piled up. But as the other employees clocked out for the evening, he noticed that only he, Hohlman and Lorenson remained behind, and that didn't seem right. He hoped he hadn't screwed up in some way, hoped it wasn't time for the *bullet in the back of the head* thing. If it was, he vowed not to let them take him easily.

Lorenson contacted him through his implants. "Please come to my office right away."

During the course of a normal day Anders used any number of tools and frequently wore a utility belt. He buckled one on now, and clipped a heavy wrench to it. It would not be unusual for him to show up wearing something like that. The wrench wouldn't do much good against a grav pistol, but it was better than nothing. He picked up a rag to pretend he was wiping his hands after being interrupted at some task.

As he approached Lorenson's office, he met Hohlman coming from the opposite direction, and the fellow wasn't carrying a weapon, which gave Anders some hope. Anders nodded toward Lorenson's office door. "What's up?"

Hohlman shrugged and shook his head. "Don't know, but I think something big." He knocked on the office door. Through their implants, Lorenson said, "Enter."

Anders followed Hohlman into the office. Lorenson sat behind her desk, and as they walked into the room she reached into a drawer. Anders tensed, stepped slightly to one side to put Hohlman in the line of fire between him and Lorenson, and prepared to grab the wrench if her hand came up holding a pistol. But all she retrieved was a bottle of kirva and three shot glasses. As she filled the glasses she nodded toward the door. "Close it, please."

Anders did so and she stood. She handed each man a glass and picked up one herself. Hohlman asked the question Anders had asked him moments ago. "What's up?"

She put the glass to her mouth and tossed back the kirva, swallowed, then took a breath. "Until further notice, we're shutting down all special shipments."

Hohlman nodded and tossed his kirva down his throat.

Anders followed suit, and enjoyed the burn as the fiery liquor made its way to his stomach. "Why?"

Lorenson sat down and shook her head, her eyes focused in a thousand-yard stare. "All I know is they're setting up something big on Viktorkinde, something really big."

Anders didn't want to seem too curious, and was glad when Hohlman asked, "Like what?"

"I don't know that either," Lorenson said, still shaking her head. "They failed to stop the diplomatic mission from the Commonwealth, so they're moving to some alternate plan, apparently something that'll really shake things up back there. It's going to take a couple of tendays to set up, maybe more, and they don't want any loose ends here, so we're going fully legit until further notice."

She raised her head and her eyes focused on Anders. "I don't know what you did, but they told me you're the only one here who couldn't pass extremely close scrutiny by certain . . . authorities. We're sending you back, now, tonight. Anything you need at your apartment?"

He needed to tell Nedda Macree of these developments, but he wasn't sure how he would do that. He shrugged. "Some clothes, a few other things. I can pack in ten minutes."

She turned her attention to Hohlman. "Get him to his apartment, then to the airstrip, and don't waste any time. They'll be waiting for you."

Hohlman led Anders to a small grav truck they used for local deliveries of smaller items. He drove Anders the short distance to his apartment building. Anders hoped the fellow would wait in the truck while he went up to his apartment, which would give him an opportunity to get Nedda Macree alone for a few minutes, but Hohlman parked the truck and followed Anders into the building.

Many aspects of life on Sarkovie were somewhat primitive, and almost nothing in his apartment building could be accessed through his implants. He carried an electronic key to unlock the front door of the building and to enter his apartment. And in the lift, a floor could be selected only by pressing a button on a panel. Nedda Macree's apartment was one floor below Anders's, and directly beneath his. When he and Hohlman stepped into the lift, Anders pressed the button for her floor. As anticipated, Hohlman didn't notice. If he had, it would have told Anders they were watching him much more closely than he thought.

They walked down the hall to Macree's apartment. Anders retrieved his key from a pocket, and passed it by the lock mechanism. Nothing happened, he frowned, grabbed the door knob and gave it a shake, hoping Macree would come to the door to find out who was there. That would put her close enough to open a secure link between their implants without going through citynet. It would be a little dangerous with Hohlman standing right next to him, but he had no choice.

He stood there for a long moment, tried to stall by looking at his key for a few seconds as if it was defective. But after that, he had to give up and play out the ruse. She wasn't there.

He looked at the door and stepped back a pace. "Oh, damn!" He glanced at Hohlman. "Sorry, I pushed the wrong button on the elevator."

Hohlman shook his head. "I envy you going back to a civilized planet like Viktorkinde."

They climbed the stairs one flight to his floor. Hohlman sat quietly while Anders stuffed his few possessions into a duffel.

As they took the lift down to the ground floor, Anders wished desperately that they would run into Macree returning from wherever she had gone that night. But luck was not smiling on him.

Two hours later, with the vibration of a ship's drive beneath his feet, Anders dumped his duffle on a bunk. Lorenson had arranged for passage on a small merchant ship. It would take at least a couple of tendays to get to Viktorkinde, and whatever they planned to do might well be over and done with before he got there.

He decided he would miss his client-server relationship with Mistress Macree.

40

One Step

TAUGRIM CAREFULLY ORCHESTRATED the transfer of John's friends. At her insistence, Neilosse made a short transition hop to within six hundred million kilometers of *Drakan Helgis*'s position, then maneuvered in sublight to a million kilometers off her bow. A destroyer against a lone hunter-killer, John's Kelk crewmates were much more comfortable with those odds.

It took three hours for *Drakan Helgis*'s assault boats to cross the distance between the two ships, pick up John's friends, then make the return trip. Taugrim sent John a bottle of kirva, and he, Carla, Leeze, Forrester and the guys had a great reunion. John introduced them to Matsen and Kolbeck, and true to form, Kolbeck focused his attention on Carla, Leeze and May. John introduced them to Nikaela as well, but she bowed out and left them to their fun.

During that time, Engineering completed the repairs on their transition drive. John wondered what Taugrim would have done if they hadn't gotten it running on time; probably some sort of bluff filled with a lot of bravado. Taugrim was not going to allow *Drakan Helgis* within targeting range of the overwhelming firepower of five Commonwealth warships, so by arrangement *Drakan Helgis* drove ahead of them by one light-year. The next day they rendezvoused with *Konigsborge*, and two days after that they met an escort from Viktorkinde. John didn't think it a coincidence that when the new escort joined forces with *Drakan Helgis* and *Konigsborge*, the combined might of the Kelk warships matched that of the Commonwealth warships almost gun for gun.

Nine days later they down-transited on the outskirts of Viktorkinde's heliosphere.

••••

Tomorrow the diplomatic mission would make history when they landed on Viktorkinde. It had been a long journey from Trafalgar, and everyone on *Lady*

Victorious felt the thrill and excitement of the moment. Faith was in the middle of packing when Strikland contacted her on a secure link through their implants. *Can you join me for dinner tonight in my suite?*

It was an audio link so she couldn't give him the inviting smile. *That sounds wonderful, darling.*

And do you think you could wear that dress I've seen you wear at the mixer a couple of times?

She had included that gown in her luggage specifically with the intent of using it to seduce him. It hadn't been necessary, but his request confirmed that her instincts were correct. *I can't very well wear it walking through the passageways of this ship to your suite, but I'll wear something really conservative and bring it with me. Before dinner I'll change into it in your bedroom.*

She could picture the smile on his face as he said, *Excellent.*

No peeking.

You're no fun.

Well, maybe I'll let you peek, but only after dinner.

That evening Faith carefully folded the gown and placed it in her briefcase, along with a pair of dysfunctional shoes that completed the look she wanted to achieve. When she arrived at Strikland's suite he answered the door wearing a tuxedo. He escorted her to the bedroom, and as she closed the door she said, "I won't be but a minute."

He smiled and said, "I'll be waiting."

She changed quickly, and when she stepped out into the lounge, his eyes widened. "You look stunning."

While she'd changed in the bedroom, someone had set up a small table in the middle of the lounge and dimmed the lights. A pristine white cloth covered the table, and in the middle of it a single candle illuminated a small sphere around it with a romantic, flickering glow. Faith had waited patiently for this moment since she had first seduced him. It was time to move beyond the simple relationship of stripping off her clothes and fucking his brains out.

Strikland held the chair for her and she sat down. He sat down opposite her and looked at her for a long moment. Then he called one of his bodyguards over and the fellow poured two glasses of chilled white wine.

Strikland raised his glass in a toast. Faith raised hers and lightly tapped her glass against his.

Perhaps he saw the question in her eyes, because he nodded and said, "Tomorrow I'll finally be able to communicate with certain friends, and I think we're going to have to make some serious changes."

"Darling," she said, "if I can help, just let me know."

He smiled. "You already have, immensely."

Strikland had ordered an elegantly catered meal from *Lady Victorious*'s galley. A couple of his bodyguards wore white waistcoats and served them. They did so with the kind of skills one saw only in waiters at one of the terribly expensive restaurants near the Capitol Rotunda. She and Strikland talked while they ate, and with each word she got a little bit closer to the real Lawrence Strikland. They finished with a light dessert wine and Strikland dismissed the bodyguard-waiters. They talked and sipped wine, and Faith considered it a testament to her skill that they continued that way for a good hour before he showed any interest in the more prurient aspects of their relationship.

••••

"The Blacksword's looking pretty smart, ain't he?"

Standing in the officer's wardroom of *Drakan Helgis*, John tried to ignore Kolbeck's banter. His stomach fluttered with nerves as he used his hands to smooth any wrinkles out of his new dress blues. Matsen sent him an image through their implants of what he saw. He walked slowly around John, giving him a view from all angles.

John didn't have any medals, but Primatov had quizzed him rather thoroughly on his time in service. He had a campaign ribbon for Reisenar, a last-recruit-standing ribbon from Miriteen, a ribbon for completing command school, a couple of specialists ribbons, his wings as a pilot, and a few others things of no great import.

Primatov said chest candy was part of the uniform, and he would look incomplete without it. *Hellfire*'s stores stocked a lot of stuff, but not ribbons of that nature. Primatov had enlisted Thealone's help to get them fabricated for John in a reasonable facsimile of what they should look like. "Don't worry, John," she told him. "If they're not exactly correct, I doubt anyone here will know the difference, and if they do, I doubt they'll care."

The dress shoes she had pilfered from one of *Lightspear*'s officers were a little large, and to make them comfortable, John wore two pairs of socks. Kristdokar said she would have proper shoes made for him once they settled in on Viktorkinde. John hoped that until he had shoes that fit properly, he wouldn't have to move quickly and do something like defend himself against a horde of armed assassins.

Matsen stood in front of him, his fists on his hips as he examined John with a critical eye. "Let me see that arm sheath."

John held his left arm out for the grandeseergent's inspection. How Matsen had accomplished it, John could not imagine. Somehow he'd gotten a long, narrow pocket sewn into the outside forearm of the left sleeve of John's service dress blue coat. They had lined it with flexible plast, which made it an excellent sheath for the butcher's blade. They had also added a small pressure clip to keep the dagger in place when he lowered his arm to his side. The bone handle of the butcher's blade rested comfortably, and quite visibly, on the outside of his forearm just short of his wrist. He could reach over, grip the handle of the blade, and pull it in an instant. The blade was for show, an act of defiance, and he dearly hoped he wouldn't actually need the damn thing, because if he did, he was probably dead already.

John consulted his implants. Twenty minutes to go. Matsen and Kolbeck sat down at a table and pulled out some odd Kelk dice. Kolbeck held them up, shaking them in his hand. "Care to join us, Blacksword?"

John couldn't sit still. "No thanks." He tried to kill time and calm his frayed nerves by pacing back and forth while Matsen and Kolbeck tossed the dice.

John heard Kristdokar speaking out in the passageway, and a moment later she, Taugrim, Primatov, Nikaela, and their two shadows, Vagle and Stinar, walked into the room. Primatov wore her dress blues with an array of ribbons and other chest candy that made John's appear paltry by comparison. The two Kelk women wore their equivalent of dress blues, which tended more toward dark gray. Their uniforms had been carefully tailored to hug their figures, which made the Commonwealth uniforms appear shapeless by comparison, though noting the way Kolbeck looked at Primatov, John had to admit the redhead would never look shapeless. Nikaela wore her butcher's blade in a sheath suspended from the belt on her uniform coat. John particularly liked the way her uniform clung to the curve of her waist and hips.

John noticed Primatov eyeing the forearm sheath sewn into his coat. She lifted one eyebrow, and he thought the scary face was only a heartbeat away, but she didn't say anything.

Kristdokar approached John, stopped in front of him and said, "I have something for you, Ensign Mathius. We have a custom in the Supremacy. If a soldier fights valiantly, but for various reasons is not recognized for her bravery, an officer of flag rank can acknowledge the soldier's valor with a personal gift. We do not allow our people to personally embellish their uniforms, but such a gift is considered an appropriate and acceptable recognition of bravery, and therefore accepted as valid insignia for the recipient."

John glanced at Primatov and she gave him a faint shrug, telling him Kristdokar had not consulted her on this.

Kristdokar extended her hand with a small, long, thin box resting in her upraised palm. John glanced again at Primatov, and she gave him a single nod of approval.

He reached out and took the box from Kristdokar's hand. He fumbled at it for a moment, discovered it had a hinged lid and popped it open. In it rested a small brass pin about the length of his pilot's wings. It contained two long, thin objects one above the other: a tiny metal fork over an equally small dagger. The handle of the dagger had even been coated with off-white enamel or something, as if it were made of bone. John stood frozen for a long moment and couldn't take his eyes off the thing.

Kristdokar's words drew his attention back to her. "I had the machine shop on *Konigsborge* fabricate that. There is a woman there who is known to be a gifted artisan. She also hates the Commonwealth and is quite superstitious, yet she gladly consented to make that for you. In a way, it's a gift from both her and me."

She smiled. "May I do the honors?"

John again glanced Primatov's way. Kristdokar followed his gaze, looked toward the Blacksword officer, and they both waited.

Primatov nodded once, no sign of the scary face. "We too are not allowed to personally embellish our uniforms." She glanced momentarily at John's modified coat sleeve. "But a military award from a foreign power does not violate that stricture."

Kristdokar turned back to John and again asked, "May I do the honors, young man?"

John tried not to stammer. "Uh, certainly, ma'am . . . uh, mistress."

She gently took the box from his hand, removed the pin, and attached it to his coat just beneath his pilot's wings. She looked him in the eyes. "I deeply regret that all you know of the Kelk culture is our unreasoned hatred. During your time here with us, I do hope you'll have an opportunity to see something in us beyond that."

John swallowed hard. "But I already have, Mistress Kristdokar." He glanced at Taugrim and grinned. "As part of Mistress Taugrim's crew I've learned a lot." He glanced at Nikaela. He'd recently learned quite a bit from her as well, but he didn't think he should mention that.

Kristdokar leaned close to John and lowered her voice. "I want you to keep something in mind, Ensign Mathius. We have rigid strictures that prohibit bearing arms in the chambers of the Executive Council or the hall of the Larscom."

She clearly wanted him to understand he would not be allowed to wear the butcher's blade in certain places. But then she added, "There is one exception to that rule: old-fashioned hand weapons worn purely for ceremonial purpose."

She straightened and grinned at John. He wondered what kind of game she had chosen to play with his life.

Kristdokar turned away from him and looked at the others. "It's show time. If we don't hurry, we'll keep Vice Skalde Nygaard waiting. And it is never advisable to keep a member of the Larscom Executive Council waiting."

John had one more thing to do before leaving *Drakan Helgis*. He turned and approached Taugrim, and stopped facing her. "Mistress, it's been an honor serving under you."

Taugrim flashed that toothy grin of hers. "Under me? And all this time I was hoping we'd find an opportunity for you to serve on top of me."

••••

John, Nikaela, and Primatov, along with their shadows Vagle, Stinar, Matsen and Kolbeck, made their way down to *Drakan Helgis*'s Hangar Deck. May Forester, Carla and the rest of her squad stood in a cluster near an assault boat, all wearing their service dress blues.

John's friends had started out intimidated by all the Kelk around them, and Taugrim had found an opportunity to bust each of their asses more than once. But that seemed to help them integrate, and after twenty-four days, they, like John, were part of *Drakan Helgis*'s crew. During his spare time John frequently joined them for gossip or a card game, if for no other reason than to compare all the weird shit they had learned about their Kelk crewmates. Two nanoseconds after John introduced Nikaela to them, Carla and Leeze somehow figured out that she had taken him off the available-guy list, and they teased him mercilessly about it. Leeze had a copy of what passed for a Kelkie handbook. She kept showing him lurid pictures of impossibly contorted positions, asking, "Have you tried that one yet?" If Carla happened to be there, they'd high-five each other and get a good laugh out of it.

They boarded the assault boat and strapped in, with Nikaela seated next to John. She leaned close to him and whispered in Lingua, "Today I think we're going to hear a lot of shit-of-bull speeches and really boring shit-of-bull stuff like that. When I get bored I need a distraction, so perhaps I'll take you as a lover."

John grinned. "And perhaps I'll let you."

The assault boat descended through Viktorkinde's atmosphere toward the city of Emkeldstadt, and settled onto the lawn in front of the old Hyvaldsborg Palace. The pilot opened the large cargo hatch in the side of the boat, and their Kelk friends spilled out of it. They had been given orders to form a defensive perimeter, but they were also supposed to do that without looking like a bunch of military people ready to shoot down anyone who got too close.

May Forester barked orders at her squad to join them, but Primatov said, "Hold on there, lieutenant. All of you remain where you are."

John had thought May's squad would precede him and Nikaela, and had stopped near the hatch.

Primatov approached him, smiled, and hooked a thumb upward. "The politicians up there are a few minutes behind us. They argued about who should be the first Commonwealth official in recorded history to set foot on the surface of the capital planet of the Kelk Supremacy. They couldn't come to any agreement, so they settled it by drawing straws, and Catarvin won."

"Oh, sorry," John said, realizing he'd been about to breach the carefully orchestrated protocol the diplomatic mission had established. "I should wait."

Primatov grinned and shook her head slowly from side to side. "Colonel Blacksword and I talked it over privately, and we feel that that person should be the young man who made all this possible."

She extended a hand, indicating the open hatch. "Please, John, after you."

It took John a moment to absorb what she had said. He nodded and stepped to the hatch, but she put a hand on his shoulder. "Oh, one more thing." She leaned close to him and grinned. "Please try not to kill anyone today."

He nodded. "Yes, ma'am. I'll try real hard."

On that day, the first Commonwealth official in recorded history to step on the hallowed ground of Viktorkinde was not a celebrated dignitary, but a simple soldier, a Blacksword.

A Comparison of Rank Equivalents

ComSec infantry rank is modeled after that of the United States Army. ComSec navel rank is modeled after that of the US Navy. Kelk rank is based on that of the Kelk Supremacy in effect at the time of this writing. A comparison of rank equivalents is provided below:

Enlisted and NCO Ranks:

ComSec Infantry	ComSec Naval	Kelk
Private (Buck)	Seaman Recruit	Unterkrieger
Private 2nd Class	Seaman Apprentice	Krieger
Private 1st Class	Seaman	Oberkrieger
Corporal (NCO)	Petty Officer 3rd Class	Unterseergent
Sergeant	Petty Officer 2nd Class	Seergent
Staff Sergeant	Petty Officer 1st Class	Grandeseergent
Sergeant 1st Class	Chief Petty Officer	Oberseergent
Master Sergeant	Senior Chief Petty Officer	Hauptseergent
First Sergeant		
Sergeant Major	Master Chief Petty Officer	Seergentmeister
Command Sergeant Major	Master Chief Petty Officer of the Navy	Kommandseergent

J. L. Doty

Officer Ranks:

ComSec Infantry	ComSec Naval	Kelk
Lieutenant 2nd Class	Ensign	Command Boss J. R.
Lieutenant 1st Class	Lieutenant J. G.	Command Boss S. R.
Captain	Lieutenant	Command Superior
Major	Lt Commander	Senior Command Superior
Lieutenant Colonel	Commander	Command Hawk
Colonel	Captain	Command Eagle
Brigadier General	Rear Admiral Lower Half	Brigadier Skalde
Major General	Rear Admiral	Major Skalde
Lieutenant General	Vice Admiral	Vice Skalde
Chief of Staff of the Corp	Chief of Naval Operations	Skalde of the Supremacy
General of the Corp	Fleet Admiral	Skalde Supreme

Acknowledgements

I'D LIKE TO thank Clyde, Tory and Dave for fixing all my dotted t's and crossed i's, and for their invaluable insight, criticism and advice, Karen for both supporting my dream and being my most valuable critic, and Steve Himes, and the whole team at Telemachus, for getting a quality product out the door.

Books by J. L. Doty

Series: The Treasons Cycle
Of Treasons Born
A Choice of Treasons

Stand Alone Novel
The Thirteenth Man

Series: The Gods Within
Child of the Sword
The SteelMaster of Indwallin
The Heart of the Sands
The Name of the Sword

Series: The Dead Among Us
When Dead Ain't Dead Enough
Still Not Dead Enough
Never Dead Enough

Series: The Blacksword Regiment
A Hymn for the Dying
A Dirge for the Damned
A Prayer for the Fallen
A Requiem for the Forsaken

Series: Commonwealth Re-contact Novellas
Tranquility Lost

About the Author

JIM IS A full-time SF&F writer, scientist and laser geek (Ph.D. Electrical Engineering, specialty laser physics), and former running-dog-lackey for the bourgeois capitalist establishment. He's been writing for over 30 years, with 15 published books. His first success came through self-publishing when his books went word-of-mouth viral, and sold enough that he was able to quit his day-job, start working for himself and write full time—his new boss is a real jerk. That led to contracts with traditional publishers like Open Road Media and Harper Collins Voyager, and his books are now a mix of traditional and self-published.

The four novels in his new hard science fiction series, *The Blacksword Regiment*, were released in July 2020. Right now he's fleshing out ideas for the next book in *The Dead Among Us*, he's writing another episode in *The Treasons Cycle*, and he's working on a new fantasy series *The Deck of Chaos*.

Jim was born in Seattle, but he's lived most of his life in California, though he did live on the east coast and in Europe for a while. He now resides in Arizona with his wife Karen and three little beings who claim to be cats: Tilda, Julia and Natasha. But Jim is certain they're really extra-terrestrial aliens in disguise.

Visit the author's website at http://www.jldoty.com
Contact the author at jld@jldoty.com

www.ingramcontent.com/pod-product-compliance
Lightning Source LLC
Chambersburg PA
CBHW032113180726

48284CB00002B/558